Sex & Death

SEX & DEATH

DEATH

STORIES

Edited by Sarah Hall
and Peter Hobbs

First published in Canada in 2016 by House of Anansi Press Inc.
www.houseofanansi.com

20 19 18 17 16   1 2 3 4 5

Library and Archives Canada Cataloguing in Publication

Sex and death : stories / edited by Sarah Hall and Peter Hobbs.

Issued in print and electronic formats.
ISBN 978-1-77089-883-7 (paperback).—ISBN 978-1-77089-884-4 (html)

Hall, Sarah, 1974–, editor II. Hobbs, Peter, 1973–, editor

PN6120.2.S44 2016   823'.9208   C2016-901318-9
                           C2016-901319-7

Cover design: Alysia Shewchuk
Typeset by Faber & Faber Limited

Canada Council   Conseil des Arts   ONTARIO ARTS COUNCIL
for the Arts   du Canada   CONSEIL DES ARTS DE L'ONTARIO
                                          an Ontario government agency
                                          un organisme du gouvernement de l'Ontario

*We acknowledge for their financial support of our publishing program
the Canada Council for the Arts, the Ontario Arts Council, and the
Government of Canada through the Canada Book Fund.*

Printed and bound in Canada

RECYCLED
Paper made from
recycled material
FSC
www.fsc.org   FSC® C103567

For Clare Conville,
brilliant and fierce,

and

for Deborah Rogers,
in loving memory.

CONTENTS

INTRODUCTION

What civil lives we lead. So mannered, so controlled. Everything tidy and safe, everything put in its place. How hard we try not to be frightened, not to let the mind and body misbehave, not to come undone. Look at us in our ties and our stockings, taking vitamins and buying prophylactics, arranging mortgages and emptying the bins, ameliorating, ordering. We've almost convinced ourselves.

But underneath, closer than we dare to think, is the reddish nature of humanity, the strong meat of our anatomy. The force that drives us on, generation after generation, the gust behind us we don't want to feel but is always felt, moves us towards the edge. How we come in, and how we go out, sex and death: these are the governing drives, our two greatest themes. The humid embrace and the cold sweat. The weight of a coffin on the shoulder, the illicit kiss or *la petite mort*; the sting of intimately split flesh and the wonder of holding a tiny howling genetic machine in our arms. These are the moments we are left staring into the void, realising, rejoicing, or fucking it all up.

With its concentrated dosage, its os into the soul, and its existential insolvency, the short story form is the perfect vehicle for our ecstasies and agonies, for reminding us of what we already know but can't quite reconcile – the cognitive dissonance of living and dying, the attempts at loving in between. By nature, the short story has immense power, as does the human imperative. That the two should meet seems inexorable, like gorgeous and terrible suitors, Eros and Thanatos in coitus behind closed doors.

I

Here, then, are twenty splendid adult versions of the truth, or the lie, however we might regard it, newly composed by some of the finest writers across the globe. Here are twenty stripped visions of the meaning of us, if we have any meaning at all. There is no hush-hush come-come, no literary analgesic or barrier salve for our most profound experiences. They move, elate, excruciate, and they arrive at the most unexpected times. In each story, there is no consolation or answer to be found, other than looking into the bare mirror of ourselves, the phenomenology of our shared and varied fates, the beauty of simply saying, ah, yes, here we are, or there we were.

Sarah Hall and Peter Hobbs

SEX & DEATH

DR PACIFIC

Robert Drewe

Don dropped dead on the sand and that was that. We'd just finished our lighthouse walk and he bent down to remove his shoes
for our swim and keeled over. He was in his blue board shorts
with the red palm trees. One shoe on and one shoe off when the
ambulance took him – his new Rockport walkers. Only seventy-
eight. Three years ago now and as I said, that was that.

Since that moment the days often look blurry around the edges, like I'm wearing his glasses by mistake. People loom around
corners when I don't expect them and next minute they're on the
doorstep. Jehovahs. Seventh Dayers. Charity collectors.

A Green type of woman in drifty clothes came by wanting to
save baby fruit bats. She said the cold snap was making them lose
their grip and fall out of the trees and they needed to be wrapped
up in bandannas and fed mango smoothies. She was collecting
money to provide the bandannas and smoothies and she showed
me a photo of a baby bat in a red bandanna to clinch the deal.

'Look how cute it is, peeping out snug and warm,' she said.

'Cuteness is a survival characteristic of baby animals,' I said.
'If you ask me, this one looks a bit confused being right side up
instead of hanging upside down.'

'But very cute, you must admit,' she said, shaking her Save the
Grey-Headed Flying Fox collection tin. It hardly rattled. She was
one of those North Coast women who look better from a distance.

The reason I was unsympathetic was that we've got hundreds
of them living in a colony in our street, raiding our fruit trees and
screeching all night and doing their business all over our decks,

especially the Hassetts' and the Rasmussens', and the council playground so kids can't play outdoors, and probably spreading the Hendra virus or Ebola or something.

Even worse than their noise and mess and being kept awake all night, the most irritating thing about them is they take only one bite out of each piece of fruit. They like to sample one bite out of every papaya and mango and mandarin on the coast – and they ruin the lot. And of course they're protected under the Wildlife Act.

Mind you, there's even people around here who are fond of brown snakes, the ones that kill you quickest. Those people need a slap, honestly. And down at Broken Head there used to be signs saying *Do Not Molest the Stingrays*. The tourists pinched all the signs for souvenirs.

I said to her, 'Let nature take its course, miss. If I was a fruit bat and the weather got too nippy, I wouldn't wait for a bandanna. I'd up stakes and fly to north Queensland.'

Another day a young woman with a bossy accent called in to convince the 'household' to switch to a different electricity provider. Sun-Co or North-Sun or something. There were lots of benefits for the 'household' in switching to Sun-Co, she said.

I told her it wasn't much of a household any more. 'Just this gnarly old bird.'

'You should go solar and save yourself many dollars,' she insisted, in a South African sort of voice. 'The sun is so harsh here you might as well benefit financially from it.'

The way she said 'harsh' it sounded like 'horsh'. Then she looked me up and down in a superior way. 'Your skin looks like you enjoy plenty of sun.'

I let that go. 'I certainly do,' I said, and gave her a big sunny grin. 'I swim every day, rain or shine. I've earned every one of these wrinkles.'

At eighty you can choose which insults you respond to. I said the stove was gas and I just used electricity to run the TV and boil the kettle. I told her I only ate cheese sandwiches and the pensioners' ten-dollar three-course special at the bowling club. A glass of brown rum of an evening. No point cooking for one.

I said, 'Miss, when it's dark and cold I just creep into bed like the decrepit old widow I am.'

She raised her drawn-on eyebrows and cut short her electricity spiel then, like I was one of those eccentric old witches with bird's nest hair and forty-three cats. Maybe I'd laid the elderly stuff on too thick. But she was a hard-faced girl.

*

Ever notice that after people pass away the world seems to have more sunsets than dawns? I try to avoid sunsets. They stand for things being over. With sunsets I think of Don in his palm-tree board shorts swimming over the trees and hills into those pink and gold clouds – that exaggerated heaven you see in the pamphlets the Jehovahs hand out. And our darling boy Nathan and his friend Carlo in '87. My own Mum and Dad. Oh, sunsets draw the sadness out.

When that sunset feeling seeps in, watch out. Don't think about everyone gone, and no grandchildren. Sorrow shows in your face. Stay upbeat and busy is my motto. Don't worry yourself about last words either. (Don's final word he bubbled out on the sand sounded like 'Thursday' or 'birthday' – I've stopped wondering what it meant.) And don't blame Carlo any more for making Nathan sick. I try to face east and the dawn and the beginning of things.

Just after sun-up every morning, all seasons, I do my lighthouse walk. It's always interesting – big blue jellyfish the size of bin lids lying there; sometimes an octopus or little stingray beached in a rock pool. One morning the shore was strewn with hundreds of green capsicums, as if a capsicum freighter had jettisoned them.

All green, no red ones, just floating there like blow-up bath toys.

What I enjoy these days is stopping to pick up shells and stones and interesting bits of driftwood to take home. I look for those rare stones shaped like hearts.

Don called this stuff 'flotsam'. He hated beach decor. 'Listen, Bet. Are we doing our exercise or picking up flotsam?' he'd say. 'Who wants to live in a beachcomber's shack?' He preferred the surfaces kept clear for his barometer collection and shiny brass telescope and Sudoku books and his cricketers' and politicians' memoirs. Books with deadly dull titles. *Afternoon Light* and *Cabinet Diary* and *A Good Innings*. God save us!

After my walk I leave the morning's beach souvenirs on my towel and then I'm in the sea, swimming the kilometre from the Pass to Main Beach like Don and I used to.

One thing's for sure – it's my love of the ocean that keeps me going. You know what I call the ocean? *Dr Pacific*. All I need to keep me fit and healthy is my daily consultation with Dr Pacific.

'Morning!' I yell out to the surfers waxing their boards on the sand, zipping up their steamers. 'I'm off to see the Doctor!'

Some of the boys give me a friendly wave. They treat me like I'm their crazy brown granny. 'Morning, Bet! Looking good!' They can't wait to hit the surf and ride those barrels. 'They're pumping today!' they yell.

You see things out there – fish galore, and there's a pod of dolphins that lives off the Cape, plus many turtles. And shapes and shadows. Sometimes there's a splash nearby, but I just keep going. I imagine the shadow and splash is Don still swimming alongside me.

*

We're on the trailing edge of tropical cyclones here on the country's most easterly point. One moment it's a hot summer's day and then Cyclone Norman or Cyclone Sharon spins south with its high winds, choppy surf and water spouts, little tornados twirling across the ocean. The humidity drives us locals out onto our decks. Everyone sits there with their beers and Hibachis and watches the weather over the sea like it's the Discovery Channel. It's all to do with La Niña or El Niño or something. Firstly, clouds bank up over the fishing boats and container ships on the horizon, then the sky turns thundery and purple, the sea looks sulky and there's distant sheet lightning over the Gold Coast. You can smell the storm racing south. The air smells of meat.

The wind's blowing barbecue smoke into your face. Pressure builds up in your ears. Then a yellowish mist drops over the ocean and hailstones begin pelting down. By now the fruit bats have got night and day mixed up and they start shrieking in this strange muddy daylight as if the sky's falling.

Just as quickly the hail stops, like a tap's been turned off, the sky's clear and the wind moves offshore. The waves spray backwards against the tide in lines of spindrift. The air's so sharp you can see the humpbacks breaching on their way back to the Antarctic.

Funny how the cyclone weather gets all the bachelor whales overstimulated. The sea's getting strangely warm for them here and they start displaying for the girl whales. Slapping their tails on the water, showing off like teenage boys. Slap, slap, over and over.

*

During Cyclone Sharon we were all out on our decks every day for a week. Even the main bat victims, the Rasmussens and Hassetts. Curiosity and anxiety plus a faint shred of hope brought everyone out. It was bedlam with the noise of the coastguard helicopters and the spotter planes and the lifesavers in their rubber duckies and jet-skis and the water-police launches. Up and down the shoreline and river mouths they were searching for poor Russell Monaghetti.

What happened was Russell's prawn trawler, the *Tropic Lass*, overturned at night in the cyclone seas off Cape Byron. Russell and his two young deckhands were believed lost. But next afternoon, the youngest boy, Lachie Pascall, crawled up on Belongil beach.

Lachie had been guided by the lighthouse and swum eleven miles to shore. He was exhausted, flat as a tack, but he told the rescue services approximately where the boat had sunk.

He said he'd left the others clinging to floating stuff when he set off to swim to land. So they concentrated the hunt and, you wouldn't believe it, six hours later they found Brendan Lutz, the second boy. Brendan was just alive. He was badly sun-blistered and dehydrated and hugging an ice box. They had to prise his fingers off it.

For a day or so that gave everyone hope. Brendan said the last he'd seen of Russell he was clutching a marker buoy. But now there was no sign of him, and after another five days the search for him was called off.

Very sad. I knew poor Russell. His boat operated out of the Brunswick Heads fishermen's marina and when he wasn't at sea he was a regular drinker down at the bowling club on Friday and Saturday nights. He was quite a big wheel, on the club committee and everything.

'How's my surfer chick?' he'd call out. He liked to flirt with me in a teasing way. 'Still fighting the surfers off, Betty?' he'd say. 'If only I stood a chance!'

'Too young for me,' I'd shoot back. 'I'm no cougar.' Russell was late sixties, I'm guessing. A good-looking silvery fellow. Lovely smile. The dashing, cheeky sort I used to go for before Don came along.

Russell knew I liked a rum or two of an evening. During the bingo he'd sneak a mojito onto the table for me when I wasn't looking. Once he pinched a hibiscus flower off the bush by the club's entrance and left it alongside the drink.

*

That strange time of Cyclone Sharon I'd be walking home from my meal at the bowling club about nine – it's only a couple of blocks – and I'd look up and the sky would be thronging with dopey fruit bats caught in the lighthouse beam. Flapping wilder than usual, squealing, and crashing into trees and electricity wires. Bats were even on the sand and struggling in the shallows. Where's your famous radar now? I wondered.

The colony had started raiding the local coffee plantations. They'd chewed up thousands of dollars' worth of ripe beans and the local growers were in a panic. As usual, Parks and Wildlife was no help.

'The grey-headed flying fox is a protected coastal species,' they said. Blah, blah. 'Try scare guns or netting the plantations.' But the nets were too expensive and the fake guns only made the bats shriek and act crazier, especially now they were addicted to coffee.

As their caffeine habit increased, the bats became even more speedy and twitchy. Their flying was more reckless, their screeching and squabbles were even shriller than usual. And they began to fall off the perch.

It took a while but the survivors eventually woke up to themselves and threw off their caffeine addiction. Mind you, there wasn't much left to eat around here by then. One full moon there was a great squawking and flapping, as if they'd come to a decision, and what was left of the colony upped stakes and flew north into the wind.

Carol Hassett's house had taken the brunt of their droppings and noise. Carol said she hoped they all had headaches from coffee withdrawal.

*

I was on my morning lighthouse walk at low tide. It was three or four weeks after the latest cyclone had rearranged the shoreline and something not regular, a bump on the smoothness, caught my eye on the hard-packed sand. A big shiny white bone had just washed up.

I stopped and picked it up. It hadn't been long in the sea. No weed was growing on it, and it wasn't eroded. It didn't look like any animal bone I could recall. Thick, quite heavy, it was about as long as – I'm sorry to say – a human thigh bone.

I know I think about things too much these days. If I'm not careful my imagination runs away with me. But as I turned it over in my hand, boy, I had that prickly sensation on the back of my neck. This old duck almost passed out there on the shore.

I said to myself, 'Betty, you're holding a thigh bone in your hand!' The sides were smooth and one end of the bone was cleanly snapped. At its widest end the bone was jagged, with a zigzag edge of sharp points, as if it had been severed by a big pair of pinking shears.

I held the white bone with the zigzag edge and my neck did that prickly thing. I was thinking of the search for Russell, and of his friendly ways, and his silvery looks, and of what I now presumed had happened to him. It took all my concentration not to collapse on the sand.

What should I do with the bone? Take it to the Byron Bay police? The cops would probably laugh it off as bait from a lobster pot or garbage thrown from a ship. ('This lady thinks she's found a femur, Sergeant!')

Lots of thoughts struck me. If it was Russell's thigh bone, would his next of kin appreciate its discovery? (He was close to his three daughters and he had an ex-wife somewhere.) Wouldn't the evidence of the bone – that sharp, zigzag pattern – be too brutal for his girls? Shouldn't there be a *thingamajig*, a DNA test? Could you hold a funeral service for a femur?

Anyway, what amount of remains, what percentage of flesh or bone was necessary for a trace of a person to be counted as a body? Would a leg bone count? Did it have a soul? I'm not a religious woman – I don't know these things. What would my pesky Jehovahs and Seventh Dayers say? God's in nature, is all I believe.

Oh, I worried over all this. The white bone in my hand now had huge significance. It carried the weight of many emotions. In the bright beach glare it had what the local hippie chicks would call an *aura*. A pale but powerful aura. The aura of a handsome kind man who'd suffered a violent death.

I continued my walk while I thought about what to do. And I decided I wanted to keep the white thigh bone. I wanted to treasure the memory of poor Russell Monaghetti. I wanted to be able to look at the femur and recall his smile and the gift mojitos and the hibiscus on the bingo table.

I had no pockets and the bone was too cumbersome to carry, so I placed it on a patch of dry sand securely far from the water, and jammed a driftwood branch into the ground to mark the spot. I'd pick it up on my way back.

Of course, as I trudged along I started feeling guilty about Don. I had no treasured souvenirs of poor Don (I'd given his cricketers' and politicians' memoirs to the Rotary market stall). All I had were his clothes hanging in his side of the wardrobe, getting musty and moth-holed, but with his smell just faintly on them. Jackets and sweaters I was too sentimental to give to the op-shop. His Rockport walkers growing mould. The palm-tree board shorts the hospital gave back to me.

How would Don feel about me having another man's thigh bone on the mantelpiece? Because already that's where I was imagining putting Russell's femur – over the fireplace, mounted on a little stand like the gold brackets that held Don's brass telescope. (Yes, on that very same telescope stand.) With its pale aura gleaming out into the room, through the windows and out to sea.

I felt strangely unfaithful and wicked for most of the walk, but young and reckless as well, almost like a teenager. My brain was fizzing with excitement. Sorry, Don.

I picked up the pace on my way back. I was hurrying along the shore to pick up the bone to take home. I reached the spot I'd marked with the driftwood branch but the marker was gone. The tide was still fairly low but obviously a contrary set of waves had swept over the patch of sand, scooped it clean of debris, left it smooth and bare as a table-top, swamped it so recently that air bubbles were still popping on its surface.

That's not unusual, of course. Waves and tides and winds seem irregular forces of nature, erratic in their evenness, but there's always a proper reason for their existence, like Cyclone Sharon being caused by rapidly warming seas.

I understand all that. I'm an old North Coast girl. I see this every day. More than anyone I understand the way Dr Pacific does things. So I waded into the sea, into that shallow green dip between the shore break and the shore itself, and the bone was lying on the sea bed, rolling back and forth in the tide. Quite easy to find, being so pale.

GEORGE AND ELIZABETH

Ben Marcus

When George's father died, he neglected to tell his therapist, which wouldn't have been such a big deal, except she could cop a mood, and she knew how to punish him with a vicious show of boredom.

He'd been deep in a session with her, maintaining that when he was younger he had discovered that there was no difference, in bed, between men and women. Literally. At the biological level. If you could wrap a present, you could make one into the other. And therefore this issue of preference had weirdly become moot. You didn't have to check either box.

'Have you ever worked with clay?' he asked her. 'Have you ever pushed pudding around in your bowl?'

George gestured to show what he meant. Spoon work, a bit of charade knitting.

Dr Graco waved for him to get on with it.

It was finally, he explained, just a shame that there were no other categories he could sample.

'So you feel incapable of surprise at the sexual level?' she asked.

'I'm sure there are things out there I haven't tried, but in the end they belong to categories that have washed out for me. Just, you know, haircuts I've already had, beards I've already worn. There's too much time left on the clock. I wish that I had paced myself.'

'Paced yourself?'

'Yeah.'

'Is it a race?'

'Yes. I just got my number. I should have pinned it to my shirt. Sorry about that.'

'You don't take this seriously, do you?'

'Well . . . I pay *you* to take it seriously. Which gives me room to deflect and joke about it and put my insecurities on display, which you should know how to decode and use in your treatment. Another layer of evidence for your salt box.'

'Do you often think about how I conduct your treatment, as you call it?'

George sighed.

'I thought about it once, and then I died,' he said. 'I bled out.'

And boom, the session was over. He was in the waiting room putting on his coat before he remembered his news, what he'd been so determined to tell her, but he had to deal with the ovoid white noise machine which turned speech into mush, and the miserable young man waiting his turn who refused to ever acknowledge George when he burst out of his appointment. It was all a bit exhausting. Were the two of them really supposed to pretend that they weren't both paying Dr Graco to inhale their misery and exhibit a professional silence about it? And couldn't they finally just unite in shame and even go sadly rut somewhere? Roll out their crusts against a building, even, or on the merry-go-round in Central Park?

Sex with sad people was something that could still deliver – in terms of sheer lethargy and awkwardness – but the demographics were stubborn. These people didn't exactly come out to play very often. It wasn't clear what bird call you were supposed to use. You practically had to go around knocking on doors. And then the whole thing could verge on coercion.

The news of his father's death had come in yesterday from a laundromat. Or perhaps it was simply a place with loud machines and yelling in the background. Someone was on the other end of the phone asking if a Mr George was next of kin.

At first George was confused. 'To what?' he asked. The word 'kin' made him picture the Hare Krishna display, human beings going hairless and sleek as they evolved. As if a bald, aquiline man couldn't swing a club and crush someone.

'All the tenants do a next of kin. I just need to know if that's you. Tenant name is . . . I can't really read this writing, to be honest. I didn't know this man. We have a lot of units.'

George very slowly said his father's name.

'That's it. Check. And are you Mr George?'

George said he was. Whenever someone tried to pronounce his true last name, it sounded unspeakably vulgar.

'I'm sorry to report your loss,' the voice said.

Try not to report it to too many people, George thought. Cocksucker.

He guessed he knew he'd get a call like this one day, and he guessed he'd have to think about it for a while, because the initial impact felt mild, even irritating. He'd have to stick his head into the dirty, hot, self-satisfied state of California and try not to drown in smugness while he solved the problem of his father's body, which he hadn't particularly cared for when his father was alive. But what was most on his mind was this question of kin, and why they had not made another call first.

There was a sister, but she'd scored out of the family. It was hard to blame her. Better food, prettier people, sleeker interiors. George read about her now and then online. She'd achieved a kind of fame in the world of industrial materials. At some point she'd promoted her ridiculous middle name, Pattern, to pole position. Like Onan, maybe. Or Pelé. Her old name, Elizabeth, George figured, was holding her back, and in a way he saw her point, given the sheepish Elizabeths he'd privately failed to grant human status in college. Sleepwalkers, enablers, preposterously loyal friends. Pattern was a family name belonging to their great-grandmother, who lived on a brutally cold little island, and who, according to their mother, had made a sport of surviving terminal illnesses. Now George's lovely sister Pattern, so many years later, was a person, a business, a philosophy, a crime. She did something in aerospace. Or to it. Had his brilliant sister once said, in a *Newsweek* profile, that she wanted to 'help people forget everything they thought they knew about the earth'? One such bit of hypnosis had apparently resulted in immense profits for her, the kind of money you get very paranoid about losing. She produced shimmering synthetic materials from terribly scarce natural resources − a kind of metal drapery that served as a 'towel' for drones − which meant Pattern was often photographed shaking hands with old people in robes on the tarmacs of the world, no doubt after administering shuddering hand jobs to them back on the air bus.

Well that wasn't fair. Probably, George figured, her staff conducted proclivity research so that it could provide bespoke orgasms to these titans of industry, whose children Pattern was. boiling down for parts, whose reefs, mines and caves her company was thoroughly hosing.

At home Pattern was probably submissive to a much older spouse, whose approach to gender was seasonal. Or maybe his sister wasn't married? It was difficult to remember, really. Perhaps because he had probably never known? Perhaps because Pattern did not exactly speak to any of the old family? Ever?

Now, with Mother in a Ball jar and Dad finally passed, George was the last man standing. Or sitting, really. Sort of slumped at home in the mouth of his old, disgusting couch. Trying to figure out his travel plans and how exactly he could get the bereavement discount for his flight. Like what if they tested him at the gate with their grief wand and found out, with digital certainty, that he super sort of didn't give a shit?

His most recent contact with his sister was an email from

soldier1@pattern.com, back when her rare visits home were bro-
kered by her staff, who would wait for their boss in a black-ops
Winnebago out on the street. Ten years ago now? His mother
was dead already, or still alive? At the time George wondered if
Pattern couldn't just send a mannequin to holiday meals in her
place, its pockets stuffed with money. Maybe make it edible, the
face carved from lamb meat, to deepen the catharsis when they
gnashed it apart with their teeth. Anyway, wouldn't his sister like
to know that there was now one less person who might make a
grab for her money? She could soften security at the compound,
wherever she lived. Dad was dead. Probably she already knew.
When you're that wealthy, changes in your biological signature,
such as the sudden omission of a patriarch, show up instantly on
your live update. You blink in the high-resolution mirror at your
reflection, notice no change whatsoever, and then move on with
your day. Maybe she'd have her personal physicians test her for
sadness later in the week, just to be sure.

The question now was how to fire off an email to his very important sister that would leapfrog her spam filter, which was probably
a group of human people, arms linked, blocking unwanted com-
munications to their elusive boss, who had possibly evolved into
a smoke by now.

Simple was probably best. 'Dear Pat,' George wrote. 'Mom and
Dad have gone out and they are not coming back. It's just you and
me now. Finally we have this world to ourselves. P.S. Write back!'

George went to California to pack his father's things, intending a
full-force jettison into the dumpster. He'd only just started sur-
veying the watery, one-bedroom apartment, where he could not
picture his father standing, sitting, sleeping, or eating, mostly
because he had trouble picturing his father at all, when a neighbour woman, worrisomely tall, came to be standing uninvited in
the living room. He'd left the door open and cracked the windows

so the breeze could do its work. Let the elements scrub this place free of his father. He needed candles, wind, a shaman. And on the subject of need: after sudden travel into blistering sunshine, he needed salty food to blow off in his mouth. He needed sex, if only with himself. Oh, to be alone with his laptop so he could leak a little cream onto his belly. Now there was a trespasser in his father's home, suited up in business wear. It was enormously difficult to picture such people as babies. And yet one provided the courtesy anyway. An effort to relate. Their full maturation was even harder to summon. He was apparently to believe that, over time, these creatures, just nude little seals at first, would elongate and gain words. A layer of fur would cover them, with moist parts, and teeth, and huge pockets for gathering money. Was there a website where the corporate Ichabods of the world showed off their waterworks, gave each other rubdowns and whispered pillow talk in an invented language? Perhaps a new category beckoned.

'Oh my god. You *can't* be George,' the woman said.

George sort of shared her disbelief. He couldn't be. The metaphysics were troubling, if you let them get to you. But day after day, with crushing regularity, he failed to prove otherwise.

The woman approached, her nose high. Examine the specimen, she possibly thought. Maybe draw its blood.

'I can't believe it!'

He asked if he could help her. Maybe she wanted to buy something, a relic of the dead man. The realtor had said that everything had to go. Take this house down to the bones.

So far, George was just picking at the skin. He was looking through his father's takeout menus, skimming the man's internet history. There were items of New Mexican pottery to destroy, shirts to try on.

Maybe he'd dress up like his father and take some selfies. Get the man online, if posthumously. If no one much liked him when

he was alive, at least the fucker could get some likes in the after-
life. Serious.

The woman remembered herself.

'I'm Trish, Jim's . . . you know.'

'Uh huh,' George said.

'I won't even *pretend* to think he might have told you about me,'
Trish said. 'It's not like we were married in any real official way.
At least not yet.'

Oh god. A half wife.

The last time he spoke to his father – months ago now – George
remembered not listening while his father said he had met someone, and that she – what was it? – provided the kind of service you didn't really get paid for, or paid enough, because fuck
this country! And that this new girlfriend was from somewhere
unique, and George knew to act impressed. Certainly his dad
had seemed very proud, as if he'd met someone important from
another planet.

So details had been shared, just not absorbed. Would she tell
George now that his father had really loved him? Pined and whatever, wished for phone calls, had the boy's name on Google Alert?

'Of course, Trish,' George said, and then he smacked his forehead, ever so lightly, to let her know just what he thought of his
forgetfulness. She deserved as much. They embraced, at a distance, as if his father's body was stretched out between them.
Then she stepped closer and really wrapped him up. He felt her
breath go out of her as she collapsed against him.

George knew he was supposed to feel something. Emotional,
sexual. Rage and sorrow and a little bit of predatory hunger. Even
a deeper shade of indifference? History virtually demanded that
the errant son, upon packing up his estranged and dead father's
belongings, would seek closure with the new, younger wife. Half
wife. Some sort of circuitry demanded to be completed. He had
an obligation.

It felt pretty good to hold her. She softened, but didn't go bone-less. He dropped his face into her neck. Lately he'd consorted with some hug-proof men and women. They hardened when he closed in. Their bones came out. Not this one. She knew what she was doing.

'Well you sure don't smell like your father,' she said, breaking the hug. 'And you don't look like him. I mean *at all*.'

She laughed.

'Oh I must,' said George. He honestly didn't know.

'Nope. Trust me. I have seen that man *up close*. You are a very handsome young man.'

'Thank you,' said George.

'I think I want to see some ID! I might have to cry foul!'

They met later for dinner at a taco garage on the beach. Their food arrived inside what looked like an industrial metal disc.

George dug in and wished it didn't taste so ridiculously good.

'Oh my god,' he gushed.

It was sort of the problem with California, the unembarrassed way it delivered pleasure. It backed you into a corner.

After dinner they walked on the beach and tried to talk about George's father without shitting directly inside the man's urn, which was probably still ember hot. George hadn't unboxed it yet.

'I loved him, I did. I'm sure of it,' Trish said. 'When all the anger finally went out of him there was something so sweet there.'

George pictured his father deflated like a pool toy, crumpled in a corner.

'He called me by your mom's name a lot. By mistake. Rina. Irene. Boy did he do that a lot.'

'Oh, that must have been hard,' said George. Who was Irene? he wondered. Had he ever met her? His mother's name was Lydia.

'No, I get it. He had a life before me. We weren't babies. It's just that I suppose I want to be happy, too. Which is really a radical idea, if you think about it,' Trish said.

George thought about it, but he was tired and losing focus. He preferred a solitary loneliness to the kind he felt around other people. And this woman, Trish. Was she family to him now? Why did it feel like they were on a date?

'It's just that my happiness, what I needed to do to get it, threatened your father,' continued Trish.

'My father, threatened,' George said. 'But whatever could you mean?'

'Oh I like *you*. You're nothing like him.'

George took that in. It sounded fine, possibly true. He had no real way of knowing. He remembered his father's new radio, which he had watched him build when he was a kid, and whose dial he twisted into static for hours and hours. He could make his dad laugh by pretending the static came from his mouth, lip-syncing it. He remembered how frightened his father had been in New York when he visited. George held his arm everywhere they went. It had irritated him terribly.

What else? His father made him tomato soup once. His father slapped him while he was brushing his teeth, sending a spray of toothpaste across the mirror.

George was probably supposed to splurge on memories now. He wasn't sure he had the energy. Maybe the thing was to let the memories hurl back and cripple him, months or years from now. They needed time, wherever they were hiding, to build force, so that when they returned to smother him, he might never recover.

After their walk, they stood in a cloud of charred smoke behind the restaurant. The ocean broke and swished somewhere over a dune. Trish arched her back and yawned.

'All of this death,' she said.

'Horn-y,' George shouted. He wasn't, but still. Maybe if they stopped talking for a while they'd break this mood.

Trish tried not to laugh.

'No, uh, funny you should say that. I was just thinking, it makes me want to . . .' She smiled.

How George wished that this was the beginning of a suicide pact, after a pleasant dinner at the beach with your dead father's mistress. Just walk out together into the waves. But something told him that he knew what was coming instead.

'I'm going to comfort myself tonight, with or without you,' Trish said. 'Do you feel like scrubbing in?'

George looked away. The time was, he would sleep with anyone, of any physical style. Any make, any model. Pretty much any year. If only he could do away with the transactional phase, when the barter chips came out, when the language of seduction was suddenly spoken, rather than sung, in such non-melodious tones. It was often a deal breaker. Often. Not always.

After they'd had sex, which required one of them to leave the room to focus on the project alone, they washed up and had a drink. It felt good to sip some skank-ass, legacy whiskey from his father's Pueblo coffee mugs. Now that they'd stared into each other's cold depravity, they could relax.

Trish circled around to the inevitable.

'So what's up with Pattern?'

Here we go.

'What's she like? Are you guys in touch? Your father never would speak of her.'

Probably due to the non-disclosure agreement she must have had him sign, George figured.

'You know,' he said, pausing, as if his answer was more than ordinarily true, 'she's really nice, really kind. I think she's misunderstood.'

'Did I misunderstand it when her company, in eighteen months, caused more erosion to the Great Barrier Reef than had been recorded in all of history?'

'She apologised for that.'

'I thought you were going to say she didn't do it. Or that it didn't happen that way.'

'No, she did do it, with great intention, I think. I bet at low tide she would have stood on the reef herself and smashed that fucking thing into crumbs for whatever fungal fuel they were mining. But, you know, she apologised. In a way, that's much better than never having done it. She has authority now. Gravity. She's human.'

'What was she before?'

Before? George thought. Before that she was his sister. She babysat for him. He once saw her get beaten up by another girl. She went to a special smart-people high school that had classes on Saturdays. Before that she was just this older person in his home. She had her own friends. She kept her door closed. Someone should have told him she was going to disappear. He would have tried to get to know her.

In the morning Trish recited the narrative she had concocted for them. Their closeness honoured a legacy. Nothing was betrayed by their physical intimacy. They'd both lost someone. It was now their job to make fire in the shape of – here George lost track of her theory – George's dad.

Trish looked like she wanted to be challenged. Instead George nodded and agreed and tried to hold her. He said he thought that a fire like that would be a fine idea. Even though they'd treated each other like specimens the night before, two lab technicians straining to achieve a result, their hug was oddly platonic today. He pictured the two of them out in the snow, pouring a gasoline silhouette of his dead father. Igniting it. Effigy or burn pile?

'We didn't know each other before,' said Trish. 'Now we do. We're in each other's lives. This is real. And it's good. You're not just going to go home and forget me. It won't be possible.'

George would sign off on pretty much any press release about what had happened last night, and what they now meant to each other, so long as it featured him catching his plane at 9.30 am and never seeing her again.

As he was leaving, Trish grabbed him.

'I would say "one for the road", but I don't really believe in that. Just that whole way of thinking and speaking. It sounds sorrowful and final and I don't want that to be our thing. That's not us. I don't like the word "road" and I definitely don't like the word "one". Two is much better. Two is where it's at.'

She held up two fingers and tried to get George to kiss them.

George smiled at her, pleaded exhaustion. It was sweet of her to offer, he said, and normally he would, but.

'You know, research shows,' Trish said, not giving up, 'that really it's a great energy boost, to love and be loved. To climax. To cause to climax. To cuddle and talk and to listen and speak. You're here! You're standing right here with me now!'

'I'm sorry,' said George. 'I guess it's all just starting to hit me. Dad. Being gone. I don't think I'd bring the right spirit right now. You would deserve better.'

It didn't feel good or right to play this card, but as he said it he found it was more true than he'd intended.

Trish was beautiful, but given the growing privacy of his sexual practice, such factors no longer seemed to matter. He would probably love to have sex with her, if she could somehow find a way of vanishing, and if the two of them could also find a way to forget that they had tried that already, last night, and the experience had been deeply medical and isolating. It was just too soon to hope for a sufficiently powerful denial to erase all that and let them, once again, look at each other like strangers, full of lust and hope.

'Is that a bad thing?' George asked his therapist, after returning home and telling her the basics.

'And please don't ask me what *I* think,' he continued. 'The reason people ask a question is because they would like an answer. Reflecting my question back to me, I swear, is going to make me hurl myself out of the window.'

Together they looked at the small, dirty window. There were bars on it. The office was on the ground floor.

'I'd hate to be a cause of your death,' said the therapist, unblinking.

'Well I just wonder what you think.'

'Okay, but I don't think you need to lecture me in order to get me to answer a question. You seem to think I need to be educated about how to respond to you. There are also many other reasons people ask questions, aside from wanting answers. You're an imbecile if you think otherwise.'

'Okay, you're right, I'm sorry.'

'Well, then, I think it must be lonely. I do. To find yourself attracted to a woman who also seems, as you say, attracted to you – if that's *true* – and to think you'd be more content to fantasise about her than to experience her physically. So it sounds lonely to me. But we should also notice that this is a loneliness you've chosen, based on your sexual desires. Your sexuality seems to thrive on loneliness. And I can't help but sense that some part of you is proud of that. Your story seems vaguely boastful.'

'Plus her being my father's widow.'

Dr Graco frowned.

'What was that?' she asked.

'You know, her also having been involved with my father, before he died. I guess I left that part out.'

Dr Graco took a moment to write in her notebook. She wrote quickly, and with a kind of disdain, as if she didn't like to have to make contact with the page. A fear of contaminants, maybe. A disgust with language.

It had sometimes occurred to him that therapists used this

quiet writing time, after you've said something striking, or, more likely, boring, to make notes to themselves about other matters. Grocery lists, plans. One never got to see what was written down, and there was simply no possible way that all of it was strictly relevant. How much of it was sheer stalling, running out the clock? How much of it just got the narcissist in the chair across from you to shut up for a while?

She wrote through one page and had turned to another before looking up.

'I am sorry to hear about your father.'

'I should have told you. I apologise.'

'He died . . . recently?'

'Two weeks ago. That's why I was away. My missed appointment. Which I paid for, but. I was gone. I'm not sure if you.'

'I see. Do you mean it when you say you should have told me?'

'Well, I found the prospect of telling you exhausting, I guess. I was annoyed that I had to do it. To be honest, I wished you could just, through osmosis, *have* the information, in the same way you can see what I'm wearing and we don't need to discuss it. It's just a self-evident fact. You could just look at me and know that my father is dead.'

She resumed writing, but he did not want to wait for her.

'That's not a criticism of you, by the way. I don't think you were supposed to guess. I mean I don't *think* I think that. Maybe. You know, to just be sensitive and perceptive enough to *know*. I am sometimes disappointed about your powers, I guess. That's true, I should admit that. I just wish I had, like, a helper, who could run ahead of me to deliver the facts, freeing me up from supplying all of this context when I talk to people. Otherwise I'm just suddenly this guy who's like, my father died, blah blah. I'm just that guy.'

'But you weren't. Because you didn't tell me. You were not that guy.'

'Right, I guess.'

'So then who were you?'

'What?'

'You didn't want to be the guy who told me your father had died, so by not telling me, what guy did you end up being instead?'

For some reason, George saw himself and Pattern, as kids, waiting on a beach for their lunch to digest, so they could go swimming. Pattern was dutifully counting down from two thousand. It was a useless memory, irrelevant here. He remembered when he shopped and cooked for his mother, when she wasn't feeling well, and then really wasn't feeling well. He cleaned and took care of her. His father had already planted his flag in California. He was that guy, but for such a short time. Two weeks? He'd been very many people since then. Who was he when he didn't tell Dr Graco that his father died? Nobody. No one remarkable. He'd been someone too scared or too bored, he didn't know which, to discuss something important.

'That just made me think of something,' he said finally. 'The word "guy". I don't know. Have you heard of Guy Fox?'

'I assume you don't mean the historic figure Guy Fawkes?'

'No. F-o-x. Porn star, but that's not really a good label for what he does. It's not clear you can even call it porn any more. It's so sort of remote and kind of random, and definitely not obviously sexual. Or even at all. I mean almost, just, boredom. Anyway, it's a new sort of thing. He provides eye contact. People pay a lot. He'll just watch you, on video. You can stream him to your TV, and he'll watch you. People pay him to watch while they have sex, of course, or masturbate, but now supposedly people just hire him to watch them while they hang out alone in their houses. Whenever they look up, he's looking at them. They are paying to have eye contact whenever they want. They want someone out there seeing them. And he's just amazing. Apparently there's nothing quite like getting seen by him. It's an addiction.'

'Ah, I see. Well I'm afraid we have to stop.'

Afraid, afraid, afraid. Don't be afraid, George thought. Embrace it.

For once he wished she'd say, 'I'm delighted our session is over, George, now get the fuck out of my office, you monster.'

Bowing to a certain protocol of the bereaved, George acquired a baby dog: hairless, pink and frightening. His therapist had put him onto it after he kept insisting he was fine. She explained that people who lose a parent, especially one they weren't close to, tend to grieve their lack of grief. Like they want to really feel something, and don't, and so they grieve that. That absence. She said that one solution to this circular, masturbatory grief is apparently to take care of something. To be responsible for another living creature.

Except George and the animal had turned out to be a poor match. That's how he put it to the dog catcher, or whatever the man was called, when he sent the wet thing back, and then hired cleaners to sanitise his home. The animal was more like a quiet young child, waiting for a ride, determined not to exploit any hospitality whatsoever in George's home. It rarely sprawled out, never seemed to relax. It sat upright in the corner, sometimes trotting to the window, where it glanced up and down the street, patiently confirming that it had been abandoned. Would it recognise rescue when it came? Sometimes you just had to wait this life out, it seemed to be thinking, and get a better deal next time. God knows where the fucking thing slept. Or if.

Did the animal not get tired? Did it not require something? George would occasionally hose off the curry from the unmolested meat in his takeout container, and scrape it into the dog bowl, only to clean it up, untouched, days later. The animal viewed these meals with calm detachment. How alienating it was, to live with a creature so ungoverned by appetites. This thing could go hungry. It had a long game. What kind of level playing field was that? George felt entirely outmatched.

One night George tried to force the issue. He wanted more from it, and it wanted absolutely nothing from George, so perhaps, as the superior species, with broader perspective in the field, George needed to step up and trigger change. Be a leader. Rule by example. Maybe he had been playing things too passive? He pulled the thing onto his lap. He stroked its wet, stubbled skin, put on one of those TV shows that pets are supposed to like. No guns, just soft people swallowing each other.

The dog survived the affection. It trembled under George's hands. Some love is strictly clinical. Maybe this was like one of those deep tissue massages that release difficult feelings? George forced his hand along the dog's awful back, wondering why anyone would willingly touch another living thing. What a disaster of feelings it stirred up, feelings that seemed to have no purpose other than to suffocate him. Finally the dog turned in George's lap, as if standing on ice, and carefully licked its master's face. Just once, and briefly. A studied, scientific lick, using the tongue to gain important information. Then it bounced down to its corner again, where it sat and waited.

Months after his father's death there was still no word from Pattern. After he'd returned from California, and cleansed himself in the flat, grey atmosphere of New York, George had sent her another email, along the lines of, 'Hey Pat, I'm back. I've got Dad's dust. Let me know if you want to come say goodbye to it. There are still some slots free. Visiting hours are whenever you fucking want. – G.'

He never heard back, and figured he wasn't going to – on the internet now Pattern was referred to as a fugitive wanted by Europol, for crimes against the environment – but one night, getting into bed, his phone made an odd sound. Not its typical ring. It took him a minute to track the noise to his phone, and at first he thought it must be broken, making some death noise before it finally shut down.

He picked it up and heard a long, administrative pause.

'Please hold for Pattern,' a voice said.

He waited and listened. Finally a woman said hello.

'Hello?' said George. 'Pattern?'

'Who's this?' It wasn't Pattern. This person sounded like a bitchy tween, entitled and shrill.

'You called me,' explained George.

'Who's on the line,' said the teenager, 'or I'm hanging up.'

George was baffled. Did a conversation with his sister really require such a cloak-and-dagger ground game? He hung up the phone.

The phone rang again an hour later, and it was Pattern herself.

'Jesus, George, what the fuck? You hung up on my staff?'

'First of all, hello,' he said. 'Secondly, let's take a look at the transcript and I'll show you exactly what happened. Your team could use some human behaviour training. But forget all that. What on earth is new, big sister?'

She wanted to see him, she said, and she'd found a way for that to be possible. They had things to discuss.

'No shit,' said George. He couldn't believe he was actually talking to her.

'Wait, so where are you?' she asked. 'I don't have my thing with me.'

'What thing?'

'I mean I don't know where you are.'

'And your thing would have told you? Have you been tracking me?'

'Oh c'mon, you asshole.'

'I'm in New York.'

She laughed.

'What?'

'No, it's just funny. I mean it's funny that you still call it that.'

'What would I call it?'

'No, nothing, forget it. I'm sorry. I'm just on a different, it's, I'm thinking of something else. Forget it.'

'O-*kay*. You are so fucking weird and awkward. I'm not really sure I even want to see you.'

'Georgie!'

'Kidding, you freak. Can you like send a jet for me? Or a pod? Or what the fuck is it you guys even make now? Can you break my face into dust and make it reappear somewhere?'

'Ha ha. I'll send a car for you. Tomorrow night. Seven o'clock.'

George met Pattern in the sky bar of a strange building, which somehow you could not see from the street. Everyone had thought the developers had purchased the air rights and then very tastefully decided not to use them. Strike a blow for restraint. The elevator said otherwise. This thing was a fucking tower. How had they done that? The optics for such effects, Pattern explained to him, had been around for fifteen years or more. Brutally old-fashioned technology. Practically cave man. She thought it looked cheesy at this point.

'A stealth scraper,' said George, wanting to sound appreciative.

'Hardly. It's literally smoke and mirrors,' Pattern said. 'I am not fucking kidding. And it's kind of gross. But whatever. I love this bar. These cocktails are fucking violent. There's a frozen pane of pork in this one. Ridiculously thin. They call it pork glass.'

'Yum,' said George, absently.

The funny thing about the bar, which was only just dawning on George, was that it was entirely free of people. And deadly silent. Out the window was a view of the city he'd never seen. Whenever he looked up he had the sensation that he was somewhere else. In Europe. In the past. On a film set. Asleep. Every now and then a young woman crept out from behind a curtain to touch Pattern on the wrist, moving her finger back and forth. Pattern would smell her wrist, make a face, and say something unintelligible.

But here she was, his very own sister. It was like looking at his mother and his father and himself, but refined, the damaged cells burned off. The best parts of them, contained in this one person.

'First of all, George,' Pattern said. 'Dad's girlfriend? Really?'

'Trish?'

'What a total pig you are. Does this woman need to be abused and neglected by two generations of our family?'

'How could you know anything about that?'

'Oh cut it out. It astonishes me when I meet people who still think they have secrets. It's so quaint! You understand that even with your doors closed and lights out . . . Please tell me you understand. I couldn't bear it if you were that naive. My own brother.'

'I understand, I think.'

'That man you pay to watch you while you're cleaning the house? On your laptop screen?'

'Guy Fox.'

'Oh, George, you are a funny young man.'

'That's actually a fairly mainstream habit, to have a watcher.'

'Right, George, it's happening all over the Middle East, too. A worldwide craze. In Poland they do it live. It's called a peeping Tom. But who cares. Baby brother is a very strange bird.

'So,' she said, scooting closer to him and giving him a luxurious hug. 'Mom and Dad never told you, huh?'

'Told me what?'

'They really never told you?'

'I'm listening.'

'I'm just not sure it's for me to say. Mom and Dad talked about it kind of a lot, I mean we all did. I just figured they'd told you.'

'What already, Jesus. There's no one else left to tell me.'

'You were adopted. That's actually not the right word. Dad got in trouble at work and his boss forced him to take you home and raise you. You were born out of a donkey's ass. Am I remembering correctly? That doesn't sound right. From the ass of an ass.'

He tried to smile.

'I'm just kidding, George, Jesus. What is wrong with people?'

'Oh my god, right?' said George. 'Why can't people entertain more stupid jokes at their own expense? Je-*sus*. It's *so* frustrating! When, like, my world view isn't supported by all the *little* people beneath me? And I can't demean people and get an easy *laugh*? It's so not fair!'

'Oh fuck off, George.'

They smiled. It felt really good. This was just tremendously nice.

'You don't understand,' he said, trying harder than usual to be serious. 'Mom punted so long ago I can't even remember her smell. And Dad was just a stranger, you know? He was so formal, so polite. I always felt like I was meeting him for the first time.'

He tried to sound like his father, like any father: 'Hello, George, how are you? How was your flight? Well that's grand. What's your life like these days?'

Pattern stared at him.

'Honestly,' said George. 'I can't stand making small talk with people who have seen me naked. Or who fed me. Or spanked me. I mean once you spank someone, you owe them a nickname. Was that just me or were Mom and Dad like completely opposed to nicknames? Or even just Honey or Sweetie or any of that.'

'Jesus, George, what do you want from people? You have some kind of intimacy fantasy. Do you think other people go around hugging each other and holding hands, mainlining secrets and confessions into each other's veins?'

'I have accepted the fact of strangers,' said George. 'After some struggle. But it's harder when they are in your own family.'

'Violin music for you,' said Pattern, and she snapped her fingers.

He looked up, perked his ears, expecting to hear music.

'Wow,' she marvelled. 'You think I'm very powerful, don't you?'

'Honestly, I don't know. I have no idea. Are you in trouble? Everything I read is so scary.'

'I am in a little bit of trouble, yes. But don't worry. It's nothing. And you. You seem so sad to me,' Pattern said. 'Such a sad, sad young man.' She stroked his face, and it felt ridiculously, treacherously comforting.

George waved this off, insisted that he wasn't. He just wanted to know about her. He really did. Who knew where she'd vanish to after this, and he genuinely wanted to know what her life was like, where she lived. Was she married? Had she gotten married in secret or something?

'I don't get to act interested and really mean it,' George explained. 'I mean ever, so please tell me who you are. It's kind of a selfish question, because I can't figure some things out about myself, so maybe if I hear about you, something will click.'

'Me? I tend to date the house husband type. Self-effacing, generous, asexual. Which is something I'm really attracted to, I should say. Men with low T, who go to bed in a full rack of pyjamas. That's my thing. I don't go for the super-carnal hetero men; they seem like zoo animals. Those guys who know what they want, and have weird and highly developed skills as lovers, invariably have the worst possible taste – we're supposed to congratulate them for knowing that they like to lick butter right off the stick. What a nightmare, to be subject to someone else's expertise. The guys I tend to date, at first, are out to prove that they endorse equality, that my career matters, that my interests are primary – they make really extravagant displays of selflessness, burying all of their own needs. I go along with it, and over time I watch them deflate and lose all reason to live, by which point I have steadily lost all of my attraction for them. I imagine something like that is mirrored in the animal kingdom, but honestly that's not my specialty. I should have an air gun in my home so I could put these guys out of their misery. Or a time-lapse video documenting the slow and steady loss of self-respect they go through. It's a turn-off, but, you know, it's my turn-off. Part of what initially arouses me is the feeling that I am about to mate with someone who will soon be ineffectual and powerless. I've come to rely on the arc. It's part of my process.'

'You think these guys don't mean it that they believe in equality?'

'No, I think they do, and that it has a kind of cost. They just distort themselves so much trying to do the right thing that there's nothing left.'

'And you enjoy that?'

'Well, they enjoy that. They're driven to it. I'm just a bystander to their quest. And I enjoy *that*. It's old-school, but I like to watch.'

'So you are basically fun times to date.'

'I pull my weight, romantically. I'm not stingy. I supply locations. I supply funding. Transportation. I'm kind of an executive producer. I can greenlight stuff.'

'Nobody cums unless you say so, right?'

'That's not real power,' she said, as if such a thing was actually under her control. She frowned. 'That's bookkeeping. Not my thing at all. Anyway, I think the romantic phase of my life is probably over now. My options won't be the same. Freedom.'

'Jail time?' asked George.

'It's not exactly jail for someone like me. But it's fine if you imagined it that way. That would be nice.'

George hated to do it. They were having such a good time, and she must get this a lot, but he was her last living blood relative and didn't he merit some consideration over all the hangers-on who no doubt lived pretty well by buzzing around in her orbit?

'All right, so, I mean, you're rich, right? Like insanely so?'

Pattern nodded carefully.

'You could, like, buy anything?'

'My money is tied up in money,' Pattern said. 'It's hard to explain. You get to a point where a big sadness and fatigue takes over.'

'Not me,' said George. 'I don't. Anyway, I mean, it wouldn't even make a dent for you to, you know, solve my life financially. Just fucking solve it. Right?'

Pattern smiled at him, a little too gently, he thought. It seemed like a bad news smile.

'You know the studies, right?'

Dear god Jesus. 'What studies?'

'About what happens when people are given a lot of money. People like you, with the brain and appetites of an eleven-year-old.'

'Tell me.' He'd let the rest of the comment go.

'It's not good.'

'Well I don't fucking want it to be *good*. I want it to be fun.'

'I don't think it's very fun, either, I'm afraid.'

'Don't be afraid, Pattern. Leave that to me. I will be very afraid, I will be afraid for two, and never have to worry about money again. Depraved, sordid, painful. I'll go for those. Let me worry about how it will feel.'

Pattern laughed into her drink.

'Sweet, sweet Georgie,' she said.

It was getting late, and the whispering interruptions had increased, Pattern's harried staff scurrying around them, no doubt plotting the extraction. An older gentleman in a tuxedo came out to their couch and held up a piece of paper for Pattern, at eye level, which, to George, sitting right next to her, looked perfectly blank.

Pattern studied it, squinting, and sighed. She shifted in her seat.

'Armageddon,' said George. 'Time to wash my drones with my drone towel!'

Pattern didn't smile.

'I hate to say it, little George, but I think I'm going to have to break this up.'

He didn't like this world, standing up, having to leave. Everything had seemed fine back on the couch.

'Here,' Pattern said, giving him a card. 'Send your bills to William.'

'Ha ha.'

'What?'

'Your joke. That you obviously don't even know you just made.'

She was checking her phone, not listening.

On the street they hugged for a little while and tried to say goodbye. A blue light glowed from the back seat of Pattern's car. George had no idea who she was, what she really did, or when he would ever see her again.

'Do you think I can be in your life?' George asked. 'I'm not sure why but it feels scary to ask you that.'

He tried to laugh.

'Oh, you are, George,' said Pattern. 'Here you are. In my life right now. Closer to me than anyone else on the planet.'

'You know what I mean. How can I reach you?' He didn't particularly want to say goodbye to her.

'I always know where you are, Georgie. I do. Trust me.'

'But I don't know that. I don't really feel that. It doesn't feel like you're even out there. When you're not here it's like you never were here at all.'

'No, no,' she whispered. 'I don't believe that. That's not true.'

'Is something going to happen to you? I don't know what to believe.'

'Well,' she said. 'Something already has. Something has happened to all of us, right?'

'Please don't make a joke or be clever, Elizabeth. I can't stand it. There's nobody left but you. What if I don't see you again? What will I do?'

'Oh Georgie, I am right here. I am right here with you now.'

*

George kept quiet about his sister in therapy. He talked about everything else. But sometimes he'd catch Dr Graco studying him, and he'd think that perhaps she knew. She didn't need to be told. She might not grasp the specific details, the bare facts – who and when and what and all those things that did not matter – but it seemed to George that she could see, or was starting to, that someone out there was seeing him, watching him. That someone really knew him and that, whatever else you could say about him, it was clear that he was no longer really alone.

At home George listened, and hoped, and waited, but his phone never made the strange tone again. He found nothing on his sister in the news, though he looked. Whoever had been calling for her blood had gone quiet. And here George couldn't decide if their silence meant that they'd lost interest, or that they had her, they got her, and Pattern was gone.

One night it was late and he'd let his uncertainty overpower him. It had been a year since he'd seen her. Where was she? How could she just disappear? He'd been saving up his idea for a moment just like this one, so he sat down at his desk and wrote his sister an email.

Elizabeth –

Is it just me now, or are you still out there? Don't write back. I cannot imagine how busy you must be! There is a lot that I cannot imagine. But that's okay, right? You're out there looking, I know. I am waving at you, wherever you are. I am down here saying hello. I love you very much.

Your brother,
George

FIXATIONS

Ceridwen Dovey

As is the way of the body, when things are going right, we are allowed to remain blissfully unaware of the fact that we are housed in sheaths of flesh. When things go wrong, however, worse than the pain, worse even than the shame, is no longer being able to ignore the body's relentless systems of audit and account: things go in, things come out, things go in, things come out, over and over and over until we die. Selene lay awake at night between feeds, fantasising about how she was going to take her body for granted again when this was all over – she was going to abuse the hell out of it, eat trans fat galore, drink buckets of booze, show her body who was boss, that it had no right to hold her hostage like this.

It wasn't the baby – though of course that had been the ultimate proof of the nature of how things go in and then come out – nor was it the breastfeeding. These processes were celebrations of the body, or at least celebrations of the higher functions of the body.

The crude bodily problem keeping her awake most nights, and in agony at least once a day, was not directly related to birthing a baby, though nobody seemed to believe her when she said that the birth itself had been a piece of cake, relaxed, downright enjoyable, compared to this. She could no longer go to the toilet – *pass a bowel motion*, was how her GP liked to put it – without being in excruciating pain from the delightfully named anal fissure that had made its presence known when her baby was two weeks old.

If Selene had to summarise what she had learned so far from the experience of the fissure (as she and her husband referred to it, so often that it was like the third partner in their marriage), it would be this. That the ultimate taboo, perhaps the only one still remaining in modern Australian culture, was to talk openly about your toilet life. Toilet humour was okay, in certain prescribed situations. But the moment Selene began to share the real, lived experience of her current toilet issues with close friends – helplessly, because she didn't really want to be sharing these details, yet she was so consumed by them that she felt inauthentic in her friendships if she didn't – she could see the desperate look in her friends' eyes as they pretended it was normal, while silently willing her to stop. It seemed to her no coincidence that it was Captain Cook who had introduced the word 'taboo' into modern English usage, stealing it, along with much else, from the Tongans, whose word *tabu* had indicated something set apart, forbidden.

How could it be that this minuscule split in a fibre of her body to which she'd never given much thought could set her apart from the rest of the teeming human life on the planet? Even from her husband, who had been nothing but compassionate. She could not help resenting his carefree attitude, disappearing into the bathroom for five tranquil minutes before leaving for work, not paying any more heed to this act of emptying his bowels than to any of his other ablutions.

It was a new low point when she said to him one morning as he exited the bathroom, the flush audible, 'I'm so jealous of you.' What on earth did she expect, for him to make the sacrificial offering of a live animal to the toilet each time in acknowledgement of his body's privilege in being free of pain?

He embraced her in sympathy, kissed the sleeping baby and left their flat to jog for the bus. Selene was left standing outside the bathroom looking with dread at the still warm toilet seat, knowing she had to face the day's first anguish. Time slowed. At least the baby was asleep, she counselled herself. Once before she had endured the agony with him strapped to her chest in the

Bjorn, her tears of pain – and every time, there were tears – dropping onto his pulsing fontanelle.

Afterwards, she sat in a hot bath, and then applied the battery of useless creams whose names left nothing to the imagination (Proctosedyl, Rectinol) that she was using in a last-ditch attempt to avoid some kind of surgical intervention. The day before, at her appointment with the specialist, after she had curled up on her side on the examining table, he'd announced apologetically that the Botox injection hadn't worked to release the muscle spasm. It was a pity about the taboo, which she was trying harder to observe after one too many pleading looks from interlocutors, because ever since she'd had the Botox injected she'd been coming up with great one-liners she couldn't use: 'You think my *forehead* looks good? You should see my sphincter!' Thank the Pope the injection had been covered by the public hospital or it would have cost thousands to render her anus wrinkle-free. And it hadn't even done the trick.

The specialist had said she would need to have a lateral sphincterotomy under general anaesthetic within a few weeks if there was no improvement. She'd come home straight away and Googled it, and discovered that, for some bizarre reason, which not even medical professionals could explain, if you made a second cut in the internal sphincter – which had gone into spasm because of the fissure – it sometimes released, and solved the problem. In his consulting rooms, she had asked the specialist what the side effects of such an operation might be, and he'd paused and gazed out the windows at his view spreading all the way to the line of blue water at Bondi. There were helium balloons – 'It's a girl!' – weighted down on his desk with a bag of fluorescent lollies. His own daughter had been born a few days previously, and he had enthusiastically told Selene that his wife wanted another baby 'immediately'. This was right before he'd looked at the rack and ruin of her bum.

'Well,' he said, 'it might mean that later in life, when you go through menopause, and there are some hormonal changes, you are left partially incontinent.'

'Sort of like it is now?' she asked. She had made a map of all the public toilets on the coastal walk near her flat, marking them like pirate's treasure with a large X, and timing the walk between them, just in case.

'Probably worse,' he said.

'What exactly does partially incontinent mean?'

'Ah – you know, skidmarks in your undies every now and again,' he said, and grinned.

As if ageing wasn't going to be undignified enough.

But she had decided, if it came to it, that she'd have the operation, take that chance, and hope that her menopausal self didn't live to regret it, and hate the younger version of herself who had ruined her ability to enjoy her retirement.

Selene had to return to the hospital a few days later, baby in tow, for the six-week post-birth appointment with the midwives. A nice little routine check-up, no need to discuss her problem, she hoped. The focus, for once, would be on her baby's health. She was actually looking forward to it. She parked in the cavernous lot beneath the hospital and took the lift up to the birthing centre. It was the first time she'd been back since the birth, and she could hear somebody labouring in the same room where she'd had her son in the bath. She felt elated to think of the lukewarm water, the feel of the edges of the tub beneath her hands.

The midwife was not from Eucalyptus Group. Selene had never met her before, and she seemed harried, uninterested in making chitchat about her water birth. Old-school Aussie, middle-aged, not one of the young women fresh from midwifery school sent out to face the onslaught of Sydney's raging baby boom. The midwife handled Selene's baby for his weighing and measuring as if

he were a choice leg of lamb, expertly palpated his still slightly swollen ballsack to check if his testicles had descended, and
then re-swaddled him so tightly it looked as if he'd spun his own
cocoon.

'Your turn. On your back, legs up,' the midwife said without
preamble, and next thing Selene was getting her stitches checked.

'There's a small polyp, I'll have to burn it off.' The midwife lit
something that looked like a long silver sparkler.

'Where, exactly?' Selene said nervously.

The midwife didn't respond. She was frowning in concentration.

It was quick, relatively painless, but still. Hot metal on raw
flesh. She had the dizzy feeling once again that she had disin-
tegrated into nothing but a collection of limbs held together by
failing viscera. She looked at her son, who was transfixed by a
black-and-white wall map, and repeated her mantra of sanity:
He's okay, he's okay, he's okay. She was quietly fascinated by how
much she could endure, but if anything had gone wrong with *his*
body, she would have broken apart. She thought of something
she'd read in one of the birthing books. It troubled her for being
both true and not true. *You have amazing reserves of self. You will
bring these reserves to your birth experience just as you bring them
to every challenging experience you have in your life. The 'you'
who births your baby does not stand outside the 'you' of the rest of
your history and present.*

'Okay, all done,' the midwife said. Her name was Agatha,
according to her nametag, for she hadn't introduced herself.

Selene pulled up her pants and moved to the chair beside Agatha, who was typing notes into a computer using her index finger.

'Now, we need to discuss contraception. It's mostly a myth
about breastfeeding. You want me to prescribe the mini-pill?'

'No, thanks,' Selene said. 'I think I'll be fine.'

Agatha looked at her suspiciously. 'Have you had intercourse
since the birth?'

Selene laughed a little too loudly, a sound verging on a guffaw. 'You got to get back on the horse,' Agatha said. 'The longer you wait, the harder it gets.'

'I'm not really planning on having sex ever again,' Selene said, half-joking.

But Agatha, it seemed, took this declaration very seriously. Her attitude changed immediately into one of bustling concern. She shuffled around in the drawer and held out a form and a pen. 'I'd like you to fill this out based on how you've felt in the past week,' she said.

'What is it?'

'It's a questionnaire, the Edinburgh Postnatal Depression Scale. It will help me assess how you're feeling.'

Selene looked down at the piece of paper. The first statement was *I have been able to laugh and see the funny side of things* and the choice of responses was: *As much as I always could, Not quite so much now, Definitely not so much now* and *Not at all.* 'Okay,' she said, 'but you need to know that in the past seven days I've had a failed Botox injection to my sphincter, and every time I've had a bowel movement I've been in so much pain I've cried. It's got nothing to do with adapting to life with my baby, or hormones. It's just about being in physical pain. So I'll answer this honestly, but it doesn't mean I'm depressed if I've had sense of humour failure recently.'

'I understand,' Agatha said noncommittally. 'Why don't you fill it out and we can go from there.'

Selene could see that Agatha was now on high alert, her post-natal depression radar quivering. She looked excited, as if she were about to bust Selene for theft, like she was anticipating a victory of sorts. Stupidly, she decided to trust Agatha, and she filled out the ten questions honestly. It felt good to tick *Rather less than I used to* in response to the statement *I have looked forward with enjoyment to things.* She was on a liquid diet for the sake of the fissure, no caffeine despite the sleeplessness, for it compounded the problem of being in semi-constant danger of shitting her pants, and she approached the bathroom each morning as she would a war zone, so yes, she believed it was safe to say that there wasn't a huge amount she had to look forward to at the moment other than the feel of her infant son's skin against her own, and his gummy, wondrous first smiles.

Her mind wandered as she filled out the questionnaire. This was the other thing she had learned in the past few weeks of pain, she realised – when your body stops working the way it should, you start to see anything involving the body as absurd, especially sex. The less of it you're having, the more bizarre it begins to seem, the more unthinkable it becomes as something anyone would choose to do. She was thinking about sex all the time, but not in a good way. She could not believe she'd ever had it, that anyone in the history of humankind had ever had any. She looked at women who were pregnant with a second child with utter incredulity: they'd actually chosen to have sex again! So it *was* possible! But when, how, why?

This wasn't prudery, it was genuine amazement. She had been placed on the outside of something and was gazing in, more perplexed by the human body than she had been as a child. Her father had once brought home a stack of blank examination booklets from his university for her when she was seven, knowing she liked to fill things in and catalogue them, and later she'd found him and her mother laughing together at the kitchen table, because opposite the box EXAMINING BODY she had written I DO THAT. She hadn't understood at the time why it was funny – in fact, the question had bothered her, the presumption that anyone else would ever think they could examine her body.

She handed her completed questionnaire to Agatha, who graded it using a mystical system of numbers.

'Hmmmm,' Agatha said gravely. 'I'm afraid we have a problem.

You're in the danger zone for postnatal depression. You've got to come back in next week and take this test again.'

Selene smiled passive-aggressively. 'But it's got nothing to do with postnatal anything. Anyone can get an anal fissure, at any stage of their lives. Men can get them. Women who've never had children can get them. It's just unfortunate that mine is not getting better on its own.'

Agatha's eyes had taken on a beatific gleam. Selene stopped talking. She wondered ungenerously if the midwives were given a postnatal depression detection quota, and she'd just helped Agatha to meet hers.

At the door, within earshot of several women in the waiting room in various pregnancy or post-birth states, Agatha said to Selene, 'Now remember. You *must* have sex. It's good for the scar tissue, too. Keeps it flexible.'

Selene imagined announcing to her husband when he got home that evening that he needed to go to the late-night pharmacy to fill an urgent prescription she'd been given by the midwife. 'A prescription for what?' he would ask, concerned, already elbow deep in their baby's yellow poo that smelled wonderful, like expensive French mustard.

'For sex,' she would deadpan.

He was always hopeful that the miracle cure had been identified, the potion of potions to put her out of her pain. The first time he'd picked up on her behalf the tub of specially prepared 0.2% nitroglycerine ointment, the female chemist had given him a knowing look and said: 'Rub a pea-sized amount around the rim of the anus twice a day. Partners shouldn't share this product, just so you know,' assuming he was gay. Unfazed, he'd returned a few days later to ask the same chemist if they sold sitz baths for relief from anal pain, and she'd said, 'You mean the bucket you put over the toilet to immerse your buttocks in hot salty water?' And he'd exclaimed, 'Yes, that's the one!', glad that she might have one in stock.

Selene knew that sex was the last thing on her husband's mind too, that his libido had gone into hiding. He was as distracted and exhausted as she was, as engrossed by his adoration for their son. Sex had never seemed more irrelevant to their bond as a couple. He had been there beside her for every minute of the birth, mildly electrocuting himself setting up the TENS machine, dancing with her in their underwear in the lounge, holding her hair back while she puked through the later contractions, gently encouraging her as their baby peered up at him from underwater in the bath, waiting for the next push to free his shoulders. Sex was great, she remembered distantly, but surely its most important function was to re-establish and affirm intimacy between two people? In which case they no longer had need of that. They were more emotionally intimate than ever before as they cared for their son together. Their relationship had evolved beyond a need for sex.

That weekend they drove out to Barrington Tops National Park for Christmas in July with three other couples. They'd kept the tradition for a few years, started by one of the husbands who was British and homesick, and who liked to experiment with different ways of cooking a turkey. It was their first road trip since the baby had been born, and Selene planned to read voraciously in the back seat beside his capsule.

The trip started out well. The baby fell asleep, and Selene plunged into an issue of the *London Review of Books* that her mum had loaned her, and that she'd been working through for what felt like months, reading one dense column at a go before her attention was demanded elsewhere. According to the page crease, she was halfway through an article about the biography of the Buddha, but she had no memory of what had come before. She gave up and read the poem on the page instead. It was by Frederick Seidel, and it began:

A man sits counting the floor tiles of the bathroom floor,
Counts silently left to right, then right to left, while pressure
   mounts,
And while, in urgently increasing amounts,
His sphincter speaks up like a kazoo and starts to snore.

'Jesus H. Christ,' she said, and her husband's eyes shot to the rearview mirror to check she was okay. She didn't explain; the wind was rushing through his window and it was difficult to communicate from the back seat.

Some people might feel better about themselves on seeing life reflected in art or vice versa, but the poet's snoring sphincter was the very last thing Selene wanted to read or think about right then. Early on in her own battle with that part of her anatomy, her mum had in sympathetic jest printed out a short poem called 'Ars Poetica' and suggested Selene stick it next to the toilet as a way to cheer herself up, or at least as a reminder that one day she would no longer have to be paying such close attention to her body's workings. It went like this:

> The goose that laid the golden egg
> Died looking up its crotch
> To find out how its sphincter worked.
>
> Would you lay well? Don't watch.

Selene had read the poem with growing horror. Did her mum not realise that the goose had *died* trying to figure out how its sphincter worked?

She threw the *LRB* to the car floor and opened up instead the biography of the doomed marriage of Sylvia Plath and Ted Hughes, which she'd been dipping into during night feeds. It gave her a special frisson to read about their mutual unhappiness from within the warm security of her happy marriage. But the section she now turned to was describing Sylvia and Ted's initial and wildly passionate love affair.

He told her that the memory of exploring her naked body lingered 'like brandy' – in his bloodstream, in his brain, warming and enlivening him, as if that brandy he poured into her the night they met at Falcon Yard had saturated her skin, and he had tasted it a whole month later . . . They wrote to each other every day, and his long marvelous letters end with pulses of pure echolocation – *loveloveloveloveloveovelove*. He longs to kiss, suck, lick, and bite her from head to heel . . . *kish, ponk, puss, wife, I am here, where are you?*

Selene looked up from the book, at the afternoon light strobing through the gum trees. They'd turned off the major freeway north now, and the shape of the country road felt more a result of historical accident than planning – its curves paying tribute to old obstacles like lakes and streams and drovers' paths. It was getting chilly. Her husband's silhouette in the driver's seat against the gold-hazed windscreen was so familiar, and filled her with tenderness. She remembered on one of their first encounters following him home in her car from a party, how she had fallen in love with the shape of his head and shoulders in the dark interior of his car and the way he had waited for her on the side of the road when she'd been delayed by a red light. It had always been a habit on road trips to put her hand on his thigh as he drove. Even if they stayed silent, each letting their thoughts unspool behind them, it meant they were connected. She missed him, she realised. *I am here, where are you?* This glancing winter light always made her nostalgic for things she hadn't properly valued in the past. She leaned forward and squeezed his shoulder, and he immediately covered her hand with his own, as if he had been waiting for the gesture.

51

Near the end of their four-hour journey, long after the sun had set, once the baby had fallen asleep again, Selene realised she needed the toilet. Her husband pulled over, keeping the head-lights on, and gave her a grimace of condolence as she picked her way through the bush at the side of the road, looking for a tree to give cover. She squatted with her undies bunched around her knees, not thinking of snakes or spiders. They were the least of her troubles. She tried to do her deep breathing but it didn't work, and she called out in torment.

For the last half hour of the trip the post-spasm pain was too intense for her to sit down. She had to keep herself partly lifted above the seat by clinging onto the coat-hanger handle. At one point she swore at her husband that he was driving too slowly, knowing even as she did it that she was being unfair.

Finally they pulled into the driveway of the historic building, an old schoolhouse converted into holiday accommodation. She could hear their friends chatting in the communal living room, and smell woodsmoke on the cold air. Without a word, understanding she needed to be alone, Selene's husband took the baby in his capsule towards the lights and laughter. She slunk off towards the sleeping quarters, claimed a bedroom with an en-suite and ran herself the deepest, hottest bath in the history of bathing. The bath stood claw-footed in the very centre of the bathroom, steam rising from it like a cauldron. Beneath the water, her skin poached pink, then red. She went to bed without saying hello to the others.

After the early morning feed, she went back to sleep, and woke later to find the house empty and a note from her husband: *Gone bushwalking with bubba and the others. Don't worry, I defrosted a bottle of breastmilk for him. Stay in bed all morning if you feel like it.* A fire was still going in the lounge, and there were sausages and eggs covered with a plate, and a coffee pot half full. She had a teaspoon of coffee. It tasted unbelievably good. She took a bite of the stubby congealed end of a sausage. Then she mashed up berries with psyllium husk powder and water for her liquid breakfast. A trussed turkey was already roasting in the oven, and on the sideboard were the beginnings of various accompaniments: raw stuffing mixture, peeled potatoes and a resting batter for Yorkshire puddings. Somebody had made mulled wine the night before, and she simply could not resist. She reheated a cup of it in the microwave and drank very slowly. She knew that later it would anger her innards and she would pay for every drop. But it tasted like nectar on the tongue.

The corridors were hung with a few sepia photographs of the schoolmaster and his family who had lived in these rooms beside the schoolhouse, now the dining room. Selene stared at the image of the wife, a woman living out her days here a hundred years ago, mother to eight children. Her thoughts turned gloomy: evidently even this woman had managed to have sex again. And again, and again, and again. Selene wished suddenly and recklessly that she had lived at a time when she would not have had a choice in the matter, and no luxury of overthinking. Her great-aunt had once described her younger son as a 'punishment baby', his conception the outcome of her not having dinner ready when her husband got home from work. Selene's own mother had implied that it was Selene's father who had decided when it was time to have intimate relations again after the birth of her babies. If she could just lower her expectations of sex, if she could think of it as something to be done to her, an act of endurance rather than communion, she might be okay. Her husband would never agree, though. Once previously in their relationship, long before the baby, she'd pretended for his sake that she was in the mood and he had recoiled, hurt that she could think that would please him.

After Christmas lunch, one of the couples – the only ones who did not have children – disappeared to their bedroom to 'sleep it off', but there was something sheepish to the way they left the lounge that suggested they were going to do more than just sleep. Selene noticed her husband also watching them leave with a wistful expression, but whether it was for the good old days of weekend napping or for the indolent pleasure of afternoon sex, she couldn't tell.

The remaining couples tried their best to pretend the mood hadn't shifted in the room, but everyone was tired and full and a bit drunk, and the babies and toddlers – who had mostly slept through the lunch itself – were getting fractious. Each couple negotiated some sort of arrangement for the long hours remaining until the children could be put to bed. Selene told her husband he could go lie down; she needed to get out, to get some air, and unlike him she'd had very little of the feast.

She and one of the other wives strapped their babies to their chests – Selene's facing inwards, the other, who was closer to five months, facing outwards with his limbs sticking out like an upturned beetle – and headed down the dirt track beside the neighbouring farm's fields.

Like all new mothers, Selene and her friend were condemned to a relentless confessional intimacy. She sometimes wondered what they would speak about one day when their children were grown and they no longer felt such urgency to brief each other on the state of their children's bodies, and their own. But still it was difficult for Selene to broach the topic that had been preoccupying her. Perhaps since it involved speaking not only of their own bodies but of those of their husbands, and that was mostly uncharted territory.

'So you know they say six weeks is *the* time . . .' Selene trailed off, trusting her friend to understand her meaning. 'It's not just about the bum thing. Even if everything was in working order, I just don't know if I'd be able to – contemplate it.'

A mist was settling. They kept walking, eyes forward, each holding their baby's feet in their hands.

Her friend was quiet for a while. 'I'm embarrassed to admit this, though I shouldn't be,' she said finally. 'I'm the one who initiated our first sex after the birth. Only at about three months, mind you. I had to talk him into it. I had this need to feel his stomach flat against mine, it had always been our thing. And I think I wanted to make my body private again, take it off the record. The way your body becomes public property, you know? My sister-in-law knew about my clitoral graze, for god's sake. Even my stepdad knew about my stitches.'

They laughed then, and Selene didn't pry any further. She was grateful that her friend didn't ask her for specifics either. But she understood her meaning, and it helped. Sex didn't always have to be about love, or even desire. Sometimes it was about nothing more than marking out the territory of self. It reminded her of the way she'd felt at eighteen, when she'd triumphantly lost her virginity and it had not mattered one iota who the man was; even at that young age she had understood he was nothing more than a placeholder, a significant zero. This had taken her by surprise, her ability to use somebody else's body to make manifest a transformation in her own. She had used him to become a woman, stepped over his naked body to go out to the dark swimming pool at midnight, caught up in her own act of courage and power.

In the early hours of the morning on the day of her operation, Selene breastfed her baby beneath the lamp in the study while reading about the first hint of rot in Sylvia and Ted's honeymoon paradise. She gets food poisoning, he thinks she is overreacting and goes cold. *The stone man made soup. The burning woman drank it.* They go for a walk at full moon, unspeaking and sullen. Years later, Sylvia writes a poem about a pair of rapturous lovers who see in the shining surface of their dining table the reflections of their doubles, unhappy, estranged.

He lifts an arm to bring her close, but she
Shies from his touch: his is an iron mood.
Seeing her freeze, he turns his face away.

The colorectal nurse had told her to fast for twenty-four hours beforehand, and by the time Selene was rolled into the operating theatre at noon, she was already floating away into the upper reaches of the room on the drug of high hunger. She felt very calm. The doctors and nurses gathered above her. She looked into their eyes, the only part of their faces left uncovered. Their eyes looked back, kind, apelike.

A bright spotlight on an adjustable base was switched on but angled tactfully at the wall. Selene knew in a few moments it would be shone directly at her nether regions. The anaesthetic hadn't even been tapped into the vein on her hand and she'd started to laugh.

'Count down from ten for me, please,' one of the masked faces said, and she realised it was her specialist, the one with a newborn daughter named Matilda. She hadn't recognised his eyes.

'Ten, nine, eight, seven . . .'

Selene was trying very hard to stay conscious. She had important things to process, she felt, things she wasn't sure she'd recall when she surfaced. In her follow-up appointment with a different midwife – Agatha nowhere to be seen – she'd lied on every depression scale question and been told she was in perfect mental health. Once upon a time she'd broken up with a lover, slapped a $20 note on the bar top and stormed out in righteous fury, all because he'd said he didn't ever want to be at the business end of a woman's birth, in case it put him off her forever. Imagine if that man, now a stranger to her, could see her like this! She pitied him his youthful greenness in the ways of the body, for not yet knowing that the flesh is designed to disappoint, that even his own would in due time put off everyone in his life, even – especially – himself.

Her husband's lustful eyes gazing down at her now, his mouth and nose covered by the pale blue mask, his hair covered by the surgeon's cap. He was lifting the edge of her hospital gown, and in his eyes was no memory of the other things he'd seen of her, the other things he knew. Was she more than the animal sum of her parts? Whittled down to portals, spirit-like? With him, she could be neither and both. She would use him to fix herself, and once more pretend to be whole.

THE POSTCARD

Wells Tower

'Let me save you a few bucks on your therapy tab,' said Cora Jakes. 'You haven't found the right person because the right person doesn't exist. You want to be happy, forget the big, pink abstractions. Find someone whose daily presence is not intolerable to you.'

'Do you put that on your anniversary cards?' asked the man she was with. '*To my husband, whose daily presence is not intolerable to me.*' Tom was this person's name. He was a photo editor with whom she had slept during a festival in Los Angeles three weeks before. The specifics of their tussle were lost to Cora, who'd been close to quadriplegia from negronis. But the experience left in her memory traces of something exciting. So now she was sitting in a dark saloon in the meat-packing district with Tom's thin knee between her thighs. Downstairs was the neighbourhood's last establishment that still packed meat. The room smelled authentically of blood.

'Is he an artist?'

'He's a non-depleting human presence. It's a talent they should give MacArthurs for. He doesn't argue for the pleasure of it. I like the way his breath smells. We laugh at the same things, and I am never lonely. The only issues, and I actually think they are relatively minor, are that I'm not in love with him, and I'm not especially interested in having sex with him ever again.'

Tom's tongue was now scouting Cora's molars. His stiff thumb toured her breast.

Outside, a blue static of falling snow haloed the streetlamps. A serious storm was in the works. Haste in Tom's bed would be necessary if she wanted to find a taxi home.

'How about we get out of here?' Cora said. She took her phone from her pocket to check the time. The phone, she saw, was on an open call to her husband. It had been that way for forty-six minutes. Cora hung it up.

'I'm very sorry,' she said to Tom. 'I have to go.'

Cora left him on the corner. When she was out of earshot, she called her husband, whose name was Rodney. The phone had been in the deepest pocket of her thick, wool coat. The bar had been a poultry house of background noise. It was reasonable to suppose that her husband had not heard a thing.

'Hey there,' Rodney said with perfect affability. 'How was your night?'

'Rife with jargon and profane young women.' Cora was a photographer. A launch party for a fashion magazine was where she had professed to be. 'But a big, dumb paycheck may come out of it somewhere down the line. Anyway, I'm getting in a cab now. Do we need anything from the world?'

'I just ate our last ginger snap.'

'Ginger snaps: check,' said Cora. Relief warmed her thorax. She could not get home soon enough. 'Anything else?'

'Actually, yeah,' said Rodney. 'Who was that guy you were talking to?'

Abasements were made. A divorce was proposed and rejected. In the weeks after the telephone call, fits of tearful self-recrimination seized Cora at restaurants, in the grocery store, in the small hours of the night.

Through all of this, Rodney was impossibly forgiving. He was not only her absolver but a spirited attorney for Cora's defence. 'Of course, it sucks and it's painful, but strictly speaking, I can't really say you did anything wrong, when we're down to what, about three IOOs a year.' The acronym came from Rodney's computer work. It stood for input/output operation, a piece of household vocabulary that, in its transition into standard usage, had ceased to be waggish and become merely apt.

'Anyway,' Rodney went on, 'we did say that if either of us wanted to be extracurricular, we would talk about it and deal with it. You just happen to have acted first.'

Cora could not recall having had that conversation. She wondered, with a touch of vertigo, whether Rodney was making it up. 'But I didn't tell you,' she said. 'I lied.'

'Well, it's not an easy thing to talk about,' Rodney said. 'But if you lie to me again, I will divorce the living shit out of you. Just so we're clear.'

Cora did not ask how much Rodney had heard of her conversation with Tom. If her husband was guilty of a cruelty, it was that he did not immediately let on that he had heard it all. Rather, he hoarded the contents of the wiretap and returned them to Cora, moment by moment, at moments calculated to cause her pain.

'For someone who didn't want to have sex with me ever again, you did a bang-up job,' is something he told her one night after a satisfying bout of lovemaking.

Lying tranquillised on the sofa of a Sunday afternoon, the curve of her skull warmly cradled by his chin, he said, 'Even if this is you not being in love with me, it seems to deliver the same basic neurochemical effects.'

Then Cora would go in for briny testimonies, swearing, no, no, no; he'd overheard only the meaningless lies of a horny lady trying to ease Tom's conscience about screwing someone's wife. 'But he'd fucked you once already,' Rodney pointed out. 'What easing did his conscience really need?'

Cora demonstrated her remorse with grand mortifications of her checkbook. She bought for Rodney a pair of $700 boots and, for $1,200, a set of Japanese kitchen knives whose whorled blue blades were so delicate they had to be stored in special scabbards packed with rust-retardant gel.

She spent thousands on a three-day reservation at a coveted hotel upstate. It was built of garbage: cardboard, shipping pallets and rendered plastic waste. The grounds were unstrollable. The glades were seeded with kitchen leavings to solicit visits from bears.

'My little six-year-old boy, who's started to act like a real little terrorist, today he asked me, "Daddy, why is it so easy to be bad?"' said a voice on the Christian radio station Cora was flipping past on the drive back to the city. 'I told him, "We're all born with a dark place inside of us, and every time we sin, that dark place gets bigger and bigger and easier to fall into."'

This caused Cora to lurch against the window glass and sob.

'Ah, fuck, okay,' said Rodney in a sigh. 'I don't think you get to do this any more.'

'What?'

'All this grief and guilt, what you're doing, you're hijacking the story. You got it on with some guy, and you're sorry about it. Only you're so sorry about it that you're the injured party now.'

'I'm not the injured party.'

'Yes, you are. You're so broken and stupefied with guilt that this AM radio jackass has you in hysterics, and now I'm the noises-off in your one-woman contrition play. It's not even good theatre. You go and do this not-nice but extremely standard thing, and now you're biblically wicked. Presto-Christo! Now you believe in sin.'

As a matter of fact, she did believe in sin. She did believe that a tar pit was spreading within her and corroding her decent parts. Tom was not the first person with whom she had betrayed her husband. He was the eleventh, in the past six months.

Her work, she felt, was to blame. A spasm of unanticipated career success had lately come to Cora. It had bent her id.

She had started out in photography with earnest aims. It was the work of Dorothea Lange, Jacob Riis, Ben Shahn and Walker Evans that incited her to buy her first camera. Her sincere, early ambition was to spend her life taking pictures that mattered of people who did not. But there was rent to be paid, and Cora ended up in the lucrative business of taking pictures that mattered not at all of those who matter quite a lot. Actors, musicians, home-run kings, senators and warlords made visits to her studio. It was exciting stuff, at first, standing in a room with Earth's most significant animals and compelling several million strangers to view them through your eyes.

In Cora's case, the shelf life of that thrill had been about ten years. The work was already unfascinating her profoundly when she did a session with Beyoncé Knowles. The singer pitched a tantrum over Cora's slave-flash, whose pinging hurt her ears. The celebrity retreated to the restroom and refused to come out. For lack of anything else at which to aim her camera (an 8 x 10 with bellows; large as a horse's head) Cora made a very pretty portrait of the bathroom door. She printed it and showed it to Rodney, lamenting that a photograph of Beyoncé unseen in a latched toilet would command an infinitely vaster audience than a snapshot of a corpse on the street. But making the image, Rodney observed, had boosted her professional spirits for the first time in recent memory. And that was true, it had. So she made more of them: a broom closet containing Derek Jeter, a rose trellis obscuring Mick Jagger, an armoire behind which Angela Merkel stood, and a few dozen more.

On a visit to Cora's studio, her agent saw the photographs. Cora explained they were just a dull joke she'd been cracking for her own sanity. The agent felt otherwise. So did lots of other art world folk. A book deal was easily arranged. First galleries and then museums, in ten different countries, hosted solo exhibitions. For the first time in her life, Cora found herself on the business end of photographers' lenses. Her face was in magazines. She was paid to give masterclasses at universities that had rejected her student application. Collectors bought prints for significant sums. In an absurd eversion of her own intent, the celebrity photographs – an aria to nothingness sung in the key of contempt – had, in her narrow corner of the world, made Cora Jakes a star.

Why the onset of her public life had sparked this uncharacteristic adultery binge (which doubled her life's count of sexual partners) was a question for which Cora had no clear answer. 'Satiable' was how she termed her appetites to the psychiatrist she visited after the pocket-call disaster. In her thirties, she testified, she had passed three consecutive celibate years with no antsiness at all. In every major past relationship, she had been scrupulously faithful.

The psychiatrist proposed that this boom year of what he called 'debauches' was Cora's method of 'scourging' herself for success she felt to be misbegotten. Cora said that though she was not, admittedly, brainlessly sex-driven, she did not confuse coitus with a cat-o'-nine-tails. She added that someone who liked to be called 'doctor' should try not to talk like a maiden aunt from a Jane Austen novel. Here, the doctor pinched his nose, which did resemble something medical: the rubber head of a tendon hammer that had been gnawed on by a cat.

Wanting to help the doctor out, she proposed three possibilities for what was going on. One was that she was getting older. She intended not to procreate. She wanted her body to have some diverting experiences before it grew too crepey and groundward to appeal to mainstream sensibilities. Two: though she knew that her marriage was over, she lacked the emotional courage to tell her husband in plain language that she no longer loved him. By a riddlesome logic, Cora feared she would do Rodney more harm with a direct conversation than by his discovery that she'd been betraying him in bulk. Or perhaps the language for that conversation did not exist. After all, he had overheard all the material points, baldly stressed in Cora's chat with Tom. Her disavowals notwithstanding, Rodney could not but perceive that the fish was trying to flop out of the boat. So what did he do? He gave her a pass. He built a bigger boat.

The third possibility, a thick-skulled non-hypothesis to which Cora privately subscribed, was that all this semi-anonymous sex was just something she happened to be grooving on at this strange and public time. Or, rather, it was what this dislocated, half-baffled version of herself was grooving on. Propriety seemed to call for it. When you have spent a long weekend at a photo festival in Nice, going from microphone to microphone, from reception to reception, amid elegant people with wine-bruised teeth, all assisting the illusion of your own significance, and at your arm through all of this is a beautiful and timid man of twenty-three, whose name is Clément and who is your Paris gallerist's assistant and whose eyes would trump a Hereford's for brownness and diameter, and who mumbles for fear that his English is too clumsy for the ears of the woman who made the celebrated photographs, and who tells you, on the final evening of the festival, in his charmingly graceless way, that he has very much enjoyed the weekend, but *honnêtement*, he has been so *stressé*, so *nerveux* in your famous company, he will be also a little bit happy when you go away – well, what can one possibly do in these circumstances but to invite Clément to one's hotel room and let him be as tirelessly oral as he wishes to be?

This she had done, one week before her barroom chat with Tom. It had been lovely. So lovely, in fact, that Cora had made arrangements to spend a weekend with young Clément, in Amsterdam, following a gallery opening in Hamburg in the spring. Of course, that couldn't happen now. The telephone incident had put an end to things. It had stripped from Cora the delusion that the receptacle for canapés, awards and critical vacuities was another Cora, a Cora whose actions did not ramify in the life of a kind husband.

The lights had gone on in the theatre. In the glare blinked a silly old woman whose marital felonies had been monstrous and insane. It went without saying, Cora had told the therapist, that she would cancel the reservation for the Amsterdam hotel room she and Clément had so looked forward to humidifying over the long Easter weekend. Cora expected the doctor to make some approving noises at this announcement, but he did not because he was asleep.

Yet weeks went by and the Amsterdam booking kept not getting cancelled. The regretful note Cora needed to write to Clément kept not getting written. These things had to be done, yet when Cora pondered doing them, an ochre feeling came over her and her thoughts went elsewhere. She had not bothered to tell Clément that she was married. During their brief collision, he had impressed her as a wholesome, fragile boy. In sending her regrets, she would need to craft a lie that would leave his feelings unbruised, and also preserve his ignorance of Cora's shabby marital scene. An illness? The death of a parent? The effort of liecraft affronted her. The chore went undone.

Winter surrendered. On street corners the grey Tetons of icy soil shrank and roiled for the storm drains. The crocuses and daffodils shouldered forth. Pollen outputs rimed the windows. In her back garden, Cora saw a bull pigeon try to mount a rat. Cora felt her own sap rising. A store of shame was in her still, but it had lost its tanginess and bite. With the spring upon her and the city, she felt the logic of guilt to be the logic of death. Not to go see Clément over Easter was an insult to the big harmonic. She decided to keep her Dutch appointment, if *decided* is the word for a thing one knew one would do all along.

The opening in Hamburg did not go well. Despite the gallerist's assurances that the press had been duly pestered, only a single critic came by to chat with the artist. He was blunt in his opinions. 'Okay, so we are obsessed with famous people. Well, yeah, pretty obvious. To me this point does not make interesting these photographs that, formally, are not intriguing.'

Speaking from a hot place in her chest, Cora retorted that she could not agree more. They were dismal photographs, but the phenomenon of the exhibit's success proved the shrewdness of its point. 'This is a little bit intriguing,' the critic allowed. 'Maybe, you put on the wall the numbers of how much money you are making with these pictures of nothing. Maybe that is the real exhibit.'

In the morning, she boarded the train to Amsterdam feeling antimagical and undeceived. Sliding rearward out of Hamburg, Cora counted her plagues. No department of her life did not have fungus on it. A divorce would happen soon. Her dog was ill, maybe terminally, with an outbreak of long blue cysts about which Cora had been too dispirited to call the vet. 'Go into the big space,' an art school professor had once exhorted Cora. For years, she had found these words useful. But when, precisely, had her 'big space' become a large damp room that smelled of rancid towels? And now four days with Clément. What a queasy bounty this would be. The prospect was appetising as a week-old crabcake left out in the rain. She would brass it out in good humour, but something had to change. From her wallet she took the index card, downy with age, on which she sometimes minutely journalled. Steadying her hand against the surgings of the car, she jotted this wisdom: 'Never do anything ever again.'

But the train ride gentled Cora: the bumping of the rail seams, the excellence of a purchased croissant, its airy tissues as organically wondrous as a living chunk of lung or brain. Retreating before the engine's nose, purple thunderheads ceded the sky to a Delftware schema of ivory and deep blue. Sheep were on the hillsides, droll yellow afros cropping weed fields to baize. Passing through Teutonic villages, she wondered Americanly at the age of stone homes. She marvelled at the absence of those architectural toxins – synthetic stucco, faux mansard roofs – that had ravaged her homeland. Beauty, beauty, here it was. Receive it, Cora. Be its willing vessel. When the train slid into Amsterdam, she told herself how pleased she'd be to see her little friend.

Cora had difficulty finding the hotel, which she knew to be a ten-minute walk from the Centraal Station along a major boulevard. For ten Euros, she bought from a street vendor a map far too large to unfold on the street. The wind rattled and tore at it. Cora balled it up and stuffed it into a garbage can. Then, in brazen English, she asked the map salesman the location of the hotel, which was right across the street.

In the lobby, there was Clément. Cora's memory had glamorised him insufficiently, if at all. Thick inches of eyelash. Fleckless flaxen skin. Cheeks nearly gory with the chill of the day. Advancing toward her was the walking likeness of a 1940s advertisement for Nazism or wheat bread. The embrace was superb. His cool, dry face fitted itself to the hollow of her neck. He lipped her carotid. Cora's legs felt thin. Greetings were uttered. In a final fit of satisfaction, Clément resocketed his face under Cora's jaw. She heard him squeaking, gently, as though trying to rid his throat of a ribbon of fine phlegm.

'Do you need a drink of water?' asked Cora, crinkling at him a plastic bottle she'd been keeping in her purse.

'I don't need anything.' Clément thumbed Cora's untweezed brow and did a thing with his mouth that was close to a pout. 'It's weird. I had fear that you were not going to come, but now here you are, so *pfff*,' he said, expelling, French-style, a morsel of air.

Their room was small but unsqualid. A desk and a bed of the futon genus. Clément disappeared into the bathroom. Cora raised the blinds. Half a lifetime of peering into other people's windows found fulfilment at last. In the apartment across the alleyway, people were in the act. The man was spherical and, even from this considerable distance, visibly striated with stiff white fur. His partner, astride, had the long bleached hair and synthetic bosom of a paid professional. She bounced upon the client and winced ceilingward in a burlesque of joy. 'Rent-seeking behaviour' was the phrase that came to Cora's mind.

A toilet flushed. Clément entered. Wet fingers braceleted Cora's wrist. 'Look, there are some people fucking here,' said Cora. Clément glanced at the humpers but briefly, as though they were the noonday sun.

'Maybe,' he said, though there was no maybe about it.

Cora put a hand to the back of Clément's skull and the other to his pants. She kissed him fiercely. His lips were marvellously supple. She hoisted the hem of his shirt and marched him backward toward the bed. 'Maybe don't do that,' he said, tugging his shirt back down over his sternum. 'Maybe I am not ready right now.'

Not unforeseeable. The microphones and gentilities aimed at Cora that weekend in Nice plus the abundance of free wine had duped Clément into thinking her a desirable commodity. But at this sober hour, in a non-luxury hotel room, by the cadaverous light of 4 pm, he saw Cora as she was: a non-athletic woman of forty-four with a deeply laddered trachea and skunk lines in her hair. She revolted him. Fair enough. Why not have it out, with no apologies, embarrassment or umbrage-taking? Nice had been nice, but this was an error. Call it off. Catch the next flight home.

But, of course, there would be apologies, shammed denials, and, unavoidably, umbrage too. Candour was enervating, impossibly so. Instead, Cora sighed, and in the politest auntly timbre said, 'Of course. Shall we take a walk? Check out the tulip market? Have stroopwaffels? Whatever you'd like.'

But even as she was saying this, Clément was unbuttoning her trousers. In a trice, her jeans and underpants were beside her on the bed, not heaped but folded, occultly, without Cora having seen him do it. And suddenly Clément's jaw was lodged at the junction of her thighs. There, for nearly forty minutes, he was an avid gentleman.

His gifts were notable. What he did to Cora was a masterwork of mouthcraft. Old Europe was somehow in this, she reflected near the half-hour mark. An artisanal standard whose line ran back through the wines of Margaux, the flying buttress and those intricate house-sized heaps of firewood built by Finnish monks. More the flying buttress. Altitude, soaring convexity were key sensational motifs.

Even after Cora's third orgasm, Clément showed no signs of tapping out. She had to bodily haul him toward her face. Even then he struggled hard to keep his shirt on. She did finally manage to strip him of it, but only after a panting grapple that felt uncomfortably close to ravishment. It took more work to crack into his trousers. The state of his penis was distressing. She had held thicker, more ardent sardines. Her hand slid north again. Clément put his face to Cora's neck and squeaked.

'Is everything all right?' Cora asked.

Clément had slipped back into his shirt with haste that seemed dire. 'Yes,' he said.

'Really?'

He exhaled slowly. A great force of will, Cora guessed, was keeping more squeaking at bay. 'I am sorry. I don't like to show you my body.'

'Why don't you like to show it?' asked Cora, unconsciously aping Clément's rudimentary English, to her own irritation. 'You have a beautiful body.'

Another sigh. 'No, it is not beautiful. It is terrible, and I hate it and I don't never like anyone to see it.'

'Oh, you poor, sweet thing, why would you say that?' Cora said. 'You have a wonderful body. I should know.'

'You knowed it only in the dark,' said Clément. 'It's normal I should hate it. I used to be horrible fat. One-hundred-seventy-four kilos.'

Cora began to say that this was nothing, and then she did the math: three hundred and eighty-something pounds!

Cooing and petting and smoothing his hair, she coaxed from Clément the story of his old body and its miraculous reduction. Large at birth, a medical curiosity at ten, he had spent his adolescence exiled within his own flesh. For years he was tormented and for years he was alone. Boys ignored him no less resolutely than did girls. When he turned twenty, he had his belly stapled. He lived on celery with mustard, and, to fend back food-longing, uppers and downers and shots of B12. He swam and he walked five hours a day. Toward his parents and the people of his little village, he felt penitent. It pained everyone, this public admission of the secret that he knew how his body looked. The pounds came off and off, one hundred and ten of them in less than a year. The great shedding left Clément with much Shar-Pei-ness, around his middle, legs and arms. A doctor's scalpel cut off sixty pounds of this. Post-operative shunts drained twenty more pounds of blood. And then the world saw fit to make him welcome. He made friends. He got an internship in an economic sector reserved for pretty people. He began to go with women but, until now, only in the dark. The thing was, there were scars.

Cora asked to see them. Clément – eyes closed, body rigid, as though this were a second surgery – obliged her. The scars were not remotely terrible. Cora told him so. 'Today is the day that you let this go,' said Cora.

Clément kissed her, and then copulated with her gratefully. Afterwards, he seemed genuinely unencumbered, and for this Cora was glad. Still, she wished she had not heard the story, which was like a giant crystal chandelier Clément had put into her hands with instructions to never set it down.

They bathed, dressed and walked out into the windy dusk in search of food.

'Ooh, so much good things,' Clément said to the menu at the

restaurant they'd selected, a pretty art nouveau bistro. 'I think I will have to be careful in this place.'

'Please do not be careful. This is a special time. We are away from normal life, and you should eat the things you like.' Why could she not stop talking this way? Clément's spoken English was not the best, but his comprehension was presumably up to par. It served no purpose to locute like Fay Wray taking King Kong out for his birthday meal.

And yet, her Tarzan-speak put Clément at ease to feed freely. He ordered steak with Roquefort sauce, shrimp cocktail, frites, burrata and several diet Cokes. For dessert, he had hot chocolate and a fluted cakelet whose centre bled raspberry magma. While he gobbled this, Cora asked him questions with which she supposed he wanted to be plied. 'So Clément, how long do you think you will be working with Hélène?'

'Not so long, I don't think,' he said.

'Good. She is wonderful, but I imagine you'll want to start really doing your own work.'

'Which work?'

'Your photographs?'

'Oh, I don't prefer to do photography,' said Clément. 'I think maybe I don't think it is so interesting, art from a machine. I have the job at the gallery only because Hélène is my mother's, how do you call, *cousine*, and my mother, she is a painter and it would make herself happy if I would be an artist, so, of course she is very happy that I am here, together with you.'

Behind Cora's ribs, an inner nozzle squirted something sour and cold. 'You told your mother about us?'

'Yes, of course, that's okay?'

'Of course, of course.'

'For us, it's normal. We tell everything between ourselves.'

'Oh, oh, how wonderful.'

'Really, she is happy that I will be with someone older. With my father, they are different by almost twenty years. Like us. And they are very happy with each others!'

Wait, hold up. What the fuck, exactly, are we talking about here? is what Cora wanted very much to say. Having confessed to Cora the secret of his old, unhappy body, did he suppose they were engaged? Was this a translation error? But with only blunt linguistic instruments at hand, Cora did not know how to clarify the matter without harming Clément's chandelier. And so, 'Oh, oh, how wonderful,' is what Cora said again.

'But my mother is a little bit angry at you that you did not ask me come to Hamburg. She thinks you are ashamed of me and you didn't want me with you at a public thing. She wants me to say shame on you.'

Cora received this absurdity with a kind of relief. She drew breath to attack the mother's lunatic presumptions, and thereby armour herself against whatever presumptions Clément was or was not harbouring himself. But Clément spoke first.

'Of course, I told her this was crazy. We are almost strangers, you and I. I love her, yes, but she is an old lady who lives in the country and her head really sometimes is full of weird ideas.' Dispelling the spectre of his mother, Clément mannishly knocked back the last inch of his diet Coke as though it were a whisky shot. 'Still I am happy we are here, Cora. I am happy we are friends.'

Cora allowed his large hot hand to envelop hers. 'Yes, yes,' she said.

The check arrived. Cora paid it. 'Now what would you like to do?' she intoned in painful monosyllables.

'Maybe we should go back to the hotel and be cosy,' Clément said. And this, because it did not involve talking, she was glad to do.

A rattling sound woke Cora from her doze. This was Clément, nesting a bottle of Piper-Heidsieck in a bucket of ice. At the first parting of Cora's eyelids, he popped the cork and handed her a spuming glass. 'I am sorry but we must drink this very fast because I have a surprise for you but we must get there in thirty minutes.'

'What is the surprise?'

'I will not tell you. Drink, drink.'

When they'd bolted the bottle, Clément conducted her to a wharf where a tourist barge was revving up. A man at the gangplank accepted Clément's tickets, which, to Cora's chagrin, bore the words 'Amsterdam Lovers' Cruise'.

The seats were hard and minuscule. Cora's chair was bolted to a juddering mechanical chase that stressed her bladder, now firm with champagne. Farther down things were stinging somewhat, the first signal flares, she suspected, of a urinary tract infection. These were blessings, in their way. By centring her consciousness in her discomforts, she was able to hear a little less of Clément's breath in her ear, and to smell a little less of his cologne, which was offgassing mightily in the close quarters of the boat.

The barge pulled away from the dock. Clément took this as a cue to start his lover-work. He put his hand beneath the table and commenced to nudge Cora's vulva through her jeans. With more force than she'd intended, she grabbed his wrist and uprooted his hand from her groin. He looked as though he had been slapped. 'Why are you being cold with me?' he whispered.

'I'm not,' she said. 'I just really have to pee.'

'So you don't talk to me and just look out the window and don't like me to touch you because you have to pee?'

'No, I was just . . . thinking about nothing, I don't know.'

'I think you are lying,' he said. 'You think this is stupid and you hate it and you hate to be with me.'

'Oh, Clément! That's not true! You poor, sweet thing.'

'Why do you call me that? I am not a thing. I am a man, so tell me, if you do not like to be with me, just tell me, please.'

'Oh, Clément, I love being here with you,' Cora heard herself say. 'I just – I am just so relaxed and so happy here that I know I will be sad when I go home. So, yes, I am sad. I am sad because of that.'

The smile returned to Clément's mouth. He pressed a finger to Cora's nose. 'Yes, of course, I love you, too. But we are here just for some days, so we should enjoy them because probably we will never see each others again.'

Had he actually said that? The three significant words? Did this need dealing with? Or did that verb not signify in the French language, wherein *aimer*, as Cora understood it, could be applied to dental floss? Nevertheless, he got the important part right. Three more days and that would be the end of this ghastly interlude. The least painful strategy was just to let it go.

A chatty bosun stopped by to deposit on their table a bottle of room-temperature rosé and a tulip made of fudge. Cora inhaled a glassful, and then another, with thirsty gratitude.

'But we don't know the future, do we?' Clément observed, between bites of tulip. 'Do you think maybe we will see each others again?'

'I hope so,' Cora said, miserably.

'Who knows? Maybe it will be years from now.'

'You'll be sixty-three. I'll be eighty-four.'

'Yes,' said Clément. 'Probably I'll be very fat again.'

'I'll be bald, except for a few long, scraggly pieces here and there.'

'Yes, but you will still look very beautiful to me and we will get married and I will take you to Corsica for the honeymoon.'

'And I will be rotting away from diabetic necrosis, and my vagina will fall off in our nuptial bed.' Cora said this more loudly than she should have in the close confines of the boat and laughed harder than this crassness warranted. Clément winced. With a kind of pugnacity, Cora leaned in close and put her lips to his cheek.

*

When the love barge had looped its hawsers around the great glansish stanchions at the dock, the lovers cleared the gangplank at a loss for what to do. It was close to ten o'clock. They hadn't yet had dinner. Clément mittened his palm around Cora's fingers. 'I think let's just go be cosy in the hotel and order something to the room.'

This prospect caused the pulp in Cora's teeth to sweat. What Cora wanted was a temporary lobotomy whose effects would not flag until she was down for the night. Though she was not a dope smoker, she said to Clément it seemed a shame to visit Amsterdam without at least setting foot in a hash bar. She proposed that they first get massively high and then go eat dinner stoned.

They settled on a modern, brushed steel hash bar where electronic music twordled at an unpunishing volume. At the counter, Cora selected from a touch screen a single pre-rolled joint of something called Dum-Dum Superkush. Its advertised effects were a 'painkiller couch-lock and steady rolling body rushes'. A quilt over the bird cage was what Cora wanted, and this seemed to be that.

Upstairs, they took a seat on a lucite bench zazzling internally with laser beams. Clément borrowed a lighter from their neighbour. She was a pale girl with straight bangs and vermilion lipstick which, in the cone of light from an overhead bulb, struck an eyepuckering chord against her bright yellow coat. She was French, as it turned out. A lilting patter sprang up between her and Clément, of which Cora understood every tenth word or so. *Séjour*, *chouette*, *formidable*, *bière*. Kids' stuff. It was fine with her to be left out. She sucked sincerely on the joint and felt her skull sear.

Projected on the far wall was a loop video of clips to delight fried minds. Footage included a baboon besieging a plum bush, an ant massaging serum from an aphid's rear, time-lapse cloud action, sealife resembling neon insoles in a rippling jamboree.

Mixed in with the trip-out clips was cross-cultural quotidiana: traffic in Beijing, Third World wedding ceremonies, old Italians playing bocce in the park. Cora chortled dumbly at it. 'You are really having a serious time with this movie,' said Clément.

'Whoever made this has a fantastic job,' said Cora. 'You could show a roomful of stoned people footage of a mud puddle, and we'd think it was the codex to the secret of the universe. How do I get into this business?'

Here, the French girl put her oar in. 'Henk made it,' she said. 'He owns this place, but he's a very famous artist, too. Is very provocative.'

At 'famous artist', Cora's hackles pricked. She suppressed a childish temptation to tell the girl who the real artist in the room was. She watched on. After a sparky clip of manholes being minted, the provocative vision of Henk the video auteur asserted itself. Here was footage of the World Trade Center in flames. The tiny figures at the lip of the smoking wound, mustering the fortitude to leap. Cora gave an audible cry.

'What is wrong, sweet thing?' Clément said, taking her hand.

'Can you fucking believe this?' said Cora, gesturing at the screen.

Clément nodded and pronounced the footage, 'Pretty intense.'

'It's not *intense*, it's fucking appalling,' Cora said. 'I guess this right here defines the culture's metabolism. Ten years is what it takes for a mass murder to become just another funky thing that went down. Still, I'd be interested to know how the asshole who made this gave himself permission to treat the deaths of three thousand people as though it were, you know, an improvisation on a theme of double rainbows or a sneezing cat.'

'You are American?' said the girl.

'Yeah,' said Cora.

'Okay,' she said, as if to say *That explains it*. 'I think you don't get Henk's point.'

'And what is Henk's point?'

'His point is that, okay, you come in here, you get stoned. There is still a real world out there. There is still serious shit going on. You can't just pretend that everything is happy and flowers and everything.'

'And my point is, if you've got a brain in your head, you are well aware that there is serious shit going on out there. That *Henk* thinks he is doing something important or transgressive by reminding us of something that nobody on the planet is unaware of reveals your friend, I think, to be not a great artist but a malignant idiot.'

'I think you do not know very much about art,' said the girl.

'Fine,' said Cora, her cheeks flushing. 'I know nothing about art. What I do know, sister, is that on that particular day, I lived on the corner of Warren Street and Church. I saw those people falling from the buildings. I saw bodies on the street. The dust filled my apartment when the towers went down. For the month after it happened, we breathed death, literally. It wasn't pretty. It wasn't trippy. And to see this dickhead transform it into a kind of visual incense is not only asinine, it's fascistic and inhumane.'

'This is really interesting,' the girl said. 'Because, really, this is what I am talking about. Yes, it happened, and for America, it is this holy thing. *Oh, yeah, this was done to us, America! On American soil! How dare they! Now we must start wars and kill hundreds of thousands.* I am sorry but this is the point of the artwork exactly. To make you look at this thing. Okay, we are in a world where this happens. How do we deal with it? But your reaction, actually, to me, it's really interesting. For you, this is your drawing of Muhammad. This is the sacred thing of America no one is allowed to touch.'

How to respond to this? While Cora was trying to marshal a storm of furious objections into a disciplined, elegant rebuttal, the words that came out of her mouth were, 'Go fuck yourself.'

Never in her life had Cora spoken this way to a stranger, but in the moment of silence that followed, she reflected that those three words most succinctly expressed the sentiment she wished to get across.

The girl stared at Cora for a moment. Then she began to laugh. 'I guess she does not like to discuss ideas,' she told Clément in deliberate English.

'Fuck you. You're a moron,' Cora said. 'Don't fucking talk to me again.'

Clément's mouth opened. He wrung his hands. The strife seemed to wound him. This deepened Cora's irritation. Clément put a hand on Cora's knee. He began to ply the girl with a torrent of apologetic French, begging forgiveness for his lover, the coarse and barbarous crone. The blood roared in Cora's ears. What was Clément saying? She could dope out a lone recurrent word: *femme* blah blah *femme. Elle est femme?* Is that what she'd heard? *She is woman* or *she is wife?*

'Woman or wife?' Cora said.

'Pardon?' Clément said.

'*Femme. Femme. Femme.* What are you talking about, Clément? Are you telling her I'm your wife?'

Confusion presided for an interval. Then the girl's sudden laughter cut a channel through the laserlit bank of smoke. '*Faim,*' she said. 'Hungry. You are a bitch because you are hungry, is what he says. Not wife. His grandmother, maybe. Don't worry. Nobody thinks you are his wife.'

Out on the street, Clément strode not quite at escape velocity, only fast enough to make it clear that he didn't care whether Cora kept up or not. They did not talk. Still immensely stoned, Cora was having a hard time tracking the valences of the fiasco in the bar. What was the thing that most needed apologising for? That she'd crushed him by accusing him of pretending to be her husband, which Clément, the Oedipal oddity, actually harboured sincere and weird fancies about? Or was he simply disgusted by her brattiness, her sanctimony, and that she'd made herself absurd?

Cora's mortification was physical: a film of cold foil plating the bones of her shoulders and her spine.

At the end of the block, Clément ducked into a corner grocery. Cora felt unwelcome to follow him in. Nor could she summon the mettle to walk back to the hotel alone. There was nothing to be done but shuffle around, feigning fascination with a kerbside banana crate as a rain began.

Clément soon appeared, eating a long, pale sandwich. So much, apparently, for their dinner plan. His other hand clutched a stack of postcards, jumbo edition, half-clad in a wax-paper bag.

'Oh, you got postcards!' Cora pointed out.

'Yes. Right now I am going to write postcards to my friends,' which population, his tone implied, did not include her.

'You write postcards! I never write postcards!' Cora gibbered. 'That's great! That's amazing.'

'Yes, I write postcards. I like to do it. I don't think it is amazing. I send them to everyone.' Using his middle finger as a tamper, Clément drove the last three inches of his sandwich past his lips, chewed and swallowed. 'The one I sent to you, you didn't get it, or you thought it was stupid?'

'You sent me a postcard?'

'Yes, of course.'

'From Paris?'

'Yes, you did not get it?'

'No.'

'Okay. *Pffft.* You don't have to look like it's serious. Who cares?'

A postcard. He had sent her a postcard. And how had he gotten her address? The gallery rolodex, of course.

The French postal system was adequate. It was wishful thinking to suppose the postcard had been lost in the mail, or to hope that Clément's clumsy jottings would be too oblique for Rodney to decode. She had been gone five days. The postcard had almost certainly arrived by now. It was probably large as a shoebox lid and as subtle as a crier with a handbell.

One other possibility, which seemed more likely because it was more hideous, was that Rodney had intercepted the postcard before the trip, that the morning Rodney saw her off with fruit, a kiss and Dramamine, their marriage had already ceased to exist.

Cora returned to the hotel. Clément went off to write postcards to the people that he liked. With the help of three sleeping pills, Cora was legitimately unconscious when her lover's body creaked into place beside her.

At 4 am her eyes opened and would not close again. Here was a trick of Cora's undependable brain. While incapable of distinguishing *femme* from *faim*, at this late hour, it was chanting, in flawless French, these words: *Jouis et fais jouir sans faire de mal ni à toi ni à personne. Voilà toute morale.* They were tattooed on the forearm of a Czech philosopher Cora had once photographed. The gist was, *Taking pleasure, spreading pleasure without hurting anybody constitutes a moral life.*

So the question, as Cora saw it, was: how to knot up the present mess with a minimum of collateral harm? Returning home was essential, as soon as possible. If the postcard was in Rodney's clutches, well, that was music she would face. If, by some miraculous postal mercy, the postcard had not arrived, she would lie in wait for it and destroy it, after which she would dedicate herself to the expert demolition of her marriage by the least explosive possible means. It was for Rodney's sake, not hers, Cora told herself, that she feared being found out. The least she could do was tiptoe backwards out of his life, to leave a minimum of footprints and derangements for his next mate to clean up.

Fleeing Clément called for tact as well. Full disclosure was out. To know that his postcard had collapsed a marriage would be a hurtful, grown-up burden for the guileless St Bernard. The only decent thing to do, Cora decided, was to tell Clément that her apartment had caught fire and that she had to board the next flight to New York to deal with the calamity. So great was her concern for Clément's feelings that she went to the trouble of counterfeiting an email from the building superintendent, bolstered with years-old insurance photos taken after her loft had indeed gone up in flames.

A little before six, she woke Clément, brandishing her laptop and wringing from her actual anxieties a simulated panic that wasn't so persuasive. 'That sucks,' ran the extent of Clément's sulky, rote condolences. His mood, however, perked up a little at the news that, if he liked, the room was his for the next three days, paid for in advance, incidentals, too. She leaned in for a farewell kiss. With éclat that seemed vituperative, Clément thrust his stale tongue into her mouth.

On the wet dawn streets of Amsterdam, Cora feels giddy, unlimbered, scrubbed clean. Suffusing her is a spirit of melancholy clarity that is not so far from joy. It does not degrade until the airspace over Boston, when the plane's descent begins.

At 6.30 pm, she debarks into a decrepit terminal. The ceiling is underpinned by conical tarps to catch rainwater and sloughing plaster. The linoleum underfoot bears cigarette burns dating to the Idlewild period. Intimations of age and dereliction season very nicely the dripping meal of despair on which Cora inwardly feeds just now. No word from Rodney, or from Clément, on her telephone.

The parking lot attendant exacts from her a punitive sum. Cora pilots her Volvo through the balky bowels of the transterminal roadway. Blocking her path are vehicles that, after Europe, seem cottage-sized. It is Good Friday. Cora rides her brake through a street fair of embracing Catholics. At last, her way is clear to the leftmost lane, where the traffic flows free. She gooses it, then screeches to a bumper-nodding stop. A middle-aged woman has selected the fast lane toward the highway as the place to board a cab. She is obese. With her is a boy of seven or eight. Cora blasts the horn at her with both thumbs.

'Would it kill you to be patient for five seconds?' the woman yells.

'Five seconds looking at your fat ass?' Cora retorts through the open window. 'Yeah, it might!'

The shock on the faces of the woman and the child is legible and pure. Even Cora is a little stunned. First *go fuck yourself* to the French girl in the hash bar, and now this.

Rodney would not have stood for it. He would have insisted that she apologise and, failing that, stepped out of the moving car and apologised on her behalf. The nastiness to strangers has something to do with her husband. It is the tentative flexion of a powerful muscle Rodney has long been trying to train her not to use. Now she can use it if she likes. Out of Queens she speeds, feeling potent and bleak.

The sound of running water welcomes Cora home. Rodney is showering. There are no packed suitcases on the kitchen floor. The postcard, Cora permits herself to hope, has not penetrated the apartment. Her lung capacity briefly doubles.

But here is the mail, heaped on the wallward end of the kitchen table, where it is always heaped. This evening the irrelevant mass of windowed envelopes and coupon circulars assumes a brazen, evidentiary quality. She rifles it. Between a catalogue and a credit card offer is Clément's postcard. It is what was once known as a 'French postcard', a cyanotype of a woman's naked torso, plastered with sycamore leaves. The text on the back is not an exact accounting of cunnilingus past and pending but close enough. Cora's aorta pumps vinegar. The shower cinches off with a baying of intramural pipes.

What will Cora do as a single woman of forty-four? She will reactivate her gym membership. She will learn to relish solitude. She will give up alcohol. She will take daily comfort in loving fatuities with her little dog. She will strive for a life of work and continence with her heart nowhere nearby.

Now here is Rodney fresh from the shower. Black underpants are all he wears. His body is a totem of amiableness. Thick skin the colour of two-minute toast, boyishly innocent of visible fat or muscle. Hairless save a furred naevus on his left scapula, shaped like a paramecium. So familiar is she with this body, she reflects, she could probably pick from a line-up any domino-size sample of her husband's flesh.

Cora dislikes personal photos. She neither takes them nor looks at them. Yet she is tempted to ask Rodney, before the hashing-out begins, if he would consent to prostrating himself on her light table and permitting every part of his anatomy to be photographed. But Rodney speaks first.

'So,' he says, twisting a pinky in his ear. 'They're doing dollar oysters at that place on the canal.'

Cora and Rodney go eat oysters at that place on the canal. The postcard goes unmentioned. In the weeks that follow, Rodney is unusually kind to Cora. He makes her coffee in the morning. In the evening, he rubs her horned, yellow feet. Cora suspects that Rodney's gentleness with her is weaponised, a force multiplier for when he finally drops the bomb. The weeks wear on and Cora's preparedness for his exit erodes. At some unsuspected and maximally harmful moment, she knows, the confrontation and departure will take place.

This keeps failing to occur. Midsummer, Cora learns that she is pregnant. Rodney is the father. They resolve to leave New York, something Cora always swore she would not do. Rodney gets a teaching job at a third-rate college in Virginia. The town is a bland Tartarus of off-brand chain stores and tract-built homes on one-acre lots. In fact, this nonreactive agar tray of a town may be the ideal place to raise their daughter, whose ultrasounds reveal a troublingly thick neck-fold. Yet the baby emerges free of Down's Syndrome and the other malfunctions associated with what the doctor terms Cora's 'geriatric pregnancy'.

The daughter is, however, a tantrum-thrower to be tranquillised only by TV or mobile phone screens. Books, in particular, seem to enrage the child.

Cora stops doing magazine work. She makes intriguing photographs of Southeastern ruralia. A university press publishes her books in limited runs. Her professional esteem is mostly local.

Rodney has an affair with a colleague. The idea of dissolving the marriage is once again raised. During this time, while cleaning the gutters, Rodney falls off a ladder and permanently loses the use of his left arm. His lover retreats. Rodney retires.

In high school, their daughter exchanges her addiction to video games for tennis, which she is frighteningly good at. She is accepted to Dartmouth on a full athletic scholarship. She goes off to school and telephones her parents no more than minimal propriety requires.

Cora and Rodney move farther out into the country, far from provocations to lead a more resounding sort of existence. In the evening, the sounds are owls and distant trains. The odours from a nearby pig farm reach their house but rarely. On infrequent occasions, they are invited to dinner parties at the attractive homes of the warm, sophisticated people in their circle. These gatherings are enjoyable. But Cora and Rodney are always happiest at the end of the evening, driving home through the deep black trees, when they observe to one another, in a kind of tender ritual, that they do not envy the life of anyone they know.

EVIE

Sarah Hall

She arrived home after work, sat at the kitchen table and took a large chocolate bar out of her bag. She said nothing, not even hello. She split the foil, broke it apart, and proceeded to eat the entire thing, square after square; a look of almost sexual concentration on her face.

Had a bad day? he asked.

She smiled faintly.

Not like you to go for the junk. Did you miss lunch?

She shook her head. Her jaw moved, slow and bovine, working the substance against her palate. She was looking but not seeing him. There was something endogenous about the gaze, something private, as if his presence in the room was irrelevant. She ate the entire bar, methodically, piece after piece, while he put the kettle on and began dinner. He heated a pre-made lasagne in the oven, opened a bag of salad and dumped it into a bowl. She ate only a little of the meal.

I guess the snack ruined your appetite.

Her eyes flickered up from the plate.

Yes. I don't know why I had the whole thing. Only, I'd been thinking about eating some for days. Then I had to.

She didn't apologise for the wasted food. Usually she would; she was the type who apologised over any minor or innocuous discourtesy. He wondered if she was angry with him, whether a passive campaign was playing out, though he could think of nothing he'd done wrong.

Over the next week she began to eat chocolate regularly. She would snap off portions while watching television or between chores. In her car there were smeary wrappers strewn on the floor. She'd never had a sweet tooth before, had never ordered dessert in restaurants. She'd always kept her figure because of it. Now, she seemed addicted. And not just to chocolate, but anything sugary: pastries, puddings, fizzy drinks. She would leave her steak or pasta half finished, leave the table, and come back with something glazed that she'd evidently bought in a bakery between her office and the house.

God, I just can't seem to stop with this stuff, she said one night.

It was true. She went with a predatory look to the cupboards. She wasn't thinking, just acting on impulse. She was drinking more too. Wine with dinner every night, a few extra glasses at the weekend; becoming gently hedonistic. They'd been for a meal at Richard's and she'd finished a bottle of Cabernet by herself, as well as the lemon torte he'd served.

Hey, hey, Richard had said, taking her hand and helping her up from the couch, after she'd slumped on the first attempt to rise. Nice to see you letting your hair down, Evie.

How gallant, she'd said, a mock-belle voice. Then, whispering, I know you want this.

She'd leaned up and kissed him. A kiss not on the cheek, but on the mouth: a deliberately erotic move that implied nothing less than seduction, as if her husband, sitting next to her on the couch, did not exist. Richard of course had been too dazed to respond. This was a glimmer from a long-desired, alternate world, where his best friend's wife was available to him instead for nightly plunder. After a moment Richard roused himself, took hold of her wrists, and looked over to the couch, as if to say, *here, hadn't you better intervene.* Evie was staring at Richard's mouth. Her lips were parted, her lashes lowered. Together they'd helped her into her coat and into the car. Once the seatbelt was buckled and the door shut, Richard had turned to him.

That was a bit unusual. Is she all right?

Evie's head was drooping to one side; she was asleep, or passing out.

I don't bloody know. She's all over the place lately. She's fine, I think.

What do you mean all over the place?

Just acting up. For attention, maybe. I don't know. She's fine. Sorry, Rich.

You're sure?

Yeah. Yeah, just had a few too many.

On the drive home the incident preoccupied him. The look of desire, the unboundaried gesture. It wasn't that she hadn't looked at him that way, of course, in the past – nights when they were at their best, their least inhibited, when the act was intentional rather than habitual. But to see her looking at another man. It'd shocked him, and Richard too, clearly. It had been exciting. Something had flared inside him. Possessiveness, naturally – she was his wife – but there was another sensation too. Pride. Or worth. He didn't quite know. She suited the attitude; perhaps most women did.

He glanced down at her legs as he drove; the skirt riding untidily on her thighs, the flesh pale in the glow of the streetlights. Her arms were cast out either side of the seat – he'd already moved one away from the gear stick – in a pose that looked supplicatory, almost religious. She roused minimally when they arrived home, walking into the house and upstairs like a somnambulist, lying on the bed fully clothed. He'd run a hand up her thigh, but by then she was unconscious.

She had a hangover the next day and he caught her in the kitchen having a shot of whisky. Her makeup was smudged round her eyes. The silk robe was loosely belted, with one breast partially exposed.

For God's sake, Evie. Didn't you have enough last night.

Hair of the dog, she said.

You're acting like a student. That's going to make you feel far worse.

Let's see.

She tossed the spirit back.

Boom!

She set about cooking pancakes for breakfast, which she coated with syrup, rolled up and ate with her fingers. He sat opposite at the table, refusing the plate of glistening batter, choosing instead a frugal bowl of muesli. He was annoyed with her; he didn't know why. She was acting a little irresponsibly, a little outlandishly – but so what? He'd always wanted her to be more cattish, hadn't he, like the girls at university he remembered who had tattoos before it was popular, who wore tiny shorts, took pills every weekend and danced on podiums in the union. And the thing with Richard; he knew there was nothing to it. Richard was too restrained, too safe, almost neuter; he was always ill with something and in need of sympathy; he'd never been a genuine threat. It occurred to him she might be pregnant, and hormonal. Though surely she would know, by now, and the drinking was very inappropriate. Evie wasn't like that.

She was washing up at the sink, her rings set aside in the small ceramic dish, her bottom shaking as she scrubbed, hips a fraction fuller under the gown, though not unattractively so. He asked her.

No, she blurted, half turning. I don't think there's much risk of that, do you?

Offended by the overt reference to their irregularity – usually they both avoided the topic with practised denier's skill – he stood and made to leave the room.

Wait, she said. Maybe, well, what do you think?

About what?

About getting pregnant.

Are you serious?

She dropped the scrubbing brush into the basin of soapy water and wiped her hands on the silk robe. The material darkened and stuck to her skin.

Actually, no. But I would like a fuck.

He was stunned. It was not the look of the previous night, but it wasn't the usual furtive pass that one or other of them made, when it had been building a while, and before an argument occurred.

Would you? she asked.

She unbelted and moved the robe away from her midriff. The pubic hair was in a neat brown strip. She had waxed. He looked at her. He was angry now, at the guilelessness, the domestic crisis she seemed intent on creating. Why was she being so bald? It made no sense. The atmosphere around her was unsettling, like irregular weather. He was jealous, and impressed by the approach, by her making a stranger of him almost. All the times he had wondered, imagined getting his cock out, stroking himself in front of her and saying, *come here and suck this*, how she would have responded. He'd never done it. Neither had she, though he'd fantasised often enough about her masturbating in front of him, kneeling, her legs apart, or on all fours. The answer was yes. But he did not speak or move. She was looking at him, her face unreadable, not ashamed, not desperate. There was only so long such a precarious, risky moment could go on, before it spoiled. He was hard. He knew what he should do. Hostility got the better of him.

What are you trying to prove, Evie? What?

She shrugged, a one-shouldered shrug, the definition of non-chalance. She left the robe open and sat down. She lifted one foot up onto the chair seat. He could see more of her cunt, the folds and dark seam. He felt hot and uncomfortable. He should be kissing her, feeling her breasts, doing what she'd asked him to. But this exchange; there was too much and too little intimacy at once. He disliked her casualness, the request as banal as to go and buy milk. He was locked in. It was absurd.

I mean, what are you doing? What are you *doing*?

Asking you to go to bed with me.

I mean, you're being just bizarre. You haven't even showered. You're a mess. You're ruining yourself with junk food. You're having whisky at ten am and saying mad things to me in the kitchen. And then last night. What was that?

I just want a fuck, Alex. That's all. If you aren't up for it, fine. Maybe later.

She leaned across the table and wiped up a viscous smear from its surface, put her finger in her mouth. She was not upset. The transaction hadn't worked, and that was that. Part of him felt ashamed for attacking her, for the impotence of his mood. But she'd walked carelessly across the tripwires of their relationship, as though through a field of mines, as if immune. And her response to the rejection was ludicrous, like a child's or an autistic's. He turned and left the room.

*

He had never really loved his wife, not with acute, debilitating passion, the kind that was idealised and sung about. He had become fonder of her over the years, and more attached. She did nice things for him – making him sandwiches to take to work and buying replacement toothbrushes when the bristles on the current one began to splay. Other men found her attractive; colleagues often commented on his good fortune, and Richard had had a thing about her for years. Richard always remembered her birthday, procuring thoughtful and not inexpensive gifts, taking her side in quarrels, though there weren't many. Objectively, she was a catch, but he'd never felt dizzyingly emotional about her. He'd never tortured himself with the idea that she might leave, or stop loving him, that she was irreplaceable.

The first thing he'd really liked about her was her name. Evie.

Like a forties starlet. He'd had a spell of dating women with interesting names, in and after university: Lola, Oriana, Kiki, Simone. They were never as interesting or free-spirited as their names suggested. He'd expected vivacity and petulance, oblique intelligence, someone who would perhaps be difficult to manage, but fascinating and worth any trouble, inspiring something torrid in him, lust leaning towards deviancy; someone who would cancel out the desire to upgrade, someone with whom he could experiment and live interestingly.

Good crazy, rather than bad crazy, that's what you want, Richard had said. A fantasy woman. But it's bullshit. You keep getting them to fall for you, then cutting a swathe. It's ridiculous.

And he had gone through a number of them, telling himself he was on a romantic quest. They were all trying for unique jobs – dance therapists, writers. Often they wore clothes that suggested originality, unusualness: red chiffon shirts with showing-through bras, men's brogues, even rebellious vintage fur tippets. They were confident at first, sometimes conceited. He encouraged them to audition for the part, which gave them licence. Once the novelty of the sex wore off, once they failed to be uniquely talented, he struggled to make a connection. Under the faux exoticism, they wanted husbands, money, three-storey town houses. Or they really were fucked up. By six weeks he was usually disappointed or bored. Or things had exploded.

The last – Simone, the children's musician – had proved disastrous. After her various antics and tantrums, he'd tried to phase her out. She'd turned up at his door, incensed, had made an aggressive pass, and they'd gone to bed. The following day, after he explained his position, she accused him of trying to get her pregnant, dragging him to the doctor's for the morning-after pill and making him watch her 'miscarry'.

By the time he met Evie he'd given up on the idea of exceptionality. They met at a Christmas party – Richard's. She was lively;

the men in the room were crowded around her. He introduced himself to those in the group he didn't know, weighed her. She was copper-haired and trim, bright hazel-eyed, but not stunning. She didn't have a bone structure that suggested lifelong beauty. They danced. She moved well, neat but suggestively. Her eyes were big and pretty. He could tell Richard liked her, even then. Richard kept bringing a bottle over and offering to top them up, trying to join the conversation.

Their dates were pleasant. Evie was pleasant. She smiled a lot and dressed well. He liked that other men were attracted to her. There was no sulking or ego maintenance. In a way it was a welcome compromise after the extreme terrain he had attempted. But she wasn't stupid. She could tell he was withholding, he was making no declarations; there was no obvious lovers' trajectory. It came up one night in a restaurant and he told her he wasn't sure exactly how he felt about her. He didn't feel anything tremendously, for anyone. There was an argument, unshouted, but definitely an argument.

I don't move you in any great way then? she asked. What am I, wallpaper? Just there in the room?

No. Listen, it doesn't affect the relationship, he said. We're having a good time.

Are you mad? Of course it does. I want more than that. Who wouldn't?

She'd stood up, unhurriedly, gathered her coat, and left. It was a superior, graceful exit. He'd tried to phone her but she ignored the messages. She started dating someone else soon after; he heard about it from Richard, who'd stayed in touch with her. This bothered him; no, it piqued him. He couldn't stop thinking about her and the new lover. He wondered if his emotions had been lagging, or had been masked. He'd lasted two weeks and then he was on her doorstep, saying he couldn't be without her, asking her to marry him. He almost convinced himself. By the end of the evening they'd had sex several times – it was as close to anything meaningful as he'd ever felt – and they were engaged. It all played out. They married. They bought a house. It was fine.

*

He remained angry for the rest of the day. He washed the car. He fixed the puncture on his bike. He stayed outside as much as he could. Evie lazed about the house eating sweets, listening to the radio and flicking through magazines. When he spied on her through the window she didn't seem to be unhappy or brooding. She made cups of tea at intervals. She painted her nails. Whatever was going on, she was clearly capable of holding out. He was angry, but he was interested too.

In the afternoon it began to drizzle, the wind got up and a proper shower arrived, darkening the tarmac driveway. He got sick of the oily stone-floor smell of the garage and the glum bare bulb overhead, so he went inside. He made a quick circuit of the lower floor. Evie was not there. He could hear faint noises from the bedroom upstairs. Halfway up he paused and listened. There was a rhythmic sound, alternating between a purr and a wail – female. After a moment it became clear what it was. He moved across the landing and opened the bedroom door. She was lying on the bed, on her side, naked, her hand between her legs. The laptop was at the end of the bed. He couldn't see the screen but he could hear the slapping of flesh, the groaning.

What's going on?

She kept her eyes on the film.

I found this site. Her voice was low, distracted. I like this one best.

A burning sensation rose up his neck. His chest was flurrying. He waited a moment, then went over to the bed. On the screen a man was fucking a woman from behind. His fingers were gripping her buttocks, indenting her flesh. There were tremors in her body every time he thrust. The camera angle showed the penis moving in and out, glistening. The image was mesmerising. And embarrassing. Not because he hadn't seen anything like it before – it was all too familiar – but because his wife was in the room, watching.

I like this bit, she said.

The man on the screen pulled out of the woman. She presented herself, wider. Her genitals were depilated, the flesh dark purple. The man knelt, put his face between her legs and began to tongue the crease. Evie rolled on her back, held her head up so she could still see the screen.

Take your clothes off, she said.

He was aching painfully. He had forgotten everything else. The automatic took over. He undid his jeans, pulled them down, pulled his unbuttoned shirt over his head. He wrestled out of his briefs. Evie knelt up. They did not kiss. She crouched and took him into her mouth. He looked down at her back, past it to the screen, where the man was pushing apart the cheeks of the woman and re-entering, higher. After a few moments Evie took her mouth away, moved back and turned round. He was rough with her. He wanted to slap her. He didn't understand any of it, but it didn't matter, everything had become reasonless. She was moaning. The other woman was moaning. A visceral harmonic. On the screen the man was pulling the woman's hair so hard that she was rearing upwards, her back bent at an extraordinary angle. He knew he would come soon. Between sounds, Evie was saying things that made no sense, some kind of rapturous, blurted language. Then:

Do that if you want. Do that to me.

He put his hand into Evie's hair, made a fist and pulled. He was breathing so hard he felt crazed. He pulled out and repositioned. He made a series of small movements. The muscle clenched and then relaxed. He worked himself in, began to move. The knowledge of its happening was exquisite. It was too much. He felt himself spasm, noise blared from his mouth, and he slumped against her.

They lay for a while, the film ended, and then he gently moved away. Evie reached over and scrolled through the contents page of the site. He looked at the mess on the sheets, pleased, mystified. Something unbelievable had happened.

It happened every night, and in the mornings, before work. They did not always watch pornography, though often she wanted to. It began with her instigating, but then he realised there was ongoing permission. For anything. They tried different ways. It was deliberate and seemed necessary, as if the arrangement required new terms. They videoed themselves on the digital camera. He saw a man like him performing oral sex, licking slowly, then frantically; he watched his wife handling herself with no inhibition. He didn't recognise the woman staring straight into the lens. She did not want foreplay or romance. She wanted candid and carnal exchange. While it happened she spoke mad words, unconsciousness.

It's inside the daylight. Making each other wet. It's all the way in. In.

There was something almost shamanic about it. She looked as if she was trancing, her pupils blown, as if the act had been incanted and was unstoppable. The expression of confused pleasure and fear and drive was spectacular. Her breasts were heavier and swung beneath her, or juddered when she was on her back. What excited him most was when she talked about other people joining them, another man.

Oh, God, both of you inside me. I'll do anything, anything. I'll do anything.

I'll watch him fucking your pussy. I want to see you ride him, make him come all over you.

The rules were gone. It was easy to say these things; easy to

undo himself. They'd suddenly found each other, through irre-
pression, means he did not quite understand. Her age, hormones,
a revival of some lost appetite, the arrival of a new one; it didn't
matter, he didn't care. He wanted to get close to her. She was on
fire. She was lit up.

Towards the end of the third week he noticed she was damaged and bleeding and asked if she was sore. It didn't matter, she
said. She wanted to carry on feeling this way; her body finally
knew what it was meant for. She made him, again. There was
more blood, an alarming streak up her rump and on the sheets.
He didn't want to stop but there was something wrong. A person did not become so extreme without cause. While she took a
bath he searched through her bag, for what he wasn't sure, drugs
perhaps, prescription or otherwise. Lipsticks, tissues, chocolate
wrappers, a discreet white vibrator, which he hadn't known she
owned. There was a letter from her work. She'd been cautioned
for inappropriate behaviour in the office. When she came out of
the bathroom he asked about it.

You dropped this. It says you've been saying things to other
members of staff. Is that true?

I don't know what the bloody problem is, she said, throwing
the wet towel onto the bed. They're just so boring, so glass. They
don't get it.

Don't get what?

What you have to do. You've got to make it happen whenever
you can.

Make what happen?

I can't explain it speaking, Alex. Come and lie down.

He lay next to her on the bed. She put his hand between her
legs. He took hold of her wrist.

No, come on, he said, softly. Try to explain, Evie. What's going
on?

Don't be angry.

Then she began to cry. Short rapid bursts, without tears. She sounded almost like a baby. A lump rose in his throat. What was coming? He put his arms round her and held her. The flesh on her stomach was plump and warm. She'd become a baroque version, a decadent. The crying did not last long. She did not wind down, but suddenly sat up, the distress forgotten, bright-eyed.

I tried to get Karl to sleep with me. Then I asked Toby. You weren't there. I wanted you to be, but you were at work.

What?

Will you help me? I have to know how it feels. I can't stop thinking about it.

About what?

Her face was hovering in front of him; open, beguiling, altered.

You and me and someone else.

He had known she was going to say it; the scenario had featured too strongly, too mutually in their role-play to be insignificant. She had decided to live forwardly, his wife, without limit or reproach. And she had taken him with her. But he knew too that there was a line, over which, if they passed, there was no coming back. The dynamic would always be changed; they would be beyond themselves.

Please. I want to. It would be amazing. Like a sun in us. It tastes like, I can taste it burning.

She put her hand to her mouth with a sharp intake of breath, as if scalded.

You say these things, Evie. They make no sense.

I have to do it. We only live. We only live, Alex. Such a tiny thing. I know how to feel. This is the truth. Do you believe me?

She moved close to him again. She put her hands on his face. Her eyes. Electrical green, and gold, powering the irises.

You choose. You choose who. You bring him. I'll do anything you want.

In her gaze was something retrograde, pure, unconstructed

desire. Somehow she had dismantled everything. She was more beautiful than he had seen.

Why is it the truth? What is it?

I don't know. It's a gift.

*

He convinced Richard to come out for a few drinks midweek. Richard asked where Evie was.

Busy. Joining us later, was all he could say.

Which sounded chary; they never deliberately excluded her. He was drinking quickly, nervously. He knew it had to be spontaneous, natural, Richard would never agree otherwise. He looked at his friend across the table in the pub. He couldn't imagine it. They'd been roommates at university but he'd never really heard any explicit details about girlfriends from Richard, or witnessed moments of intimacy. Perhaps going with a stranger would have been better, but that seemed reckless. He bought them both another pint and then a whisky.

Whoa there, slow down, Richard said. I'm going to get hammered. I am hammered.

Yeah, sorry. Just wanted to cut loose a bit. I tell you what, let's leave these. Come back to ours and we'll have a nightcap with Evie?

I thought she was coming here?

No. Come on.

They left the pub and walked back towards the house. They walked without coats. The air was warm. The world seemed looser.

You and Evie are okay though?

Really great. Revolutionary!

Oh. Good. God, I haven't felt this drunk in a while, Richard said. Thought you were getting me loaded so you could confess something bad. Like an affair. I'd have killed you.

No, he said. Just fancied a fun night. We're not that old yet.

True.

The lights were on downstairs when they arrived, but Evie was not around. He called up, saying Richard was here for a drink. He was numb enough to make an attempt, but was sure he sounded like a bad actor, overdoing lines, like the hammy utilitarian films Evie had been watching. He didn't know how she would play it. She'd been so direct, so layerless lately, it was possible she'd scare Richard by moving too quickly. Whatever was in her now used no subtlety. They'd talked about what might happen, what kind of lover Richard might be, how receptive, but the truth was there was no predicting; shock, disgust, willingness. They were gambling.

She came downstairs wearing a nightgown, her hair wet, as if just washed. She smiled at them both. The room seemed charged. Precognition. It was going to work.

Richard, she said. She kissed him on both cheeks and then on the mouth, playfully, laughing.

Richard's face was flushed, from the beer, the walk, from the pleasure of seeing the woman he cared for. She sat down on the couch and began to talk in the way she did now, synaptically, brilliant and baffling. She had uneven, intense theories about life. She was impressionistic. He could see Richard listening, trying to follow, enjoying her. He left them and went into the kitchen and took a bottle from the wine rack. He uncorked it, poured and drank a glass, then brought the glasses and bottle into the lounge.

Let's have a really good night, he said, too loudly.

They drank the bottle and opened another. It was fun, it was ridiculous, they played stupid games, Evie flirted with them both, he and Richard conspired. She leant against their legs, against their chests. She dropped the shoulder of her gown and showed Richard a small new tattoo. It began soon after. It began almost unnoticeably, like a season, a regime. It was unreal and then it became serious. The protests – there were only a few from

Richard, of, we should stop now, come on guys, this is madness – were overridden. Evie reassured him. He reassured him. Once she was unveiled, once Richard saw her, allowed her to take his hand and place it, once he began to believe there was nothing prohibitive, even in himself, that there was just love, everything accelerated. The laughter died away. They were clumsy and aroused. Richard was surprisingly confident. There were no condoms; they knew each other. It went on for a few hours, each of them took turns. She always invited the other back in. He wanted to watch from the chair; he watched her being touched, grasped, opened, watched her responding. He began to understand: jealousy was only desire; it was wanting to do what he could see was being done to his wife. They went upstairs and fell asleep. Once he woke to see Richard going down on Evie. It was amazing to see, more sensual than anything he'd imagined. He reached over. He felt ill and elated. They were still drunk but there was clarity. They slept, woke. He remembered a moment, or he was in a moment, when Evie was bent over in front of him; he was moving behind her, Richard was kneeling in front and she had him in her mouth. The two of them were joined by Evie's body. They were facing each other. It would be all right afterwards.

He slept again. The next time he woke it was because Richard was calling his name and hitting him on the shoulder. White dawn light. His head was splitting, his mouth tasted evilly bitter.

Alex!

He looked over. Evie was lying on her front on the bed, her legs apart, jerking. She was making long, low sounds, bellows, almost cowlike.

She just started going, Richard said. I don't know why. I was on top of her. Help me turn her over.

He moved to Richard's side and the two of them rolled her. There was foam across her face and in her hair, the smell of bile and alcohol. He tried to keep her head still but her neck muscles were snapping up and down. Her eyes were white in her skull, her jaw clamped, the spit oozing out.

What the fuck. Evie! Evie! Call an ambulance. Should we drive her?

No. I'll call.

Richard leapt up and went downstairs. The convulsions were so strong it felt as if her spine would break. Then they began to ease. Richard came back in. He had trousers on. His face was ghastly.

They're coming. Christ, what the fuck is the matter with her. What kind of fucking depraved game is this?

*

A junior doctor asked him questions in the family room of A & E. About the fit. About whether she'd had headaches lately, or vomiting, vision or memory loss – he did not think so, he said. And her behaviour: had there been any changes? In what way? Had he been concerned?

They had ruled out stroke, toxicity. She was sent for a CT scan. The junior was evasive, professional, but the scan was not a good sign, he knew. Richard had followed the ambulance in a taxi, had sat with him on the hard plastic chairs while they'd sedated her and run tests, had fetched coffee. But they did not talk. *I didn't know*, he wanted to say, though no blame had been directed. The silence was blame. The repeated enquiries about his wife's state that he'd been fielding from his friend for the last few weeks were blame. There was no point in them both waiting. He promised to call Richard with any news.

A consultant came and found him in the family room. The scan had shown an area of the brain that appeared abnormal, in the prefrontal cortex. They didn't know yet what it meant. But the appearance was suspicious.

Do you mean a tumour?

We need to investigate.

The same questions were asked, more focused, the chronology of her cravings, her confusion, her promiscuity, the man nodding at the answers, as if already confirming a diagnosis. When they let him see Evie she was asleep. He found her hand under the sheet. She didn't wake. In the light of the small overhead lamp she looked normal, unextraordinary.

Everything after was the penalty for some unknown crime. The MRI pictures. The whitened shape. She was lucky and unlucky, they said. The mass, though probably benign, was big. He couldn't remember the word after the meeting and had to look it up. *Meningioma*. It was not in the important tissues – he did not really understand what could be unimportant inside the brain – but pressure was swelling the surrounding area, interfering with her functions, her cognition, her self. Over the next few weeks she had more fits. The second broke her wrist. She choked on her vomit and infected a lung.

She was given drugs to control the seizures. They began radiotherapy. The operation was scheduled. He could barely stand to think about the procedure – the position was difficult, she was ineligible for Gamma Knife or endonasal surgery, she needed a craniotomy. He looked online. The pictures were medieval. Rent-open heads. Pinned-back scalp. Lilac membranes and manes, so horribly wet and delicate. In one video a surgeon described the sound of cracking the skull, *like opening a can of Coke*. They would try to keep the incisions behind her hairline, but plastics might be required. The risks were extensive; leaks, aneurysms, coma.

She still wanted sex. She still strung wrong words together, talked like a charismatic, her mind slipped and was instinctive. But she knew what it was now. She was self-conscious, and fought for rationality; she contained it. When they were in the act she would claw away and start to howl and they would stop.

This isn't me, she'd say. I don't know if it's me.

She was not afraid. She knew she would live. Recovery would be tough, unpredictable, relearning; she might not be or feel exactly like the same person, ever again, but she would live. He didn't know if it was her, believing, or the lambency, the mania of the illness. It was an illness now. It had a name.

They had told Richard soon after the final diagnosis, convincing him to come over for dinner, saying that the meeting was vital, not a set-up. He had wept. Evie looked at him, expressionless, and left the room.

Jesus Christ, Alex.

She'll be okay, he said. She's tough.

Richard shook his head.

Do you not understand. What don't you understand.

They sat without speaking, sipping their drinks, until the evening dissolved.

Richard phoned the morning of the surgery but did not come to the hospital. He phoned regularly but did not visit. The decision to withdraw was obvious, even gracious. It was difficult, but he didn't mind. He was glad that it wasn't completely broken off. On the phone they talked about things of no consequence. Work, weather, the past. They never talked about that night, though he thought of it, often, more often than he should.

THE DAYS AFTER LOVE

Yiyun Li

Imbody, Lilia said, spelling for the two children. Patience was not her virtue, but if she had enough to live to her age, there was no reason she could not spare some for the third-graders. Or were they in second grade? It didn't matter. She would long be dead before they'd grow up into anything remotely interesting. 'Make sure it starts with an *I*,' she said. Lilia, née Church, had kept her second husband's last name because it was too precious to give up for Milt Harrison, whom Lilia had married only because she had not felt ready for a permanent widowhood. 'A gentle giant' was what Milt's children had put in his obituary, and after that, Lilia had given her life some thought, and decided that three marriages were an adequate record – not everyone could be Elizabeth Taylor. 'Mrs Imbody,' Lilia said now. 'Not Mrs Embody.'

The boy checked his notes before raising his face, the black and white of his eyes in shocking contrast. One only saw droopy lids and fogged-up eyes these days. 'Mrs Embody, would you like to go by your first name or last name for this interview?'

This was one of the days when she could benefit from playing truant from this life. Coffee lukewarm in the morning; Phyllis Nielsen taking a seat next to Lilia (uninvited) and talking in a circle about what to buy for her granddaughter's birthday (who cares); Elaine Moniz demanding everyone's participation in the school project – the head teacher was her niece, Elaine had gone from table to table with the announcement, her two loyal followers trailing behind her (as always one could hear their 'double double toil and trouble'); and now a child who seemed to be on the verge of tears under Lilia's stare. 'Call me Mrs *Im*body,' she said.

The boy nudged the girl and whispered that it was her turn. 'Is it okay if we record this interview, Mrs Imbody?' the girl read, and then explained that a Post-it would be placed in front of the camera and only her voice would be recorded.

'Where's the camera?' Lilia asked.

The girl turned to the boy and he pointed to the top of the laptop, which was set facing Lilia, though she had forgotten to bring her reading glasses so nothing on the screen could be deciphered. It would be perfectly fine with her if they left the peephole uncovered; Lilia wondered if she could request that they remove the Post-it. What could they see, though, these children whose undiscerning eyes would not tell the difference between Lilia and Phyllis or perhaps their own nondescript grandmothers tucked away in some nursing home. If indeed their teachers wanted them to understand anything about the world, they should be trained to look and listen at the same time, but there was no need to further this discussion. Lilia could sense Elisa and her assistant unwrap packs of cookies in the kitchenette next door. The flyers advertising the morning activity – meeting students from a local school for their oral history project – had promised cookies, clementines and hot chocolates with marshmallows. Lilia imagined Elisa peeling a clementine and handing a smaller half to her assistant – infringing on the residents' rights; a theft, strictly speaking, though no one here was strict with petty crimes. When you're closer to death, you're expected to see less, hear less and care less. Care less until you become careless, and that's when they pack you up to the next building. Memory care unit: as though your memories, like children or dogs, are only temporarily at the mercy of the uncaring others, waiting for you to reclaim them at the end of the day. You have to be careful not to slip into the careless: the care-full live; the care-less die; and when you are dead you are carefree. 'But who cares?' Lilia said aloud.

The boy studied Lilia's face. The girl patted him on the back of his head and said again – she must have memorised the line – that they were only recording voices. Around Lilia most residents were talking with their interviewers one on one. Only she was assigned a precocious girl who could not wait to mother an infantile boy. Lilia leaned close to take a look at the girl's ear studs. 'Are they diamond?'

The boy looked too. 'Do you know there's a diamond called Hope?' he said, addressing the air more than Lilia or the girl.

Normally Lilia would have reminded the boy that it was rude to speak when a question was not addressed to him. But somewhere in her body – Mrs Imbody's body, she called it when it made mischief to inconvenience Lilia – there was a strange sensation. Sixty years ago she would have called it desire, but now it must be as wrinkled as she was – the memory of desire. Certainly the staff at the next building would be happy to confiscate it.

The girl touched her earlobes. 'These are crystal. My cousin in Vancouver made them for me.'

'Are you Canadian?'

'My dad grew up in Canada.'

Lilia thought of saying something – so rarely did she get a chance to discuss the country with another person. On a second thought, she turned to the boy. 'Cheaper than your Hope, aren't they?' Hope, the diamond that had once been the subject of a post-lovemaking talk with Roland – but any conversation between them had taken place after sex. Lilia wondered if she could locate the mention of Hope in his diary. Not that she would see herself on the same page – Lilia had appeared in the diary only three times, and all three entries she had memorised, page numbers included. Footnote from the editor on page 124: L, unidentified lover.

'My mom took me and my brother to see the diamond last year,' the boy said.

'Did she?' Put a woman and a diamond together and you get a thousand stories, all uninteresting.

The girl nudged the boy. 'Do you want to start with the first question?' she said to him.

Lilia would rather discuss jewellery with the boy. She regretted that she hadn't thought of wearing something for the day. She could've shown him her favourite ring and quizzed him on the stone (green amethyst – he'd never have guessed that); she could ask him to venture an estimate about the ring's age (fifty-six: a present naturally, not from Roland but one that had made him jealous). 'I bet you a hundred dollars that your mother is one smart woman who knows how to raise a son.' Men in training – no doubt that was why the mother had taken the boys to see a diamond instead of zoo animals.

'I don't have a hundred dollars.'

'I don't have with me either,' Lilia said. 'It's just a way of saying.'

'But my mother died.'

By now the girl was more on the verge of tears than the boy. She looked around, searching for an intervening adult.

'I'm sorry to hear that,' Lilia said. 'But it's okay. Everybody dies. It's not up to you and me to say when.'

The boy opened his mouth and looked straight ahead as though he had not heard Lilia. She turned around, and, not to her surprise, Phyllis was sobbing into a cluster of Kleenex. Elisa and her assistant had already arrived at the crisis scene, trying to calm her, and the teacher bent down and whispered to Phyllis's interviewer, a girl who seemed too embarrassed to raise her eyes. The children around the recreation room gaped, but the residents tried hard to draw the interviewers' attention to their own memories. Let Phyllis cry – this was the chorus that went unheard by the children.

'Do you know –' Lilia whispered to the boy and his companion. 'That woman there, ask her anything she turns herself into a faucet.'

The boy's face, not expressive to start with, turned oddly flat. Look, here's an exemplary child for Phyllis to learn a few things about stoicism: after a lifelong career of wife-ing and mothering and grandmothering she still could not forget that she had begun as an orphan.

The teacher gestured to the children to go back to their work. 'Mrs Imbody, when and where were you born?' the girl asked. (Mrs Imbody, Lilia thought, has no use for obedient little girls.)

The interview was shorter than Lilia had expected. Five questions, harmless (but for Phyllis) and uninspiring. Where and when were you born? What was your family like when you were a child? Who was your favourite teacher when you were in school? What was your hometown like when you were a child? What's one thing you've done that you're proud of?

'One thing I'm proud of? Hard to choose. There are too many. How about I once knew a man who tried to borrow that diamond of yours –' Lilia nodded at the boy, '– for an exhibition.'

'Did he get it?' the girl said.

'I said he tried.'

'And they wouldn't let him borrow it?'

'His country. They wouldn't let his country borrow it.'

'Why?'

'Well, ask your friend here.'

'I don't know,' the boy said.

'I thought you saw the diamond with your own eyes.'

'My mom took us there.'

And your mom is dead. 'Where did Hope come from?' Lilia asked the boy, who shook his head. 'Not from this country, you know that, right?' Perhaps the boy didn't know anything. 'But once put into the museum, it rarely travels again. Remember, I say rarely, not never. It did travel, but not to my friend's country.'

'Where did it travel to?' the girl asked.

'Well, young lady, you should've asked where it was not allowed to travel,' Lilia said. That was what mattered to the story. 'Can you do me a favour,' Lilia said to the girl. 'Run to the lady there, yes, the one standing by the cart. Ask her if you could help her with the hot chocolate since we're done with your interview.'

Lilia moved closer to the boy when the girl went away. 'How did your mom die?'

'From a heart problem.'

'What kind of heart problem?'

The boy shook his head. The black and white of his eyes were never for a moment blurred. (Dry-eyed-ness, Lilia said to herself, is a virtue Mrs Imbody endorses.)

'Who do you live with now?'

'My grandparents.'

'And your brother, too?'

The boy nodded.

'Where is your dad?' (Or: do you have a dad?)

'He lives in San Diego.'

'Did he move there before or after your mom's death?'

'Before.'

Lilia thought of pulling the teacher or her young assistant aside and asking if the boy's mother had killed herself (and if so, in which way). They might be horrified, but so what? A distinction was essential: a woman dying from heart attack was different from one dying from heartbreak. Lilia had earned the right to know every single detail even if it was a stranger's death: enough people had died on her, starting with her parents. Too bad the boy was born at a wrong time when orphans were no longer an everyday phenomenon. Let me tell you a story from a long time ago, Lilia thought of saying, and this would then become one of those Russian stories she used to read with Roland, when an aristocratic soul, after enough food and drink, sat down by the fire and recounted the past, his or other people's. By the end of the story the boy would pretend nonchalance and yawn, but Lilia would know that something in him was changed. You don't just tell a story to a random soul.

Elisa clapped her hands and herded the residents to the snacks. The boy looked at Lilia uncertainly, so she prompted him to thank her for the interview. He did, and instantly rolled on the carpet with another boy.

Elaine went from one resident to the next, making sure they had co-operated with the children. 'Do you notice that there's no middle ground with your niece's students?' Lilia said.

'What do you mean?' Elaine said, and Lilia pretended that she had lost interest in the conversation. From neck up Elaine was made of marble, and Lilia was not a craftswoman to make anything out of that beautiful dumbness. Had Roland been here, Lilia would have pointed out that the children were either too skinny or too plump. No middle ground – children at this age were like politicians he used to laugh at: they had made entertaining subjects for post-coitus conversation. Children would do, too.

From the corner someone started to play a Bach minuet, tentative at first, but when even the noisiest boys quieted down to listen, the pianist became bolder. Ever so expectedly, it was Lilia's girl interviewer who was enchanting the roomful of people. Always eager to be more than what she was, Lilia thought. Already she could hear Elaine and her two wayward sisters expressing their amazement afterwards; Phyllis must be drowning in a fresh flood of tears; those who had finished their snacks were looking for a spot to sit down; Walter Berns, one hand on his cane, was conducting with the other arm. When you're closer to death, you don't need much of an excuse to play at being alive again.

Lilia shuffled around the room, looking for the orphan. He was sitting under a table, on which sometimes cut flowers would be on display but today the vase was empty. Again his face took on the obtuse look. Lilia beckoned him, and he, defeating her in a staring contest, did not move.

Had she been alone with the boy Lilia would have crawled under the table. There was a lesson for him, which nobody but she could teach him at the moment: any other person's death would be his gain. It was never too early to instil the wisdom in a child. The world might not love him; the world might not ever be in love with him.

'All I ask you is to be unselfish,' Roland had once said to Lilia. 'Always let me be the selfish one.' To be absent and present at once was what Roland had demanded: Lilia was not to be in the newspaper clipping where his bride held birds of paradise in her hands (26 January 1947; what a cold day in Ottawa that must be, for the flowers and newlyweds alike); Lilia was not to be the minor poetess whose decades of love letters to him had elevated her to some infamous status ('Sentimentality seems to calm her sexually,' one reviewer, not without malice, said of her letters). But didn't Lilia defeat them all by staying alive, present long after they had vacated their worldly positions?

Boy, let me tell you something your teachers and your elders don't know: one can – and should – live on a minimal diet of feelings. People expect you to always remember the sweetness of your mother's affection or the bitterness of losing her; they will come into your life with offers of other food and unnecessary spices. But trust Mrs Imbody's words: the days after love are bound to be long and empty. Let others seek in vain to satiate themselves; you and I know that only a cleansed palate prevails.

WHERE HAST THOU BEEN

Jon McGregor

When I first met God I was desperate and lost and my balls were leaping about within me from the lack of use. I was twenty-two years old and I'd never been laid. For a time I was stoical about the situation but that time had passed. I'd taken to scanning the faces in whatever room or street I was passing through as though looking for someone I'd lost when in truth there was no one to lose, and in this way I'd come to see how many people were odd-looking or sad or turned-in-upon in their own special way. My face was looking much the same and I tried to hide it but the hiding only made it worse. The state of most people it was a wonder anyone ever got laid. I was twenty-two years old and I felt that time was passing. University had finished and I was stuck for ideas. It was the summer time. There was a party and I went because the others were going. Tony the Dutch and Jimmy James and X, the X-Man. Tony was from the Netherlands so we called him Tony the Dutch. The X-Man's name was something Greek that no one could pronounce. We were living in Leeds and the party was in Hebden Bridge so we took the train, shunting past the back-streets and burning wastelands towards the narrows of the Calder Valley. There was a watery light washing over the hills and the air was charged. Jimmy James was already on his second can. Tony the Dutch was quiet and he kept rubbing his hands like he had a plan that would soon come together. X-Man was rolling a joint. He was saying a lot of words but it was a job to know what all of them were. The train crossed a canal and in the middle of the canal was a boat so slow it could have been there since the day before. The man at the tiller was watching the train with a patient kindness as though he'd always known our paths would cross and he would one day see us with our faces turned to the glass. We went into a tunnel and there was darkness and we came out into the light.

At the party the kitchen was full so we went through to the back yard. We couldn't see anyone we knew so we just stood around for a while. There was corduroy and there were conversations about Derrida and Brazilian dams. It was an academic crowd. Whose party is this anyway, X-Man wanted to know. Tony nodded through the doorway towards a woman with black hair and thick lashes who was holding up a long cigarette and tilting her head back to laugh. He said her name was Sofia and she was teaching Silent Cinema at Leeds Met. A smile crept over his face and he wiped it away with his hand. X choked on a laugh and the smoke streamed out of his nose. Jim opened the fourth of his cans and fell back into a white plastic chair. He was on a teacher-training course and the workload always had him wiped out. I went inside for a drink of my own. As I walked through the kitchen I heard the German Expressionist talking softly about the next on her list. I took a beer to the back room, where there was food on a table and Nick Drake on the stereo and still nobody I knew. I edged through the crowd and by the time I reached the buffet I could tell this was another night I wouldn't get laid. I had an instinct for it. There was a pattern I couldn't get past. I saw a large bearded man at the savouries and before he'd even turned towards me I knew this was God himself. For a moment I was afraid to look upon his face. I'd known him by reputation long before we met and what I'd heard hadn't led me to expect that we'd be friends. Full of himself, was the impression I'd formed. The kind of northern chancer who turns up at parties empty-handed and is drinking the best wine by the end of the night. His real name was Godfrey but he never answered to that. A big lad, with a beard he'd grown to go with the name and talk that he could handle himself in a fight. No one I knew was likely to handle themselves, in a fight. Those weren't the circles we moved in. We framed this as a question of non-violence but in truth we were sheltered and overfed. We stayed out of the town centres in the evenings and we kept our eyes lowered in the poorer neighbourhoods where we lived. God didn't sound as though he lowered his eyes for anyone. He turned to face me. His mouth was full and when he spoke he spat pastry flakes.

'Eh up,' he said. 'You tried these vegan sausage rolls? They're well mint.'

Later there was djembe drumming and God said there were better places we could be. We followed him and we didn't ask where. As we left there was a girl with red hair who looked like she thought she knew me but I hadn't seen her before so I nodded and followed the others. The streetlights were just coming on. There were seats on the train but I couldn't sit down. There was something urgent clicking through me. I asked X-Man did we know the girl with the red hair and he said he didn't think so. I wondered if I should have stayed behind to talk or if I would have been wasting my time. I watched through the window the lights of Hebden Bridge slip away around the corner and I didn't know how I would ever get laid. The ache of it was all over me. God took us off the train at Bradford and led us through the littered streets. He had a light-footed swagger that didn't fit with his size. The swagger was from Manchester, though he'd done his growing up in towns further north with far less spring in their stride. We ducked round some bins and down an alley and he knocked on a red steel door. When it opened there were handshakes and God introduced us and we followed him down some stone cellar stairs. There was a wet heat coming up to meet us and a noise that was mostly bass. We asked him what this place was and when he said it was the Mormon Social Club it took a moment to realise he was kidding us on.

*

That was the summer I worked at a bread factory on the edge of town, one week on night shifts and one week on days, and the havoc this played with my sleep only added to the trembling state of confusion I was in. The work was lifting tins and wheeling trays and sorting the subs from the batches as they hurtled down the line. It was heavy work and hot. The line moved fast and there was a fear of falling behind, the bread backing up and tumbling to the floor while the mocking shouts rang high. I thought the hours of work would make me stronger but they only made me tired. I lost weight. Most nights I spent the whole shift thinking about sex. I once made the mistake of mentioning this to God, while the two of us stood by the punch bowl at a Green Party fundraiser near Roundhay Park.

'That'll be the yeast,' he said, as though the problem was famil-iar. 'Whole place reeking of it, our kid. All that rising action. Stuff of life.' The party was quieter than we'd hoped for and this wasn't a conversation I wanted overheard. God had a voice that could project. It was an older crowd on the whole and the women had a strong commitment to knitwear. In the back room there were bald men with homemade guitars singing paragraphs of Foucault to a twelve-bar blues. We finished the punch and were halfway down the road before Tony thought to ask where we were going. God said there was a party in Headingley and we had time so we might as well walk. The evening was long and the shadows were longer and we had all the time in the world. We were lost and we had to cross a dual carriageway and cut through some woods. In the woodland there were three boys standing around a fire and two girls sitting on a mattress and nobody spoke as we made our way past. In a park James fell down a grass bank and it took a few minutes to get him back on his feet. This was how that summer went: walking around looking for the next party or gig, jumping on buses and trains, chasing rumours of lock-ins and open-mic nights and gallery shows and often this long veiled light of the sun going up or coming down. We never made arrangements but God always showed up. It was a long time before I even knew where he lived but I had started to think of him as a friend. I didn't know if he considered me the same. We came into the leafy streets of Headingley and God put his arm around me and said maybe this would be the night I found my way to the bread-oven door. I must have looked puzzled for a moment too long.

'Bush, our kid. Boggy hollow?' I nodded, but he carried on. 'Olive grove, mangrove, peaches and cream?' I told him I'd got it but he persevered. 'Lady garden? Garden of tears?' X-Man said something in Greek which he later translated as secret harbour. I told them all I had got it, and God said getting it was exactly my problem, and as we came to the house where the party was he started singing 'Like a Virgin' to the tune of 'Ilkley Moor Baht 'at', and he was still singing as we walked through the door. God always liked to make an entrance.

I didn't know how lost I was. It wasn't that I didn't know how to talk to girls but there were some things I just couldn't say. Some of my best friends were girls and we talked a lot. I never knew how to get to where the talking would stop; if there were cues I was missing or questions I was failing to ask. At heart I assumed that no one would want me so there seemed little point taking the chance. The beds I slept in were all too big and I was kept awake often thinking of these things. The summer came to an end and the autumn was wet. I didn't get the funding for my PhD and sometimes after work I went for drinks on campus with a girl who had. She'd been on my masters course and was writing a thesis on hypertext. These were the early days of the internet and I didn't always understand what she said. Her name was Isobel and she had eyes that were hard to avoid. She had a way of holding a gaze. She'd ask what I was reading and my answers made her sad. One night she took me to a benefit gig for a group called Soldiers for

Peace and before the music started there were people talking on the stage talking about checkpoints and demolitions. This was in the Wesleyan chapel in Shipley. One of the speakers was a woman who'd served in the Israeli army and she challenged the audience directly while Isobel took notes on her use of rhetorical device.

'It's nice that you came tonight,' the woman said; 'it's nice that you are concerned and you care, okay. So what are you doing to change things? Who are you challenging? What good is your concern to us?' She looked angry, and I noticed that her eyebrows were dark and incredible and how attractive she was in her scorn, and I knew if I didn't get laid soon my politics would be lost in a haze of objectification. The band started playing, and when Isobel touched my arm to ask what I wanted from the bar it was the first time a woman had touched me for weeks. I kept my arm still so the sensation would take longer to fade. I saw God and Jimmy James talking to the Soldiers for Peace, reading their leaflets and signing petitions. Later when they said they were leaving I asked Isobel if she wanted to join us, but she had somewhere to be and for the rest of the evening I felt raw with shame for having asked her at all.

There was a gallery opening in Saltaire, and a warehouse party in Manningham, and by the end of the night we were getting henna tattoos on our hands to raise money for the Zapatistas. The logic of these things wasn't always easy to follow. At some point in the evening God told me he was adopted and I couldn't work out how the conversation had begun. He'd never known who his real parents were but his adoptive parents were so good to him that he waited until they died before trying to find out. He told me this like it was something he'd read in a book. We both kept our hands very still. I wondered how long the henna would take to wash off. After the second funeral he went to the archives and looked out his birth certificate. He made it sound easy. The tattoos were done by then and we stood up but the woman told us not to leave until they'd dried. Wave your hands around, she told us.

'When I found it there were no father listed,' God said. This stuff just rolled out of him sometimes. We both stood there with our hands in the air. 'But my mother's name was Ruth Schalansky.' He looked at me like I should know what he meant but it took me a moment to cop on.

'So – God's Jewish?' I asked. He shrugged.

'Who knew?'

*

One night in the spring we were thrown out of a party in Sowerby Bridge. I'd been talking to a concrete poet from Kingston-upon-Hull who had just started teaching in Tony's department. She had pale eyes and freckles across her nose and a skirt that swung thinly around her thighs when she danced. She was dancing while we talked and I was trying to keep looking at her eyes. Once I realised how long we'd been talking I got nervous and ran out of things to say. She didn't seem to mind. There was a silence between us. A shout went up from across the room. Jimmy James had fallen asleep in an armchair and wet himself, and the BBC producer whose party it was started shouting about the chair being genuine Eames. He tried pulling Jimmy to his feet, and we told him to get his hands away. Someone came through with a bucket and sponge, and the producer told us all to get out. As we were leaving the poet said something I couldn't hear. I didn't even get her name. When we came out of the house a drunk driver skidded on the corner and crashed into a row of parked cars. It happened with a chill kind of slowness and a great racket and by the time it had stopped God was already in the road. These things followed him round and he took them in his lengthy stride. He opened the door and snatched at the keys and told the driver to go ruddy nowhere. He pushed the man's face hard against the steering wheel to be sure. We were away down the hill before the police arrived and at the station we had to carry Jim onto the train. By this time we knew Jim had a problem and his drinking wasn't funny any more.

The next morning I woke with a pain in my neck and the many faces of Noam Chomsky looking over me from the bookshelves above where I'd slept. There was an open patio door beside me and a cold wind coming up from the river below. The patio was thick with bottles and ashtrays. Past the patio the garden fell steeply away. I had a blanket around me but it was thin and I felt exposed. I was still in Mytholmroyd. We'd turned up late the night before and it looked like I was the only one left. It was the leaving party for a semiotics professor from Isobel's department who wasn't quite retiring but going on extended research leave. There'd been a restructuring. The party had been tense and most people had left by two. When I'd fallen asleep God was still out on the patio talking to Tony the Dutch about the Soldiers for Peace. I'd heard him say something about going to Bethlehem. It seemed far-fetched. The morning was bright and there was an elaborate smell of coffee. I saw the semiotics professor in the kitchen reaching for some cups, bending for the milk, setting a loaf and a knife on a board. Her movements were flowing and light. When I tried to stand I felt like an old man. She watched me creak towards her and said good morning. There was classical music. The coffee machine on the counter was beginning to steam and she asked if I wanted one. I leant on the counter across from her. My neck was so stiff I had to move my whole body when I tried to nod. She flinched. I said it was nothing and she talked about posture, and when she mentioned the Alexander Technique I thought she was talking about sex.

'Imagine your head as a ping-pong ball, floating on a cushion of air.'

'It's more like a cannon ball,' I said. She smiled, and reached over to put one hand on the back of my neck. The other hand pushed flatly against my chest. Her fingers were cold and smooth.

'Let your shoulders fall,' she said. She had her hands on me and we were listening to classical music and she was making coffee and instructing me and this was the closest to adulthood, I'd yet come. 'Let yourself really stretch,' she said. 'Keep those shoulders down.' She was talking quietly because she was standing so close. She had faint lines around her eyes that looked like experience. I wanted her to experience me. It was true she was older but by then my parameters were broad. She asked if I felt any better. I wanted to say please don't stop. There was the sound of a toilet flushing. A door opened, and God appeared before us.

'Now then,' he said. The professor dropped her hands and turned to the coffee machine. I asked if she'd been introduced.

Later Tony surfaced as well and the three of us went looking for a bus. God asked outright if I'd nailed the professor and I told him I didn't like his tone.

'It's objectification,' I said. 'It's problematic.'

'Problematic, my arse. You were objectifying her all night.' He punched me lightly on the arm and it hurt like hell. God didn't know his own strength sometimes. 'You missed a chance there, pal. Body language were bang on.'

'Signs and signifiers,' Tony said. 'She was signifying, for certain.' I had no idea if they were winding me up or what they were saying so I asked what all the talk about Bethlehem had been in aid of. Tony looked at God and threw up his hands. God said he'd signed up to rebuild demolished houses in Bethlehem, and to take direct action against evictions. It seemed like a joke but it wasn't a joke. I asked if he thought that would be safe, and Tony said he'd already asked all this. God didn't reply. He had a face on him like he thought we were missing the point. There was a silence as we walked down the hill. I asked if he'd even be allowed into the West Bank, being Jewish.

'Who's Jewish?' God said. 'That birth certificate means nowt. I'm toto intacto down doors. I don't even know when Passover is. And what about my father, anyway? He could have been a Catholic, or Muslim! He could have been a Palestinian, pal. Who knows?'

'This seems unlikely,' Tony said, and he had just enough of a smile on him to get God riled.

'Fuck you know about likely, Dutchie?' God grabbed hold of Tony's collar and held his face close. Tony looked him in the eye. 'Fuck you know about any of this?' I stood and I watched and I didn't know what to do. It was all falling apart. Tony apologised and God let him go and at the train station we stood on different platforms, waiting for different trains.

*

The parties dried up for a time after that. I was working week-end shifts to cover my rent, and X-Man went back to his parents' house, and no one saw Jimmy James for months. God kept out of sight. Then came the news that Tony the Dutch was getting mar-ried, to the concrete poet from Kingston-upon-Hull. There was surprise and later there was complacency. We were too young to notice what this first marriage meant. The weekly whirl of gigs and shows and traipsing around looking for strange beds to wake up in was coming to an end. The pairing off had started in earnest. Soon the babies would come and the parties would stop. This would be it, now, until we hit our forties and the divorces started coming through.

There was a stag weekend. Tony barely understood the concept but let himself be talked into a minibus with Jimmy James at the wheel, heading for the Lakes. Having Jim drive was the best way of keeping him sober. Everyone else was drinking as soon as we hit the M62. The first stop was a paintballing centre, which was a surprising choice. Most of us came from backgrounds of co-operative play, and this was the first time we'd held anything that looked like a gun. Within minutes of the briefing we were crawling through the brambles and the killing had begun. I kept getting taken down by a Peace Studies lecturer who hid in a thicket of birch trees and only ever needed one shot. He was a Quaker. He was very good at sitting still. At one point I got stuck in a ditch with Tony the Dutch, pinned down by two gender theorists from York St John. We sat it out and he lit a cigarette. He asked if I knew what my problem was. I asked were we talking about paintballing or something else.

'You're just waiting for something to happen, always,' he said. 'All these years I've known you, just waiting. Like you're entitled.' The smoke from his cigarette curled up into the air and a volley of paintballs burst against the trees overhead. 'You won't get the girl by standing around looking pale and interesting. You don't look interesting enough for that.'

'That's nice, thanks.'

'None of us look interesting enough for that, come on. All these years I keep hearing the no-one-will-want-me bullshit.' This was starting to feel like advice. It was hard to take advice from a Dutchman in a face mask and a camouflage gilet. 'It's very safe for you. You never have to take the chance of being turned down.' My face mask was starting to fog. What did he know. He had no idea. The paintballs were coming faster now and we could hear movements towards us in the trees. Tony and I had been friends since the first week of university and he'd never talked like this. He finished his cigarette and caught my eye and we ran from the ditch in a final desperate charge. We didn't get far but we went down together.

And then came the incident, which wasn't planned although it must have seemed that way. It was the last rest break of the day and everyone was ready for a drink. The light was starting to fail.

God was talking about the instructors only covering their backs with the warnings they'd given. 'It's nonsense,' he muttered, running his hand through his beard, stroking the words away. 'These pellets won't break skin at any distance. That minimum range talk is a crate of guff. It wouldn't do any damage. You could shoot a man in his hind-parts from right here and it wouldn't do owt. Would be funny and all.'

He was looking up into the trees as he spoke. He caught my eye for the briefest moment, glanced at Tony the Dutch, and looked back into the trees. Tony was bending to retie his bootlaces. I could feel the weight of the gun in my hands. As I shifted it the paintballs rattled in their hopper. I felt the tiny plop as one of them slipped into the chamber. Tony was taking a long time to tie his bootlaces. Almost as though he was waiting. As though the thing was ordained. The afternoon light filtered through the trees. The instructors were talking amongst themselves. God turned his back slightly, as if to say *let it be so.* I lifted my gun and from no more than six inches I shot Tony the Dutch in his hind-parts.

There was a reaction.

Tony dropped to the floor and roared something animal-like and unintelligible, something Dutch. The others gathered around to watch, and he looked up at us in a state of agonised continental disbelief, asking with his sad blue eyes how anyone could have done such a thing.

'I couldn't help it,' I said, knowing I sounded absurd. 'God made me do it.'

*

The only reason I still went to the wedding after that was because I was Tony's best man. It was awkward. We barely spoke and his wife didn't look at me once. When they walked down the aisle he was still limping. I didn't know how to make things right. At the reception I kept my speech short and I left before the first dance. It was a long time before I saw Tony again and our friendship was never the same. I blamed God and his habit of stirring up situations, and for once I took the risk of telling him so. He called me a gobshite and said I'd been acting on my own free will. He laughed and reminded me of Tony's reaction, and I told him I didn't think we could be friends for a while. He looked surprised. He told me we'd never really been friends. For a while I kept hearing about him and then he drifted away, and I'd given up feeling any regret about it until I found myself at another wedding the following year, standing by a buffet table and remembering our first meeting back in Hebden Bridge.

This was the wedding of Jimmy James. I hadn't seen him for a long time either and I was surprised to be invited. When I got there I couldn't see anyone I knew. The ceremony was brief and there was a long delay before any drinks were served. When the photographs were taken I hid at the back and got talking to a girl who was hiding as well. She was on teaching placement at Jimmy's school. She introduced herself and held out her hand and when I went to shake it she thumbed her nose instead. It was so unexpected that it took me a moment to remember her name. Marion. I didn't see her again until after the speeches, when the wine was eventually served. I told her I thought she'd left and she said she was looking for someone, and when I asked who she gave me a look I couldn't translate. She walked away to the bar and I could hear God telling me to do something. I could hear what Tony had said when we were stuck in that ditch. There was dancing and I found myself moving to the back of the room and running out of reasons to stay. I got stuck in a conversation with the semiotics professor from Mytholmroyd. And then somehow I made it through the crowd to the buffet table and Marion was beside me again.

'Hey,' she said. 'It's you.' Her mouth was full, and she held up a hand to cover the crumbs. 'Have you tried these vegan sausage rolls?' I looked at her. 'They're basically rank,' she said, laughing as flakes of puff pastry tumbled down the front of her dress.

We talked about her teaching practice, and what it was like working with Jimmy, and the PhD I still wasn't doing, and we kept finding more things to say. The music was loud and we had to stand close to be heard. There was a moment when she stopped talking and looked around the room, and I knew I had to do something to keep her from going away.

'Do you want to dance?' I asked her. She gave me a sideways look.

'Not really, no. Why, do you?'

'Should we go out for a smoke?' She scanned the room again. She seemed to be looking for options. She nodded and led the way out to the terrace. It was quiet outside and cold. I checked my pockets.

'Do you smoke?' I asked. She shook her head. I told her I didn't either and she laughed.

'So what are you checking your pockets for?'

'No idea.' There was quiet and we looked at each other. It was cold and she shivered and stood closer.

'So, what now? Do we go back inside?'

'Maybe if we've run out of things to talk about we should do something else.'

'Something else?'

'Yeah. If we're going to stop talking.' The words fell out of me and I had no idea how they came. I was out of the ditch and walking towards the guns and none of the paintballs were knocking me down.

'You're probably right. You'd better keep talking then.'

'Keep talking?'

'Be on the safe side.' She moved closer again.

'I've got nothing to say.' I leaned closer and kissed her and it was the first time I'd kissed anyone in years and this wasn't how

I'd had the evening planned out in my mind. It was a long kiss and there were hands and I didn't feel cold any more.

'Is that what you meant, instead of talking? Why didn't you just say?' She was smiling and she pulled me by the hand. We left the terrace and the wedding and we walked away. There was no hurry and no word of where we were going and the conversation went back to Jimmy and the school. She said she thought he was on top of the drinking now. She asked where I was staying and when I told her she said we'd get to her hotel first. I thought there was a catch, or some misunderstanding. I thought at the hotel entrance she would shake my hand goodnight. I thought that inside her room there would be a man with a stick or a knife who would take all my money and push me out of the door while they both laughed. She was leaning closely and matching my step and there was a smell coming off her of red wine and perfume and the chance of it seemed well worth the while.

In the room she sat on the bed and asked if this was what I wanted. I told her it was. And as we lay across the bed I was struck by how simple it was, when for all those years I'd been making it something complex and out of reach. She kissed me, and I kissed her back. I thought of the opportunities thrown up by all those parties, all the friendships that had grown up and drifted away over the years as the social circle reeled apart under its own centrifugal force. She unbuttoned my shirt, and slipped her hand against my chest. I thought of the house on the side of the hill in Mytholmroyd with the bookcase full of Chomsky, and she wriggled out of her dress, and I thought about Tony rubbing his hands all those times and whether we might get back in touch, and then the two of us were naked on the bed and it was all so unlikely that I felt as though I was watching the scene from above. She was kissing my neck, and lifting herself from the bed against me, and I worried about all the things I might be doing wrong. I wondered about God and where he was now, what he'd told them if he ever got as far as Tel Aviv. I could imagine him talking himself all the way to Bethlehem and standing in front of bulldozers, rebuilding houses, washing teargas from his eyes. I hadn't thought of him for months and now I missed him, now of all times. Marion was pulling my hand between her thighs, and although I felt clumsy it seemed from what she was saying that I was doing at least something right. At one point she actually said, *oh, God!* and it was so surprising that I almost laughed. It seemed self-conscious, the way she said it, as though she'd heard that this was the thing to say, and I realised that perhaps she wasn't much more experienced than I was. The mechanics of the thing itself were awkward and there was a moment of confusion before we could carry on. And when I heard her call out, *oh, God,* a second time, more tentatively, I thought of my lost friend again, and found myself muttering his name in reply, God, and she heard me and laughed as though it were a joke, and she yelled, *oh God!* much louder this time and we both laughed, and it turned out that laughing during sex made it something else entirely, when I'd always imagined that sex would be earnest and solemn, and so then we were both yelling *oh God! oh God! oh God!* until one or other of us eventually came – this was the way I thought of it later, although it wasn't her and eventually was far from the right word – and the two of us in that small room were soon yelling loudly enough that I imagined God himself might hear us and look up from a house he was rebuilding, in the shadow of a watchtower or beside a burnt-out olive grove, look up and hear our call and smile to himself and say *nice one finally our kid* as he mortared another breeze-block into place. And these thoughts – of my absent friend and all we'd been through together, of my years of missed opportunities, even of Marion and how there would soon come a time when I would wonder where she was and whether she thought of me at all – these thoughts all brought me close to crying, close enough to want to hide the fact by getting down on my knees and burying my face in her garden of tears, where I opened my mouth and murmured soft distractions until she pulled my hair and whispered *oh God* once again, as though saying it for the very first time.

10-ITEM EDINBURGH POSTPARTUM
DEPRESSION SCALE

Claire Vaye Watkins

1. Since my baby was born, I have been able to laugh and see the funny side of things.
- • As much as I ever did.
- ○ Not quite as much now.
- ○ Not so much now.
- ○ Not at all.

2. I have looked forward with enjoyment to things.
- • As much as I ever did.
- ○ Not quite as much now.
- ○ Not so much now.
- ○ Not at all.

My husband beside me in the waiting room, reading over my shoulder, frowning. That's rather evasive, isn't it? 'As much as I ever did.'

You think I'm being dishonest?

No, but.

But what?

This should be short answer, not multiple choice. He rocks the car seat with his foot. Short answer or essay. Don't you think?

As much as I ever did.

It becomes our inside joke, the answer to the questions we're afraid to ask.

1. Since my baby was born, I have been able to laugh and see the funny side of things.

We try to find you a nickname in utero but nothing fits so well as the ones we have for your father's scrotum and penis, your brothers Krang and Wangston Hughes.

An app dings weekly developmental progress and fruit analogies. Every week we write our own.

> This week your baby is the size of a genetically modified micropeach, which itself is about the size of a red globe grape. Your baby's earholes are migrating this week. Your baby can hear you and may already be disappointed by what it hears.

> This week your baby is the size of a medjool date knocked from the palm and left to soften in the dust. Your baby is now developing reflexes like lashing out and protecting its soft places. It is also developing paradoxes, and an attraction to the things that harm it.

> This week your baby is the size of a navel orange spiked with cloves and hung by a blue ribbon on the doorknob of a friend's guest bathroom. Your baby is developing the self-defeating emotions this week, among them doubt, boredom, self-consciousness and nostalgia. It may even be besieged by ennui!

> This week your baby is the size of a large, thick-skinned, inedible grapefruit. Your baby has begun to dream, though it dreams only of steady heartbeats and briny fluids.

2. I have looked forward with enjoyment to things.

Sushi, beer, pot brownies, daycare, pain-free BMs, getting HBO, my in-laws going home.

Erica visits and asks, Does a person really need a doula? No, I tell her, not if you have an older woman in your life who is helpful, trusted, up to date on the latest evidence-based best practices and shares your birth politics, someone who is nonjudgemental, won't project her insecurities onto you, is respectful of your boundaries and your beliefs and those of your spouse, carries no emotional baggage or unresolved tensions, no submerged resentment, no open wounds, no hovering, no neglect, no library of backhanded compliments, no bequeathed body issues, no treadmill of jealousy and ingratitude, no debt of apology, no I'm sorry you feel that way, I'm sorry you misunderstood me, no beauty must suffer, no don't eat with your eyes, no I cut the ends off the roast because you did, I did it to fit the pan.

Erica says, So it's basically $750 for the mother you wish you had.

3. I have felt scared or panicky for no good reason.

There are little moths drifting twitchy through our apartment, sprinkling their mothdust everywhere. I cannot find what they are eating. I brace myself each time I take a towel or a pillowcase from the linen closet.

Our baby is born runty and jaundiced. We wrap her in a hot, stiff so-called blanket of LEDs, to get her levels right. She's at twelve, they tell us, without saying whether the goal is fifteen or zero or a hundred – not knowing whether we are trying to bring them up or down. I don't know which way to pray, your dad says. Little glowworm baby, spooky blue light-up baby in the bassinet, hugged by this machine instead of us, a gnarly intestine-looking tube coming out the bottom. Jaundiced and skinny skinny though neither of us are. *Failure to thrive*, the diagnosis. In the car we agree that a ridiculously lofty standard. Haven't we every advantage – health insurance and advanced degrees, study abroad and strong female role models? Aren't we gainfully employed, and doing work we do not hate, no less? Didn't we do everything right and in the right order? And yet, can either of us say we are *thriving*? We remind ourselves it's not so bad, the jaundice, the smallness. Erica says, I was little and look at me! We remind ourselves of the Nick-U and paediatric oncology, which we walk past on the way to our appointments. I remember the apparatus we learned about in breastfeeding class that the lactation consultants can rig up for a man: a tube from a sack at his back taped up over his shoulder and to his pectoral, to deliver imitation milk to the baby as though through his nipple. I comfort myself with the dark, unmentioned scenarios wherein that would be necessary.

A box on the birth-certificate paperwork says *I wish to list another man as the baby's father (See reverse)*. I see reverse, curious what wisdom the hospital has for such a situation, what policies the board has come up with to solve a clusterfuck of such magnitude, but the reverse is blank.

My husband has hymns and spirituals, but when I sing to the baby I can only remember the most desperate lines from pop songs. If you want better things, I want you to have them. My girl, my girl, don't lie to me. Tell me, where did you sleep last night?

Q: Do you think having a baby was a good idea?
A: As much as I ever did.

4. I have been anxious or worried for no good reason.

Erica says, Your phone is ringing.

What's the area code? There are certain area codes I categorically avoid.

What about home?

Especially home.

In my Percocet dreams our blankets are meringue but quicksand thick, suffocation heavy, and the baby somewhere in them. From the toilet I shout it out.

She's not in the bed, my husband says from the hallway.

How do you know?

Because she's in the bassinet.

But how do you know she's in the bassinet?

Because I'm looking at the bassinet and I see her in there.

But, I want to know, how do you know that you are really seeing?

5. I have blamed myself unnecessarily when things went wrong.

A postcard arrives addressed to both of us but meant only for my husband: *Funny how some people feel like home.*

Q: Do you still want to be married?
A: As much as I ever did.

The world slips out from under us approximately every hour and a half.

6. I have been so unhappy that I have had difficulty sleeping.

Over Skype people say things about the baby I don't like – she seems small, she seems quiet, she's a princess, she will be gone before we know it – and I slam the computer closed. After, I send them pictures of the baby and small loops of video, to prove I am not a banshee. I am a banshee, but cannot get comfortable with being one, am always swinging from bansheeism to play-acting sweetness and back. I cannot play nice and don't want to, but want to want to, some days.

7. I have felt sad or miserable.

I can hear the whispers of my own future outbursts: I wiped your ass, I suctioned boogers from your nose, I caught your vomit in my cupped hand and it was hot! I cut the tiny sleep dreads from your hair and blew stray eyelashes off your cheeks. I can feel the seeds of my resentment as I swallow them. When you couldn't sleep I lay beside you with my nipple in your mouth. For hours I did this!

I can feel lifelong narratives zipping together like DNA, creation myths ossifying. You would smile but only if you thought no one was looking. Your hands were always cold, little icicles, but pink and wrinkly as a man's, little bat claws, little possum hands. Your dad cut the teensiest tip of your finger off trying to cut your nails, and after that we let them grow. That's why you have socks on your hands in all your pictures, to keep you from scratching yourself. When we took the socks off you had little woolly worms of lint in your palms, from clenching and unclenching your fists all day. We had a machine that rocked you and another that vibrated you and another that made the noises from the world you'd never seen – breakers and birds, rain on a tin roof – but they soothed you anyway. Robo-baby, I worried you'd become, since you liked the machines so much more than me.

8. I have been so unhappy that I have been crying.

Ours is not even a bad baby. She sleeps so much I have to lie to the other moms, pretend to be tired when I'm not, commiserate lest they turn on me. In truth ours sleeps through anything, even two adults screaming at each other, crying, saying things they can't take back, making up, and screaming again – our baby sleeps through all of it, waking only when we stagger into our own bed.

When her cord stump falls off I put it in the pocket of my bathrobe. I don't cry until the robe is put in the wash.

Creation myth (his):
He broke his collarbone falling off a fence. He was trying to get to the neighbour girl.

Creation myth (hers):
When they brought her baby sister home from the hospital she tried to deposit the bundle in the trash.

Q: Do you still love me?
A: As much as I ever did.

9. *The thought of harming myself has occurred to me.*

And also the profound pleasure of sitting in the back yard on the last warm day of fall, the baby and her dad on a bedsheet on the grass, me in a lawn chair because I cannot yet bend in the ways that would get me to and from the ground, in my lap a beer and a bowl of strawberries.

Q: Do you appreciate being alive?
A: As much as I ever did.

10. *Things have been too much for me.*

On Christmas Eve the upper-class grocery store is a teeming jingle-bell hellscape. I decide to play nice for once, an exercise, my Christmas gift to the universe. I strap the baby to me and do not pretend not to notice when strangers gape at her there. I stop and let them say oh how cute and even oh how precious and when they ask if the baby is a boy or a girl I do not say, Does it really matter? nor A little bit of both! nor You know, I'm not sure, how do I check? And when they ask how old I do not say, Two thousand eight hundred and eighty hours, nor A lady never tells. Instead I round up and say four months today! I wag the baby's hand and make the baby say hi and bye-bye. I spend too much money on stinky cheeses and chocolate coins, stovetop popcorn, armfuls of cut flowers, muffin tins I will never use, pomegranates that remind me of home. I do not use self-checkout, the misanthrope's favourite invention, and when the nosy checker asks me to sign my name on the electronic pad I do not write 666 nor draw a big cock and balls and instead I sign in elegant cursive the baby's name. And outside I do not look away when more lonely people ask me with their eyes to stop so that they might see the baby and touch her and instead I do stop, in the fresh snow falling and padding the parking lot, let them hold the baby's hand and let them tell me how I will feel in five years or ten years or twenty years or at this time next year, let them tell me where I will be and what will be happening and how I will cherish every minute.

REVERSIBLE

Courttia Newland

London, early evening, any day. The warm black body lies on
the cold black street. The cold black street fills with warm black
bodies, an open-mouthed collective, eyes eclipse dark. Raised
voices flay the ear. Arms extend, fingers point. Retail workers in
bookie-red T-shirts, shapeless Primark trousers. Beer-bellied men
wear tracing-paper hats, the faint smell of fried chicken. There
are hoods, peaked caps, muscular puffed jackets. There are slim
black coats, scarred and pointed shoes, red ties, midnight blazers.
A few in the crowd lift children, five or six years old at best, held
close, faces shielded, tiny heads pushed deep into adult necks.
New arrivals dart like raindrops, join the mass. Staccato blue
lights, the hum of chatter. They pool, overflow, surge forwards,
almost filling the circular stage in which the body rests, leaking.

A bluebottle swarm of police officers keeps the circle intact,
trying to resist the flood. Visor-clad officers orbit the body, gripped
by dull gravity; others without headgear stand shoulder to shoulder, facing the crowd, seeing no one. Blue-and-white tape, the
repeated order not to cross. A half-raised semi-automatic held
by the blank policeman who stands beside a Honda Civic, doors
open, engine running. His colleague speaks into his ear. He is
nodding, not listening. He looks into the crowd, nodding, not
hearing. Blue lights align with the mechanical stutter of the heli-
copter, fretting like a mosquito. Its engine surges and recedes,
like the crowd.

The blood beneath the body slows to a trickle and stops. It
makes a slow return inwards. There's an infinitesimal shift of air

pressure, causing fibres on the fallen baseball cap to sway like seaweed; no one sees this motion. There's a hush in the air. Sound evaporates. The body begins to stir.

One by one, the people leave. They do not hurry. They simply step into the dusk from which they came. The eyes of adults widen, jaws drop, mouths gape and snap closed. Children's faces rise from shoulders, hands are removed from their eyes and they see it all. They crane their necks, tiny hands splayed starlike on adult shoulders.

The crowd step back. The uncertain suits, the puzzled office workers, the angry retail assistants. Chicken shop stewards, the cabbie, Bluetooth blinking in his ear. They step back until there is no one left but a trio of young men, Polo emblems on their chests, hands aloft, calling in the direction of the police.

The police shimmer and stir, lift and separate. Arms and legs piston hard, five officers backstepping faster than the crowd. They speed away from the body until they enter a parked ARV, three in the back, two in front. The vehicle gains life and roars into the distance. One of the remaining officers, a tall, gaunt woman, reels in blue-and-white tape, eyeing the young men with a glare veiled by an invisible sheen. When the tape is a tight blue-and-white snail in her hand, she also retreats, climbs inside a car with her partner, starts the engine and they roll away backwards. The visored officer joins his visored colleagues, where they gather like a bunched fist, semi-automatics raised and pointing.

The body lifts, impossibly. Ten degrees, twenty degrees, ninety; the fallen baseball cap flips from the ground, joins the head, and the man is half crouched as though he might run. He holds his left arm up, fingers reaching for sky, one bright palm facing the officers while his right hand clutches his heart. Drops of sweat fly towards his temples, as his head turns left, right. Thicker beads of red burrow into three puckered holes in his Nike windcheater, exposed beneath his fingers. He blinks one eye, as though he's winking.

He is not.

Tiny black dots leap from his chest like fleas. Three plumes of fire are sucked into the rifle barrel. He stands and raises his right hand to his blinking eye, almost wipes, and then both palms are raised. He is shaking his head. His mouth is moving fast. His eyes are shifting quickly. Streetlights turn from orange to grey.

The young man is stepping into the Civic. The police officers are stepping across the street. The Polo youths on the opposite side of the road turn their heads, beginning to brag that road man's time has come, and seconds after, of Wiley's tweets about Kanye. They're laughing. They have no idea. On the street, the young man drops his palms and crouches inside the Civic. He sits, puts his hands on the steering wheel and waits. The police officers stop shouting, they back further away. Beside the empty ARV, they lower their semi-automatics until the weapons are pointing at the dark street. Three get into the shadowed rear seat. Two climb in front. They roll backwards, away. The Polo youths reach the nearest corner. A flash of illumination from Costcutter lights, and they are gone.

The young man reaches down, starting the Civic. He puts the car in gear and its tyres turn anticlockwise, following the ARV; he could almost be in pursuit. He is not. He's looking into the rearview, chewing on his inner cheek, a habit he has learned from his mother. He's trying not to look at his blue-faced Skagen. A prickling disquiet, palms sparkling like moist earth; his hand lifts from the wheel and he marvels at this. He remembers; he must watch the road.

He wants to text his girl, but he's afraid to pull over. He wants his right foot to fall, but knows where it will lead. Yards roll beneath him, and he stops paying attention, ignores his rearview mirror. There's a song he doesn't recognise on the radio. He taps the steering wheel in time. His palms are dry. He might even be

singing; it's impossible to tell. There are blue lights in every mirror. He hasn't noticed.

Noisy blue dims into black silence, but he doesn't see this
either. Few pedestrians notice the ARV rolling backwards, or the
baritone engine. Baseball-capped youths follow its passage, only
tearing their eyes away as it leaves. Broad slabs of men duck
towards the blank wall of shops, hide their faces, relax shoulders
and return to upright positions. An elderly woman tries to loosen
her spine, swivels too late and frowns, sensing a presence she
can't quite see, pulling her trolley towards her stomach. School-
girls in askew blazers and stunted ties, pink Nikes and petalled
socks, lift their gaze from the pavement and become grim por-
traiture, before they retreat into a dusty corner store. The warped
door shudders closed.

The young man palms the steering wheel anticlockwise, turns
left. The sad-eyed windows of unkempt houses within an inch of
dilapidation. The regressive spray of thick green hoses inside a
hand car wash, a dormant hearse and driver. Mustard brick new-
builds and the glow of a Metro supermarket, tired women stood
on corners the closer he gets to home. They try not to stare in; he
tries not to stare out. He does not see the green Volkswagen van
creep behind him for another half mile. He palms the wheel left
again, backs into a dead-end street. The green Volkswagen slots
onto the corner of his block. He passes by its idling rumble, eases
into a resident's bay, and shuts off his engine. Pats his pockets
ritually to make sure everything is there. He gets out and stretch-
es, bent backwards, reaching towards sky.

The sun on his cheeks, the occasional chilled breeze. Patchwork blue and grey above. The tinny chatter of a house radio,
shouts of neighbours' kids playing football. His windcheater flut-
ters like a flag. There is tingling warmth inside him. It's bathwater
soft, soothing, and for one moment he smiles. He waves at the
kids, who leap to their feet, yell his name.

Ray.

He is.

He doesn't see the man on a street corner talking into his lapel. He misses urgent eyes that scan the road and fingers pressed against one ear. The lonely intent.

He enters the house, back and further back, immersed in turmeric walls, imitation pirate's maps of back home, studio photos of himself, his mother and troublesome sister. He slows in the narrow passage. Smiles wider. His phone is pressed to his left ear, he's grinning. It makes him look younger. The phone drops into his jeans pocket. He enters the kitchen.

His mother holds him close like a promise, one hand grasping the back of his head. Her eyes are shut. She rocks him in silence, as though he were still a boy. She knows and does not know. He is muttering about being late, but she refuses to listen. On the dining table a plate is dotted with rice shards and pink slivers of curried mutton, dull cutlery laid prone, fork cradling knife, a smudged glass sentry beside them. He wrestles from his windcheater and throws it onto the back of a chair. He sits.

THE NEWS OF HER DEATH

Petina Gappah

By the time Pepukai emerged from the kombi at Highfield, it had just gone half past nine. She was thirty minutes late. Kindness had said she should come at nine or just before. She had followed the directions in the text message: take kombi to Machipisa, get off at Gwanzura, cross road, walk past Mushandirapamwe Hotel, go left after TM, go past market, saloon (that is how Kindness had spelled it) is next to butcher.

She found the salon with no problems. On one of the French doors that led into the place was the picture of a simpering woman whose hair flowed out and curled into the letters 'Snow White Hairdressing'. From the butchery next door came the whirring sound of a saw on bone. Everything about the salon spoke of distressed circumstances, the peeling paint outside, the worn chairs and dirty walls inside, the faded posters for Dark and Lovely and Motions hair relaxers. This place made her usual hair place in Finsbury Park look like the Aveda in Covent Garden. Then again, none of the Nigerian or Kenyan women at her salon in London would have done her hair in long thin braids that lasted four months and cost only fifty dollars. If they had, it would have cost her £500 and two days or more, if she was lucky.

There were five women inside. Four were standing talking together in a huddle, while the fifth swept the floor. They could have been a representative sample of the variegated nature of local womanhood. One was large with a big stomach and bottom and skin like caramel, another was her opposite, thin and sallow with long limbs and dark gums, the third was medium-sized in everything, height, breasts, bottom, complexion, while the last was short and slight with delicate hands and bones and skin so light it was translucently yellow.

The one thing they all had in common was their hair. It was dressed in the same weave, a mimicry of Rihanna's latest style with dark hair tumbling to the shoulder, and reddish hair piled up over one eye so that they had to peer out of the other to look at anything. It was a hairstyle that neutralised features rather than enhancing them; it suited none of them, giving them all the same aged look. Pepukai thought back to the Greek myths she had loved as a child. They looked like the Graeae might have done, had they had one eye each and had there been four of them.

Away from the group of four, the youngest of the women, not a woman at all, Pepukai realised, but a teenage girl of maybe sixteen or seventeen at the most, was sweeping the floor, leaving more hair behind her than she swept before her. Her hair was not in the Rihanna weave of her workmates, but was half done, with her relaxed hair poking out in wisps from one side of her head, while the other half was in newly plaited braids.

All five looked up as Pepukai entered. She was the only customer. She felt their eyes on her, giving her that uniquely female up-and-down onceover that took in every aspect of her appearance and memorised it for future dissection.

'Can we help,' the largest of the women said.

'I am here for Kindness.'

'Kindness?' they exclaimed together. The large, caramel-skinned woman threw a hand to her mouth. The sweeping girl stopped, her hands on her broom, and looked at her open-mouthed.

'Yes, Kindness, I had an appointment with her at nine.'

Almost simultaneously, they turned to the right to look at a hairdressing station above which the name Kindness was written in blue and red glitter. Pepukai's eye followed theirs. There were bottles and brushes and combs, but no Kindness.

'Kindness is late,' said the large woman.

'I am also late, quite late in fact,' Pepukai said. 'How late do you think she will be?'

'No, I mean late *late*. She is deceased.'

'I am sorry?' said Pepukai.

They did not hear the question in her tone.

'Yes, we are all very sorry,' the black-gummed woman said. 'She passed away last night. We are actually waiting to hear what will happen to the body.'

'She has gone to receive her heavenly reward. She is resting now, poor Kindness. May her dear soul rest in peace,' intoned the small slight woman.

All five of them came to her and, one after the other, offered her their hands to shake, as though they were condoling with her. As she shook hands with them, Pepukai did not know what to say. Things were now more than a little awkward. She was sorry, of course, that this woman that she had never met was so suddenly dead, she was about as sorry as she could be at any stranger's death, but, after all, she had not known Kindness. She had never even talked to her – she had only exchanged a series of texts arranging the appointment.

The truth was that she was feeling slightly panicked at this news. Her flight to Amsterdam was at ten that evening. Her afternoon was to be given to a whirlwind of last-minute shopping at Doon Estate and Sam Levy's and farewells that would see her criss-crossing the city. She had only this morning left to get her hair done, and, according to her sister, the now late lamented Kindness was one of the rare hairdressers in the city who had both the skill and the willingness to do the kind of braids she wanted.

Even as these thoughts pressed on her, she did not think that she could be brutal enough to say, effectively, that the death of this unknown woman was a major inconvenience for her, but she need not have worried because the women came to her rescue.

'What did you want done?' said the black-gummed woman.

'Braids,' Pepukai said. 'I would like long, thin braids like this.'

On her phone, she showed them her profile picture on Facebook.

'Oh, you are the one who wants the Shabba?'

'The what?'

'Kindness told us that there was someone who had sent a text to say she wanted those Shabba Ranks braids. We could not believe it, they are so old-fashioned, why not just get a weave like this?' The black-gummed woman caressed her own hair as she spoke.

'Well, I like my hair done that way.'

'We can do it for you that way if you really want,' said the large woman. 'We would have finished off your braids even with Kindness here, she would never have finished alone in one day. It would have been the five of us doing your hair at the same time. It will be eighty dollars, and it will take all of us three hours. Do you have your own extensions?'

This was not the fifty dollars and two hours that Kindness had promised her, but Pepukai did not have the heart to argue. She handed over the extensions she had bought at Daks in Finsbury Park. They settled her into a chair at a station belonging to Matilda, who, Pepukai gathered, was the largest woman. The others introduced themselves. The black-gummed woman was MaiShero. The small, slight one was called Genia, and the medium-sized everything one was Zodwa. As MaiShero combed out Pepukai's hair to prepare it, the other three separated and prepared the extensions.

Pepukai broke the silence by asking what had happened to Kindness. Even as she asked, she knew what the answer would be. It would be the usual long illness or short illness, the euphemism for an HIV-related disease. Wasn't it one in four dying, or maybe it was slightly fewer now that cheap anti-retroviral drugs were everywhere. Kindness, who had gone to receive her heavenly reward, would probably be another death to add to the statistics.

'She was knifed by her boyfriend,' said Matilda.

'Not knifed,' said Genia. 'She was shot.'

'That's right, sorry,' said Matilda, 'at first they said she was knifed but it turns out that she was actually shot by her boyfriend.'

'You mean to say by one of her boyfriends,' added Zodwa.

This exchange was so entirely unexpected that the only thing that Pepukai could ask, rather feebly, was, 'Where?'

'Northfields,' said Zodwa.

'Northfields?' Pepukai asked.

'You know, Northfields, those flats opposite the sports club where they play cricket when the Australians and South Africans come,' said Zodwa.

MaiShero said, 'It is that expensive complex where they pay three thousand dollars a month for rent.'

'Three thousand, who has that sort of money?' asked Matilda.

'Obviously dealers, just the type Kindness would go for,' said MaiShero. 'She was killed right there in one of those expensive flats, you know they have lifts that open up to the whole place. She will probably be in that *Metropolitan* paper tomorrow.'

'You mean you go from the lift straight into the flat? You don't say?' This was Matilda.

'They call them paint house sweets but I don't know why,' said MaiShero. 'They are actually bigger in size than many of those houses in the suburbs, you can have a whole floor just for yourself alone. The only thing you won't have, being so high, is a yard.'

'You don't say,' said Matilda.

'Well,' MaiShero continued, 'the cleaner came at six this morning, got in the lift, went to this paint house flat, and there she was, Kindness, just lying there, all shot, with bullets and blood everywhere.'

'You mean she was shot with a gun?' said Pepukai.

'She can hardly have been shot with a cooking spoon now, can she?' retorted MaiShero.

'All the dealers have guns now, all of the ones in Northfields anyway, they need the guns for their deals and, well, you know,' said Genia.

From the doorway came a loud voice, '*Ndakapinda* busy Mai-Mwana, but listen, I have no more airtime. No more airtime. I said no more . . . *ende futi* Econet.' The voice belonged to a woman in her fifties who wore the blue-cloaked uniform of the Catholic Church, with a white headscarf covering her head. In one hand she had her phone, and in the other, a roasted maize cob. Her overloaded handbag seemed to drag down her left shoulder.

'*Hesi vasikana*,' she greeted as she entered.

'*Hesi* MbuyaMaTwins,' said Matilda.

'*Hesi* Mati,' MbuyaMaTwins said. '*Kokuita chidhafinya kudaro, kudhafuka kunge uchaputika?* Why so fat now, seriously, Matilda? Are you pregnant or something?'

As she spoke, she poked at Matilda's stomach with the pointy end of her maize cob.

'*Mukawana nguva mundikwanire, ndinonhumburwa nani* Steve *zvaariku*South?' said Mati. 'How could I get pregnant when my husband has been away this long?'

'There are those who are able, it is not just husbands and Steves who can do it.' MbuyaMaTwins gave a coarse, leering laugh that shook her chest and the rosary beads around her neck.

'Besides, I have been on Depo how long now, since my last born, you know, the one who was born legs first,' said Mati.

'Depo?' said MbuyaMaTwins.

'Yes, Depo, the contraceptive, the one you inject.'

'So it is injections that are making you so fat? Better to be pregnant in that case, at least you get something out of the fatness. *Ndigezese musoro* Mati, I want just a shampoo and set today.'

'Shylet will do that for you. *Handiti* you know she is now my junior?' said Matilda. 'Shylet!'

The sweeping girl came over.

'Do MbuyaMaTwins. But mind, I'll be watching you.'

Shylet walked with MbuyaMaTwins to the sinks.

'Did you hear about Kindness?' MaiShero said. 'She is now late.'

MbuyaMaTwins, who was about to sit down and lower her head into a sink behind her back, said, 'What do you mean?'

'She was killed by her boyfriend.'

'What are you talking? What are you telling me?' MbuyaMa-Twins forgot that she had been about to sit and remained crouched above the seat in a half squat, her face twisted into a rictus that was almost a caricature of disbelief, the maize cob in her hand stopped just before her mouth. 'How is it that this came to be?'

'She was shot by her boyfriend.'

'What are you telling me? Do you mean the boyfriend who drove a silver Pajero, the junior doctor who worked at Pari?' MbuyaMaTwins said.

'What do you know about her boyfriends, MbuyaMaTwins?'

'Who did she not tell about her boyfriends? Everyone in High-field, from Egypt to Jerusalem, knows about her boyfriends. She told me about this doctor one when he picked her up after she did my hair just the other week. *Hede!* I said to myself, what kind of a doctor, even a junior one, would want to marry a saloon girl?'

'Ha, MbuyaMaTwins, are we saloon girls not women also?'

'No Genia, you know what I mean, there are saloon girls and then there are saloon girls. You and Kindness are very different types, she was her own type, that one.'

'Anyway, myself I think this boyfriend is the one who drove a red Mercedes,' said Matilda.

MbuyaMaTwins heaved herself into the chair below with an exclamation and laid her head on the sink. Shylet opened the taps and put a finger under the water to test its temperature as she asked, 'Are you talking about the man who bought lunch for us the other day? The one she went with to Victoria Falls? Because that one did not drive a silver Pajero.'

'No, that was someone else. He did not drive a red Mercedes either,' said MaiShero. To Matilda, she said, 'Tell your junior to stop interfering in news that does not concern her.'

'You mean she had three going at the same time?' said Mbuya-MaTwins. As Shylet ran water over her hair, she continued to chew at her maize cob, almost absentmindedly, her face still frowned in disbelief.

'*Kuda zvinhu*, Kindness,' said Matilda.

'*Makwatuza!*' saidMaiShero.

'*Makwatikwati*,' said Zodwa.

With MbuyaMaTwins's quizzical prompting, the four women speculated over which of the three boyfriends could have been her killer. It could not be the junior doctor, said MaiShero, because he did not live in Northfields.

'But imagine if he followed her there, MaiShero,' said Zodwa. 'Maybe he found her with another man, what would you do if you were him?'

MaiShero said Kindness had been seen two nights ago in the red Mercedes. But the night before, she had been in the Pajero.

'Maybe,' said MbuyaMaTwins, struck by a charitable thought, 'maybe it is the same man. You know these dealers, they all have different cars. Maybe it was the same man, just in different cars.'

'Then,' said MaiShero, 'he must have changed his body type too, because I saw the men and they looked different from behind. Maybe they are alike in the front area.'

'*Makwatuza!*' said Genia.

'*Makwatikwati!*' said MaiShero.

At that moment, a young man came in through the open door. The wide smile on his face was almost as big as the large box in his arms. '*Hesi vana* mothers,' he said. 'Today I have crisps, doughnuts, *maputi*, sausages, fish, belts, afro combs, phone chargers and cellphone covers. I also have a very good traditional herb for period pain that can also keep wandering husbands close and that's also good for teething babies and for curing bad luck.'

'Let's see the fish,' said MaiShero. 'Is it fresh, Biggie?'

'It is very fresh. Fresh smoked fish just for you,' said Biggie.

'Biggie you are back with that smelly fish of yours, when will you learn we don't want it. It's that Lake Chivero fish that swims in people's faeces and urine, isn't it?' This was Zodwa.

'From Kariba straight, mothers,' said Biggie. 'This is fresh fish fresh from Lake Kariba. Do I look like I would sell you fish from Chivero?'

'But what is to say that it really is from Kariba?' Zodwa pushed him. 'Did you go yourself to catch it yourself with your own two hands, Biggie?'

'Mothers, when have I ever sold you something that was not genuinely and really real?'

'Biggie, where do I even start? You once sold us relaxing cream that made the hair even harder after you relaxed it.'

'And there was that soap that he said had glycerin in it but it produced no suds, *yaisapupira kana* one day,' said Zodwa.

'And what about . . .'

'Okay, mothers, okay,' said Biggie. 'Why can't you just forget some of these things? Even Jesus made mistakes. But maybe the clients are interested?'

He thrust the box before Pepukai, who shook her head.

'Don't shake your head,' said Matilda, 'I am planting the braids now.'

'What about you, MbuyaMaTwins?' said Biggie.

'*Undikwanire semari yebhazi iwe*,' MbuyaMaTwins said. 'Last time, you sold me those batteries that didn't run. You still have not given me back my money.'

'What about you, Shylet? A smoking girl like you needs something to make you even more smoking. How about some smoked fish for a *chimoko*?'

Shylet giggled and said, 'Ah, you also, Biggie.'

At Shylet's giggle, the four women around Pepukai eyed and nudged each other.

'I will take the fish,' said MaiShero. 'I am thinking maybe Ba'Shero might like it.'

'If Ba'Shero can eat that fish,' said Zodwa, 'then he is a man among men.'

'Biggie,' said MaiShero, 'I will give your money tomorrow.'

'*Kahwani* mothers,' he said. 'No problem at all. Any excuse to come back.' He grinned at Shylet as he spoke. She smiled behind her hand. He was about to say more when his phone rang. He answered it on speaker. Into the salon, a tinny voice shouted, 'I have no airtime. *Ndiri kwa*Mushayabha . . .' before the phone cut.

As he pocketed his phone, Biggie said, '*Nedza*Kindness. Someone in the butchery says Kindness was axed by some man?'

'She was shot, not axed,' said Zodwa.

'There was no axe? Are you sure? I heard it was an axe.'

'But even if there were, she is still late, *nhai* Biggie.'

'So what is going to happen?'

'We are waiting to hear where the mourners are gathered. As soon as we are done with this one, we are off.'

'But mmm, that Kindness, well, I shall not say, but mmm, she was special that one.'

'*Iwe*,' Zodwa rebuked him. 'You should concentrate on selling your smelly fish and one-stop herbs, what do you know about Kindness?'

'Sorry mothers, *pa*laters.'

'MaiShero,' Zodwa continued as Biggie left, 'how can you buy that smelly fish? You can't keep it here otherwise we will all end up smelling of fish. You had better ask Matilda's junior to take it to the butcher next door.'

'Shylet,' MaiShero called.

The junior had finished washing MbuyaMaTwins' hair, setting it in rollers, and had settled the client under the hairdryer. She abandoned her chair near the sink, where she had been plaiting her own hair, and came over.

'Take this to the butcher. I will pick it up when I go home.'

The girl shuffled out.

'I bet you she won't come back in a hurry,' said Genia. 'You saw how she was with that Biggie. She has been making eyes at that butcher boy too, next door.'

Making her voice louder to be heard over the sound of the dryer, MbuyaMaTwins boomed, 'You mean that pimply boy who looks like he has not had a shower since nineteen *gochanhembe*?'

'Ah,' said Matilda. 'She would even go with a *hwindi* this one, she is not fussy. She will drop her pants at the sight of a Coke. These are some of the Kindnesses in the making.'

'*Makwatuza!*' said MaiShero.

'*Makwatikwati*,' laughed Zodwa.

'*Kuda zvinhu*,' said Genia.

Shylet returned as they laughed and Matilda immediately turned the conversation. 'Imagine. People like Biggie, of all people, are now commenting on Kindness, can you imagine?'

'Who did not know about Kindness?' said Genia.

'Even in Engineering, even in Five Pounds, they know about Kindness,' said MbuyaMaTwins.

They looked up at the sound of a sleek, silver car pulling up to park outside. The woman who emerged from the driver's seat wore a dark grey suit, elegant heels and sunglasses. Her cropped hair framed her face. As she entered, she pushed up her glasses.

They looked at her in silence.

In a low, pleasant voice, she said, 'Afternoon ladies, I am looking for Judith.'

'Judith went to China two weeks back,' said Zodwa.

'Oh yes, she did say she may be going,' the woman said. 'When
is she back, do you know, because I have been trying to reach her.'

'She comes back Thursday.'

'Oh, thank you, I will call her then.'

'Is there anything we can do?' MaiShero asked.

'No, that's fine,' she said with a smile. 'I have to take one of
my children to play in a tennis tournament this afternoon. I could
have stayed if it was not for that, so I will just wait for Judith.
Thank you, ladies,' she said.

Several eyes followed her to the door and to her car. Even
before she had driven off, MbuyaMaTwins was asking, 'And who
is this tennis tournament one?'

She had poked her head from under the dryer and was trying to
scratch her scalp with the rollers on her head. Shylet jumped to
attend to her and reset the rollers.

'That is one of Judith's clients, you know Judith goes out more
and more these days, she is making herself exclusive to a few
clients,' said MaiShero. 'She goes to their homes, they don't have
to come here.'

'*Hoo*,' said MbuyaMaTwins, 'is that why she was looking at us
like we were something under her shoe? Because she is a special
tennis one who gets her hair done at home?'

'I thought she was nice,' said Shylet as she shifted the rollers.

'Nice *chiiko*, you should talk what you know about,' said
MaiShero.

'Did you see that car?' said MbuyaMaTwins. 'How did she buy
it? With money from where? Do you think such money is clean?
There must be something behind it. Harare *yabatabata vasikana*.'

'*Vanobatabata!*' said MaiShero. 'You read that story about that
small house in Borrowdale, sleeping with that mad man. This is

exactly the sort of thing women like that do, you think it is money from just working?'

'Ah,' said MbuyaMaTwins, 'are you saying that woman is a small house?'

'She isn't any man's kept mistress,' said Shylet. 'Judith said she has a very good job, she runs a big bank in town. She is not a small house.'

'Exactly what I mean,' said MbuyaMaTwins. 'You would not believe the things that go on in banks. My own husband once wanted to take a job in a bank. I said to him, and this is what I said, no thank you, I said to him. I know those bank women. I would rather we suffered, yes, I would rather eat plain vegetables, even cooked with no cooking oil, than have you work with women like that. Even up to now, he is not working.'

'She probably got into the bank through being a small house,' said MaiShero.

'She is a widow,' said Shylet. 'Her husband died in a car accident three years back.'

There was a silence until MaiShero said, 'Well, some of these widows, you would never believe they are widows. There was this funeral I went to last week, at the church of Ba'Shero's cousin brother, and can you believe the widow wasn't even covered in a wrapper cloth or headscarf or anything, she wore a smart dress, *kashiftso*, and it was not even black-black but blue-black. She had high heels on, can you imagine, high heels at a grave site, just like that woman, and sunglasses too, just like that one.'

'*Achitoti akatopfeka* sorry?' said MbuyaMaTwins. She was back in the dryer, her face aghast with shock at what she was hearing. 'What sort of mourning outfit do you call that?'

'It was like she was going to a wedding, she even had makeup on, and a black hat.'

'There will be something there,' said MbuyaMaTwins. 'Mark my words. Before the year is out, you will have heard something.'

'Ah,' said Matilda, 'it would not surprise me at all.'

A sharp-eyed woman in a TM supermarket cashier's uniform entered, bringing with her the strong smell of the orange she was peeling and eating. Her TM name tag indicated that her name was Plaxedes. As she greeted the others, she approached Pepukai to admire the now almost completed braids. Pepukai could smell the orange on her hands as Plaxedes gathered up the plaits to examine them closer.

'This is nice, girls, this is nice,' Plaxedes said. 'Maybe I should have this next time, what do you think?'

Without stopping for breath, she said to Pepukai, 'Is your hair natural?'

She pulled at the little of Pepukai's hair that still remained to be braided. Again, Pepukai was hit by the smell of oranges.

Pepukai said, 'Yes, it is, it is natural.'

'Hoo. Ende futi makazochena. What perfume are you wearing?'

'I think it's called Jardin sur Nil,' said Pepukai. She was now being suffocated by the orange smell.

'Jadan chii?'

'Jardin sur Nil,' said Pepukai. The smell of orange was threatening to overpower her.

'What language is that?' asked Plaxedes.

'Erm, French, I think.'

'Hoo, saka munototaura French?'

'Not really, no,' Pepukai said. 'I don't speak French.'

'It smells expensive. It must be expensive. Is it expensive? How much is it? Where do you live?'

'NdeveLondon ava,' said Genia, with an air of ownership.

'London! Zvenyu! But why is your skin so dark? You don't look at all like you live in London. When do you go back?'

'My flight is tonight,' said Pepukai. 'I leave at ten tonight.'

'Zvenyu!' said Plaxedes. 'My sister went there only seven months, she was in London but not London exactly, she was in

Men Chester, do you know it, and she was almost as light as a Coloured when she returned. She was deported. Do you have a white man? But you don't look like the *ngoma kurira mbira dzenharira* type, that's what white men like in Africans, women who just look rough so.'

'Stop going on about white men,' said MaiShero. 'Have you not heard about Kindness?'

'Kindness?'

'Kindness is late. She has passed away.'

'*Haa?*'

In her surprise, Plaxedes pulled at Pepukai's hair.

Pepukai winced, but the other woman did not notice.

Plaxedes pointed to Kindness's empty station. 'Do you mean this Kindness, this one right here?'

'That Kindness,' MbuyaMaTwins called out from under the dryer.

'*Uyu* Kindness *wekuzvinzwa uyu*, who walked like her feet did not touch the ground and talked like she was chewing water?' said Plaxedes.

'That very one,' said MaiShero.

'That Kindness?'

'That Kindness.'

'How?'

'She was shot by her boyfriend.'

'She was shot by her boyfriend?'

'She was shot by her boyfriend.'

'But that one had so many boyfriends!'

'That is just what we were saying,' said Matilda. 'She wanted to be upper-class, that one, and she thought the way to be upper-class was to go out with an upper-class man, now look at her.'

'*Ii*, I should let my sister know,' said Plaxedes.

For Pepukai's benefit, she added, 'That's the one who was deported from Men Chester, but she is quite well up now. She lives in Ashdorn.'

Into her phone, she said, 'Hello. Hello, Kuku. *Ipa mhamha phone. Ipa mha* . . . Hello, MaiKuku? . . . *Ende futi! Iwe*, you won't believe it. Kindness is late . . . Kindness! . . . Kindness *mhani iwe, wekunoku*Fiyo . . . The hairdresser . . . Don't you remember Kindness? . . . You met her that time at the Food Court at Eastgate, remember? . . . We had gone to watch that film, what was it called? *Rabbit, Habit* something, the one about those creatures who look like *tokoloshis* but act like normal people even though they are not actual people. Yes. *Hobbit*. That's the one. We had gone to watch *Hobbit*. And she was walking in front of us and I said to you, MaiKuku, I said, I know that bottom . . . Yes . . . Yes . . . Very big . . . *Chivhindikiti so* . . . Yes . . . That's the one. She wore a tight red trouser and a white blouse . . . Yes . . . *Hanzi* she died . . . Shot . . . I said shot . . . Yes, shot . . . Yes . . . Shot with a gun . . . *Ufunge* . . . Yes . . . Some boyfriend . . . I don't know, *mira ndivhunze.*'

She turned to Matilda. 'Where did this happen?'

'Northfields, in town,' said Matilda.

Plaxedes turned back to her phone. 'Northfields . . . Northfields. In town. I said North . . . Ah, I have run out of airtime.'

'*Inga i*horror,' she said. 'But I have to go. My break is over but I will be back in an hour to find out more. If you are not finished with the braids, I will even come and help.'

Pepukai breathed at last.

Plaxedes's phone rang as she left, and they could hear her say, 'Northfields . . . Northfields . . . Yes . . . She was shot at Northfields.'

As soon as she was out of hearing, MaiShero said, 'Is there a bigger gossip than that Plaxedes?'

'You know, don't you,' said Zodwa, 'that her husband's sister and aunt actually beat her up once because of her gossiping?'

'She is not the type that you can tell anything,' said Mbuya-MaTwins.

As she talked, MbuyaMaTwins moved from under the dryer to a dressing station. Shylet stood behind her to unroll her hair from the curlers and style it. MbuyaMaTwins admired her reflection in the mirror. Pepukai thought the wash and set made her neck and head look like a very small mushroom on a particularly bulbous stalk. As Shylet sprayed liberal doses of a particularly smelly moisturiser over the finished hair, Pepukai tried not to cough.

'*Ende machena zvekwa*MaiChenai *chaizvo*,' said MaiShero. 'That looks so nice.'

'*Ndachenaka?*' said MbuyaMaTwins. She preened in the mirror as she turned her head, the tips of her spread-out fingers lightly tapping her new hairstyle. 'We have a function at church. This time, *bambo vekwangu* will have to come, I won't hear any more of his excuses. What sort of golf is it that is played at all hours?'

The women nudged each other. MbuyaMaTwins, unseeing, continued to admire herself in the mirror. They all looked up as a voice came from the door. '*T'ookumbirawo rubatsiro vanhu vaMwari. T'ookumbirawo rubatsiro vanhu vaJehovah.*'

It was a blind beggar who was led by a small boy of no more than seven or eight years of age. The man wore tattered blue overalls while the boy wore a shirt and shorts that belonged to two different school uniforms. They were both barefoot.

Matilda said, 'Does anyone have a dollar?'

MbuyaMaTwins rummaged through her overstuffed bag. Pepukai opened her purse. Genia let go of Pepukai's hair so that she could dig into her trouser pockets, MaiShero and Zodwa went to their stations to get their handbags. As the boy went from woman to woman collecting money, the old man dropped to his knees in thanksgiving, raised his voice in blessing and clapped his hands in gratitude.

'*Mwari wenyu vakukomborerei, vakukomborerei, vakukomborerei.*'

They left the salon.

MbuyaMaTwins took twenty-two dollars from her bag and handed it to Matilda. 'I will give you an extra two dollars for a drink,' she said.

'Thanks MbuyaMaTwins,' said Matilda. 'Shylet!'

Shylet's face brightened.

'Go and give this to Plaxedes at TM. I owe her thirty for the relaxer. Tell her the rest is coming.'

Shylet's shoulders drooped as she walked out.

'Right, girls,' said MbuyaMaTwins, 'I have to go, but before I do we need to pray.' Without further prompting, the women melted from Pepukai to gather around MbuyaMaTwins in the middle of the salon, their heads bowed. Unsure of what to do, Pepukai joined them.

MbuyaMaTwins's face became twisted with effort.

'Bless Lord everyone in this salon, Lord, and especially this daughter who is taking a flight today. Send her journey mercies, dear Lord. Do not put evil thoughts in the mind of the pilot, Lord, let the pilot land the plane with no incident, let him not crash it deliberately.'

'Amen,' said Genia.

'We ask you to receive into your loving arms our sister Kindness, take her into your glory, Mwari Baba to you she has come to rest Lord, *Ndimi* Mwari Baba *vemasimba*, Mwari Baba *munogona*, Mwari *munogona kani*, Mwari Baba *munogona*!'

'Amen,' the women chorused.

'We ask you to guide us today in everything we do, so that all that we do may be to honour your holy name.'

'Amen,' said Genia.

'This we ask in Jesus's name. *Muzita ra*Baba, *nere*Mwanakomana, *nere*Mweya Musande. Amen.'

'Amen.'

MbuyaMaTwins crossed herself and kissed her rosary. She picked up her bag off the floor, stuffed her white headscarf into its capacious depths and with a radiant smile said to Pepukai, '*Wofamba mushe dhali*, travel well,' and to the others, '*Ndiyoyo vasikana*, see you next week.'

'Mati,' said MaiShero as soon as the client was out of hearing, 'isn't that woman supposed to be a Roman Catholic?'

'You know she is,' said Matilda. 'You saw what she is wearing, so why do you ask?'

'Because she prays like a Pentecostal, that's why,' said MaiShero.

Shylet piped up from the sink. 'She apparently wants to set up her own church. A women's ministry.'

'That is a smart move,' said Genia. 'There is so much money to be made in these new churches.'

'And she will need all the prayers she can get with that husband of hers,' said MaiShero. 'He is the busiest unemployed man in the city.'

'And he is never alone either,' laughed Genia.

'*Makwatuza*,' said Matilda.

'*Makwatikwati*,' echoed Zodwa.

'*Kuda zvinhu!*' said Mai Shero.

They laughed and clapped their hands to each other.

It took a little more talk of Kindness and another hour before Pepukai was done. The braids fell beautifully and lightly from her head, in hundreds of long thin ropes that were perfectly even. The last thing was to soak the ends in hot water to seal them and make sure that they did not unravel. Genia held up a mirror to the one before her so that Pepukai could see the back of her head.

The women beamed as they admired their handiwork.

'You are so right,' Matilda said, 'this is very old-fashioned but it really suits your face.'

'Perfection *sipo yekuwizira chaiyo*,' said MaiShero.

'*Maoresa nhunzi yegreen*,' agreed Genia.

Shylet approached, shaking the can of the stinky spray. Pepukai held up her hands as if to ward off evil. 'It's really okay, thank you, Shylet,' she said. 'I do not need the spray, I will do that later.'

She paid the eighty dollars that Matilda had requested, and gave her an extra twenty. 'This is my *chema* for Kindness,' she said. 'I hope it all goes well.' As she spoke, Matilda's phone buzzed out a new message.

'It's from the cousin sister of Kindness. She has no airtime, but she says we have to come now,' said Matilda. 'The mourners are gathering at their house in Warren Park.'

'Is it okay if I just wait here for my hair to dry a bit?' Pepukai asked.

It was fine, Matilda said, Shylet would stay to lock up. They said their goodbyes and bustled out. Pepukai continued to hear their voices until they turned the corner past the butcher's. In thirty minutes, her hair was dry enough for her to leave. The last Pepukai saw of Snow White Hairdressing was Shylet sitting at Kindness's station, plaiting the rest of her hair.

That night, on her flight to Amsterdam, Pepukai chose the chicken over the fish. Nor did she eat any of the orange segments in her fruit salad, choosing to eat, instead, the grapes and cubed melon and the delicate slivers of apple.

VISITATION

Damon Galgut

Money had kept everything sweet for the last few years, but now
it had all gone wrong. He was in bad trouble, and it was because
of money. He couldn't see any way out of the situation except to
run, and so here he was, taking the train without telling anybody
he was leaving, without saying goodbye.

From the moment he got on board he was reminded of what
awaited him, what money had been protecting him from. Only
poor people took the train these days. The other passengers were
threadbare, stamped hard by life. The few white passengers in
particular had something granular and common about them. He
didn't want to share a compartment with any of them.

He himself was young and attractive and liked to dress well, but
he didn't want to be noticed today. Although his suitcase was full
of expensive clothes, he was wearing jeans and a green T-shirt,
along with a cap and sunglasses. It was the way he'd looked when
he'd first arrived in Cape Town seven years ago.

The train was quite empty and he was still alone in the compartment when the whistle blew. He took off his sunglasses and
watched the city fall slowly away, though the mountain stayed
visible for the first hour, a blue stain on the horizon, gradually
diminishing. He was restless to begin with, lying down, standing
up again, pacing the corridor. But as the train climbed away from
the greener landscape at the coast toward the interior, he became
more settled, and then introspective.

By the time they arrived at Laingsburg in the late afternoon, he'd
been immobile in his seat for an hour, brooding on the turn that his

life had taken. He was slow to become aware of a lone figure on the otherwise deserted platform, and only saw a passing glimpse of a sorry-looking old man, bald and battered, toiling with a heap of luggage toward the carriage door. Immediately he had an odd certainty that the old man would be with him in this compartment.

When the train pulled out again, the sun was going down. The reddish light gave a soft, benign look to the stony hills they were passing through, but the scrubby bushes, festooned with rags of plastic, were vibrating in a cold wind. After a few minutes nothing had happened and he started to relax.

Then came a knocking and a tugging at the compartment door.

'Who is it?' the young man called, though of course he knew.

'It's me, Corrie.'

He unlocked and opened the door. The old man was outside amidst his baggage. Two bulging suitcases, a rucksack and a plastic bag. All his life in these worn-out containers; you could see it at a glance.

'I'm in here,' the old man – Corrie – told him. Holding his ticket in his hand.

'There's lots of space,' the young man said. 'You could be on your own.'

'Sorry?'

'Don't you want to be alone?'

He looked at the ticket, confused. 'No,' he said. 'I'm in here.'

As he started stowing his luggage, the young man went out and down the corridor, looking into other compartments. If he could find one that was free, he might take it. But by now there were more people on the train and no more vacant spaces. He went back to his own compartment, where Corrie had seated himself on the opposite bench and was running a comb through a few lank strands he'd greased down across the top of his scalp. He put the comb away in his shirt pocket and studied the young man through thick, black-framed glasses.

Finally he said, 'I didn't catch your name.'

'I didn't tell it to you.'

'Sorry?'

'Robert. My name is Robert.'

They nodded uneasily at each other. Two men in a metal box, rushing across a landscape.

'How far are you going?' Robert said.

'Johannesburg. All the way. And you? What about you?'

'Me too. All the way.'

No escape then, till midday tomorrow.

'You live in Johannesburg?'

'In Morningside.'

He could see that the name meant nothing to Corrie, though a quick, indefinable emotion passed across his face. 'I've never been before,' he said. 'This is my first time.'

'Never been to Johannesburg in your life?'

'No. I never had a reason.'

Robert watched him and could see what the old man was trying to hide from himself. Corrie had nothing to show for the past and was very afraid of the future. He glanced sideways at Robert and asked, 'What work do you do?'

'I'm a lawyer.'

'A lawyer!' Corrie whistled through his teeth. 'Man, that sounds to me like a real job.' A moment later he was studying Robert in bemusement. What was a lawyer doing riding on the train?

'Do you live in a big house?' he asked.

'In a flat. With my fiancée.' He looked calmly at the old man. 'It's a huge, old block and we have the penthouse. Twelfth floor. Great view of the city skyline. On a clear day you can see across to the Hartbeespoort dam from the bedroom windows. Floor-to-ceiling glass.' As he described it, the life composed itself around him, even though he had borrowed its parts from somebody else, a man he'd once known. None of what he'd said was true, not even his name, which was actually Johan.

The old man was openly worried now, fidgeting on his seat. He dragged one of his suitcases out and rummaged through it till he found a box of cigarettes. He offered one to his fellow passenger, who shook his head, then retreated to the corridor outside to smoke. Johan could see him through the open door, staring at the darkening view. He had that quality of thoughtfulness certain smokers have, as if contemplating weighty matters while they puff. Though Johan doubted there was anything important to think about in this case – nothing but bad choices and missed chances.

The conductor came by to check their tickets and to ask whether they wanted bedding for the night. There was a fifty-rand charge, which Johan reluctantly paid. Corrie said no.

When the conductor had gone, Johan said, 'It's going to get very cold in the Karoo tonight. Below freezing.'

'I know.'

'How will you keep warm?'

'I've got a *trick*,' the old man said, and winked at him.

Johan didn't want to know about any tricks, but the question had set Corrie off. His reticence had gone and now he wanted to speak. For some reason he launched into an account of working for a fisheries company ten years ago, although he hadn't been there for long. It was only one of a series of useless jobs he'd had, all of which he was describing to Johan, spreading out his life in a patchwork of one-horse towns and bright ideas that had quickly burned out. He'd been living in Laingsburg for the past four years, ever since his wife had died of cancer and his only child, a daughter, had become estranged from him. He'd had a plan to get a carpet-cleaning business going there, but it hadn't worked out. There just wasn't a big enough market, he explained dolefully, but he brightened again as he talked about going to Johannesburg and making a fresh start. He would be staying with the brother of his late wife, who was a good guy and would help him. Life had given him a few kicks, it was true, but he had some big fish on his line and it was all going to turn around soon. He could feel it. There was a note of genuine hopefulness in his voice, as if this time, at last, against all the mounting odds, something would fall into place and his luck would finally change.

While he spoke and spoke, Johan studied him with the clear eyes of hatred. He saw the marks of old food on his jacket, the frayed cuffs, the nicotine stains on his fingers and moustache, and all these things told a story that the young man knew by heart. It felt to him suddenly that he couldn't listen for another second.

He stood up abruptly and said, 'Excuse me, I'm going to eat.'

Corrie was halfway through a sentence, his mouth open. Johan pushed past him and went down the corridor. On the way to the dining car he turned into the bathroom. The mirror above the metal basin was scratched and old; his youngish face floated in it. He judged himself coldly, as he judged others, not liking what he saw – his fading prettiness and also the corruption it concealed. Though he was only twenty-seven, his expression had started to thicken and set. Something evasive in the eyes, a petulance in the downturned corners of the mouth.

He had used his looks well in his time in the city. They were his only real asset, like a bright blade with which to cut a path for himself, and he had cut and cut, and some people had bled in the process. He'd never paused for long enough to care, but the edge of the blade had become duller lately and life had slowed down. There were younger, prettier faces now, supplanting his, even before what had happened. This – the Event That Changed Everything – was something he didn't like to think about, not directly. When sometimes it came into view, he flinched away. It was too big, too dangerous, the consequences too scary to imagine.

He thought about them now. He took a sharp breath, looked his reflection in the eye and told it, 'You killed somebody.' The words sounded flat in the grubby little cubicle. The memory of it was also far away and somewhere else, faint pictures that didn't fit together. Cocaine on a mirror, a hotel room with a brown-green carpet, an argument going badly out of control. Money at the heart of it all. For him, money was somehow always the main cause.

For a moment he saw clearly what might happen to his life and this was far more vivid than what he'd done. He yanked quickly away from the mirror, ran water into the basin, splashed his face. Better to keep moving, not to think too much.

He left the cubicle and went to the dining car, though he wasn't hungry. He sat at one of the tables and drank bad wine and tried to stop his mind from turning as he stared at the blackness pouring past the window. He had a sense of fate gathering inward, toward some central point in the future. It hadn't been that way till just a few days ago. Up until then, he'd believed he was in charge.

When he got back to the compartment, his bed had been made up and Corrie was sitting on the bottom, unmade bunk, grinning, wearing a puffy, padded white outfit, something like an astronaut's space suit. White gloves and jacket, white pants. He pulled the white hood up over his head and goggled smugly at Johan.

'I told you I have a *trick*,' he said.

Very pleased with himself.

'What is that?'

'When I worked for that fisheries company I mentioned, in the warehouses with the frozen foods, you know, they gave us this stuff to wear. This is all I need, my friend. I am A1. I tell you what, I won't be cold tonight.'

You may not be cold, Johan thought, *but your life will always be your life*. His heart was hardened anew with contempt against Corrie and his kind. There was nothing you could do with some people.

*

He himself slept restlessly, and every time he woke it seemed to him Corrie was standing in the corridor in his bunny suit, under the fluorescent lights, smoking a cigarette. But in the morning, when Johan climbed down, the old man was lying on his back on the bottom bunk, hood up, eyes closed, still wearing his glasses in his sleep. The compartment was thick with stale air.

He opened one of the shutters and raised the window a little. The landscape had changed in the night, bleached grass replacing stones, emptiness giving way to houses, roads, people. The world was filling up. He stood staring, his brain like a dirty windscreen that the cold air was wiping clean. Eventually he could see through it to what the rest of the day contained. Beyond that, everything was obscure.

When he turned back from the window, he could tell immediately that the old man was dead. There was a total stillness about him that was almost like a colour, though all the actual colour had drained away.

'Oh,' he said, himself going still. Something should have followed on, but didn't. There were no words.

He gripped Corrie tentatively by one arm and shook him, to make sure. But there was no doubt. A coldness, a heaviness had taken over. The old man had become an object. Some time in the night, with Johan just above him.

He had seen only one dead body before. It was what he was running from, would always be running from, and it had followed him here. That other scene welled up in him, and for a moment he was in the sickening aftermath again, not able to believe what had happened. What his hands had done.

Now, as then, he very quickly became practical. He moved to the door, making sure it was locked. It was obvious to him what should happen. He didn't want any kind of scene; he didn't want to be questioned and have his details recorded. He was travelling under a false name and no clues would lead to him, if he just acted fast. The old man was nothing to him. He didn't owe anything to Corrie.

He dressed in the same clothes as yesterday, the T-shirt and cap and dark glasses. He packed everything away that belonged to him and left all the old man's things exactly in place, including his wallet with its pathetic clutch of notes. Then he sat ready in the darkened compartment, watching over the corpse, like a mourner or a mortician, for the next couple of hours, until they were entering Johannesburg. There was a general commotion on the train and he slipped out into the corridor with his suitcase, at a moment when nobody was passing, closing the door behind him, and walked down to an exit three carriages away to wait.

*

A bus, an hour of hitchhiking, another hour on foot. Then he was coming along the dirt road above the house, the Hartbeespoort dam glowing red with the sunset in the distance. He stopped at a bend to look down on it all, cupped in a bald hollow in the veld. The tin roof, the back stoep, the tree with its old swing made from a car tyre. The walls just slightly askew, not properly aligned with each other. None of it any different, as if he'd only gone that morning.

Even his father had apparently not moved since Johan had left. Still on the couch in his vest, watching the television. Though the lines on his face were deeper and his hair was grizzled. He hadn't shaved for days.

He seemed to think that Johan was somebody else. 'Did you take the empties?' he asked, then blinked rapidly in confusion. 'Oh, hell, it's you,' he said.

'*Ja*, Pa.'

'Just like that.'

'*Ja*, Pa.'

They were speaking Afrikaans to each other; it was their language. An earlier self had immediately reclaimed Johan.

'I thought you were dead,' his father told him.

'I've been sending money. I wrote a few letters.' He put the suitcase down on the floor and rubbed his throbbing arm. 'Did you not get them?'

His father made a sound and looked away. He had become an old man – in such a short time. Or perhaps he'd been old before.

'You didn't tell me you were coming,' he said eventually.

It was all unbearable, like a pain building up that only a scream could release. Instead the silence was nearly complete, underlined by the sibilant sound of wind in the dry grass, the rustling of the old tree in the yard.

His room had been stripped down, all his things packed away, out of sight. The marks of Prestik on the wall where his Christian posters had been. Hooks in the ceiling where his model planes had hung. He'd left most of his clothes behind, but they were gone too, only empty shelves and hangers in the cupboard. It was the bare bones of a room, just the bed and the desk and chair, the faded orange curtains on the window. But it was enough to begin with, or would be when he'd got it cleaned up.

Everything was dirty, veneered in dust, but so was the rest of the house, all of it ignored, overlooked, slowly piling up or subsiding. His father had used to work for Telkom, installing telephone lines the whole day, and then coming home and drinking at night. But he'd retired seven years before, around the time Johan had gone, and now he just drank.

He'd always been an aggressive and accusing drunk and he got stuck into Johan while they sat out on the back stoep that night, downing boxed red wine out of tin mugs. An old scene, one he'd run to Cape Town to escape, but here they both were again, speaking their lines. Though Johan was mostly quiet, sometimes interjecting, then falling silent again. It was his father who talked, on and on, a fervent sermon, the moral of which was that he, Pa, had always known – had always pointed out, in fact – and yet was still amazed by, the utter lack of talent or promise that constituted the character of his son. He wasn't even a disappointment, because that would be something, and he was a nothing. It was his mother's side, a useless family with weak blood. It wasn't Johan's fault. He'd been born that way and couldn't change it. He was a nothing. He'd gone away for years and years and now he'd strolled back in again and what did he have to show for it? Nothing.

'That isn't true,' Johan said. 'I've been places. I've done things.'

'Pah.'

'You didn't see. You don't know.'

'What have you done?'

'I've been working in Cape Town.'

'Doing what?'

'Different jobs. I was the maître d' at a famous restaurant. I worked at an art gallery. Then I was an assistant to a fashion consultant. One of the clients really liked me and took me on—'

'Pah.'

'I did these things,' he said, suddenly close to tears. 'Pa, believe me.' And in that moment he almost believed it himself. All these other vocations, these ghostly identities, he'd heard talked about in casual, throwaway phrases by the men he'd been with. He knew nothing whatever of the world behind the words, though he'd learned to try on its language, in the same way you might put on a hat.

'Pah,' his father said again, though less certainly this time. He gathered his rancour for one last judgement. 'When you left, you said you'd never come back. Now here you are, with your tail between your legs, after five years. Aren't you ashamed of yourself?'

'Seven.'

'What?'

'I've been gone for seven years. Yes, Pa, I'm ashamed.'

The shame did burn, a faint red glow, like cheap wine.

His father got to his feet and as he lurched off inside Johan fought again the need to cry. More than that: to weep, to howl. *I am in bad trouble, Pa. I have nowhere else to go.* Instead he stayed on alone, weary and drunk. In the morning, he knew, the conversation would finish, but it would be his father who'd weep. He would take Johan's hand and ask for forgiveness, for what he'd done and also for what he'd said about Johan's mother. She was a fine woman, one of God's angels, and he, Pa, was the bad person, who had driven all of them away . . .

This, too, was an old story.

Yes, he had nowhere to go, but he also couldn't stay. That was what it came down to. And wherever he went, how long could he keep in one place? No matter how many names and other identities he took on, it was always possible that somebody might be on the case, following up. Following him.

An old couch had been abandoned in the corner of the yard, near the tree and the swing. After a while he got up and wandered over. It exhaled a smell of damp as he sat down. With his head tilted back, he could look into the massive frieze of stars. Great coldness and vastness, so that he knew the smallness of his warmth. It was oddly consoling: in only fifty years, nothing would matter.

*

He must have fallen asleep, because then he woke. Into a soft, pre-dawn whiteness, everything very still and exactly placed. He was calm and cold inside, as if the white light had touched him too.

Something had woken him, a soft, repetitive creaking sound. He turned toward it, knowing already what he would see. There was no shock, no alarm, though the white figure in the swing was a weird sight. Rocking gently backward and forward, the only thing moving.

'Corrie.'

The head didn't turn. With the hood and the gloves, no skin showed; perhaps nobody was there.

Johan felt nothing. His inner mood was joined to the numb white light outside, so that he was empty, maybe even asleep. Except he knew he was awake. He was sitting on the old sofa, it was almost daybreak, he was talking to a dead person in the swing.

'I'm sorry,' he heard himself say.

Then the old man did turn his head and look at him, those horrible spectacles framed by the encircling hood. Why was he wearing the white outfit when he was dead? Did the dead also know nothing?

'I'm sorry for walking away and leaving you,' he said.

'It's all right,' Corrie said.

'If I'd stayed I would have got into trouble. I *am* in trouble.'

'It's why I came to see you.'

'Because I'm in trouble?'

'Because you didn't stay.'

Johan brooded on this.

'I have to say goodbye to somebody,' Corrie explained. 'It's the rules.'

Johan had no idea what rules were being referred to. This entire conversation was only possible, he thought, if all the rules had been broken.

'I don't have anybody else,' Corrie told him. 'Even if you don't like me. It's all right,' he said, when Johan started to protest. 'Lots of people don't like me. Didn't, I should say. You lied to me about everything.'

'Yes.'

He looked at the crooked little house and shook his head. 'A lawyer in Johannesburg. What's the matter with you?'

Johan gazed at his feet, dark against the pale ground. 'I don't know,' he said.

'Well, I don't know either.' He shook his head ruefully. 'It isn't going to work out, is it?'

'What isn't?'

'Your life.'

They looked at each other and for an instant Corrie was like a face glimpsed in a crowd, somebody he'd known once and couldn't place, passing before he could speak.

'There's still time.'

'I have to go now.'

'Wait,' Johan said, and he felt a strange pain and sadness. 'Stay with me.'

But the old man was out of the swing already and moving away. He took a few steps and was gone, as if he'd walked through a door. Somewhere else entirely, if he was anywhere at all.

*

He must have fallen asleep, because then he woke. Arms wrapped around himself, shivering. The white light was the first paleness in the sky, objects gradually becoming visible. The swing hung down, inert and empty.

A dream after all. A dream of being awake, though the soreness was real, almost physically so.

'There's still time,' he said again aloud.

It was the coldest hour, just before dawn, everything bunched together against the coming sun.

FRANK'S LAST DAYS

Guadalupe Nettel
Translated by Rosalind Harvey

Before he died, my uncle Frank spent three weeks in hospital. I found out about his stay at the clinic due to a coincidence, or what the surrealists used to call 'objective chance', to describe those fortuitous events that seem dictated by our destiny. Around that time, my best friend Verónica's mother was suffering from very advanced cancer and had been admitted to the intensive care unit. That morning, my friend asked me to accompany her to the hospital and I didn't feel I could refuse. We left university, situated in the same neighbourhood, and instead of going to our Latin etymology class, we caught a bus. As I wandered through the corridors waiting for Verónica to visit her mother, I entertained myself by reading the names of patients written on the doors. I just had to see his to realise he was a relative of mine, but it took me a while to figure out exactly who he was. After a few baffling minutes – a sensation comparable to when we come across a tombstone in a graveyard with our own surname on, without knowing who lies buried there – I figured out that the person in there was Frank, my mother's older brother. I'd heard of him but didn't know the man. He was the outlaw of the family, as it were, a man almost no one spoke of out loud, never mind in front of my mother. In spite of the curiosity I felt at that moment, I didn't dare go in, afraid he might recognise me. An absurd fear, as it happens, since as far as I could recall we'd never met.

I stood there for quite a while, not knowing what to do, focusing on my heartbeat, which only grew faster, until the door opened and out of the room came two nurses. One of them was carrying a breakfast tray with dirty plates on it.

'That guy eats more than a St Bernard. You'd never think he was so ill.'

I was amused to discover that the nurses joked about their patients, but also at the possibility that my uncle was an imaginary invalid like Molière's, who we were reading in drama class.

On the bus ride back to university, I told Verónica about my discovery. I also told her everything I knew about Frank. Like my mother, he had received a religious education, first at a Marist school and then at a Jesuit one. He had obtained brilliant marks from primary school all the way through to the final year of the baccalaureate, as well as the admiration of his teachers. His reputation at school was impeccable and for this he was always able to count on the collusion of my grandmother – so I had heard my mother say – who glossed over his absences from class just as she did his misdemeanours at home. After completing the first year of an engineering degree, he left university to devote himself to the arts and, later on, to drifting about all over the world. His vices and addictions were spoken of too, although I never heard anyone specify what these were, exactly. He was never present at big family occasions, such as my brother's graduation from college or the coming-out ball the nuns organised for my fifteenth birthday, events where, as if by spontaneous generation, clusters of relatives would appear to whom I had to introduce myself several times. All my aunts and uncles, except for Frank. From time to time, I would hear old friends of my parents enquire about him with morbid curiosity, the way we ask about someone when we know the answer will be outrageous. It was impossible – at least for me – not to notice my mother's discomfort when she replied to these questions about the whereabouts of this brother of hers. 'I do know he's in Asia,' she would say, or, 'He's still with his girlfriend, the sculptor.' The things I knew about him I had heard in passing, in conversations with other people such as this one, but at that time Frank's life didn't matter a great deal to me.

The following day I was the one who asked Verónica if I could go with her to the hospital. This time we missed our ethno-linguistics class, the most boring one of all. We got to the hospital around noon. When my friend went to her mother's room, I waited a few minutes and, after making sure there were no nurses in there, I knocked at Frank's door and went in. It was the first time I had stood before his bed, where I was to return countless times. My uncle was a thickset man with a full head of grey hair who, sure enough, did not have the look of someone unwell. What he did have was a set of features very similar to my own. His expression, unlike that of other patients, such as Verónica's mother, was lucid, and he was aware of what was going on around him. A catheter connected his left arm to a drip, which was full of various drugs, but beyond this, and a slight paralysis to the left side of his face, he looked ready to leap out of bed.

'We don't know each other,' I said. 'I'm Antonia, your niece.'

For a few seconds I felt that, rather than being a pleasant surprise, my presence had scared him. It was a fleeting sensation, the merest flash of intuition, but as unmistakable to me as the shock I'd felt the previous day outside the door to his room. Before he replied, a seductive smile played across his face, the same smile he would give me every time I went to visit him.

I have always found it strange the way we establish a familiarity with someone we don't know as soon as we find out we are related. I'm sure it has nothing to do with an instant affinity but rather with something as artificial as culture, a conventional loyalty to the clan or, as some people say, to a surname. Nonetheless, this wasn't what occurred between my uncle and me that morning. I don't know if it was because of the irreverent reputation he enjoyed in my family, or because of the disobedience that talking to him entailed; the fact is, I felt a sense of wonderment similar to that inspired in us by characters from myth.

He asked how I'd found him and asked me not to tell anyone. I explained, so as to ease his mind, that it had been by accident. I told him about Verónica and her mother, and assured him he could count on my silence.

Back then I found the smell of hospitals and their patients intolerable. So instead of sitting in the visitors' chair, situated by his bed, I stationed myself on a little concrete ledge by the window, through which a pleasant breeze blew. I sat there for over an hour, answering the questions my uncle asked me about university, my literary tastes, my political opinions. It was the first time someone in my family took seriously the fact that I was studying literature, without assuming that my choice was down to a lack of any particular talent or that it was a degree designed for women who expect to devote their whole lives to marriage. I was surprised, too, by how much he had read. There wasn't one writer I mentioned that morning whom he hadn't read at least one book by. Then Verónica knocked and, from the doorway, motioned at me to leave.

I didn't kiss him goodbye. I walked towards the door without looking him in the eye, with a shyness he clearly found amusing.

'Come back soon,' he said.

On the bus, my friend began interrogating me. 'He's still really good-looking,' she commented, excitedly. 'He must have been quite a catch when he was younger. Be careful, though. There's a reason he's not liked in your family.'

It was a Thursday. We were in the middle of the rainy season, and I arrived home dripping wet. My mother and brother would be out until late, and so the kitchen and all the other rooms were in darkness. Only in the living room was the last of the evening sun filtering in, illuminating the furniture with a dim light. I put down my schoolbooks and, without wasting any time, went

straight to the study to look for the box where my mother kept
her childhood photographs: two carefully ordered albums covering the first few years of her life. There she was with my uncle
Amadeo and an older boy with huge brown eyes, who could be
none other than Frank. In several of these images I saw them
smiling quite happily in a swimming pool, a park and out on my
grandparents' patio. A couple of pages in, the little boy mysteri-
ously disappeared. Aside from those albums, there were a few
other photographs scattered at the bottom of the box. In these,
Mamá must have been around thirty. Her clothes were unchar-
acteristically bohemian: traditional Mexican blouses, skirts with
indigenous-style embroidery, flares. Occasionally, my brother
and I appeared in our parents' arms, wearing pyjamas or in our
underwear. In the most recent ones I was probably around five
or six years old. Many of these photos had been systematically
cut. I suspected, and I don't believe I was mistaken, that what
had been erased was in fact the head or the entire torso of Uncle
Frank. Probably, in some long-ago period, he had lived with us,
a fact neither he nor my mother had ever mentioned. Looking at
the way the photos had been cut, it was easy to imagine some
furious scissor action. What could he have done to deserve such
a vigorous attack? And in any case, why not get rid of the childhood photos too, where brother and sister appeared so close? I
thought of Juan, my own brother, three years my senior. Ever
since he'd become a teenager we'd been living in the same house
as each other with a complete lack of camaraderie. The closeness we'd developed at some point during childhood had been
forgotten a long time ago. Even so, it would never have occurred
to me to entirely remove his silhouette from our family photos. I
heard the key in the lock. My brother had come home from university with a couple of friends, and they went to sit in the dining
room. I put the box back on the bookshelf and returned to my
room without a sound.

The next morning, I went back to the hospital. As soon as I walked into his room, I saw a satisfied expression on my uncle's face. This time I was the one who asked the questions. I asked him to tell me his story, starting with the time he lived in my grandparents' house, what his childhood had been like and his time at university. His story did not contradict the one I had heard my family tell, but he added a dose of ridicule and a sense of humour that made it far more enjoyable. In his version, family dramas became comedy and the reactions of relatives a faithful caricature. In almost twenty years he hadn't forgotten any of their personalities, and could mimic them uncannily, making me laugh out loud several times. The only one who escaped his barbs was my mother. That week I found out about a few family secrets: of my aunt Laura's first love, which had led her to seek an abortion, of my father's obsessive jealousy, of the mysterious death of a neighbour, which some people blamed on my grandfather . . . If they all had some dark episode in their history, why was he the only exile?

I asked him in the most tactful way I could and he replied that he had been the one who chose to cut all contact so as not to feel judged by each one of his acts and choices.

'But don't you miss the support of a family?'

'If I liked families, I would have started one myself, don't you think?'

My eyes must have grown wider than expected because my uncle burst out laughing.

'Don't make that face! One day you'll see that I'm right. You're not like them. I've known that ever since you were very little.'

His comment sent a shiver down my spine. I was flattered that Frank thought me smarter than the rest of our relatives, in whom I too could see countless defects, but I was also afraid to be different. Even though I liked literature, even though I was attracted to transgressive, eccentric types like him, I did want to get married and have children. I worried an awful lot about never achieving these things and, in particular, about finding myself in hospital one day, without the support of anybody.

'So you already knew me?'

By way of a reply, Frank took my hand. It was the first time he had touched me – at least in my memory – but in spite of the circumstances, I felt in his warm, protective palm an indisputable intimacy. Somewhere, probably in one of those medical magazines that floated around in the hospital and to which I had become instantly addicted, I had read something about the trace left in our memory by the people we have contact with in our first few years of life. Imprinting, I think they call it. According to the article, family ties are based on this initial physical impression. We stayed like that for a few more minutes, his huge hand enclosing mine. Not even the presence of the nurses made us let go of each other. To me it was a silent pact, the tacit promise that I wasn't going to leave him there to his fate.

It was the start of the weekend. Even with accompanying Verónica as a pretext, it was going to be tricky to slip out of the house without anyone noticing. In any case, we had a wedding to go to on the Saturday and a dinner party to host on the Sunday.

When I told him this, my uncle asked me to at least try to call him on the phone.

'I was all right before you showed up. Now, after seeing you every day, I've got a feeling I'm going to miss you.' I assured him I felt the same way.

That afternoon, before going back to the university, I asked to speak to his doctor. The specialist wasn't there at that moment, but the doctor on duty explained a few things to me: he'd had a tumour in his brain for several years and there was no longer any possible treatment for him. They were administering palliative care so that his final few days wouldn't be so bad.

I had to hide in the toilet so Verónica wouldn't see me crying.

My friend had been trying with all her might to stay afloat while her mother lay dying – what would she have thought if she'd seen me crying my heart out for a man I barely knew?

The time I spent in the company of my family yet far away from him seemed endless. During the wedding, I had to try hard not to laugh as I remembered the imitations he'd done of them all. I would far rather have been in his hospital room with its smell of disinfectant than listening to those dull, repetitive conversations. I thought of how different all of our family celebrations would have been if he had been present. The reasons one falls into disgrace with one's own family are strange. Over the years I have seen all kinds of cases and I've come to believe that they are never related to moral questions or principles, but rather to internal betrayals, perhaps invisible to everyone else, but unforgivable to the clan they belong to or, at the very least, to one of its members. On Sunday afternoon, as I helped my mother prepare the food, I tried to bring the subject up.

'What did Uncle Frank do to make you stop talking to him?' I asked, trying to play down the importance of the matter. Her answer was brief.

'He acted like an asshole.'

She was in a good mood that day and it reassured me that she had taken my question lightly. Almost immediately afterwards she left the kitchen to go and welcome her guests.

When I got to the hospital on Monday morning, I found Frank with a ventilator in his mouth. I tried to hide how upset I was. I made a joke about the device and he smiled beneath the mask.

That was the day we began the custom of watching films together on his computer. First we put on *Blow-Up*, and then *The Best Intentions*. I sat in the visitors' chair and, from there, we held hands again, touching each other in a totally relaxed way. They were casual caresses, almost distracted, on the nape of the neck or along the arms, but to me they were delicious. We would spend hours like that, touching the other's skin in silence, while on the screen a story unfolded to which we hardly paid any attention.

Every afternoon, on the return bus journey, I gave Verónica a run-down of these visits. I told her of the affection I felt for my uncle and gave her a detailed progress report of how close we were growing: 'Today he brushed his fingers against my lips'; 'today he just touched my ear.' One afternoon, however, my friend let me know she was not on my side at all.

'You don't seem to have a clue what you're doing,' she said, her voice sharp. 'You're running a real risk. You'd be better off not coming to the hospital at all.'

It was shortly after this, perhaps a day or so later, when Verónica unexpectedly opened the door to our room to announce that her mother had lapsed into a coma. She was sobbing more than howling and, although it was completely justified given the circumstances, I couldn't bear for Frank to see her like that. And so I suggested we leave the room and go down to the cafeteria.

Once there, she ordered a coffee and let the cup grow cold in her hands. I, meanwhile, gulped mine quickly down, eager to return as soon as possible to the intensive therapy ward, but not quite daring to leave my friend on her own. Neither of us said anything. She stared at her coffee, I at the visitors coming and going through the main doors of the hospital. In the midst of this multitude I suddenly made out my grandmother, accompanied by my mother and my uncle Amadeo.

'They're going to Frank's room!' I said to Verónica, desperately. 'How did they find out he was here?'

'I told them,' she confessed, without looking up. 'Forgive me, but I thought you were in danger.'

I almost smacked her.

'Go home and pretend you don't know anything. Do it now while they're going up the stairs.'

Instead of taking her advice, I ran over to catch up with them.

As soon as the lift doors opened, I heard my mother's angry voice in the distance, but her words were completely indistinguishable. Once I was in the corridor where Frank's room was, I pressed my face up against the door to listen, and what I managed to hear was the following: '. . . twenty years and when you find her you try and do the same thing to her.' At that moment, a nurse came past with a trolley full of medicine and gave me a knowing smile. My uncle's reply was drowned out by the clinking of her medicine bottles. I wondered what family secrets came to light in that ward every week or, alternatively, would remain hidden forever. I couldn't wait any longer and opened the door with no thought to the consequences. As soon as I was inside a pristine silence fell, only faintly interrupted by the heart monitor, which made clear Frank's agitation through its fluctuating display. The air in the room was unbreathable. There was pain in my mother's eyes and humiliation in my uncle's face. I felt bad for them both.

Without adding a single word, my mother took me by the arm like when I was a little girl. I felt the pressure from her tense fingers on my skin, the same fingers that had fed me, dressed and undressed me my whole childhood. No ideology, not even the tenderness my uncle brought out in me, could resist her touch. Out of all the imprints of my childhood, hers was without doubt the strongest. I let her lead me downstairs and then out to the car park where she had left her car. My grandmother and Uncle Amadeo remained in the room. I wondered what it would be like for Frank to have his mother's hands close by.

I spent that night wide awake, watching as the rain grew heavier, then lighter. I must have got up at least ten times to see if my grandmother had come home. On one of these occasions, it occurred to me to go into the study and look for the photographs I had seen a few weeks earlier. This time I didn't stop to look at the childhood pictures. I took the images that had been sliced into and spread them out on the carpet like someone about to piece a jigsaw puzzle together. My task was to imagine or guess at the missing pieces. Unlike my grandmother's, my parents' bedroom was at the other end of the house. The risk of them catching me in the act was minimal. What I hadn't thought of was that, like me, my mother couldn't sleep that night, either. When there wasn't room for one more photo on the floor, I looked up and saw her watching me in silence from the doorway. Her long nightdress that fell to her ankles made her look like a ghost. I had to make an effort not to cry out. Her bloodshot eyes revealed she'd been crying recently. I kept quiet for a few minutes to see if she felt like giving me some sort of explanation, but my strategy didn't work and I chose not to push it. Outside, the rain had stopped. My mother sat down next to me on the floor and helped me to gather up the photos. When we'd finished, we put the box back in its place and settled down on the sofa to wait in silence for the sun to rise. I looked sideways at my mother, wrapped up in her own thoughts. She must also have had lots of questions with no answer, which, out of respect for me, she chose not to formulate.

The next morning I went to the clinic without spending even an hour in the lecture theatres at the university. My grandmother let me in, her face distorted with tiredness. I asked her to leave us alone for a minute and, to my surprise, she accepted wordlessly. Frank was semi-conscious. With a hesitant gesture, I put my hand under the covers and took his, searching for some kind of answer. All that I found in his skin that morning, however, was a cold, motionless piece of flesh, an entirely unrecognisable feeling.

PORTO BASO SCALE MODELLERS

Alan Warner

Porto Baso Scale Modellers – all three of us – were out the retail park and vectored for home, motoring up the slow lane of the *autopista* to the very familiar sound of King Crimson's *Larks' Tongues in Aspic* – stuck in the CD player of Norman's old Peugeot since summer 2010.

Clear of Benidorm, Norm was insisting, 'Bob Fripp. Real honest-to-goodness, dynamic front man; his uncle Alfie was last of the 39ers you know.' Norm's fingers scampered for the solitary CD case then quit. 'You never tire of the classic Crimo.' He turned his smile aside for the briefest instant from the carriageway.

I looked out to my right. 'You've mentioned this.'

Henri is from Luxembourg and didn't leave it long enough before asking from the back seat, 'May we please change over to radio please?'

I can report our en-route weather conditions for that one-hour journey home were highly favourable; clear alarms of full summer in the wild rose of the motorway central reservation. For a week roaming, balmy winds had been rampaging across the north country then down through our region; high cirrus bandings were fixed in the blue sky like the white streaks on fatty bacon. But the tags of chop on the sea were gone, so the day had turned still and warm – the car air con fixed at 1. Right out over the Med, a solo contrail dragged across the clearing roof of the afternoon.

'What equipment's that?' Then Norm immediately answered himself, 'Airbus 320.' His chin had sunk, his eyes looked up under his ginger lashes. He never wore shades.

'Not a 737? The squat fuselage.'

'That is an Airbus, my friend.'

'Henri?'

We heard Henri unclip his safety belt and shift across the back seat in order to peer upward. 'Where?'

'Starboard, two o'clock.'

'That's a three-seven.'

Norm used his irritated voice. 'That's an Airbus.'

'It is the Boeing. Put on some Rayban.'

There was a tense pause. 'Well then, Henry.' (Norm always anglicises the name.) '800 or a 900?'

'Cannot tell unless you bring up flightradar24 on your phone. Probability would say an 800. Commercial traffic is boring today.' He shifted across and put the seatbelt back on. Then as a bitter nostalgic coda, 'Not like the seventies.'

Norm grunted. Reluctant agreement.

I asked the old plane-spotter's classic, thinking Henri might never have heard it up in the Benelux realm. 'What kind of hot snacks is the trolley serving then?'

Henri took in a breath and I thought he was going to offer some accurate suggestions, but he held an obscure peace.

Passing down to our right, with its white cells of new moorings and erect phalanxes of yacht masts, was the huge new super-marina, recently dug out the edge of this country. Aligned with us, the sun caught each hammered wavelet and fired it back like ten thousand polished dustbin lids.

The speed limit was 120 but Norm held a steady eighty, until every possible variation of vehicle seemed to have overtaken us. He buzzed the Peugeot off at toll 63, each of us thrusting respective widower, bachelor or divorcee pot bellies upward, groping down into our pockets for loose change.

We crossed through the terraced orange groves behind Cal-aborir, the cypresses black in the late afternoon high above the wide bay, then descended through Villafeliz into Porto Baso. As is usual on the return from our adventurous little jaunts to the Benidorm retail park, I had phoned ahead on my ancient Nokia and we parked in beside The Brave Gurkha.

*

I myself keep the www.portobasoscalemodellers.net website up and running: spry and of-the-moment.

Not to boast, but we have all the latest links to the official Air-fix, Revell and even Humbrol model paint websites; all slapped up there smartish by yours truly, especially when prodigious developments transpire: such as when Airfix took the Armstrong Whitworth Sea Hawk FGA6 out of 1:72 and did a limited edition in 1:24! And not just in 1959–60 Fleet Air Arm colours of 806 Naval Air Squadron out of RNAS Brawdy either. You could have painted that big sucker in RNHF colours out of RNAS Yeovilton, if that really tickled your fancy.

Now we at PBSM are always striving to boost membership and to bring in a somewhat younger constituency – younger than our-selves that is – to draw the youth off the Facebook, get a set of assembly instructions into their left hand and a modelling air-brush in the right. The male youth that is.

As well as patience, dexterity and a need for sobriety, scale modelling gives you a sense of history that didn't do us any harm when we were younger blokes. Did it now? But this is why I don't want photos of Norm, Henri or me up there on our website, bran-dishing our latest completed aircraft – one look at us, smiling by the barbecue with our bellies, our baldness and our bad shirts, and any potential young lads would scarper.

I'm not being stuffy and all *Daily Mail*, but I don't expect any

Spaniards to join up with three old expats like us – there's this bloody language barrier thing, though Henri has the lingo off – more or less; your standard life-is-for-living Spaniard has no intrinsic hatred of the well-made aero scale modelling kit. Admittedly, the Spanish air force never fielded a very interesting native fleet, unless you give a little credit for the civil war's old Polikarpov I-16, with, hopefully, a natty Popeye insignia painted on its upper rudder. But certainly any younger blood of any nationality would be very much appreciated by us in Porto Baso Scale Modellers – some spry fellow who could throw himself with real enthusiasm into Gulf War One/Two aircraft – or even these bloody drones – who would want to build a 1:24 drone? Search me. Yet several kit companies do offer them. It takes all kinds in the universe of scale modelling.

There have been several email responses to our website 'Contact'. Well, two. Both of which I responded to promptly. One was from a young lad called Joe ('sent from iPhone') who was clearly English but he vanished when I invited him to pop round Henri's for our next meeting. Then the other email was from a camera shop in Valencia, offering to rent us reflectors and synchronised standing lights – labouring under the unfortunate misunderstanding that the modelling we were involved with was of the glamour variety: poolside nude photo shoots.

*

There is full disclosure among we Porto Baso Scale Modellers that Henri's place is best for our Saturday meetings and occasional group construction sessions. The old Luxembourg civil service pension speaks for itself. Henri has a three-bedroom villa up in the pine range with its own pool and barbecue terrace. In each room the dusted cabinets, even tallboys (he has a cleaning lady in three days a week), are filled and topped with expertly completed and painted plastic model kits in all scales.

Henri's tastes run exactly similar to Norm and me – namely classic aviation – 1960s and 70s civilian airliners, seaplanes, WWII props and Cold War jets; but we start to wind down with the onset of the boring F-15 era, though we'll never sniff at a Tornado or a Starfighter. It's not just planes for Henri though. You will see a gallant representation of German WWII battleships, torpedo boats, landing craft, Allied and Axis tanks, Apollo 13, armoured cars, light and heavy artillery pieces with operating gun crews and even two D-Day dioramas with lettering, entitled 'Ruined French House' and 'Gun Emplacement'.

A tall glass case (locked) is in his front room, sheltered from the scourge of the summer sun which can fade a colour scheme in just two months. Here Henri has the models he is proudest of. Some are especially rare: the Kabozi Co.'s much sought-after mid-1980s kit of the Messerschmitt Me 262 – in perfectly rendered mottled camouflage. There was also the Bohums DC-8 Super 61, boldly reproduced in the mad Braniff colour scheme. Here also is his De Havilland Mosquito in 1:24, completed when Henri was just fourteen years of age in Clervaux. It is hard to discern any drop in his high level of modelling skill, even at that early age when the eyes were so sharp and daring was so great – though I would just point out that the embossing of the silver cockpit frames shows a slight and displeasing thickness which wouldn't escape Henri's exacting standards of today.

That afternoon we gathered around Henri's spacious kitchen table. Even here Henri had placed some finely completed models on top of the cupboards. With Norm's cautious driving, our takeaways from The Brave Gurkha really required a bit of a reheat in the microwave. Norm lectured us at length on the thermal mass properties of microwaves and how you must heat the curry sauce and the rice separately. It was all a bit of a production line, getting the rice, main curry sauces and side dishes piping hot, and then, amidst this hubbub of rather anxious, peckish old chaps who love their snap, came the clanging of that hand-rung Don Quixote doorbell. Norm's aloo gobi was going round and round on the revolving plate; Henri was stooped down to closely monitor it through the microwave view window and spoke slowly, 'John, would you go to the door, please tell Mrs Kroll her cat is not in my rear garden, please.'

Norm, in the tone of reading back a checklist, announced, 'All curries are now at optimum temp.'

I stepped along the corridor where the grandfather clock of Henri's mother clucked with the faint aroma of its insecticide-crammed interior. I opened the front door.

'Hey!'

Fiercely, I blinked once – said, 'Look. We're not interested. You've got the whole wrong idea.'

They had actually sent in a bloody potential participant to Henri's. Since the bankers' recession, things must have been pretty grim in the camera trade. She couldn't have been north of thirty. I mean better, twenty-seven, twenty-six? And English to boot; break your heart just passing her on the street: sun-mashed hair and big cowboy boots at the end of skinny bare brown legs, denim shorts and wrist bangles, every finger decked with golden rings – apart from the matrimonial one – those coloured false fingernails like a Disney cartoon. I immediately glanced left into the villa garden of Mrs Kroll. With this one calling round, it looked like we'd not only ordered in food but also a Ukrainian private dancer from the White Love Club.

'We're a model *aeroplane* group, love. Toy models.' I turned round and I swept my hand beyond the grandfather clock, along the corridor to the arched doorway where you could see into the front room above the pool. Models which Henri had constructed with their undercarriages fixed in the down position were lined up all along the sideboard, their engine nacelles angled proudly high.

A Pacific Operations catwalk: Grumman Hellcat, Jap Zero, Beau-fighter. 'We don't need flashgun reflectors or cameras, whatever. We're just three old blokes making toy *model* aeroplanes. Bloody daft little hobby, you know? Just whiling our time away.'

'Cameras?' One tiny wonky tooth among a rack of dazzlers – a smile that would have crushed the entire sports team bus. She continued, 'What you on about? I know. I'm Josephine. Emailed a month or so back and you give *me* this address. Didn't you? You said Saturdays. I'm up the hill, sat by the pool, stuck your address in the satnav, just popping my head in, aren't I?' She swung her hair around; beyond the crenellations of Henri's ornamental wall and the tangles of mature bougainvillea upon it, she indicated a silver SUV shape parked out on the road. She laughed very quick, two long earrings – a sequence of gold droplets – leaping excited-ly beneath each lobe.

'Joe! Sorry. I thought you were someone else entirely. Embarrass-ing. I'm John Bishop.' I held out my hand and she took it, her fingers felt like pretzels and the bangles clattered. 'The blokes are here right now actually. If you feel okay. About coming in to meet them?'

'Just a jiff; grab something out the car.' She lifted her gold sunglasses from where they hung on the neckline of her blouse and popped them directly onto her tanned face. She stepped out the shade and down the semicircle of stairs, all in just two long strides, wrists jingling, cowboy boots clicking, she was across that patio and out the gate in seconds, the car-key fob held straight out before her like a pistol; a little purse of skin at the elbow of her golden arm. I stood in the porch staring after.

Norm glanced up from the table in a profound bafflement as I returned to the kitchen, accompanied by a stunning young woman, holding in her arms an object wrapped in a lightweight fleece blanket. Later, with great concentration – as if struggling to describe the manifestation of a holy apparition on some mountainside – Norm repeatedly told me that he first thought this woman had run over a dog out on the road and had carried the poor creature in to place before us, seeking assistance.

In her mildly croaky voice, she called, 'Hello all. Lovely day; is this all of us? You rascals having a sneaky curry while the sun's out, are you?' She held her head back with the burden in her arms and inhaled sharply through her prim nostrils. 'Mmmmm. Where can I plonk this one then?'

We all froze, guilty at the abundance of food, paralysed by her unlikely youth and sudden beauty right there in Henri's kitchen. Henri just opened his mouth slightly. The curry dishes were slid aside so she could place the burden down. I did quick, polite introductions of names but she hardly looked at any of us and they just stared back at her. She unfolded the blanket and glared at what was there. 'What do you reckon then?'

In the middle of the table, surrounded by tikka laziz, Goan king prawn curry and Brave Gurkha special chicken, was a beautiful 1:24 scale McDonnell Douglas DC-8 Super 61 – just like the one in Henri's display cabinet – the impossible-to-obtain Bohums limited edition, but instead of Braniff colours, this one was in the perfectly rendered, long orange-red-blue cheatlines of United Airlines' mid-seventies fleet.

Norm nodded. 'Gosh. Exceptionally done I must say.'

Henri placed his fancy designer reading glasses on his nose very, very slowly. 'The Bohum.' He clucked his tongue and frowned, moving his head around the model, which was just beneath his chin. 'Who made this then? I'd like to talk with him; your small brother? Your young son maybe?'

'How do you mean, lovey? I don't have no kids. I made it.'

Henri blinked up over his lenses, quite appalled.

She smiled round the three of us.

'How did you obtain this particular model?' asked Norm, with a sort of feigned English indifference.

'I'm not with you. Obtain it? Like balance it, once the wings were on, or put a putty weight in its nose?'

Henri had a caustic smile, which didn't become him.

I said, quietly to her, 'It's an out-of-date but very rare model among old collectors like us. They don't make these any more and you just don't see them for sale.'

'Oh. Really? How about that then? I got it for nothing. Just came by it up in this old house in Hampshire back home. This is the first model I ever made, isn't it?'

Norm gave me a funny look, like he was going to remove a notebook and jot this information down for future use against her in a court of law.

Henri enquired, 'And have you been doing this long?'

'Two years, seven months and eight days.'

Henri sneered, 'It took you that long to complete this one model?'

'Nah. I did this one in a week, lovey. You're not getting me straight here. I've a load of these that I've all done; just thought I'd cart this over for you to see how it's come out. It's a sudden hobby I've got; isn't it? Like a sudden hobby I can see all you fellows share.' She shook her earrings and held both her palms up in the air, which seemed to signify Henri's collection all around us. 'That's about all I do now, building these fellows up, painting them, putting their cute little sticker things on.'

'The decals.'

'I'm addicted,' she mumbled, apologetically.

Henri very carefully hoisted the model and studied her work on the underside of the fuselage, his lips parting silently in French. Then he asked in English, 'You are using airbrush then hand brush on some smaller parts?'

'True enough. A hand brush on bits of that but I use more airbrushes now.'

'What type of airbrush? What type of compressor?'

'I don't know the names, lovey. My husband used them in the workshop for his bloody Harley and now I use the littlest ones.'

'Your husband?' Norm said cautiously.

Henri nodded, in an impatient way. 'These discolourations on the wing surface are from wet landings, dirty runways, just in front of the flaps and the staining here. Very skilfully done. And what was your approach?'

'To be honest. Henri is it? To be honest, Henri, I get most of my brainwaves all off my iPhone. You just type it in the net and you get all the sites and Myspaces; lots of blokes' tips, but I try to do my own thing too. I try to put in unique touches. Do you know what I mean? Guess what I used there? To get that mucky effect round the what's-it? The exhaust thing.'

'The cowling.'

Henri told her, 'You used a touch of charcoal, maybe cigarette ash on your fingertip.'

'Nah, that's too obvious, lovey, and besides, I seriously quit the smokes.' She let out a brash laugh. '*That* is using just the tiniest flake of mascara. Lancôme Doll Eyes. Good stuff too,' she pointed a bright finger up at her own smoky eye, crowned with lagoon-blue eye-shadow, and out came that laugh again.

Norm and Henri looked at one another.

'I know fine what you bunch is all thinking and yous are too much gentlemen to say out loud, but you're thinking that building up planes from all their little bits and pieces is just a boys' game and what's she doing, getting stuck in about it, but I'll let you all in on a little secret about me, boys – if you want to know?'

We all three leaned a little closer to her.

'I'm a trained beautician. If you can use tweezers to whack a pair of false eyelashes on a hungover housewife in Colchester, then it's a doddle gluing these plastic things all together; it's basically IKEA flatpacks, but littler. Isn't it? Nail technician too. So I'm fairly handy with the smaller brush.' She shot out her

ringed fingers and the bangles chipped together once, displaying
for us the gaudy, woven, fantastically intricate patterns on each of
her long fingernails. 'I got pretty steady hands, fellas. These days.
Hey. Go break us off some of that naan, why don't you?'

Norm hesitated, then he leaned across and did so. She took it
from him and tugged away at the bread chunk in her fingers using
the front teeth, chewing at it as if she now had a plug of tobacco
behind her sunken delicate cheek.

Henri viewed her very carefully. He stood and he went through
to the side room where earlier, from the boot of Norm's Peugeot,
we had each carried in our retail park purchases. I had finally
bought the Short Sunderland flying boat; not the classic Airfix
Mark III, which I already owned when I was a nipper, but the
Italeri Mark I in 1:72, just reviewed as 'kit sensation of the year'.
Norm had gone and got himself that MiG-15 in 1:48 by Revell.
Chinese Air Force colours. Inspired by the Korean War era in
Benidorm and money-no-object, Henri had bought the beautiful
Hasegawa 1:48 F-86 Sabre with its distinctive yellow bandings
and amazing cockpit detail, choice of speed brake positioning
and decorated drop tanks. Henri placed these three boxes on the
counter top at the sink side and he told Josephine, 'Today we were
at the retail park in Benidorm.'

'Were you now? I go to the toy shops there sometimes, but I
write down the names of the planes and then order off the internet. The shop markup is quite stiff now and I'm always careful
since I'm divorced.'

'Divorced?'

'Oh. Divorced?'

'You're divorced?'

'Yeah,' she looked left and right and back again between us,
smiling. 'You know what they say, Spain: divorce capital of Essex.
We had a good five years. My husband, he was in securing of
oil rights, India, Venezuela, ends of the earth. When we split he

left Spain taking bloody Marie Carmen with him. Didn't he? Our fff-ing accountant. Shoulda known he couldn't be spending that much time. Two-timing *and* double accounting. Got to admit I was seen all right – moneywise, wasn't I? But I've always watched the pennies since I was a little girl, apart from a wild period.' She looked at the kit box and wiped her palm across the picture so the bangles jinkled once more.

Impatiently, Henri said, 'This one is mine,' and he lifted the F-86 box. 'I wish very much for you to have it?'

'Me? I couldn't do that, lovey. That's a nice mark that, pricey, I've seen them.'

'Why not that you begin it and then next week we too see how much you are getting along?'

'Really? Then I can be in your modelling club too?'

She seemed charmingly happy but Henri laughed indulgently. 'Well, we'll see, my dear.'

I had to speak out. 'Steady on now, we're not a Surrey golf club. I mean surely, the more the merrier?'

'Tell you fellas,' she said, nodding, 'the more the merrier. That's what I've often said in life. I can tell you. Look, Henri. I'll work on it and I can just text you a photo to your phone on how I'm getting along.'

'Ah no no no. I think. No text please. I have no mobile phone. I think next Saturday you come along here to us and bring how much of the model you've made so I can examine?'

'Oh. How much,' she smiled, gently. 'All right then, lovey.'

There followed a bit of blether about summer being here at last and the water company digging up the road at the top of the hill. Then Josephine grabbed a last bit of naan and, chewing, she departed, with Henri's new €180 scale model kit in her arms. I helped her out to the car with the old Dick 8-61 in its blanket and we placed it carefully into the hatchback: a silver Range Rover, the one with all the fancy stuff stuck on. Fifty grand's worth at least. She beeped as she drove off up the hill, the automatic gears dropping and upgrading easy in the ascent towards the larger villas on the summit, where I'd never been.

The three of us sat for some time over the cooled food and we had little interest in reheating it. Subconsciously we had all begun diets. We stared at each other. Henri said, 'I refuse to believe she made it. A woman. This terrible ex-husband perhaps. Did you see? Hey. Guys. Come *on*! It was one of the best made models I ever seen.'

'It is. It is just remarkable,' I nodded. 'Sickening really.'

Norm shook his head. 'But a young woman. A girl even! A girl in our group. I mean it'll change everything. Henry.'

Henri nodded.

Norm flustered over the gender issue. 'And not just a woman, I mean, but a . . .' He blushed but spat it out. 'A divorcee. And a damned attractive divorcee. Damned, damned attractive. Well I find her damned attractive.'

'I think we're with you on that one, Norm.'

'She's. Very saucy.' Norm spoke this in a complex tone which seemed to hint that the poor young woman would now be exposed to his own attractiveness and that this would be a sudden and unfair burden upon her.

I turned to Henri. 'You gave her the Sabre to see if it's really her making them, eh?'

'*Oui*. I just cannot believe, the look of her. I mean, *trop belle pour toi* but all of this and just a beautiful child. What age is that child?'

'Twenty-five? Six?'

'Good God,' Norm blinked, 'my niece Pippa is twenty-four.'

'Thirty at a push.'

'At our age it gets harder to tell.'

'But it's just, socially . . .' Norm frowned, despondent. 'Socially we need to face up to the fact there will be differences. I mean she's a bit. She's damned attractive but a bit.'

'Not *farouche*,' said Henri.

Norm stated it clearly. 'How can we discuss, with a girl like that, all the latest surface-to-air weapons systems?'

*

Wednesday night at my place, immersed in National Geographic channel, tucking into a six-pack of mini pork pies from Iceland; Henri telephoned the land line. He would only say it was urgent and better if I could come directly, Norm was picking me up in five.

King Crimson were mercifully silenced outside Henri's garden wall when Norm twisted the ignition off. I was disappointed to see no silver Range Rover parked there.

Henri sat at his kitchen table staring down at what lay before him in full sparkling silver. It was the freshly minted F-86 Sabre he'd given to Josephine. Henri had placed the model on a piece of mirror so we could fully appreciate the workings on the undersides. For the unpainted aluminium factory-finish effect, she had used silver foil and pre-grained it; she had sanded the raised lines flush, working to give each piece of metallic skin which formed the aircraft a distinct and flawed identity. I noticed she had used a galvanic, goldish piece of discoloured foil to simulate the overheated metal around the jet pipe. A technique I'd heard of but never dared attempt.

In a quiet voice, Henri told us, 'She is building them for sure. I had to ask what techniques she used and she explained some to me. Ideas I have never considered. She dropped it off one hour ago. The quality itself is barely credible but that she did this in less than four days. She cannot have slept.'

I tipped my head down to look in the mirror at the hand-painting on the drop tanks. They were each perfectly matched.

Norm sighed, 'She has even got some of the raised rivets to show as worn-through silver, on the painted wing band sections.'

I nodded.

Henri leaned backwards and extended his two arms out before him, his unlikely, strong, short fingers gripping the table edge. 'Gentlemen. To my mind, we have the privilege of being in the presence of one of the greatest scale modellers I have ever witnessed. Perhaps who has ever lived.'

*

Next Saturday, the males of Porto Baso Scale Modellers all became visibly nervous as the silver Range Rover crunched in on the gravel beneath the portico. A rare privilege, Henri had parked his Mercedes in his garage to clear the turning place; his main gates had remained flung open in welcome all morning.

It was also difficult not to note sudden transformations in our own physical appearances; gone were the baggy tropical shirts, darkened with the gelatinous tug of underarm sweat stains, cast aside were the bum bags strapped onto each of us, stuffed with watch tools, receipts, old barley sugars and magnifying glasses. We were all wearing suspiciously ironed slacks and chinos, in preference to the baggy tropical cut-offs that normally revealed our pale, skinny and shapeless legs, or Norm's ankles, hammered into a blue cheese by varicose veins. Despite the warmth, Jesus sandals – often with black socks – were now replaced by deck shoes or in Henri's case, Gucci loafers. We all seemed to have paid unmentioned trips to the barber for a tidy trim to what was left of our vanishing, yet still unruly hair.

Henri was extremely attentive; he shadowed Josephine, hovering at her right shoulder like a president's translator on some state visit; nodding and speaking quietly, always in agreement. Often, when she was not looking, I caught Henri gazing steadily at her bleached eyelashes. Norm kept his distance and directed his shyness towards his MiG-15. Without sisters, educated from an early age in various obscure, male-only independent English boarding schools, and a lifelong bachelor, Norm viewed women with mixed fascination and suspicion – but never distaste.

We had – each of us – rather shameful works in progress: Norm his MiG, I had started in on the Sunderland, and Henri – from his vaults – had produced a big Airfix Mustang P-51 in 1:24.

She had surprised us by arriving with no work in progress. Instead, already, she now toured and examined our own sorrier efforts, pointing out and praising a nifty piece of paintwork on Norm's, or suggesting to me – despite the fact it would be concealed inside the fuselage – that a rogue blob of hardened adhesive, which just showed, could be smoothed down. She produced her own pink emery board from the soft leather bag she had swung round her torso and which bounced upon her buttock. The emery board was stained with the colour of her painted fingernails.

I had forgotten how physically busy she always seemed to be. It was difficult to imagine her fulfilling the still, sedentary hours at a work surface required to build scale models to her own dazzling standard. Yet at one point, taking an interest in the cockpit section of Henri's P-51, she suddenly sat down on the chair beside him with great directness; a tense, tightly controlled, determined stillness overcame her, the pretty face aggressively focused upon the model part.

When we broke for three Tetleys and an espresso for Henri, she sat Christine Keeler-style on a kitchen chair, chin rested on the golden hairs of her arm, joking with us, but she soon stood, spun the chair and sat again with her calf flung over her knee, jiggling a horizontal leathery sandal and golden anklet. Her mouth was working at gum but she still drank her tea down while continuing to chew. It was now clear from various unselfconscious movements which caused her vest to shift and bending in her short skirt, that the suntan was an all-over concern, maintained by private poolside sessions. Sipping her cuppa she suddenly asked,

'Any you fellas, you ever have problems here and there?'

'Problems?' Norm smiled.

'Yeah. That's how I got into building model kits stuff; started them when I was in hospital; the last time for three months.'

Norm said, 'Gosh. I'm, I'm sorry to hear that. Ill health or bit of an accident? Medical insurance was my line before retirement.'

'No, Norman. My whole life was in a bit of a right tiddle. Put it this way, I was wearing my Sunday socks on Wednesdays. I had a massive cocaine and sex addiction. And a forty-a-day fag habit. Had to go to rehabilitation three different times, didn't I?'

I bit my teeth down. Norm turned slightly away from her – his views on casual drug use were never located at the liberal end of the spectrum.

'All puffed up on the devil's dandruff, me and the ex, running wild round this town for three years on his silver Harley, dawn to dusk riding with god knows who. He couldn't fulfil contracts by then – could he? – so strung out he took sabbatical. At one point Chucho, our usual coke dealer, was round our villa so much we just asked him to move into the guest apartment and work exclusively for us. Got him cleaning the pool and pottering in the garden too some days.'

Henri sipped urbanely at his small cup. His English was excellent but I wondered if he was fully understanding all of this in her quick-talk accent.

'Too right I needed a hobby. When I was through the clinic that first time in England, which didn't work, I talked to this older fellow. Now he was a serious old-timer. About you guys' age.'

I winced and Norm slightly raised his teacup in protest.

'Alcohol was his vice, could have poured him straight into the corners and he told me he had once shaken off a long smack habit back in the eighties. Not in a posh clinic or nothing we was in then but just on his jack jones in some bedsit. He tried twenty times but nothing clicked until a little Airfix aeroplane kit. Who would ever have credited it eh? He explained how reading some big long book, or getting aerosols and doing your own graffiti, or watching DVD box sets is all very open-ended, unstructured stuff, not with what you'd call a clear set outcome. Is it? Not when you're trying to come off and then stay off and your life is in chaos. Now have a ponder: building a model kit is perfect therapy; a way forward. A start, a middle, an end. No matter how bad that old bloke was feeling, long as he went down the instructions, step 1 to 2, 3 to 4, it give him order and he'd get through withdrawals. Long as he had more of them models to build. When he got out he'd been skint, hadn't he, but he'd shoplift kits to keep him straight: days, months, years, with no urges. Admit it,' she indicated Henri's collection all around us, 'when we build these models, we're making a perfect little world, all of our own, the only one that we can control, where we can make this world stop and have stillness and ask it to stay that way, calmed forever and ever. That's what's so beautiful about them. Isn't it? Have to be frank with you though. First time I heard all this from the geezer, I thought it was a right load of old bollocks and I come out that clinic and straight back onto the sniff and – even better – the fags.'

Norm interrupted. 'If it's, if it's not at all an impertinent question, may I ask, may I ask, the drug addiction, the tobacco addictions you appear to have conquered. I am presuming the sexual . . . ? Conquered that yet?'

Good old Norm, straight in there, and this coming from a geezer who had recently told me his only idea of a dream week was to be left alone, naked, just him and his tube of haemorrhoid cream, applying it at will round the house.

She barked that hard and experienced laugh of hers. 'Don't you fret, Norman, I'm like a nun these days. The sex stuff came from cocaine the way hay fever comes from pollen. But things did get wilder and more out of hand up at the old villa with my ex. Even Chucho made for the hills – didn't he – coke paranoia and the

fears, right convinced he was that the Guardia would come calling what with the consumption amounts, all our car-key parties,
prossies in the swimming pool and out on the speedboat all that
summer. Dogging. Me and the ex got into that too. A right proper
little buzz. We was into what they do here in the summer moonlight – jet-ski dogging at night, out behind Tanga Island. There's
people out there from all over Europe and bleedin' beyond; but
the nationalities break down, don't they just? I've had a few
cross-border experiences behind Tanga Island, haven't I? I can
tell you.'

Henri confirmed my translation fears, frowning benign-
ly towards her. 'You are fighting dogs on jet-skis behind Tanga
Island?'

'I'll explain later, Henri,' I said softly and tapped his shoulder
to allow Joe to continue. 'I'll explain later.'

'That's me. I like to feel exhilaration *and* shame at the same
time. One's no fun without the other, that's for sure. This's what I
found out about myself, nights in the bay and the beach behind
Tanga Island. Didn't I?'

Norm helplessly spoke again. 'If I may chip in with a not impertinent question, just a question, my dear, but from for instance the
medical insurance point of view, if I could say, on a, on a, on a
practical level. How do you. *On* a jet-ski? Does one face one way
or perhaps another way?'

'Norman. Aren't you just chock-a-block with curiosities? So
was I, once. Watch out now, 'cause they have three- and even
four-person jet-skis these days and I've seen it all in the field
of personal water craft, haven't I? Dogging's not really swinging,
mostly, it's more about watching and being watched, isn't it?' She
called this loudly, projecting her words through the open kitchen
window as if she was expecting an answer from someone out there
– working in the garden perhaps, pruning the swaying faces of
pink poinsettia beyond the insect screen. She shrugged. 'Or that's

how it starts, then I do more coke and it gets more swingy and I want a bit of everyone. But for beginners, a two-person jet-ski is a secure place to be. No one can climb up very quick, folk float around in circles out there, and jet-skis float round them, so everything that does happen is very consensual. On the beach: lot more comfy in this climate, isn't it, all bikinied up like the other gals – but not for long of course. Different class, isn't it, than a steamed-up Mondeo in a forest near Braintree, some heavy breather white-van-man, leaning in through your wound-down rear window? Mind you Norman, I seen some gruesome sights out there on Tanga Island in August that would put you right off your lunch. Monster of the Black Lagoon meets *The Jeremy Kyle Show*. But sometimes there'd be lovely-looking young couples out there. Or girls. Wouldn't there? Get so high I didn't care. Some nights I'd let them all have a shot at me while my husband and others watched like the paparazzi on a convicted celeb. Having it on with some right old gas men, wasn't I, and a lot of us given up bothering with condoms by then. Main prob' was just keeping our snorting grammes dry among all that bloody water. And bodily fluids round the nostrils and what have you?'

There was something of a pause.

I asked. 'Literally gas men?'

'Nah-nah. That's just an expression we had, didn't we: they'd serviced a right load of old boilers every night. Then me. Don't forget. Exhilaration plus shame equals happy Joe! Thank you for successfully pumping up all my tyres.' The harsh laugh, then she leaned over, opened the cupboard beneath the sink where the hinge movement both swings out a small litter bin and flips up its lid; here she spat a great pink-coloured gob of gum.

I reached and touched my forehead.

'Third time the husband sent me through rehab in that big place in Hampshire. Realise now he was so keen on packing me off to English health farms to give himself more time with that bitch Marie Carmen from Churchill and Crozer; tucked up together in our king-size, cooking the books among other things. I felt a little bit of a prat over there but I eventually thought of that old fella, asked about an Airfix-type model to pass the time and the staff in the rehab rec room thought they had one. They dug round up the back of some old cupboard and sure enough, there it was. Been there years, hadn't it; that same one I brought round here last week. Got my cement and paint and went to work; wised up that I had a bit of a knack for it as well. Stopped cocaine two years seven months and fifteen days ago; building them kits ever since and if I didn't, one toot of the jizz and I'd be out behind Tanga Island with my bum up in the warm moonlight,' she laughed joyously, completely forgiving and understanding of herself.

Before she had reversed her Range Rover out Henri's drive that weekend, he had presented her with yet another gift. 'Take your time with this one, do please,' he told her. It was a De Havilland Mosquito, the same updated model Henri himself had built at age fourteen and still displayed in the glass cabinet. 'Go carefully now,' he said. 'This is balsa-wood body, not plastic, so a bit harder to start off – like the real aircraft had a wooden body too so this is a tribute to accuracy – what do you say – a way to come very close to controlling the world. Follow the instructions. Enjoy. Delight,' he smiled. He opened his arms but got it slightly wrong, 'Be exhilarate.'

Balsa wood modelling was damn tricky but I reckoned it took more than a toy plane to exhilarate and shame Josephine.

We waved her off from the balcony as she backed out of the gravel drive and then the Range Rover accelerated uphill. Henri turned directly towards me, saying quickly, 'Explain, explain,' and when I did a look of hurt came upon Henri's face and he groaned, 'She's not even French.'

*

The Thursday night following, my apartment buzzer sounded and when I put on my trousers and answered, Henri was right there in the communal corridor shoving a piece of paper at me. 'It was crushed into my letterbox. Perhaps you need to translate but I believe I understand.'

I frowned, walking back in toward my living room and Henri followed leaving the front door wide open. He is taller than me and had to move his head from side to side with irritation to avoid my model aircraft hanging from threads on the ceiling. On lined paper featuring coloured macaws printed at each corner, in a childish hand, big looped circles over the i's:

*Listen here Henry the 8. Two years 7 months 18 days – your
balls all model I couldnt do and thats me back on the bloody
sniff. Arent I. Thought toot wd help me along to finish
the thing but did not. Shouldnt have joined your PortoB
Modellers.*

   goodbye Joe x x

'Isn't kidding on is she?'

Henri stared, astonished. 'Kidding on? *Non, non.* I have been to her villa ringing the video phone. Talk to her neighbours. They tell me they have not see her and on Tuesday night, a commotion, the garage door remained wide open as she drove off down the hill in her Range Rover and she hasn't been back. That's not all.' He opened his eyes wide. 'The neighbour permitted me in, to look over the wall which separates their properties. Those are very large villas but you can still see into her rear gardens. Just floating there in her very big infinity pool with its rock waterfall.'

'What?'

'Thirty or forty plastic kits. All just beautifully constructed things as well – absolutely perfect but now ruined, floating in there. It is a real, real tragic thing to see, John. I wanted to remove them with the pool net.' He paused. 'I noticed the balsa-wood Mosquito floated there too. Half complete.' He gave a wry smile, which angered me. He had obtained satisfaction at last.

'Where has she gone?'

'John. Behind the Range Rover she was towing her jet-ski.'

'Oh I see. Like she said.'

'She will destroy herself. We've got to get out there and after her. For the sake of scale modelling.'

'I beg pardon.'

'To find her.'

'Out where?'

'To the back of Tanga Island,' he pointed to my front window. I hadn't even bothered to put my blinds down though the tennis court apartments overlooked me. I stepped across. In the parking area of my residency below was Henri's Mercedes. And there was Norm sat in the passenger seat wearing his King Crimson tour T-shirt. And behind the Mercedes on an aluminium trailer was a long, lime-green-coloured jet-ski.

'Henri. You must be joking, where did you get that bloody thing?'

'Antonmeister.'

'What? Where?'

'Antonmeister. My Austrian friend. A three-seater; took me out this afternoon for several hours to show me how to operate. It's easy to conduct. In fact it's wonderful. The throttle is like bike brakes on handlebars, vroom, vroom, in case you fall off so the power is cut. It even has a brake. Don't tell Antonmeister we are using it in night times though.'

'Henri, I am detecting the mother of all bad ideas here – it's dangerous at night. You're not even meant to take jet-skis out on water in darkness.'

He chuckled. 'This is Spain, all laws are advisory and it has done little to prevent the development of certain subcultures. Get your bathing costume. Norman is awaiting.'

'Henri, please. Just because you have taken a shine to her and you're curious about the things going on out there. We're too old. We'll kill ourselves. Drown Norm.'

'Hey. You think I'm crazy? We have three good life jackets.'

The sheltered waters off the coast of Porto Baso lie between two distinctive headlands positioned five miles apart; on the promontory of each, a tall lighthouse is suspended high on the point above the rocks and waters. Those steady white pulses, which seemingly signal from one lighthouse to the other and back again, have become familiar to us at night – their rhythmic light crawls over the whitewashed walls of obscure apartment buildings and across tiled roofs in our small town. Down the years of retirement you discover those surprising beams everywhere, signalling through the branches of orange allotments, in car parks behind restaurants you have never visited before. Yet you can only see both lighthouses simultaneously when you sail far enough out from the coast toward the east and are roughly two miles offshore. Two miles further out to sea lie the main shipping lanes and forty miles beyond that the Balearic islands.

Upon this black Mediterranean, a mighty gibbous moon laid down an unsteady slick of pinkish light which jittered on the surface. Through this element Henri steered us on our three-hundred-horsepower steed, with the lighthouses of home steady on our stern.

Our faces were dry yet coated in salt. We had gone so very, very fast in the darkness, when I leaned to starboard, out into the slipstream from behind the shelter of Norm's shoulders, my cheeks and lips had blubbered like the flesh under a forceful hand dryer in some men's toilet.

I was seated on the very back saddle and though the spray was dampening the rear of my life jacket, I had two good rubberised hand grips by my thighs. I noted occasionally, Norm placed his arms around Henri's ample waist as we crossed a patch of rougher water.

Henri very cautiously throttled back in increments and the water craft sank slightly deeper. It had been impossible to talk before but now Henri turned off the engine completely.

'What's wrong?'

'Nothing. It's just, so very strange out here.'

It was true. The water slapped slightly at the lips and flanks of the sleek-shaped hull but with the abysmal depths below and the settlement lights of the coast so far distant, there was indeed a curious silence far out here upon these waters. I shivered and drew up my feet a little further from the black surface. I noticed the three of us were breathing hard as though we had all just ceased some illegitimate sin.

Henri slightly turned round, more in gesture, to speak. 'My God, you guys. I'm gonna have to buy one of these.'

'They really are something.' Norm nodded.

I pointed. 'Tanga Island isn't its real name, that's just a nasty tourist name. The island on satnav is called Isla Granbolo, just over there about two miles south and further in too; we've come out a bit too far, Henri.'

'Yes, yes.' Henri nodded and he wiped something aside from his face.

Norm coughed and announced, 'I don't hear a thing.'

'What do you expect? The howling of wild beasts? Joe's laugh?'

Henri chuckled in the dark. 'With Homer, is it not the Sirens singing their promise of love which lure men and their ships to destruction upon the rocks?'

'Exactly,' I said, coldly.

'Some people,' said Henri, 'believe all of Homer happened on this side of the Mediterranean, that charmed Odysseus fell for Circe right here in these waters.'

'Bollocks. That's an invention of bloody hippies on Formentera in the sixties. You don't need to pull out classical allusions to gloss over what you two are up to. Get over there and satisfy your curiosity.'

Even Norm was ready to foil my line of attack. 'Don't be vulgar, John. She's in trouble and we need to help her, like gentlemen. Get her home and get those models out of her swimming pool. The future of Porto Baso Scale Modellers is our responsibility. She is a fellow member in need of assistance and guidance.'

'Well when you meet the cannibals on those shores you better sew your swimming trunks to your T-shirt.'

Norm added, 'You know none of us will be covered by our med insurance for activity like this.'

'You can say that again.'

The plastic key hung from a string attached to a bracelet on Henri's wrist. He started the engine and we began to steam south, parallel to the coast, watching the lighthouses but also squinting ahead for possible obstructions on the surface. We did so for about three minutes before Henri suddenly cut the engine again and the jet-ski slowed down to a halt far more abruptly. We floated.

'It's that flashing red light?' Norm was nodding round Henri's back at the dashboard on the handlebars.

Henri was taking something out the front pocket of his life jacket. 'Now I put on my reading glasses it reads "Fuel".'

'I did point that light out to you back at the canal, Henry, I thought it a bit fishy that it was flashing.'

'I thought it was the power setting. And please, my name is Henri, please.'

After a few moments of contemplation, Norm reached into the pocket of his life jacket and an eerie, unnatural illumination shone upon the dark wavelets by the side of the jet-ski. With a disinterested voice he said, 'No reception.' The light was curtailed.

We sat that way, one in front of the other. Henri leaned on the handlebars, our six legs thrown over our mount. None of us spoke as we rocked lightly from side to side. Now I thought I could actually hear gleeful shouts of abandon towards the south, but we seemed to be drifting another way. Eastward, out to the shipping lanes.

The moon had sunk much lower and high above us in the vaults of heaven two cherry lights crossed, linked by a steady pulse of cyan. A moment later we heard the low turbo-prop groan which just as quickly faded. All three of us had turned our heads upward as if this might – inexplicably – be the coastguard already. In the dark, Norman lifted his bare arm with its wristwatch and rustled his life jacket. Norm told us – and that ancient, uncaring sea all around – 'I say, that'll be the Iberojet ten to midnight, out of Ibiza for Madrid. Seems to be running a touch late.'

FIN

Lynn Coady

They had just moved into a new house when he told her he wanted out. It was such a great house, too – they'd never been able to
afford to rent a whole house in the city where they used to live.
And the rent was half what they had paid for their last apartment.
The house had two bedrooms, a finished basement. It was cute,
forties-era, unostentatious in that timid, post-war mode of cautious optimism. An outlook that seemed in line with what was
happening in their lives. That is, their life, together.

It had a massive back yard, with black, needly trees looming
above, squirrels scrambling up and down the trunks. The cat went
insane for them. The cat stayed out all day, stalking squirrels,
stalking birds, stalking crickets. She would bring the crickets
inside, look around to make sure someone was watching, and gulp
down the frantically clicking insects in a kind of performance.
These were the happiest days of the cat's young life.

They bought a barbecue and there was enough room to set up
the croquet wickets in a fairly challenging course that wound its
way around the picnic table and the fire pit. The cat went around
examining each of the wickets like a foreman investigating a construction site. Once they had finished making friends in this new
city, they would invite the friends over for barbecue and croquet,
was the plan.

Anyway. He didn't want to be with her any more.

He had been going to work every day and she had been looking
for work. She had also been looking for friends. She was lonely
and about to get lonelier. She didn't know that. She was trying

to be upbeat. She was being upbeat about everything because he seemed so nervous about the move and his new job and was drinking so much and saying cold and pessimistic things when he did and she was trying to be supportive. She, in her turn, was being cheerful and optimistic. He had a job! They had a house! After more than a decade in their grad-school, low-wage holding pattern, at last real life could begin.

He blurted it out. One night when he was really drunk. He had to get really drunk and blurt it out because all the months of getting drunk and saying cold and pessimistic things hadn't made her want to leave him. All the times he woke her up in the middle of the night to accuse her of sleeping with other people hadn't made her want to leave him. The time he stuck one of his ear-buds into her ear in the middle of the night when she was fast asleep and started blaring music into her head – that didn't do it either.

She had been so worried about him. She was trying to be supportive.

After that, it was nothing but blurtings moving forward. He would blurt, You never say anything! You never said a word all this time. Everything was crumbling around us and you wouldn't say a word.

It wasn't true, exactly. She would say things. She would say she was concerned, the next morning, and ask for reassurance, and he would give it. He would hug her and say everything was fine. But now he was angry at her for believing him, that's what he was angry about. He was angry at her for not reading the signals, not being the grown-up and insisting they both come clean and lay their cards on the table. It had been a standoff of conflict-aversion.

But why did he expect her to be the grown-up all of a sudden? The whole relationship was about no one ever having to be the grown-up.

So they broke up, as the euphemism goes, like ice in the

ever-warming Arctic. They broke at the close of summer. He moved out. He had to start work again in the fall, he needed his head clear, he couldn't be dealing with all this.

He did that thing that men do when they move out – she only learned this afterwards, that men did this thing, she learned it from talking to people like herself – he moved out and took only what he needed, a few items of clothing and toiletries – and left everything else behind. He packed light.

So, here she is now – as we move into the now. She is a sudden caretaker. She oversees The Museum of Us, the place where they were once a couple who lived together, showcasing the physical yin/yang of their cohabitation. His art, her CDs. His rocker, her knitted throw, thrown atop. Her desk, his chair, the former tucked neatly inside the gap beneath the latter.

She oversees his sweaters and his shoes and his one formal suit and his books on Derrida and his books on Agamben and his books on Deleuze and Guattari, and one of the things he blurted that he was so mad at her about, that he hated her for (because – *blurt!* – turned out he'd been hating her much of these final months), was that he couldn't talk about Deleuze and Guattari and all those guys with her. She wasn't keeping up with his research.

Here's the thing, though – this is the thing right here: he comes back whenever he needs something. He does this – just plucks random items from the museum, her museum, to take away. It's getting cold, the weather. He comes back for a couple of sweaters. His winter jacket. His winter coat. His boots. He calls her to make an appointment, then picks up whatever he requires as the cat follows him around, meowing, perplexed, openly haranguing in a way you might expect the woman in this situation to be doing.

They have a massive dining-room table. One of the displays in the museum is a massive dining-room table – that they bought together, specifically to fill the spacious dining room of this very house, a grown-up purchase anticipating guests, feasts, lively evenings playing host/hostess. One day, she gathers all his things and piles them on the dining-room table. No – she doesn't actually pile them. She puts them in boxes. Neatly – folding whatever needs to be folded. Astoundingly, she is still looking after him. In all the years of their couplehood, she never thought she was that kind of woman, in fact they made jokes about her not being that kind of woman, it was a leitmotif of their relationship. But it turned out she'd been that kind of woman all along without either of them quite realising it. It's like with the cellphone bill. He took the cellphone, still in her name, because the house had the landline. So she gets his cellphone bills. Secretarially, she emails him, every time a bill arrives, so he can pay it.

The fact is, she is worried about him even now. She wants him to be okay.

Anyway. He shows up one day to pick up a scarf and his Portable Foucault or whatever. He is shocked when she points him to the table and the boxes. He indicates his shock by smirking – puffing air out from between his puffy lips.

Oh, he says. Are these the 'fuck off' boxes?

His feelings are hurt, you see.

*

Anyway.

The first sign was that he started saying 'whatever' all the time, like his students did. 'The young people today,' they used to joke with one another, as if they didn't really believe they were growing old themselves – as if the idea was laughable. He'd come back from teaching and complain bitterly about colleagues during their brief dinners together, how they were conspiring to destroy him, and it should've occurred to her to wonder how it was he could be feeling such scalding anger and betrayal toward people he had only just met. Anyway, he'd always end these angry soliloquies with this new word. 'Whatever.'

'Anyway,' he'd say. 'Whatever.' And head outside to drink alone on the step.

And sometimes he'd say it like this: 'What. *Ever.*' Gesturing with his hands for emphasis.

Imagine feeling the need to *emphasise* such a word!

*

She is in a city where she doesn't know anyone and the weather is growing cold and the only job she can get is talking to people all over the world who want to write stories. They call her at strange hours to talk, because of the varying time zones at play. A woman named Nancy – a bouncy-haired, 1970s name like the blonde daughter from *Eight Is Enough* or the friend who grew breasts before Margaret in *Are You There God? It's Me, Margaret –* is writing a story about a wife who bashes her cheating husband's head in with a Farberware meat tenderiser. They talk for a long time about Nancy's choice to include the brand name of the murder instrument. On the one hand, it's a little distracting because Nancy never just calls it 'the tenderiser', she doesn't employ any quick euphemisms like, say, 'the little hammer' or something. It's always 'the Farberware meat tenderiser'. It gets repetitive. At the same time it's one of those grounded-in-reality details a creative writing teacher should approve of.

The story is called 'Meat Hammer'. It's meant to be a 'playful' title, says Nancy. 'Meat Hammer' refers to the Farberware tenderiser, of course, but also the husband's penis.

But really all the talk about the Farberware meat tenderiser is just preamble before they can get to a more troublesome aspect of the story. She's not quite sure how to raise this with Nancy. The husband comes across as an unrepentant villain, is the problem.

It's okay for the wife to think of him that way, but the first half of the story is in the husband's point of view. And it's not realistic. He drives around in his sporty car luxuriating in thoughts of his horny, sexy mistress. And these thoughts comprise the most detailed and intricate part of the story – are clearly what Nancy laboured hardest over. The husband and the mistress fuck and bray like goats, and Nancy goes on for paragraphs about the way they grunt and shudder and lie around afterwards laughing 'throatily' and stinking of sweat and genitals. At any moment you expect the floor to belch a sudden, fuming hole into itself and a red, scaly hand to yank them both, still stuck together like a pair of moths, into the waiting furnace below. Meanwhile, his poor dolt of a wife wanders in their lonely yet beautifully appointed home (he's a big moneymaker, this bastard husband), pausing every once in a while to gaze with a certain vacancy at their sweet, oblivious infant son who lies sleeping in his crib, reeking of innocence.

I don't think, she tells Nancy, the guy would actually think this way. I don't think he'd exult in his deception. I think he'd rationalise. He'd want to think of himself as basically a nice guy trying to do the right thing. That's how anyone would want to think of themselves in his situation – we all try to excuse our worst behaviour. Unless he's a sociopath. Is the husband meant to be a sociopath?

I don't know, says Nancy. I just know he needs to get his brain bashed in with a Farberware meat tenderiser.

The conversation stalls. She and Nancy listen to the landline silence that isn't quite silence, but a distant, inexorable hum.

Nancy? she calls across the line after a while. Nancy lives far away, northern BC, Prince Rupert to be exact. Nancy told her at the beginning of the phone call that she is sitting on her front step watching the sun dip into the ocean like 'God's great, shining toe'.

Nancy? she says. It reads like a revenge story. It reads like a revenge *fantasy*. You have to think of the guy as a real person. As someone like you. I know that's hard. You have to put yourself in his shoes. He's not a monster. The story can't be realistic if he's a monster. It would have to be a different kind of story if that were the case. What are your other stories like?

I have no other stories, says Nancy.

I mean what stories have you written before this?

I haven't written any other stories, says Nancy. I only ever write this story, Lynn.

*

Anyway. She keeps getting bills from the cellphone company and every month the unpaid balance at the bottom of the gently phrased corporate reminders gets bigger and bigger. Pretty soon correspondence from the cellphone company becomes less breezy in tone, more standoffish. I thought we were friends, the tone says. But frankly, I don't know where we stand in relation to one another any more. I'm not sure you're the person I once supposed you to be.

Herewith we descend into the squalid, petty domestic details of a North American couple as it disentwines. She emails him about the phone bill. He emails back that he's very busy because of his job and he has a lot of expenses now that they are living apart. A different kind of woman, say a woman in a Nora Ephron movie – someone smart and sassy, vulnerable yet take-no-shit – someone who is *going to be okay* – would have many wry, sardonic things to say at this point in the correspondence. She would sputter, briefly, in disbelief before unleashing a stream of verbal devastation. But this woman, sitting in front of her computer, has no such resources. She has nothing to say. She never says anything.

She starts to email him back after sitting there for twenty minutes. But something starts to burn on the stove and she goes to turn it off. It is, was, a sausage. She realises she has been trying to cook it for the last three hours. She had been thinking: Sausage is easy, you just fry it. If I can just get this sausage cooked I can steam some broccoli and then I will have eaten dinner. But it's been three hours and the sausage plan has failed.

She sits back down and types: You have been using the phone and I have been getting the bills. I sent you the bills and you haven't paid them.

He protests that he hasn't been able to pay the bills because the phone is in her name.

At which point the Nora Ephron character she isn't throws her hands into the air and stalks back and forth across the room, muttering.

She emails back that every time she forwarded him a bill, she explained what he needed to do to pay them – he just had to enter her password. It takes her another hour or so just to compose this short message. Because it's impossible, this exchange. It is lose–lose. She can feel the portrait taking on clarity every time she emails him back. The version of herself, in his eyes, that she is helpless not to become. Portrait of the Artist as Vindictive, Grasping Ex. Clinging to petty grievances. Trying to punish him with this small-time bill-paying bullshit.

There was the thing with the candles for example, which she knows is in his mind as they bat their terse missives back and forth. She'll never be able to live those candles down. But the inner Ephron still insists that she was in the right. She had a collection of pillar candles that she'd bought for the house and artfully placed in the blocked-up hearth of the house's former fireplace. She saw it in an Ikea catalogue and thought it looked nice – you could have a little fireplace even after the official fireplace had long since been taken away. Anyway. He'd asked for a couple of the candles. For his new apartment. He needed, he said, something to 'warm the place up'.

She'd thought: *May you be cold*, and told him no.

Listen, says the Ephron spitfire, those candles weren't cheap. You went out of your way. You were trying to warm *this* goddamn place up, for all the good it did you.

For all the good the Ephron does her. The Ephron does no good, she's just a voice, another impotent voice dictating what one is supposed to do and say in various hackneyed circumstances if one is a contemporary female North American. The break-up is the most hackneyed circumstance of all. How could a life event that popular culture has so diligently undertaken to prepare her for – with its songs, films and prime-time dramedies all to do with love and loss – leave her so completely at sea? She can't send an email. She can't cook a sausage.

Pop culture has only offered comfort in the aftermath. Like that moment a few days ago when music started speaking to her. It started talking to her directly, of heartbreak. All music. Even bad music. Bon Jovi. Roxette. When she had to stop what she was doing and sit on the kitchen floor and listen because suddenly she realised that she was being addressed. Someone else's pain was messaging her own, like an animal locked in a basement, howling away, rousing her own animal to start howling in return.

How would the Ephron spitfire send an email? Sassily! How would she cook a sausage? Fuck the sausage. She'd call up her besties and go out for Martinis and – what, what kind of food signifies rebellion and indulgence to the Ephron? Cheesecake? Fondue? See, she doesn't even know. There is that *Kids in the Hall* sketch where a bunch of office ladies pour a bottle of Irish Cream on top of a cheesecake. But she is lactose intolerant. She can't eat cheesecake, pizza, ice cream, any of the more celebrated foods understood to indicate feminine self-love and self-care and a certain fuck-all-y'all *je ne sais quoi*.

I did it all for love!

But maybe she didn't do it all for love. Perhaps she did it all so she would never have to feel like this.

*

At the end of the summer he came in from the step where he had been drinking. She heard him calling back and forth to some students making their way down the alley. The tone of the conversation was jarring because he sounded cheery and convivial. She could tell from its lazy jocularity the students were drunk too. The two parties greeted each other as friends, because of what they had in common.

He came in and she asked him, Who were you talking to? And he told her: None of your business.

That was the point things had got to and what was terrifying was that she had no idea how. She gulped. She was doing a lot of gulping around then. She said: Why won't you tell me?

It was awful the way asking a completely reasonable question could sound like a screechy harangue when you knew the other person was primed to hear it that way.

Like the nightmare when you find yourself on stage, in a role, expected to know the lines, but you don't. So you wing it, badly, as the audience heaves with resentment – you can feel it as you hear it, the outrage: a low but steady rumble, seething like a human soup.

You don't like me talking to young people, he said.

She repeated the sentence word for word back at him, changing the appropriate pronouns.

Then she sputtered at him for a while. Why wouldn't he tell her who he was talking to? This was madness. What was happening? He refused to say. All he'd say was she didn't like him talking to young people, which was what he had been doing outside, and because of that, he would not tell her.

It was a code, he was talking in code, she realised.

He was telling her, I don't want to owe you anything, any more.

Of myself. Even the smallest things, the most inconsequential courtesies or snippets of experience. From this day forward I begrudge.

He said: When are we going to talk about what's happening with us?

Which was a fair enough question. But by then she was too far gone to reply to a fair question.

*

The next day he was red-eyed sober and all business: We need to ask ourselves why we are together. We haven't ever really sat down and asked ourselves that.

So this was what they were going to pretend, now that it was morning. They would pretend to be analytical. That it was really just a matter of drawing a line down a page and listing reasons, good ones and shitty ones, pros and cons. Taking grown-up, responsible action, something they should have done long ago, that it had been irresponsible and shortsighted of them to put off, like buying RRSPs or mutual funds.

I mean: what do we want? Do we even want the same things? Do we want kids, do we want . . .

We have been together all these years without wanting kids.

You don't care about my work . . . We don't like each other's family.

I like *your* family!

. . . Each other's friends.

Friends? There was no way she was letting him get away with this. *You're* the one who doesn't like your friends. *You're* the one who doesn't like your family. You hate my friends *and* your friends. You hate my family *and* your family.

This faux-masculine, head-versus-heart bullshit he was suddenly trying to pull. *Let's just think about this for a minute.* But his analysis was incoherent. His analysis was incoherent. When they were twenty-five and spending entire days in bed, gleeful at their own poverty, that they literally could not afford to do anything but what they were doing right now at this moment, he never once sat up, the quilt bunching around his jutting hip bones, to declare: *We need to ask ourselves why we are together.*

He said: I know you want kids – you treat the cat like a baby.

She looked up from the cat, whom she happened to be cradling in her arms. There she sat, the first woman in the history of the world to behave in a maternal fashion toward her cat.

Furthermore, she was perfectly content to be cradling the cat and he knew it.

*

So even the sober conversations were bullshit – that's what was so difficult. That's why it got so that every time he tried to talk, drunk or sober, he would open up his mouth and she would hear: I want to get away from you so bad. So bad. So bad, I'm just making up random shit at this point. In all my panic; in my desperation.

It got so she could only gulp: I can't hear this any more, I can't hear this.

And he would say: See? We can't even have a conversation. Because he was the reasonable one.

One night, maybe around day three of what she came to think of as 'the talks', she started whooping. She ran into the down-stairs bedroom and flung the door shut in a panic because she was whooping and she couldn't stop. She heard him upstairs saying, Oh come on – as if to the universe. Finally he came down to find her. He said: You run off and slam the door, come on. We don't need this melodrama. We need to talk. But she was still whooping and he became concerned. He lay down beside her on the bed and they spooned as she whooped. She tried to get words out and explain the situation. I (whoop) can't (whoop) talk. I (whoop) can't (whoop) talk. He rubbed her back.

Because it was astonishing! To wake up in her own home, smack in the middle of this life she had chosen, and find herself despised.

*

She walks into the room she uses for an office. It's flooded with summer daylight. She looks up to see that the roof has blown off the house – at least this side of the house. It must have happened in a storm – a storm she must have slept through, because she never noticed it raging. On the one hand, this can't be a good thing, the roof blowing off the house. She doesn't know how to deal with it, logistically – whom to call, where to begin. On the other hand, it's a beautiful day. Birds and treetops overhead.

She wakes up and the roof is still on. But it's not summer any more, it's winter. Now the task at hand is to get through winter. She'd forgotten about winter, and now it's here, and she has to get through it.

The grocery store is a five-minute walk away, the drugstore is in the same plaza as the grocery store, the liquor store across the street from the drugstore, the gym is ten minutes away, the organic grocery store is about nine – she can stop in there on the way from the gym – yoga is about ten minutes in the opposite direction, except she can't afford yoga any more.

Godzilla Video and DVD, with a rampaging dino glaring down from the roof, about to leap onto traffic sending massive, apocalyptic fissures into the pavement, into which cars teeter, their occupants screaming. About a twelve-minute walk.

So: if you get up in the morning, feed the yowling cat, reply to emails, do some kind of work, you'll look up and it will be about noon.

Then, say, you cook a sausage or an egg and listen to the friendly and sympathetic CBC announcers while you eat it.

Then, maybe, you need groceries. Or you should really go to
the gym. It's important to take care of oneself. Self-care, that is a
woman thing. You read about it in the magazines, you hear about it
on television. It mostly has to do with yogurt and various creams.
Nobody ever talks to men about yogurt. The gym at the university
is free because as far as the university is concerned, you are the
spouse of one of its fine employees, which gets you perks.

Massage and physiotherapy for example. That is, until the
university bureaucracy catches up and this present unreality
receives an administrative gesture of some kind – a form, likely, that will be filled out, deeming things official. And that form,
she reflects, will be all they ever have by way of divorce papers.
Because they never 'made it official' as the saying goes. Which
is why this whole process has been, and will continue to be, so
incredibly easy. Two people live together. One of them leaves. A
year or so later, a university administrator notes a discrepancy,
crosses out a name, pushes up her glasses, decides to grab a coffee. *Fin.*

And if at the gym you have a lingering shower, pull on your
various winter-city layers, wind your scarf around your raised
hood? It could well be three or four o'clock in the afternoon by
that point.

So you might as well stop at the organic market on your way
home, laboriously unwind your scarf, pull down your hood and
contemplate the varieties of wheat-free pasta on offer.

When you ask a woman in an apron which brand is most popular with her customers – realising as the words form that it's your
first conversation of the last couple days – she says: I don't know.
Why don't you ask someone else?

Outside, it is thirty-five below zero Fahrenheit. Time to go
home. Dark. Maybe approaching 5 pm.

Once home, you cook dinner. Maybe a sausage or an egg. We're closing in on evening now. Two glasses of wine tops.

From Godzilla Video, a popular TV series. A man lies on his back in the middle of the jungle. He hears screams, shouts of distress all around him. He opens his eyes, awaking to panic. Looks around. He doesn't know where he is or how he got here.

IN THE REACTOR

Peter Hobbs

When I get back to my desk in the morning the chat box is blinking in the corner of the screen. At the top there's a message from Barbara, my personnel manager. She doesn't write very often. The message reads: *Good Morning, Todd. Let me know when you log in.*

Hi Barbara, I type. *I'm here.*
Hi Todd. Sorry about the weather today. How are you? Not too lonely?
I'm fine. Not lonely.
Bad news then. We've finally cleared a new co-worker for you. She'll be arriving at 2. Can you go meet her?
Sure, Barbara. No problem.

I'm always a bit nervous with new people, but it's been nearly three months since my last co-worker left, and I've been doing the day shift, then having to get up in the night too when an alarm goes off, to check the monitors and see what the problem is. So it'll be nice to relax a bit, and share the responsibility.

I take lunch early, and make an effort to tidy up the work station, smoothing the crumbs onto the floor and giving the screens a polish. I've developed some bad habits, working by myself, and I'm going to have to remember to eat in the snack area, rather than at the control panel. I clean the floor too, then when I'm done I make some tea and sit in the swivel chair to drink it. I nurse the hot mug for a while, enjoying the emptiness around me, while it lasts.

*

I don't get up to the coach bay much. To get there you have to head up to the glass viewing screen, where the tours go to look down over the power plant. There's a visitor centre on the other side of the site, where tourists go in and ask questions and get answers, before going home and turning their heating up to full. Then you leave the control centre and take the long covered corridor which runs like a furrow up the hillside. From the top you get a great view of the plant beneath you, in all its odd and immaculate geometry. It looks like someone has installed a gigantic kitchen appliance of uncertain purpose right in the middle of the moor.

The coach bay is just a lay-by with a shelter and a small bench. I don't get outside much and it's cold waiting under the shelter. I begin to wish I'd brought some tea.

After a while a tiny coach appears on the road and slowly grows to life-size. It parks up beside me, the door exhales and opens, and an enormous rucksack attempts to climb down the steps. From somewhere behind the bag I hear swearing as its owner – I catch a glimpse of some battered jeans and canvas basketball trainers – twice tries to make the last step from the coach. The rucksack, in green army camouflage, keeps getting caught in the doorway. Eventually it shoulders its way through and bobs groundwards, revealing a young woman about half its height. She has a frown crinkled just between her eyebrows, and with a practised concentration she swings the huge bag onto her shoulders, then works at tightening the straps attaching her to it. She blows sharply upwards from the corner of her mouth in an effort to clear a stray strand of hair from in front of her eyes. It resists the attempt.

'Oh hi,' she says. 'Todd? I'm Sally.' She extends her hand and the rucksack lurches forward over her head, as though it were keen to give me a hug. I step back.

'Sorry,' she says.

'Would you like a hand with that?' I ask.

'No thanks,' she says. 'I've got it balanced. Don't want to shift it now.'

I give Sally the tour. I show her the bunk rooms with their camp beds. I point out the TV/VCR and the stack of old movie tapes. I show her the cupboards with the spare blankets, even though it never gets cold enough to need them. I show her the snack area and where we keep the mugs for tea, and the medical cabinet with our supplies of pills. I show her the locker room, and she gratefully dumps her rucksack, swinging it to the ground then attempting to stuff it whole into her locker.

'Sorry,' I say. 'I should have brought you here first.'

'What's with all the lockers? I thought there was only the two of us.'

'Everyone gets a locker.'

'Everyone, huh?' she says.

She has to lean against her rucksack to squeeze the sides in. It's not clear that she'll be able to get it out again.

'What on earth do you have in that?' I ask.

'Oh God, I know. It's like everything. I'm between houses at the moment.'

'Well, at least it's a big locker.'

'Great,' she says. We stand there a moment, until I realise why she's continuing to look at me.

'I'll be outside,' I say.

She comes out after a few minutes, hair tied back in a hasty ponytail. The jeans and trainers have been replaced with scuffed shoes and smart, though creased, black trousers. She gives me an embarrassed grin and tries to smooth out her blouse, but the wrinkles keep regrouping on her. She looks upset.

'There's an iron,' I say.

'It's a nuclear power station,' she says. 'Lots of ions.'

I look at her suspiciously. 'I've only seen the one,' I say.

*

Lastly I show her our control room, and how to operate the CCTV screens. She nods along.

'You didn't show me the reactor,' she says, when I've finished.

We go back up to the viewing screen and I point out the white-painted dome sticking out from behind the control centre. All that's visible is part of the outer concrete shell. Inside that there's a steel containment vessel, then a concrete liner. Beneath that, the reactor chamber. And within that, absolutely nothing, nothing at all.

'How do we get there?'

'We don't,' I say. 'It's not our area. I mean there's a corridor, but it's locked.' I pause, and then add, 'But you know it's empty, right?'

'What do you mean?'

I think about this for a moment. I wonder if I'm not supposed to tell her that none of it is real. That the whole thing, as immaculate and perfect as it all looks, is fake. *Pastiche*, Barbara calls it sometimes. *How's our pastiche today?* The production values, admittedly, are amazing. God only knows how much it all cost, enough for a million wind turbines, I imagine. They've even done out the walls around the reactor in radioactive paint. And the workers on our screens, for the most part, are just drone robots in hazmat suits. A few weeks ago one of them broke down when there was a crowd of tourists at the viewing screen. It slowed in its movements then ground to a halt, taking on the slightest stoop. A yellow-suited figure standing perfectly still in the middle of nowhere, looking as though time had frozen for it. No one seemed to notice, or else they just assumed it was normal, a scientist lost in thought. Maybe they imagined his hair grey and crazy under the suit. I called Helen from Tech Support and when the visitors had gone she sent out a guy to get it running again.

Still, I would have thought that someone would have told me if I wasn't supposed to tell Sally about it. I make an executive decision that this is information she needs to know, in order to do her job. I lower my voice, even though we're the only two people in the control building.

'It's not real,' I say.

'Well, duh. Everyone knows that. But what do you mean, empty?'

I remember the chamber, just a big empty space, seamless and white-tiled, an inside like the outside of an egg. I remember a low, pervasive hum, soft and calming. I remember liking it.

'Empty. You know. Like there's nothing inside it.'

'Did they *tell* you it's empty?'

'It is empty. I saw inside it when I got here.'

'Like, completely empty?'

'Like empty empty.'

'Hm,' she says, her frown nestled back between her eyebrows. It fits there pretty well. I don't meet many girls, it's true, but even allowing for this, I realise that Sally is what many people might describe as attractive.

Later, we sit for a while and watch the CCTV together, and views of clean corridors where robots pretending to be scientists wobble slowly along. I show Sally how to switch to the outside cameras, with their shots of heather and razor wire. There's almost never anything of interest on those cameras, unless a protester has trekked over the moor and got caught in the wire and I have to see if someone's free to go and cut them loose.

'And then what happens to the protester?'

'I don't know. Nothing.'

'Just point him in the right direction and send him home?'
'Sure.'
Sally gives me a look.
'What?' I say.
'Never mind,' she says, and looks around. 'And that's it?' she asks.
'Pretty much.'
'It doesn't sound like fun. You know,' she says, when I don't reply, 'fun?'
'No,' I say. 'It isn't. Shall I make some tea?'
'In a bit,' she says. 'I'm going to take a look around first, get my bearings.'

I'm a little hurt by the implication that my tour wasn't up to scratch, but I know how I am when I'm in a new place, so I leave her to get settled in her own way, and I get back to my desk. I message Barbara to tell her that Sally arrived on time, and then I switch back to the camera screens. I click the mouse and flick between views. It really isn't much fun.

*

Our employers are a group called Low Carbon Fuels, which is a local division of what was once an American corporation, then part of a Middle Eastern consortium, but which is now, as far as I understand, owned by a Chinese conglomerate. I fell into the work by accident: a couple of years ago I was going through a tough time and got into a bit of trouble paying one or two bills, and, eventually, my rent. Due to some things which happened in the past and which I don't want to talk about, going home wasn't an option. So instead I covered for a while by borrowing money and moving things around on credit cards. After a sequence of letters with a colour scheme that shifted rapidly from black to red, and came with an increased use of block fonts and underlining (all of which I carefully recycled), they sent some bailiffs round to seize the only asset I owned, which turned out to be myself.

It was at this point that I learned that my landlord and the companies I owed money to were, coincidentally, separate subsidiaries of what was then the American group that used to run Low Carbon Fuels. We've since negotiated a payments programme to consolidate my existing debts into one easy monthly payment, converting money owed (of which I had none) into time available (of which I had plenty), and handing myself over to the company for that period to do whatever it was they told me to do. It was either that, they said, or they harvested my organs. I have never been good at telling when people are joking, so it seemed best to go along.

And it's turned out to be an arrangement that works well. It's good for me, after all: food and accommodation are provided. I don't have to pay any electricity bills, and most of the time I don't have to talk to anyone either. I like having everything looked after, and not having to worry where my next meal is coming from (it's coming from the snack area). And they like employees they can rely on.

Low Carbon Fuels, of course, due to that accident with the cabinet minister, is well known as one of the companies the government contracts to build fourth-generation nuclear power stations. Except it turns out that it isn't, and what it actually is, is one of the companies the government uses to pretend to build nuclear power stations. Or rather, to build pretend nuclear power stations. After the last incident, they're scattering a few of them around the countryside, much as they did with inflatable tanks in the Second World War. As I understand it, they're built to pretty much the same specification as the real nuclear power stations, so even the people doing the building aren't able to tell whether they're working on a fake or the real thing. No doubt the building of actual nuclear power stations is subcontracted to companies whose names I don't even know, and is done deep underground, well out of harm's way.

I know all this because Barbara told me about it not long before the plant opened, while she was showing me round. It was my first day at work.

'Wow,' I said. And thought it best to add: 'Don't worry. I won't tell anyone.'

'I won't worry,' she said. 'One of the reasons we like you is that we think you're very good at keeping secrets.' She tapped her nose exaggeratedly as she said it.

This seemed like a nice thing to say at the time, and I smiled with her. I've thought about it a bit since then, and the more I think about it, the less nice it seems, but I also think that she's probably right.

Perhaps the strangest thing about this place is that though it's essentially useless, it is apparently more profitable than the real thing. Once when I was talking on the phone to Kurt from Accounting about where I was up to with my graduated payments programme, we got distracted and he ended up showing off about how much work it was running the numbers for a place like this. It turns out that although the facility isn't exactly productive in terms of energy output, due to a liberal spread of solar panels among the roof tiles it barely uses any either. We're a loss-making institution, still, but the sums involved are pretty minor, and are offset by the gift store and the cafe in the visitor centre, both of which bring in good money.

'Hell,' said Kurt, 'if you factor in decommissioning, and the environmental cost of all the radioactive waste you're not producing, that place is a gold mine.'

*

Sally settles in well. She's happy with the night shift, and it turns out she likes tea (though she takes it with too much sugar), which is good because I structure my day around regular tea breaks. We get into a routine of meeting for breakfast (dinner, for her) and then again for dinner (her breakfast). Sometimes she comes to fetch me before she finishes her shift, when I'm still waking up, so we have time to hang out before I take over.

'Hey kid,' she says, putting a mug of tea by my bunk. 'Sleeping?'

This is a trick question, because the only honest answer is no.

'Well, up and atom,' she says.

Then after we've chatted for a while she settles into bed and starts watching movies. It helps her unwind, she says, though there's not a great deal to get wound up by. I think the thing with Sally is that she doesn't much like being alone, and the TV helps. It occurs to me that this may not be the best job for her in the long term, but that's not something I can control, so I don't see the point in mentioning it.

'So how long since the last guy left?' she asks, one morning.

I shrug. 'A couple of months,' I say. It is eighty-seven days and nineteen hours. Not that I've been counting, but some events stick in your mind.

'He just quit, did he?'

I give her a look.

'Sorry,' she says. 'Not my business. But you've been all by yourself since then?'

'Yeah.'

'Wow. No days off?'

'I can't really afford to take them. There's nothing to do, anyway. I'd probably just end up watching the screens.'

'Wow,' she says again. 'I'd hate to be here by myself.'

'There are worse things.'

'Not for me,' she says. 'Leave me here for a week on my own

and I'd go crazy. Seriously. You'd find me sleeping with the worker drones or something.'

For me it's the other way around. I miss the feeling of knowing that there's no one else near. I like Sally's company, but there are times when I'd like to be able to choose to be without it. Sally seems to need a lot of conversation to feel at home, and though I do my best to accommodate her, occasionally it's a struggle. She has picked up on this.

'Warning,' she says sometimes, when she wakes me up with a mug of tea, 'chat mode fully operational. Prepare to engage.'

One day, when the talking gets too much for me, I tell Sally I'll be back in a few minutes and I wander up to the glass viewing walkway. I look down over the power plant. The morning is murky and grey, but the buildings shine chemical bright. In the gloom behind them are the familiar shapes of the cooling towers, barely visible in the blurring dark. Then out there beyond them only the open moor, then the sombre sea. It's the saddest place, really; even I can feel that, and I like working here.

I stay there until I've restored some of my solitude, then mooch on back to the control room. Sally's shift is over, but she's still staring at her screen, a small notepad cupped in her hand and a frown on her face. The instant she sees me she puts the notebook down and starts chatting in my direction. I like hanging out with her, but I wish she'd talk a little less, and smile a bit more.

Sally stays at her monitor all day. She doesn't seem to need as much sleep as I like to get, but I know from experience that back-to-back shifts like this aren't healthy. You have to pace yourself, or you won't last. I start to worry that perhaps she's already bored in the job. During my break I go to the snack area and get two mugs of tea. She empties three sachets of sugar into hers, plays around with a fourth in her hands while we talk, and then twists that open too and stirs it into the tea. We drink our tea and compare our pills. They look the same, which is reassuring. One of the first things I was made to sign was some kind of indemnification form. I worry about that. I realise that they have to tweak the area's health statistics – to provide some evidence of increased rates of leukaemia – but I always assumed they'd just fiddle the statistics, rather than the actual rates of leukaemia. Now I'm not so sure. I wonder if there's a list somewhere with leukaemia quotas waiting to be filled.

'What do you think they are?' I ask her.

Sally takes one and instead of swallowing it whole as usual, bites the pill in half. She crunches it between her teeth.

'Sugar,' she says, and grins. 'Definitely.' She eats the other half.

*

A few days later the chat box pops up on my screen with a message from Barbara. The message reads:

Good morning, Todd! I hope the weather isn't getting you down. How are things working out with Sally?

I think about this for a while, then I write:

Sally is great. She's very professional and a pleasure to work with. We're getting along great.

I consider writing that she doesn't make the tea as often as I do, but I'm not sure they'll get that I'm joking. I wouldn't want them to take it seriously and fire her for not making the tea.

It occurs to me that my problem with establishing whether someone is joking or not might be because I don't have a very good sense of humour. I'm not sure how easy it would be to tell.

I don't know why I lied for Sally. It's true that she's mostly a pleasure to work with, but I don't follow everything she says. Last night I had some music playing quietly on the computer when she arrived for her shift.

'Is that radio active?' she asked.

'It's just the computer,' I said. 'I'll turn it off.'

'Well, let's not fall out over it,' she said.

I stared at her.

'Oh, brother,' she said.

I kept out of her way for the rest of the evening.

Also, I don't think she's very professional at all. She should be spending most of her time in the control room, sitting at her desk and watching the screens, or if I'm there with her, perhaps chatting a little about what the weather is like outside. In fact what she's spending most of her time doing is wandering the corridors with a Geiger counter in her hands. I'm not sure where she found the Geiger counter, because I don't remember there being any Geiger counters. I assume she brought it with her, in her rucksack. She's been taking long walks through the corridors over near the reactor. I've warned her about the radioactive paint, but she's having none of it.

She waves her Geiger counter at me and it makes a disturbing, lurching, clickety wheeze.

'Paint,' she says. 'Sure.'

*

A week or so later I roll up for my shift and there's no sign of Sally, just a yellow Post-it stuck on my screen with a note that says: *Gone fission*. I peel it carefully off the screen so I can get on with work, and stick it to one side.

Two hours later I look at it again, and my heart does an odd double jump of alarm.

In the corridor, the door leading towards the reactor chamber is ajar. It doesn't seem to have been forced, merely unlocked, and I'm pretty sure that Sally doesn't have the keys, because I have the keys. I pause at the door. I've always been able to go through if I wanted, but I've never wanted to. After all, I can always watch it on the monitor. I think about how it looks on the screen, grey and empty, and I think about how it will look with me walking down it. It seems a shame that it will be the most excitement the corridor has seen for ages, and there'll be no one watching.

'Sally?' I call down the corridor. The sound makes a thin echo, dying as it goes. I scuttle after it.

At the end of the corridor, the steel door to the reactor chamber is thickly, defiantly shut.

'Sally?'

There is a long silence and I'm about to give up and go. Then a muffled voice comes from the other side of the door. 'What?' it says.

'It's me. Hey. Open the door.'

'No.'

She sounds grumpy, as though she's sulking.

'I told you it was empty.'

'Go away,' she says.

I think about this for a moment. It seems a good suggestion. I turn round to leave three times, but each time I feel that I'm somehow letting her down. But I can't quite work out how to express this, and I don't think my concern is fully communicated by what eventually comes out.

'What am I supposed to do?' I say.

'Do whatever it is you usually do. What do I care?'

There is a pause.

'You could make me a cup of tea,' she says.

I walk back through the corridors to the snack area. The air feels unnaturally warm. I wonder if there's a problem with the heating, if I need to call Debbie in Maintenance. I think it over as I make the tea. I put extra sugar in Sally's. It sounded like she needed it.

I bang on the reactor door. There's no reply.

'I'm leaving your tea here,' I call. 'Don't let it go cold.'

I wait a moment, and then retreat the way I came. If I had a tail, it would be curled between my legs.

I spend the rest of the day watching the cameras showing the door to the reactor chamber. I bite my nails down until the soft flesh underneath starts to ache. Eventually the door opens and Sally comes out, sloping sadly along the corridor, her mug dangling loosely from one finger. She shuts the doors behind her, and tries them to check they're locked. I give a sigh of relief, exaggerated- ly loud, as though just by hearing it I'll feel twice as reassured. Then, so Sally doesn't catch me looking at the screens where she's been, I switch to watch outside. Things are quiet. The heather ruffles in the wind. A grouse flies by.

What seems like a long time passes and Sally doesn't return to the control centre. I can't find her on the screens so I get two teas from the snack area, load one up with sugar, then head off to look for her. I check her bunk, to see if she's gone back to bed, but she's not there. I finally find her sitting on a bench by the glass viewing screen, staring sadly at the work area. I give her the tea, which has gone cold. She doesn't seem to mind.

'What are you doing?' I say.

She doesn't reply for a while, but then makes a visible effort to perk herself up and points down to the laboratories below.

'I'm giving the robots names. Listen,' she says, 'that one is John, and the one over there that's listing slightly is Don. And the fellow in the corner is Ron. Which one do you think we should elect leader?'

I start to point to Don, mostly out of sympathy.

'Think about it,' she says. I lower my hand. I try to furrow my brow the way she does.

I think about it for a long time, until it comes to me.

'We should elect Ron,' I say.

I glance at her, and for a moment it looks like there's a smile playing around her lips, but she hides it quickly behind the edge of her cup so that I can't tell any more.

'Attaboy,' she says, quietly.

*

Some time early the next morning I'm reminded how small the bunks are, and that they are in fact only big enough for one person, when Sally climbs into bed with me.

'Budge up,' she says. 'It's you or the robots.'

I shuffle as far as I can to one side, but it's still a tight fit keeping us both under the blanket, and we're pressed pretty closely together. Her skin holds a faint sweet smell of perfume and sweat. When I work up a bit of courage I move my hand so it's resting on her bare arm. I marvel at the heat.

'You're really warm,' I say.

But Sally, unusually, doesn't seem to be in the mood for conversation. She squirms around, and I'm worried she's going to push me out of the bed, so that I'll have to go and sleep somewhere else. As I try to keep my place in the bunk I grab hold of something soft and warm, and I realise that a lot of her squirming was so that she could take off her pyjamas. At this point it occurs to me that she should probably still be on her shift, and I'm about to mention it when she leans over to nuzzle her forehead against the side of mine, and then sticks her tongue inside my ear. After that I get so distracted I forget to bring it up.

*

When I get up for my shift the next day Sally is sleeping in her own bunk. I stand beside her for a while, wondering if I should say something, but she stays unhelpfully asleep, and eventually I have to go to start my shift.

Beyond saying hi, Sally ignores me for the next two days. In the morning when she finishes her shift she goes straight to her own bunk. I stay in my blankets for longer than I usually do, hopeful, but all that happens is that my shift starts without me and I begin to feel guilty about it. In her bunk, Sally snores, convincingly.

Every time I see her in the day and go to talk to her she gives me a grin as though she's pleased to see me, and then walks away before I get to her. The first time it happens I follow her, thinking that maybe she's heading back to the bunks, but she just makes a big loop around the control centre and ends up right back where she'd been. As I trot in after her she is already sitting at her monitor looking somehow pleased with herself and I don't know what to say.

On the afternoon of the second day, I'm at my desk flicking through the monitors when I see Sally standing in one of the drone-patrolled corridors near the laboratories, waving patiently at the camera, waiting for me to see her. I'm a little surprised to see her there, as that corridor is usually locked, and I thought she was still in bed. I focus the camera on her and zoom in a bit, and she sees the lens move and stops waving. Then she turns her back to me and slowly, carefully, starts to undress.

She's down to her underwear when a hazmat-suit-clad robot whirs up behind her and pauses, detecting something in its path. Sally turns around and mouths an exaggerated 'oh' to the camera, putting her little finger to her lips. She starts to step out of its way, but at the last minute just bends forward to pick up her clothes, so that the drone gently bumps into her. She slips out of the rest of

the clothes, and leans backwards against the robot's yellow rubber suit, moving her hips against it, closing her eyes and reaching
back behind her with one arm. Then she glances at the camera
again, gives it a wild and frankly terrifying grin, turns round to
face the machine and starts to climb it.

The drone just stands there and takes it. I don't think it's been
programmed for this. I have some sympathy. My hands hover over
the keyboard, not knowing whether to switch to a different monitor. After a while I take them away. I watch for quite a while.
When Sally walks into the control room later, smirking, I don't
know where to look.

*

For a couple of days after that everything is all right and we have
a good time. We bring our sandwiches from the snack area and eat
them together while watching the screens, scattering crumbs over
the surfaces. Sally takes her turn making the tea, and remembers
not to put too much sugar into mine. When we take our pills I
make her laugh by cramming as many as I can into my mouth
and then trying to talk to her, pretending to be unaware that my
mouth's full. When things are quiet, we squeeze together in one
bunk and watch old movies on the VCR.

'Sally?' I say one evening, when we're curled up in blankets.
We're naked and sleepy, a single, glowing heat. Our skins are
pressed so closely together I'm no longer sure what is me and
what is her. Outside there's a storm blowing, black and wild. The
heather is whipping in the wind, and the wind is howling at the
windows.

'Yeah?'

'What did you do?'

'What do you mean, do?'

'To get sent here, I mean.'

'I did the usual thing. I applied.'

My mind bends in a way it wasn't designed for. 'People apply?' I say.

'Sure,' she says. After a few seconds she looks back at me with that frown on her face and says: 'Wait. What did you do?'

*

'That's all wrong,' she says, shaking her head firmly. 'They can't do that.'

I shrug.

'It's bonded labour,' she says. 'That's practically slavery.'

'It's kind of my own fault,' I say.

'It's completely out of order.'

'It's not, really. You don't have to be so critical.'

'Oh, I'm supercritical,' she says, quickly. 'You have to be.'

'What?' I say. 'Why?'

'You need supercriticality,' she says, extra slowly, 'to achieve fission.'

I gape at her. Her forehead crinkles.

'Did you, like, study any science at all?' she asks.

'It wasn't my best subject,' I say, defensively.

*

When I wake the next morning, something feels wrong. I lie in my bunk for a while, hoping that Sally will come in to wake me and everything will be okay, but Sally doesn't come. The unease coalesces as I doze, almost forming into nightmare, but just as I'm on its threshold something pulls me away, and I lie with my eyes open, feeling terrible. Eventually I become aware of a distant beeping sound. I'm not sure how long it's been sounding. I get up, get dressed and trace the beeping to the control room. There's a message from Barbara on my computer, marked urgent. The beeping stops when I click on it.

Good morning, Todd, it says. *I hope you're enjoying the good weather. Please reacquaint yourself with the contents of the manual 'In Case of Nuclear Excursion'.*

I think about this for a moment. I remember the manual. Barbara pointed it out when I started work here, though I never read it, just put it away in a drawer somewhere. I always assumed it was a prop. I always thought it was a joke related to the holidays I don't take.

The manual is where I left it. It begins: *In case of critical excursion, do not under any circumstances attempt to leave the facility. Ensure all bulkheads are firmly closed, then proceed to your station.* What the manual omits to mention is how I'm supposed to know if there has been a critical excursion. Presumably something will light up on the control panel, but it would be nice to be clear. I go to check, but there are no new lights, and I decide that reading the manual is probably just a precautionary measure. The first thing to do is to find Sally.

I look everywhere twice before I'm sure that Sally has locked herself in the reactor again. The thought of it makes me uncomfortable, and oddly sad, and that sensation runs in circles around my chest until I realise that I'm starting to panic. It's the exact same feeling I used to get when I had all that debt and I'd wake in a sweat with something twisting inside of me. I count back the days since Sally arrived, and get to twenty-nine. It seems an appallingly low number. How did everything go so wrong so quickly?

I make some tea to calm myself down. I drink it while it's still hot and it burns my tongue, but the warmth feels good in my throat. Then I fiddle with a panel in one of the cupboards until it comes off in my hand. From a hook behind it I take the emergency key, and then I head over to the reactor chamber, my heart listing slightly in my chest.

The reactor chamber is empty. It's round and white and bright, with no sign of Sally. There's just the white-tiled interior, interrupted only by a single black tile in the centre of the floor. I go over to take a look.

The single black tile turns out to be a white tile that has been removed and placed neatly on the tile next to it. The black tile is an opening in the floor. Just below the rim is the top of a ladder. A breeze, slight and sleepily warm, breathes from it. My foot nudges against something on the ground and I bend down to find, neatly camouflaged, an empty white mug. It's cold to the touch. I look behind me, back to the door. I look at the mug. Then I take a few deep breaths and I lean over and look down the hole.

*

My trainers ring softly on the metal ladder, then pad down onto an invisible floor. It's dark at the bottom, the black filtered by a faint red glow. It takes my eyes a while to adjust, and when they do I can just about make out that I'm standing in a small alcove, with the ladder behind me and the outline of a door on the wall in front of me. My foot nudges against something again, and on the floor I find Sally's basketball trainers, the laces pulled loose, their cloth tongues lolling. Beside them, in a neat row, are her Geiger counter, a torch, and what turns out to be a small, cloth-wrapped case with tools inside. I don't recognise the tools, but it seems plausible that they might just be the kind – slender, pointy and precise – that would fit inside locks.

I stand and look at the door, which avoids my gaze. I run my hands along it at the level where the handle should be, but the surface is smooth. I give it a push, but the door continues to ignore me, and I stop pushing.

After a while I realise that the red light warming the area is coming from a small LED in the ceiling. I look up at it and try to make out if it belongs to a camera. If it does, it wouldn't be one of mine, or else I'd recognise the place I was standing in. My brain eventually remembers I have Sally's torch, and with it I can see that there is indeed a concealed lens there. I stare at it a moment, stupidly, and it stares back. It doesn't blink. I wonder if the light is good enough for whoever is watching to see through my eyes, and along the nerves into my core. Deep inside, my heart is beginning a slow decay.

I look away. I look back. Then I give the camera a wave and a thumbs-up, collect up Sally's things and climb back out. I put everything away as tidily as I can in her locker, though I still need to lean against the door to get it shut. I avoid looking at the other lockers. There are a lot of them, it's true, but if we carry on at this rate we're going to need some more.

Back in the control room I begin to write an incident report to send to Barbara. I don't feel very good about it, and have to stop three times to make myself some tea, but eventually I get it done. Then I file a final work evaluation on Sally, giving her the highest marks I can. The numbers may get queried by Personnel, but I'm a bit past that point. After that I don't feel very well at all, and have to lie down for a while.

When I get back to my desk the chat box is blinking in the corner of my screen. Barbara is waiting for me to log in.

Hi, Todd. Sorry Sally didn't work out. I know you were getting on well.

That's okay.

Well, we feel bad about it. Like we let you down a bit, recruitment-wise.

That's okay.

You'll be all right on your own again for a while?

I'll be all right.

Chin up, she types. *The weather should be picking up soon.*

Barbara logs off, and I close the chat box. There's a warning light flashing on the control panel. Something has got stuck on the barbed wire again, and I'll have to check to see if it's a sheep, or a protester, and then find out if someone's free to go and cut them loose.

BRUNHILDA IN LOVE

Taiye Selasi

Halfway through the spa detox Brunhilda takes a lover.

This comes as a shock to all of us, including Brunhilda herself.

To state the plainly obvious: Brunhilda is not attractive. Realistically (if not statistically) speaking, few Brunhildas are. The name is too heavy, too thick in the waist. A sign of things to come. The things that came were: childhood teasing, weak-willed parents, excellent grades, a pitying husband, an underage mistress, a quick and expected divorce. On the bright side the weak-willed will often excel in the dullest of corporate contexts and Brunhilda's parents willed her all they'd saved before they died.

Quiet people. Suburban Germans. Thrifty, self-denying. Every time they saved some cash they bought a small apartment. One in Florence, two in Shoreditch, four in former East Berlin, together worth the kind of sum that lightens psychic loads. Even without the life insurance payout she'd have quit her job and booked the three-month detox at Espace Henri Chenot. But Brunhilda's parents, bless their hearts, died instantly in Munich when a tower crane collapsed: a painless, profitable way to go.

Hundreds injured, two struck dead.

Apology accepted.

In life they'd left her to fend for herself. In death they made amends.

At forty Brunhilda is single, childless, rich and overweight. For five and a half of their six years of marriage, Dirk was chubby too. Then, at his company's annual retreat, he met a personal trainer. Heiko is this trainer's name. A veritable Adonis. Sprayed gold skin and dyed gold hair and gleaming muscles carved from marble, born and raised in Elmau, smelling still of fresh-chopped wood. That year, due to a global recession, the corporate retreat was not on Kos but rather at the luxe hotel, ten minutes from Dirk's office, where Heiko taught a morning dance-cum-fitness class called 'Rise and Shake!' adapted from his disco days to suit his clientele. Who's to say why Heiko took an instant shine to shaken Dirk and offered him free access to the hotel gym on weekdays? Monday, Wednesday and Friday evenings, faithfully, Dirk lifted weights, returning home aglow with joy, a gleaming suckling pig.

Brunhilda thought, and delighted to think, that Dirk was in the closet; that her rapidly shrinking husband had become his trainer's lover. It aroused her intensely to picture this, Dirk's pale and fleshy buttocks offered up like heaping mounds of clotted cream on fork-split scones. She'd always preferred (and still prefers) gay male porn to other genres. She particularly likes the nomenclature: Bear, Twink, Daddy, Verbal, Dominant. Such meticulous categorisation. As if, devoting his life to research, a taxonomist had classified all sexual fantasies, pinning them down like butterflies.

'Verbal Daddy' is Brunhilda's favourite. In truth, she doesn't know why. She never felt anything close to lust either for or from her actual father, a kind but physically distant man who rarely hugged or kissed her. The only time she ever felt his fingers on her body was the time he placed her sixteenth birthday gift around her neck.

'Almost . . .' he'd murmured, standing behind her struggling to do the necklace up. (Her father always murmured, as if shamed by making noise.) Her mother was waiting in front of them beaming and holding a camera, obscuring her face, while recently blown-out candles wept their wax tears on the cake. As Brunhilda had no friends at school apart from one young teacher, Mr

Engel, who taught classics and wore tweed suits every day, the party was small: just the dinner at home for her and her parents and Fido their cat. She'd invited Mr Engel but, surprisingly, he'd declined.

Like her, Mr Engel had no friends. His colleagues found him awkward. Nervously huddled and painfully shy; it pained them to engage him. Brunhilda often ate lunch in his classroom, the two of them chewing and reading in silence. She liked the soft sound of their turning their pages, waves lapping shore or else breeze stroking leaves. 'But a male teacher's attending a female student's sweet sixteen', he'd said, 'might raise some awkward questions.' Brunhilda said she understood. There was the awkward question of why said student had no better options than said teacher: skinny, fidgety, a sad old man at thirty years old. (When, years later, she learned that Mr Engel, a raging paedophile, had been sent to prison she wasn't stunned but palpably offended. On all those sunless afternoons he'd never paused to lower Ovid, lift his gaze and leer from where he sat, across the room. She had, and often, glancing up to see if he was glancing too. No. Just nibbling crackers, snowing crumbs on his tweed coat.)

Bittersweet sixteen. Fido sleeping. Mother beaming. Candles weeping. A gift of atypic extravagance from her penny-pinching parents. Brunhilda opened the velvet box and shyly drew the necklace up: a white gold chain from which hung, catching light, a diamond heart. Her mother wanted a Polaroid. Her father could not close the clasp. Brunhilda touched her chin to her chest as if to give him room. Between curtains of hair she closed her eyes and prayed that he would fumble on, that the magical tingling at the back of her neck would carry on for hours. He succeeded in seconds then reached around to nudge the pendant into place, his fingertips brushing the broad expanse above her heavy breasts. '*Alles gut*,' he murmured as he drew his fumbling fingers back.

'Look up, let me see,' her mother said. 'Oh darling, why are you crying?'

Whatever its root this penchant for the Verbal Daddy category really can't be traced to anything her father ever did. In thirty-nine years she never saw him touch her mother lustfully, nor she him for that matter. Here again she couldn't say why. Both were plain- and pleasant-faced, much slimmer than Brunhilda is, the sort of harmless couple found in medical brochures. Each one seemed to like the other. They often went on nature walks. They called each other *Schatzi* and they rarely disagreed. But she never saw them clasping hands, barged in to find them nude in bed or watched her father's fingers idly graze her mother's ass. She'd presume they were asexuals if not for knowing better – for the world presumes the same of her and look how much she masturbates.

Her favourite position is prone in bed, a toilet roll between her legs. The roll must be approximately seven-eighths finished, the width of a so-called Monster Cock. She'd mastered the method at fourteen years old, having previously used her pillow, faithfully, bunching it up in a ball at her groin and grinding down against it. The problems were two. The pillow was soft and she, its lover, heavy. Her mother also wondered at the faint stains on the case. Like an underage mistress the toilet roll was soft yet firm, would hold its form, and when it lost its usefulness could simply be discarded. In six years Dirk never thought to ask why the cardboard cylinders never showed brown, why they always vanished, an eighth left to go, replaced by fresh and fluffy ones.

Verbal Daddies and toilet rolls.

Brunhilda's chest of secret joys.

To which at the end of her sexless marriage she added: homosexual husband.

Imagining Dirk on his hair-dusted back in a happy baby yoga pose, his small cock resting sweetly on his stomach, out of use;

imagining Heiko plunging in, his buttocks taut (from her bird's eye view), his broad back flexed and rippling – made Brunhilda come in seconds. The more explicitly violent the fantasies were – the harder the thrusts, the louder the squeals – the more aroused Brunhilda became. Soon she abandoned her laptop. She no longer needed the visual aid and so became more mobile. She masturbated madly whenever alone and once while Dirk was sleeping. If after she came she always felt an overwhelming flood of guilt, she couldn't let the sex scene go; it felt so thoroughly *right*. At last her husband's uselessness – his passivity, his inferiority, his fundamental weakness as a man, his flab – had been put to good use.

Brunhilda had never been happier. Dirk had never been happier. A balance had entered their daily lives, the tenderness born of guilt. Couples keeping secrets are remarkably affectionate ('Would you like a bit more clotted cream on your fork-split scone, my love?'). Brunhilda was keeping two secrets, mind: the one the sexual fantasy, the other the peace and the sense of relief that she felt when she thought *Dirk is gay!* This was a secret she kept from herself. *Why else had he married her?*

Brunhilda is brilliant and wickedly funny and told, as heavy women are, what lovely skin and hair she has – but what was this to Dirk? There are men who value intellectual agility over physical attractiveness. In Brunhilda's experience such men are unusual and unusually intelligent. To recognise brilliance is easy. To enjoy it requires native brilliance. As Dirk has none, Brunhilda never knew why he'd proposed. Her reasons for accepting were clear enough. He loved her repetitive cooking. He kissed her goodnight on the back of the neck. He loved his repetitive job. To know *his* reason finally and to relish it in secret she now felt for him a love-like blend of loyalty and pity.

And so to the violent sex scene Brunhilda added her own healing hands: cradling Dirk's head in her lap as he squealed, pinned and wriggling with pleasure. Heiko, thrusting athletically, was not her competitor but her avatar. Through his perfect body flowed her scorn, her pudgy hands her love.

Never had she felt such honesty. Such equilibrium. Such euphoria. Believing Dirk in love with Heiko, Brunhilda fell in love with both. We can imagine, then, what she must have felt when Dirk came home one Wednesday night and kissed her neck then backed away and said to her, 'I'm leaving.'

Brunhilda was frying pork chops in their American-style kitchen, meaning the sound of sizzling onions rather drowned out Dirk's announcement. When she heard again, 'I'm leaving,' she said, 'Good. Please buy a tannic red. And try to be back within thirty minutes? The chops are better warm.'

'No, I mean I'm leaving you,' said Dirk, now sweating badly. He rested his bag on the island counter but didn't remove his coat. 'I'm leaving you for Heiko.'

Brunhilda laughed. 'What fun! At last.'

Dirk was virtually dripping wet. Brunhilda was facing the stove. He raised his remarkably high-pitched voice. 'I'm leaving you, I said!'

'I heard you, dear.' She wiped her hands. 'I'm happy for you both. May I just ask: do you plan to leave me after dinner or before?' As we said, Brunhilda is funny. But Dirk lacks native brilliance. He looked at her, sweating and blinking and red, a lost and bobbing apple.

'I'm in love with Heike,' he blurted out and still Brunhilda heard *Heiko*. A timer went off. She lowered the flame. The kitchen fell suddenly quiet. 'I'm in love with Heike.' Dirk started to cry.

'Who on earth is Heike?'

Heike is a hotel receptionist, a deep tissue masseuse, and Heiko's best friend. Heike is gay. Dirk, alas, is not.

Two days later Dirk moved out. He had lost ten kilos. He left the clothes that did not fit. Months later they divorced. Three weeks after her parents staged their apology-death in Munich, Heike left Dirk for an ageing masseur and Brunhilda made haste for Merano.

THE CLOSING DATE

Alexander MacLeod

This happened not far from where we are now. The Bide-a-While is still there, but when the whole story came out – or at least most of it – they had to change the name. The place closed down for a couple of months before they staged a grand reopening as part of the larger Sleep Station chain. Now the sign is blue instead of faded orange and there are stars and moons around the words, but from the outside it looks like business is about the same. Long-haul truckers and highway work crews, salespeople with samples in their trunks, contractors on short-term jobs that have to be done right here and right now. All the in-betweeners: they still need beds. They still need places to rest when they are away from home, and this building, with its single storey of a dozen rooms in a line, can still do the job. Sheets and towels are changed and there is a person who will pluck unsightly dark hairs from the white porcelain sinks. Lipstick smudges and grey fingerprints are wiped away and all the glasses are rinsed and rewrapped in a special kind of paper that promises sterilising power. Waste baskets emptied, carpets vacuumed, tiny soaps and shampoos restocked. The stubborn red circle of rust around the bathtub drain is scrubbed and scrubbed again. The last guest leaves just before the next guest arrives and different credit cards are swiped. A rotating privacy is what they sell and we were part of the cycle for a little while. In and then out.

We only stayed because it was cheap – half the cost of the Super 8 or the Quality Suites down the street – and because it was exactly where we needed it to be: two blocks away from the house we had just bought, the permanent home we moved into two days later. This was back at the very start of everything for us, when this was a new city and we'd just got the new jobs and almost a new set of lives or at least a new strategy for the way things were going to be. Our daughter, Lila, was four years old and Maddy was seven months along and nearly ready to go with Jack. Between these two pregnancies we'd been through one very sad, very late miscarriage and we were trying to be extra careful this time. No sudden swervings, no need to strain unnecessarily. We made a detailed but not very ambitious plan for our move and the Bide-a-While was part of it. Two double beds, a mini-fridge and a coffee maker for $63 a night. After the Montreal apartment had been cleared, we were going to drive to Halifax and stay in the motel for a couple of days while we waited for the movers to arrive. Our closing date, the moment of the official transfer, had been locked in for months and June 1st was stamped on all our documents, but before the house came to us, we were going to pause and reset. We wanted to be ready for the change.

I think everyone has spent at least one night in a place like the Bide-a-While. When we were kids, my parents used to search for exactly this kind of no-nonsense motel, a bargain option with drive-up parking where they might let us swim in an unsupervised, unheated outdoor pool, twenty feet away from the trucks and the steady stream of highway traffic. There were five children in our family and whenever they could find them, my parents would ask for adjoining rooms. The owner would hand over this strange extra key – usually chained to an oversized block of wood or a thick piece of plastic – and we'd get to turn the secret silver doorknobs and then run back and forth through that opening in the wall that normally stays sealed to most people.

The paired rooms were identical but opposite, mirrored images, with four beds pushed against the two outside walls. We'd burn off whatever energy we had left jumping across the chasm from one bed to the next and our parents would let us stay up late to watch strange TV in one room while they went across to the other side together. They might bring along a six-pack or a bottle of wine and maybe a bag of chips or some leftover pizza. After half an hour, one of them would get up and quietly close the door on us. I remember the click. We'd be alone, together with just ourselves but separated from them, for maybe an hour before they'd come back and we'd split up again along different lines. A couple of the children would sleep on one side with Mom and a couple of others in the next room with Dad.

When the news story came out, pictures of the motel were everywhere. Police cars and flashing lights, caution tape and pylons, men in hazmat suits entering and leaving the mobile forensic unit. It was what you'd expect, the rerun of a show you have already seen. Half a dozen satellite trucks pulled into the parking lot for that first week and a line of people of different races, all with perfect hair, reported live for the national shows. It ran in the papers for months, almost a full year. For a little while, it felt like the whole world was paying attention – nothing animates us more than a dramatic loss of life – but for Maddy and me, there was always something extra in it. The story held us differently and claimed us as characters though we didn't want those roles; it saved room in its plot for our lives. Like walking through a thick fog at street level, the story surrounded us completely and we had to breathe it in. At breakfast, over cereal and orange juice, we'd watch the shows and read, consuming something much higher than the recommended daily allowance of photographs of the victims, accounts of their sad backgrounds, editorials, in-depth analyses, searches for explanation.

*

The murderer, as everybody now knows, ran a plumbing business. His truck was already there, parked in front of room 107, when we pulled in the first time. On the driver's side door, he had a rectangular magnetic sign that could be slapped on or peeled off as the truck moved back and forth between its work life and its other life. There was a basic clip-art icon of a bucket catching five separate drops and underneath it said, 'Want it done right? Call 902-454-7111'.

We didn't see him at all that evening as we unloaded our bags and our toaster and kettle, our box of road food. Juice and bananas and bread and marble cheese and crackers. This was the night of May 30th. It is important to keep the dates right and put everything in proper order. The next day was the 31st. At about eight thirty in the morning we left our rooms at the same time: Maddy and Lila and the murderer and me. We closed our side-by-side doors and entered the outside world at exactly the same moment.

We had errands to run and forms that needed to be filled out. Insurance, and a trip to the lawyer's office and then back to the realtor again and the utilities and the phone. The list was com- plicated and disjointed – more work than we had expected – but every separate task needed a separate line put through it.

Maddy was hustling Lila towards the back seat on the pas- senger side. I can see it exactly: her perfect four-year-old sum- mer clothes, the dress and the sandals and the floppy hat. There were yellow straps tied in bows over Lila's shoulders and a little puff, an extra floof of air in the skirt that made it stick out away from her legs. The shoes had red flowers on the toes and her skin was still shining and greasy from the heavy dose of spray-on sun- screen we had just applied.

As Maddy and Lila passed by the murderer, he smiled and held out his right hand for a high five and Lila gave it to him hard.

He wore blue cargo pants with lots of pockets and a grey tucked-in shirt with more pockets on the chest. In his left hand, I remember, he was carrying some needle-nose pliers and he had a roll of duct tape hanging on his wrist like a bracelet. Again, this was the morning of the 31st. We've been over it. There was nothing strange about the way he walked out of that room, nothing strange about the way he handled these objects. He opened his door and threw the tools into the cab and when he turned around he saw Lila still standing there holding out her hand for the return high five. He gave it back right away.

'Have a good one, Little Miss Lady,' he said. And he looked over the roof of the car and smiled at me and nodded his head. I unlocked my door and pushed the automatic button that opened up everything else. I watched him bring his right hand up to his nose and sniff. Then he made a big show of raising his eyebrows and shaking his loose fingers and pretending like the powerful tropical sunscreen smell burned his nostrils.

'Hole-lee coconut!' he said, and he waved his palm in front of his face.

Lila laughed in that delighted way that only she could do. She had that laugh for only a couple of months, somewhere in between the middle part of three and the first part of four – I don't think anybody can hold it much longer than that – but it was there in that moment and she was giving it up for the murderer. A pure kind of wonder – straight-up happy surprise – untouched by anything else. I loved that laugh so much, loved that she could bring up that sound without any effort.

'Sill-lee,' she decided.

Then, 'Silly, silly, silly,' up and down, like a song. She pointed directly at him, then directly at me.

'Silly man,' she told me.

'Why thank you very much,' he said, and he gave her a little nod.

He pulled a pair of sunglasses off the visor and put them on. They had reflective lenses and when he looked at us again, I saw myself and Maddy and Lila held there on the surface of the glass.

'Have a good one, buddy,' he said to me. 'You sticking around for another night?'

I nodded my head and he gestured at our doors.

'Maybe we'll see you later on.'

We got in and turned our keys. The engines started and I waved at him to go first. He gave me a thumbs-up, then quickly stuck his tongue out at Lila as he pulled away.

*

Before we found this house, Maddy and I used to stay up very late searching for it, a laptop computer balanced between us in bed. We'd scroll through the internet real-estate listings, dozens of them, maybe a hundred a night, and we got very good at moving the earth with our little gloved computer hand. Lila would go down around seven thirty and not long after that, we'd make a kind of nest of propped-up pillows and then take turns gently swirling our middle fingers on the mouse pad. The computer rested on both our inside legs, pressing down evenly, and I remember the heat of the battery and the buzz of the processor rubbing up against my cock. The machine kept kicking off this steady blue glow as the pictures flashed in front of us and sometimes, when the backgrounds changed from light to dark, I caught a glimpse of our faces pressed close together and staring back out of the screen. Our expressions were blank and our mouths hung a little bit open, but our eyes were sharp and intensely focused. We looked like different people, strangers lit up by this weird trancelike concentration, a couple who did not know they were being observed.

'This one,' Maddy would say and she'd dart at it quickly and click and point and click and point again. The tip of her tongue

slid back and forth on her top lip as she thought through the possibilities and I could hear the fluctuations in her breathing, the
catches and releases, surges and disappointments. Her hair was
down and she was wearing her glasses and her pyjama bottoms
and the tank top I liked.

'Focus,' she said, and she tapped the screen.

It was always summer in the photographs – full trees and lush
gardens – and there were never any people in the frame, even
when we switched to the Google Earth street view. I think there
must have been an algorithm, an elegant bit of code, that went
into the images and automatically subtracted the pedestrians or
the dogs or anything that might distract a buyer. We made our
way, block by block, one house at a time, moving up and down
the abandoned streets. Eventually, we got a feel for the market
and a sense for the cost of things. The numbers we read seemed
to make a pattern we thought we could understand and we started
to see everything as a mathematical equation, a pure exchange.
The places we didn't like were ugly or insanely overpriced – only
a fool would live there – and all the places we wanted were special and unique, good long-term investments, and certainly worth
the kind of debt we would have to take on to get started. We were
looking for something on the edge, a hidden gem that did not
announce itself in an obvious way, a house with a special potential that not everyone would be able to see.

*

When the detectives came to us the first time, they had all their
facts in order. Credit card receipts and the motel's log and the
one long-distance call we made to her parents, even the Interac
transactions for the groceries and for the thirty dollars in gas I'd
bought from the station down the road. This was incontrovertible
evidence, rock-solid data drawn from the permanent digital record

of the world. The information plotted us into a single square on a tight piece of graph paper. Our location at that particular time and in that particular space could not be negotiated retroactively.

'Think back,' one of them said to us. He had a yellow notepad and a digital recorder. Maddy and I were sitting around our kitchen table and both kids were upstairs and asleep. Later, they took us to the police station and we made separate statements in separate rooms.

'I want you to put yourself back there on May the thirty-first and I want you to visualise exactly what you were doing and exactly what was happening around you. Tell us everything you saw, everything you can remember. The smallest detail may turn out to be important.'

He rolled his pencil between his thumb and his middle finger. The red light on the recorder stayed solid.

'Just look at it again,' he asked. 'The thing we need may not have been something you noticed the first time around.'

*

The weather records backed up our statements. May 31st was unseasonably warm, ten degrees hotter than the day before and well above thirty by the late afternoon. Our errands with the car had gone poorly – we couldn't find anything on the first try – and Lila had been straining in the back seat, sweating and complaining for hours. We needed supplies and a break so it was decided that I would drop the girls off at the room and then run to the grocery store. It was four o'clock when we pulled into the motel parking lot and a wave of heavy boiling air rolled out and washed over us when we opened the door.

'Great,' Maddy said. Her face was pale and I could see a thin purple vein throbbing at her temple. Her hair was matted on the back of her neck.

'Too hot,' Lila declared. 'Too too hot.'

There was no air conditioning, but we flipped on the overhead fan and opened the back windows and popped the screen on the door to create some feeling of circulation. After five minutes, the air was moving, but the stored heat still radiated off the floor and the walls and the beds.

'Let me run and get the stuff,' I said. 'At least some drinks and a bag of ice and some fruit. And if it doesn't get better in the next hour, we'll find somewhere else for tonight.'

'Okay,' Maddy said, 'but be quick.'

It took forty-five minutes in the end, maybe almost an hour, but by the time I got back, everything had changed. When I came through the door – the handles of five plastic bags digging into my fingers – I found the murderer sitting on our bed and only Lila left in the room. She was still wet, hair swooped back with leave-in conditioner, and she was bouncing up and down on the other bed in just her underwear. The murderer watched her calmly and I did not think – I still don't think – there was anything out of the ordinary in the way he looked at her. Lila was chanting, 'Up-and-down-and-up-and-down-and-up-and-down.'

She had a jumbo Mr Freeze in her hand, a thick blue tube of softening ice, and the murderer was sucking on an orange one, holding it at the bottom with one hand and sliding the cold syrup up to his mouth. The melting dye leaked out of Lila's face and dribbled down her chin, her neck and her stomach. It ran in two parallel rivulets that seemed to come together and pool in her belly button. She saw me and smiled and her teeth were almost purple. The murderer waved his finger at me, his only acknowledgement.

'Hello?' I said, and then I called out, 'Anybody else home around here?' louder than it needed to be.

The bathroom door opened and Maddy came out, wearing one of my old T-shirts with just a towel wrapped around her waist.

The slit came almost all the way to the top and her belly pushed against the yellow fabric of the shirt, her cold erect nipples showed through. Her hair was slicked back like Lila's and her face was bright and beautiful, recovered and cool and happy again. She had her own half-eaten Mr Freeze, a red one, and her mouth was dark at the corners too.

She pointed at the murderer.

'Thank God for this guy,' she said and then she rushed through her story.

'So we come in here after you left and I'm thinking, "Maybe a shower, a cool shower, to blow the stink off." But then, of course, the taps aren't working right and all we have is hot, scalding hot, like it's pouring right out of the kettle – there's no cold anywhere.'

She shook her head and waved her hand back into the flawed bathroom.

'So I go to the desk, but there's only a kid there and he doesn't know anything and he says he has to call the manager and that we will probably have to wait till tomorrow. So I'm completely losing it now and I'm walking back to this freaking hole and I can't believe this is happening and then I turn and I see the truck parked right there and I think, "What the hell?" So I knock on the door and this is Mark and I tell him our situation and he says, "No problem at all." Out he comes and he's got all the right tools in the truck and he opens that little hatch under the taps and two seconds later the hot is off and we have complete cold and it's perfect. So, so perfect, not glacier cold, just cold enough. So I give Lila a quick little hair wash and a cool-down rinse and when I come out Mark is back at the door, but he's gone across the street to the store to get every-body Mr Freezes. I ask him if he'll watch Lila just for a second so that I can get my turn in the shower and he says no problem again and now you're back and that's it. Here we all are.'

Lila kept bouncing up and down through all this, nodding her head, and the murderer did the same.

I thanked him.

'What do we owe you?' I said. 'For the rush job, you know. These kinds of things, last-minute rescues, don't normally come cheap.'

'No,' he said and he waved me away. 'Come on. It was nothing. Took less than two minutes.'

He leaned back on the bed, resting on his elbows, and he looked up at the ceiling fan, watching the blades make their whirling cuts through the air. There was a little bit of a breeze coming down now and I could see his hair rustling where it stuck out from beneath his cap.

'Whenever you need the hot back, just give me a shout, and I'll crank her back open.'

He jutted his chin to the inside wall that separated our rooms and he laughed.

'If we could open that door there, I wouldn't even need to go outside. Could slip in here and get it done while you were sleeping.'

I hadn't noticed it before – probably because I had not been looking for it – but it was there, painted the same colour as the wall to make it blend in. I doubted it had been touched in years. Families were smaller now and people did not travel in large groups any more. Maybe for baseball tournaments, I thought. A baseball team might need to open that door.

'Just give me the signal and I'll leap into action,' he said. 'On call twenty-four-seven for all your emergency needs.'

This was the evening of May 31st. If what they say in the papers and on the news shows is true – and there is nothing, nothing anywhere, to suggest the reports aren't completely accurate – then he killed the second person, the woman, that night. Probably just a few hours after his time with us and maybe ten inches away. He went from our taps and our Mr Freezes, our bed and our fan, and he walked out of our room and on to his next task. The young man had been days earlier, before we arrived, but there is a chance – more than a chance – that the woman was already there with us, waiting on the other side while he sipped from a cold tube of sugar water wilting in his hands.

Of course, none of this was known and none of it mattered to us at the time. We had other things, our own things, to worry about, more lists to go through. It took more than a year, almost two, before we started to understand what had happened.

*

The first time we saw this house, we recognised it. It felt like the place was sending out a signal that only we could pick up. Maddy wrote an email at 1.27 am and we called first thing the next day to set up the viewing and the inspection. The realtor picked us up at the airport in a silver SUV and it took her maybe thirty seconds to figure us out. She took one look at our shoes and our sunglasses and our haircuts.

'Yes,' she said. 'This should work out well. This is exactly the kind of place that people like you like.'

High ceilings, chunky mouldings, heavy iron grates and radiators, plaster and lath, all of it left alone and original. An old fireplace, untouched for a hundred years but still working, grandfathered in before the rules and the building code changed. We liked that there were no renovations and nobody had messed with anything or tried to put in a propane insert.

'These old character places are great,' the realtor said, 'as long as you're okay with the problems.'

The inspector showed us cracks in the foundation and pointed out actual sea shells that were decomposing in the sandy cement of the basement walls. The roof was definitely going to need money some time in the next five years, and the chimney was going to be trouble of course, but we blurred through all that and worked it out. We had the higher numbers from Toronto and Vancouver and Ottawa popping in our heads and we allowed ourselves to use the word 'bargain' before we sank ourselves in completely.

'I'm going to put my chair right here,' Maddy said, and she pointed to the tight corner, the nook she still loves. 'And my lamp will fit there and this will be my spot to read. Close enough to the fire, but not too close. I can rest a cup of tea on this ledge.'

I put my palm flat against the old wall like I could send and receive messages that way.

'Does this mean it's done?' I asked. 'We're done?'

Maddy looked at me and her eyes were wide and she was smiling hard.

'Yes,' she said and she gave three quick crisp claps. 'Yes, for sure, for sure. This is exactly who I want us to be.'

The job and the new city and one little girl and a lost baby, but another on the way. Now the house. Forces were working on us and there were chain reactions that couldn't be controlled. Our bodies were a mess of tissue and bone and nerve endings, primal synapses and firing receptors. Sporadic electrical currents surged in our brains and all the signals were confusing. They say there is a name for this experience, a raw nesting instinct that hits during pregnancy and drives us forward to prepare for a new life. Maybe that explains it or at least provides a little cover. Maybe we were in a phase, a period of extreme change like puberty or menopause, and maybe hormones and chemistry did have something to do with it, but I'm not sure. I don't think it was limited to the female body because I felt it just as hard as Maddy and I was caught up in the same way. I wanted this house, this particular house, and I wanted to put it in order. Long before we actually owned the place, when it was still the property of other people, I used to dream of what I would do to it. Rip out the hedge in the front and tear off the rotting back deck. Then gut both the bathrooms and take them all the way back to the studs before repainting every single surface on the inside.

*

In those first days, the murderer was the only person we knew in the whole city, our only connection. When we saw his face on the news, almost two years later, it felt, at first, like he was one of our old friends, someone we'd lost touch with.

'Is that Mark?' I asked Maddy, and I pointed at the TV. The famous mug shot was there filling the screen, the one where his lips are slightly parted and his eyebrows are pushed down low and there's a little V in his forehead that gives him the look of a person who is thinking very hard about something.

'The plumber from the motel, you remember? The guy who fixed the taps. Is that *our* Mark?'

It turned out that Mark actually was his real name and that he was a kind of missing piece, the essential link no one had noticed before. Like a constellation or one of those tricky 3-D optical illusions that slowly emerge from the background only after you learn how to look, Mark was a pattern, a set of connections that had always been there but could only be seen once they were pointed out. The distances he had travelled seemed too far and there was no consistency in the people or the places or the timing or the way things unfolded.

In split-screen TV interviews, expert criminologists tried to hide their admiration as they marvelled at the perfected randomness of his actions. They called his behaviour 'highly irregular' but I am not sure about that either. I think there was a system, a special way of looking that let him see something in his people, a common aloneness, or a sort of halo that glowed around them and guided him or pulled him forward to seek out others who moved through the world like he did. People connected by separation, people who did not have other people looking for them or asking questions about where they had gone. Every one of his files was considered cold before he reactivated them. A woman from northern New Brunswick, five years earlier, then later, a young man from around Kenora, Ontario. A slightly older lady from a completely francophone community in the Gaspésie.

The girl from Esquimalt, BC, practically downtown Victoria, was the first. I think of her often, stepping out of that place with all the gardens and the flowers and the trees that seem like they could hide dinosaurs. Nine victims in total, three on top of three on top of three. Everybody knows the grid of their stacked photographs. It was on all the front pages.

They stopped him in Saskatchewan. A female hitchhiker felt a current coming off of him and declined the ride, then wrote down his licence plate and called it in with a description of the truck and driver. The plate was stolen and the police immediately pinged the GPS in her cellphone – the chip inside a cellphone is what ended it all. They pulled him over, fifty clicks down the road, half an hour later. When he stepped out of the truck, he calmly told them everything: names and dates, specific sites where the remains would be found. He pulled the little lever and leaned the seat of the cab forward. He had an array of different licence plates and a set of different magnets for the truck all with the same slogan, the same bucket, the same drops, but different area codes. He could pass for local almost anywhere.

He told them about a motel in Nova Scotia where they still rented rooms by the week or the month. He'd been there almost two years ago at the end of May. There had been a man in his late twenties and then a woman in her early forties, eight days apart. They were the fourth and fifth. He was precise about his practice and spoke calmly about ether and duct tape and bungee cords and plastic. He told them what he knew about chemical solvents, and drain cleaners, and active bacteria. They passed a purple light over his tools and it all showed through. The police cars and the rolling lab pulled into the parking lot hours later. A team of expert dogs trained for exactly this task went into the woods outside of town and came back in twenty minutes. It was easy for them to follow the smell when they were pointed in the right direction. In the past, they'd found mass graves that were more than sixty years old. No amount of scrubbing or time could hide these facts from them. The satellite truck and the cameras appeared the next morning.

*

Right after this, just when the news broke and the crews were on the scene and the details were still unclear, a woman I barely recognised – somebody from way up the street – knocked on our door. It was in the evening and Jack and Lila were almost ready for bed. The woman had a tea light burning in a small mason jar and she held her hand over the top, gently, like the flickering glass held a butterfly she'd just caught and did not want to lose.

'Yes?' I said.

'My name is Candace,' she announced, very formally, like a grade-school kid. 'The people from the community are organising a little memorial and we thought you might want to know that, this evening, there will be a small candlelight vigil for that poor couple from the motel.'

It was clear she'd said these lines many times before, on all the other porches before this one.

'Nothing too fancy, just some candles and flowers, I think. Some people are going to sing or play music, but you are welcome to just stand silently. We are going to start in about half an hour.'

'Thank you,' I said.

Nothing like this had ever happened to me before and I don't think the opportunity will come again. The invitation was made and there must have been a chance, a second when I could have accepted, when I could have been taken in and carried along, but I did not go for it. A clinical part of my mind, something colder than it should be, kicked in and I spoke when it would have been better to stay quiet.

'Oh, I didn't think they were a couple,' I told her. I can imagine my blank face staring into hers. 'My wife and I, we heard, we thought it was two separate things, two separate incidents. We heard that the people didn't know each other at all, maybe didn't even see each other. We didn't think there was any connection.'

An expression of deep confusion rose up in Candace's eyes and flexed across her forehead, then switched to anger, almost disgust.

She said the word: 'Incident?' And then she snapped. 'Well they are a couple to me. And lots of people around here like to think of them like that, together and not alone.'

She turned and stamped away from me. The candle almost went out.

· ✳

This is the rest of it. This is what really happened, just to us, on May 31st, the night before our closing, the night before we moved into our home, the night he killed the woman and made her disappear.

On our side of the wall in the Bide-a-While motel, we had bought a big cheap bottle of sparkling wine – 1.5 litres of not champagne – and we put it in a waste-paper basket and poured half a bag of ice over it and let it stand for an hour. Then we packed up the rest of our loose stuff and we loaded the car. By eight o'clock we were set and everybody was in their sleeping gear and it was my turn to take the freezing shower. When the water first hit my chest, I gasped hard and I felt all the air leaving my lungs, but then I gradually got used to it and I relaxed a little and I was able to at least rub the small soap over my body and rinse. It took maybe five minutes and then I dried off and pulled on the last of my fresh underwear and my final clean T-shirt. I tussled my hair a bit and walked into the bedroom.

Maddy was waiting on the other side of the door and she held up both her hands, palms flat and right in my face. She pointed at our daughter and made the shush sign with her fingers on her lips.

Lila was face up in the middle of the other bed, arms and legs starfished beneath one thin blanket. Her eyes were closed and her breathing was deep and regular and steady.

'How did that happen?' I whispered. 'Tranquilliser dart? Something in her milk?'

'Nope,' Maddy said and she smiled. 'Nothing we did, just a summertime miracle.'

She raised Lila's limp wrist about a foot off the mattress and let it fall back down.

Nothing registered. The girl's breathing kept that steady pace.

'Gone,' I said. 'Completely gone. Unbelievable.'

We were both clean and we smelled better than we normally do. There was an opening.

I kissed Maddy and when our tongues touched, it felt like both our mouths were wetter than usual. She put her hand on the back of my head and I felt her fingers going through my hair directly to my skin. She stroked the ridge where the back of my skull tapered into my neck.

We took the bucket and quietly went back into the bathroom and closed the door almost all the way, leaving only a crack. There was barely enough space to stand so I put the bucket in the tub and stepped in there with it. When I pulled it out, the bottle was wet and sweaty and I undid the tinfoil and twisted out the little wire. I shook it a bit, enough so that the white plastic cork flew with a muted pop and hit the ceiling before rattling back down.

The fizzy wine ran up and over my hands and we quickly poured it into the bathroom glasses.

'Here we go,' I said, and I held out my glass for her to clink it. 'To this.'

'Yes, to all of it,' Maddy laughed and she gestured to the lump of wet towels shoved into the corner behind the door.

We clinked and downed our glasses in one gulp and then quickly refilled. This was the first drink Maddy'd had since we found out about the baby, but we were only a few weeks away now.

'One more of these is not going to hurt anybody,' she said and she drank again.

I stepped out of the tub and we sat there on the edge and leaned into each other. Our pinky toes touched. The carbonation made a kind of mist in the glasses and everything in the room was so tight and so compressed, it felt like you could almost hear every separate bubble bursting.

I put my hand on the soft part of the inside of her thigh and my thumb grazed the edge of her underwear. We stayed still and silent for about thirty seconds, thinking it through, and then we went for it for real, kissing again, harder. There was no room and we had to kind of spin around and almost elbow each other in the face as we tried to get our shirts off. As we kissed, she ran her fingers down the bones of my spine and then brought her hand around so her palm was flat on my chest. I pulled her in close and hard.

It had been a long, long time for us. Every little flutter with Jack's pregnancy worried us and all we wanted to do was get through unscathed. Again: there were mysterious chemicals flowing through our bodies and our brains, especially in these final stages, and we felt like there was a delicate balance that shouldn't be fooled with. There were words, names, in our *What to Expect When You're Expecting* book and we said them out loud like a kind of incantation but we did not know what they meant. It seemed like no one knew for sure. Progesterone, oxytocin, prosta-glandins. Nothing behaved in the same way every time and there were reactions and counter-reactions that could only be experienced and never explained or predicted. The doctors had told us that our miscarriage was nobody's fault and that nothing had gone wrong. A completely natural occurrence, they said, a thing that happened all the time, but we did not feel that way. Now though, at last, in that tight bathroom, it was all coming back and it felt like everything inside us was working again, accelerating and rushing down the right channels.

'Maybe just a lick,' she whispered. 'Please.'

We took the last good towel from off the rack and put it down on the toilet seat. Maddy spread her legs, resting one foot on the edge of the tub and the other in the dip of the gooseneck from the tiny sink. She braced her hands against the wall and I went down on her. My left hand moved back and forth, resting on her stomach or touching her full hard breasts, while the fingers of my right hand went in and out of her, very gently, and my tongue stayed on the right spot.

'Slow,' she breathed. 'Go slow.'

It was perfect. I could feel her tensing and relaxing, tensing and relaxing and blowing out these long, long breaths.

'Good,' she said. 'So good.'

After a few minutes she put her hands in my hair and pushed me back. I moved to the left instead of the right and I smashed my head on the stainless-steel leg that propped up the sink. She wanted me to stand up, but when I backed against the bathroom door, one of the hooks jabbed me in the neck.

'Smooth,' she laughed. 'Very smooth.'

'This is not easy,' I said.

'Now you,' she said. She put the towel on the floor in front of me and knelt down on it. Then she pulled my shorts down and put my cock in her mouth and worked the shaft with her hand. Too many things were happening at the same time, the new and the familiar were mixing and I couldn't keep up. I looked around the room and imagined our next move. Us trying to do it standing up in the tub or somehow crouching down into this square of tile. The angles were all bad and I didn't think any of them would work. We were running out of space and time.

'Out there?' I whispered. 'Do you want to try out there?'

I opened the door. The curtains to the parking lot were still half open and a beam of end-of-day light fell directly onto Lila's face, but she didn't stir. I took two or three quick strides across the room and pulled the velour drapes closed so that they only glowed around the edges.

Maddy was on her back on the other bed, on top of the blankets. We would have no cover if Lila woke up.

'Are you sure?' I asked.

'Yes,' she said. 'We're fine. Come on. Right now.'

In the beginning, all I could do was concentrate on Lila, watching her for any sign, and imagining how Maddy and I could maybe both roll off the side and duck down behind the bed if we needed to. I did not want to get caught by a four-year-old and end up leaving some scarring image that would be seared into her brain.

Then we shifted positions, standing up with Maddy pushed against the wall. The pressure was rising and the pace increased. From that stage on, I closed off and did not care any more. I don't clearly remember exactly what happened or the order things followed. Something gave way inside of me, in both of us, and after months and months of stillness it felt like we were moving again, doing what we were supposed to.

'On top,' she said after a little bit. 'I want to be on top.'

I rolled over onto the bed and she straddled my legs and put her hand on the headboard. She pushed down very hard and I pressed back up against her. We were getting closer and there was no concern for Jack any more. Raw sounds were coming out of us and we were saying words we would not normally use. I could just vaguely sense that things were getting louder and louder, more insistent, but I wasn't sure any more. Maddy's eyes were closed and she was grinding down and sliding herself back and forth very fast. The headboard was making steady regular contact with the wall and the lamp shades were moving. We both had all our weight, all our strength, behind every movement.

I was breathing hard and my legs were actually starting to burn. I was just going to say something when we heard these three booming blows coming out of the wall on the opposite side of the room. The spacing was even and methodical, like a machine with a two-second delay between each movement. A thud and then a thud and then a thud. We glanced at each other, both our chests expanding and contracting. We were close, but we could not be sure if this sound came in response to what we were doing or if it was entirely its own action. The two were likely connected – the timing too close – but we could not be certain.

It felt like the blows were coming through the whole wall, like a repeating wave of sound, the echo from some piece of roadwork machinery, or the concussive vibration you feel in your chest after a firework explodes or when they are excavating for a new underground parking garage in your neighbourhood. It did not seem like this could be the work of a single hand or a forearm or a shoulder hitting just one spot. When I turned to look at the wall I thought I watched a crack opening up and actually moving down through the plaster. In the dresser mirror, I saw the two of us, still moving furiously. Her back pounding down, my hips rising up. We were seven months pregnant with our second child, but he was not in the world yet. In the other bed, Lila, his big sister, did not stir. The noise from us and the noise from the other side did not reach her.

I looked into Maddy's face. Our eyes locked and she shook

her head. Before I could say anything, she reached down and clamped one hand over my mouth. Our rhythm increased.

'Do not stop,' she said.

We carried through all the way to the end. Our actions did not trigger the premature birth of our son, and our daughter slept through to the morning and no other sound ever rose from the other side. No secret door knobs were turned and no phones ever rang and no inquiries were ever made. The night of May 31st faded quickly and completely into our shared past and on the morning of June 1st, our new lives began and continued on for almost two years.

But then the TV showed his picture and the other story – the bigger one that includes us all – began. The detectives visited our house and sat around the kitchen table while the children slept upstairs. We told them almost everything – our move, our plan for the Bide-a-While, the house, the sunscreen, the taps and the Mr Freezes – but we kept the last part only for ourselves and we never gave that away. The booming signal sounding in the night – the message that may have been sent directly to us, or maybe through us into the larger world – did not make it into the official record and it did not become information and you will not find it in any of the reports. When they took us to the station, Maddy and I gave our independent statements and we delivered them in different rooms to different officers, but when they were placed side by side, they matched up perfectly, the same gaps inserted into the same spaces. For years, we have kept that sound just for ourselves and it is not something we share with other people.

I think about it a lot, though. Or maybe I think that we think about it a lot or we hear it repeating in our memories. The sound and our silence are combined now and the consequences of our choices – the things we did or did not do – are hard to understand even though I have tried to play out all the different scenarios. Perhaps our quietness saved our lives and saved the lives of our children. Perhaps we were spared. Or perhaps the noises we made and the noises we heard but never reported led to very different results for other people living their lives in other places. Perhaps we are partly responsible for what happened to them. Perhaps the strange possibilities he was trying to open up on his side of the wall shut down other possibilities in our lives. It is hard to know. I cannot tell where privacy ends and the rest of the world begins.

But I know that our lives are much quieter now and that there is a different kind of stillness in our house. Maddy gets tired earlier than before and we go to bed at different times and we do not share the computer any more. Now we have our own devices, amazing cellphones with hand-held video screens, and we use these to usher ourselves into our own unique versions of sleep. It does not feel strange. The kids go down and we clean up the kitchen together and we take our showers. Then we sit for a couple of minutes before she says, 'I think I'll go up now,' and we kiss. In separate rooms, we choose the shows we want to see and the pictures and the sounds we select bring us a specific comfort. They help us rest. I think she watches old sitcoms or YouTube episodes of *Grand Designs* or *House Hunters International*, but I am not entirely sure. I never ask and I know she is not interested in my sports teams or wherever I go when the games are over. When I come upon her in bed, I try not to disturb her, or even touch her body, as I take my place beside her. We both have to be ready to go in the morning.

This house has served us well and we have never regretted our decision. All the old character is still there in the walls and the mouldings and the place is filled with the histories, the trace elements, of other people who came through before we arrived. Some nights when I have the fire going, I can imagine them, the former residents, generations of strangers, staring into this exact same spot and stretching out their hands towards the heat and the light. But they are all gone and this place belongs only to us now. We have made it the way it is. Our particular actions and inactions, our most intimate longings and revulsions, have come together to form a daily domestic shape that only we designed and only we can fully recognise.

But I go back sometimes and I see us at the beginning of everything. We are together in the mirror of the motel bedroom and we are seven months pregnant with Jack and we cannot help ourselves. Then the wall dissolves and now I am looking down from above and I can see him too, just a few feet away, his hand in the air, waiting for a signal. At other times I picture him sitting silently in his own kind of quiet room, the cell where they keep him today. I imagine a cot and some books and the stainless-steel toilet. Mark and I and Maddy and Lila and Jack: we do not know where we are in the arc of our lives – old or young, safe or exposed, closer to the beginning or the end, brushing up against death or far away from it. We do not know if the decisive moment has arrived or if it is yet to come. Led only by what we desire, we go out into the world and we make our way. And then we sleep, each of us in temporary beds that will one day be occupied by other people.

THE FORTUNE FISH

Clare Wigfall

'So it is you,' she said, coming up alongside as I was getting myself a glass of Zinfandel.

I'd only just stepped into the party and not even had the chance to check it out. She was younger than myself, with curly sandy-blonde hair and a good figure; a little shy-looking maybe, but that only made her all the more attractive. My type for sure, but nothing about her was familiar. I glanced over my shoulder to check it was me she was addressing.

'Don't remember me, do you?' She kind of laughed, but like she'd just realised something stupid. She looked away a second before turning back again, and it was in that movement that I saw the girl I once knew.

'Arlette?' Must have been near fifteen years since I'd spoken that name, but the memory of her came back to me. A girl I'd run around with one summer. Sexy. Young. A little bit high most of the time.

'Ray,' she replied, and the way she studied me, like I was something surprising to her, something she'd misplaced, it was intense; this could get interesting, I thought. And so I smiled at her, but she was still too absorbed to smile back.

'Always imagined maybe I'd bump into you one of these days,' she said. 'You're looking old.'

I'd first met her on Haight. An afternoon – that crazy summer of '67 – when I'd driven across the bay to visit an esoteric book-store a guy at work had told me about. There she was on the sidewalk, trying to make a buck reading tarot. Her hair was loose and long, down-to-her-ass long, and her fingers flipped the cards on the grey paving. She was sitting cross-legged, in a long Indian skirt and a bunch of ethnic jewellery – beads and bangles, and these heavy silver rings on her skinny fingers. Like a little kid playing dress-up who no one had told not to speak to strangers. When I came out the store she was still there, and she looked up and smiled. Her face was very open, very young, and two bucks didn't seem like a lot to talk to this girl. I offered her a ride along the coast after. We smoked a few and watched the sun go down. She was sleeping on a girlfriend's couch in the Upper Haight, everything she owned in an army duffel bag almost as big as herself. I helped her carry it up the stairs to my apartment when she moved in.

'I teach their daughter dance,' she said now. 'And you? How do you know them?'

'I play squash with Ted.'

'You play squash?' she said.

'You teach dance?' I countered.

She shrugged and smiled. There was a reserve to her manner that was new, but when she smiled it disappeared again. It was a nice smile. Her lips were full and glossed, her teeth straight. She'd changed a good bit since I'd seen her last – matured into her features, lost the skinniness, changed her hair – and it suited her well.

The mention of squash had made me draw in my stomach instinctively. I keep myself pretty trim, eat healthy – vegetarian for the most part – but for all the squash I play there's a bulge I just can't seem to shake any more. I'm vain enough that these things bother me – like the way my hairline is receding, or the grey in my beard – even if I know that for a guy of my years I'm looking pretty good. I still keep my hair long, though mostly I wear it tied back now, and my beard I keep neat; I take care of my appearance. Today I'd dressed nice for the party; a slim-fitting shirt unbuttoned at the neck, Levi's, a string of Himalayan prayer beads.

It was Ted's party. An architect I'd met on the courts down at the Y. We'd had a few games together. He was a good player and we were well matched. He laughed easily, even when I beat him, which is a trait I admired because hell I wish I could take losing so lightly. He and his wife Marion, a professor of women's studies, had just bought a house up on Stanford Avenue. 'We're having a housewarming potluck Saturday,' Ted had said, last time I'd seen him, wiping at his forehead with a hand towel as we headed back to the changing rooms. 'Want to come along?'

I knew it wouldn't really be my scene. Architects and academics from the university, all of them talking gender politics and timber cladding, their noisy kids ducking through our legs and knocking over plates of food. I'd planned on bringing a date, a recently divorced yoga instructor called Judith who I'd been seeing on and off, but she'd cancelled on me that morning because her cat had vomited; I had a feeling already things weren't going to work out with Judith.

So I was a bit bummed to be going alone, and might have backed out but it was my first day off after a string of double shifts and I figured I'd just swing by, check it out.

'So what are you doing these days?' Arlette asked, talking over the noise of the party.

'Working in a vegetarian kitchen,' I told her. 'Rosa's Pantry?'

'You're still cooking?' she said, surprised.

It's true I used to hate the job. It was only meant to be something I'd do until something better came along: I was working on a poetry chapbook, thought I might take up carpentry, considered enrolling on an anthropology programme, I wanted to travel. But I never really got my ass in gear to change anything, and anyhow I'd come round to kitchen work over the years. You can be pretty

Zen about food preparation. And Rosa's is a co-operative so really it's more than just a job.

'But hey, I don't wanna talk about me,' I told her, because what I really wanted to do now was steer our conversation round to her. 'Let's talk about you.'

'Oh,' she said, blowing out through her lips like her story was hardly worth telling. 'Oh, yeah, okay.'

I suggested we go out to the deck because it would be easier to talk out there. I eyed Arlette's hips, how they swayed to the music, as we moved out through the crowded living room.

With the trees and the hills and the bay sparkling down below, the view from Ted's deck was impressive. The air smelled of warm eucalyptus. Anyone would have felt a little envious with a view as phenomenal as that; I'd have liked a place up in the hills myself. We leant against the railing. In the back yard beneath us they'd set out a yellow Slip 'N Slide on the grass. There were kids in bathing suits screaming excitedly as they slid down the hill. A red setter ran up and down alongside them, barking maniacally, its dopey energy relentless.

'Looks like fun,' I said.

'Sure does.'

Her glass was near empty again so I fetched a bottle to refill it.

'God, I always drink too much at parties where I don't know anyone.'

'Doesn't everyone?' I reassured her, topping up my own glass.

Her smile really was pretty.

It turned out she'd become a dancer. She'd trained in New York and had only been back on the West Coast a couple of years. It explained why we'd not run into each other before now. 'I did shows in NYC for a while,' she said. 'It was fun but I'm too old now. Too old to dance professionally anyhow. So now I teach.'

'You're looking great.' She lowered her head at the compliment. 'I like what you've done with your hair.'

'It's a perm,' she said self-consciously, then a moment later a thought struck her. 'I was still a hippie back when you knew me, wasn't I? Wow! I cut my hair soon as I got to New York. It was a whole different scene over there.'

'Still reading tarot?'

'Tarot!' She couldn't help laughing.

I caught her eye as she looked back up and there was a flash of something, of the attraction there'd once been between us, I could tell she felt it too. I was feeling good about the way things were going. 'Yeah, you read my cards,' I reminded her. 'Told me I was gonna meet a beautiful girl who'd break my heart.'

'I did?' She coloured, then a moment later looked unsure. 'I said that, really?'

I kept my gaze on her. Shrugged in place of answering.

'Wasn't your heart that got broke though, was it?' she said matter-of-factly, and then she relieved the moment's tension with a laugh. 'Honestly, the tarot? I didn't know what the hell I was doing. I just needed money.'

There were a lot of young girls like her in the city back then. Run away from small-town life, from parents who didn't care or cared too much, looking for something that didn't feel like everything they'd known up until then. They didn't have a clue. For a guy like me, it was like being handed a platter at a party.

I'd been in the Bay Area a while already, long before the place was swinging. Came to take an engineering major at Cal, largely because it was what my father had wanted to study, but then I got stuck on the idea I didn't want to be the realisation of his failed ambitions so I dropped out. I was young and stupid. He cut my monthly allowance and never really forgave me. I had rent to pay and the only work I could find was in kitchens. On my nights off I'd go out and visit jazz clubs and try to meet women. I wasn't the kind to settle down, I knew that already, I liked variety. After a while of this I was wanting something new and maybe I would have quit town again, moved on someplace else, but then the scene started to change and suddenly everything got kind of crazy and fun. These young kids began to arrive. I liked their music, the attitude, I liked their drugs. And most of all I liked the girls. It wasn't hip to cross your legs back then, even the shy ones were easy.

Arlette used to keep that tarot deck of hers in a little Indian purse around her neck, along with some of her other fortune-telling junk – a dowsing pendulum, baoding balls, dumb little crystals. She'd read strangers' cards when we were out. Nobody cared if she was making it all up. It was a nice summer we spent together. She was fresh, uncomplicated, good in bed. So it took me by surprise when one morning I woke up and she'd cleared out – the armchair was still pulled up next to the wardrobe where she'd climbed up to fetch her duffel bag down, but her clothes, her journals, her toothbrush from the tooth mug by the sink, all of it was gone. The only trace of her was a tarot card she'd left on my dresser. I couldn't tell you now what it pictured; honestly, I think I tossed it in the trash. I assume she meant something by it, but at the time the gesture seemed juvenile, a little corny. Other than that, no note, no explanation. I wasn't used to having a girl leave on me. Normally I was the one who broke things up, getting out before it all got too heavy. I figured she must've run away back home. Maybe she'd met another guy. I figured maybe a letter would arrive in the post. I was kind of pissed about it for a week or two but the fact of the matter was there were plenty other girls out there.

'So, are you married?' I asked. 'Kids?'

She shook her head.

'But you've got a guy, huh?'

'No,' she said simply, and in that moment she looked away

like I'd made her uncomfortable. I was annoyed I'd broken our easy flirtation. She shook her hair back over her shoulders and straightened up. 'Can I get some more of that wine?'

As the party started winding down, we realised we were amongst the last guests left out on the deck. I suggested we take it elsewhere.

She left me waiting a moment for her answer and then said, 'Yeah, all right. Let me just run to the bathroom.'

Leaning on the deck rail, I finished my wine and watched the sail boats far out on the bay.

I was trying to think what I could remember of her. Small things I'd had no cause to recall for years: how she liked her food spicy; that she'd been named after a Belgian grandmother, or maybe it was an aunt; riding the Tilden Park Merry-Go-Round together on acid. It had been fun talking with her again, time had passed easily, but I couldn't help noticing that she was different from how I remembered her. She seemed more guarded. And for a dancer she came across as, like, a little tense, if you know what I mean.

After some minutes, I realised Arlette had been gone a while so I figured I'd go in and find her.

The living room was less crowded now, potluck table looted, a Carly Simon song playing on the stereo.

That's when I saw her – at the door, about to leave. One foot already past the threshold, her jacket on, pocketbook over her shoulder. Evidently Ted's wife had hindered her; she was telling Arlette something, laughing, their daughter hanging on to one of Arlette's hands.

I could have stepped back out onto the deck. Maybe I should have let her go, she obviously wanted to, but it was a matter of self respect; when a girl's already walked out on you once you're not going to just stand back and let her pull that again. There was a full moment before she saw me, and when she did, her face flushed with a guilty expression. 'You two know each other?' asked Marion, surprised.

'Used to,' said Arlette, 'a long time ago.'

'That's wild.'

The daughter dragged Marion away soon after, and I turned to Arlette with a smile. 'Ducking out on me?'

'No, no,' she said, evidently embarrassed. Then she laughed. 'Actually, yeah.'

She didn't live far. 'You want to just follow?' she suggested. She was a careful driver, especially considering the wine she'd drunk.

When we pulled up and parked she turned off her engine but didn't make any move to get out.

I locked my own car, then stepped up and opened her driver door, thinking maybe that was what she was waiting for. 'You okay?'

'I'm great,' she replied, and yanking her keys from the ignition she swept herself up from her seat.

I don't know what I'd expected but her apartment surprised me some. A boxy conversion on the first floor of a family house. She had her own entrance round the side of the building. It was very clean, everything in its place, but it wasn't exactly homely, more like it was someone else's apartment she was just staying in temporarily.

If you'd have asked me before that evening where I'd have pictured Arlette, I'd have bet you she was living someplace nice, with a guy who loved her, a couple of beautiful kids, maybe a puppy dog.

Standing now in her living room, the evidence of Arlette was scanty: a purple foam exercise mat rolled up beside the TV; a film poster for *Chinatown* thumbtacked to the wall above; a shelf of paperback novels.

A photograph framed on that same shelf caught my eye. It showed a guy standing in the suburban back yard of a light-blue clapboard house, an Oldsmobile parked in the drive. He was wearing a blue apron and a button-down shirt, holding a set of cooking tongs and smiling.

'My dad,' she said. She was kneeling below me, rooting through a shoebox of cassettes. She picked one out and put it in, a Windham Hill Sampler from a year or so back. 'He passed away just before I moved out here, not so long before I met you. Pancreatic cancer.'

Had she told me that before? Probably.

'You were close?'

'Yeah.'

Arlette's father, he was of similar colouring and build to myself. Born not so very long before me either, if I were to hazard a guess. Shouldn't have surprised me really; it's not like she was the first girl looking for a father figure.

I set the frame back on the shelf. 'You know I'll be fifty next year?'

'No way,' Arlette said as she stood back up. It gratified me that her surprise seemed genuine.

I kissed her as she made the coffee. She was faced away from me, standing at her kitchen counter, and I scooped her hair into my hand and kissed the skin at her neck. She stopped, her hands on the counter top, still holding a coffee spoon.

I reached to pull up her skirt and had just hooked a thumb under the elastic of her panties when she whispered, 'Not like this.'

Taking my hand, she led me through to the bedroom. She didn't turn on the light.

'Slow,' she said, as we sat together on the edge of her bed.

She lifted her fingers and ran them over my face, like she was trying to reacquaint herself, then stroked them through my beard and slow across the lines the years had left on my skin. Sliding her hand to the back of my hair she pulled away the elastic that held my ponytail. 'This is how I remember you,' she said with a small laugh, as my hair fell over my shoulders.

I reached for her belt. Heard the snag in her breath as I unbuckled and pulled it through the belt loops. I lifted her dress next, her ass lifting from the mattress for me, arms raising so I could pull it up over her head. Her white lace bra and panties showed in the dark.

'You sure?' I said.

'I don't know,' she replied, and pulled me towards her.

Greedy, a little wayward, that was the kind of lover Arlette used to be. She was good in bed still, her body trim and lithe from her dancing, but she was holding back. Each time I went to kiss her mouth she'd turn her head, which was weird, but I let it go because it's not like I'm going to make a woman kiss me.

And then, as we lay there afterwards, she said something that I guess explained a lot. 'You know, I was in love with you, Ray. You were the first guy I ever loved.'

I made to say something but she touched my lips with her finger. 'It's okay. It really is okay,' she said. 'You fall too deep with your first. It sticks with you, you know?'

I wondered how much she'd thought about me over the years and almost felt a little badly that I hadn't even recognised her earlier on. I wondered if I'd lived up to her memories, but I didn't ask.

A question came to me. 'How old were you when we met, Arlette?'

There was a pause.

'Seventeen,' she said. 'I'd have been seventeen.'

'You were a child.'

'I didn't feel like a child,' she said. 'Sometimes I feel like more of a child now.'

I reached over and stroked the hair back from her face.

'You must have been round about my age now,' she said after some reflection. 'What were you doing hanging around with us kids?'

I didn't answer. 'It's not like you're so old,' was all I said.

'You still do drugs?' she asked. 'Smoke grass and whatever?'

I shook my head no. I didn't do any of that any more. Hadn't even smoked a joint in several years. 'The stuff was killing my libido,' I joked, although it wasn't so far from the truth. It was easy enough to let it all go. I've never had an addictive personality.

Not for drugs anyhow.

Maybe she could tell what I was thinking or I don't know but when she spoke next it was hard to read her tone. 'You haven't changed so much though, have you?'

We lay there together in the darkness and when I didn't say anything eventually she rolled away from me onto her back, then got up for some water.

When she came back I asked, 'So what was the deal with you leaving like you did? Sneaking out on me without even saying goodbye?' A part of me wanted to remind her that even if I'd been no prince she hadn't been totally faultless back then either. By her silence now I got the impression this had worked.

'Running away was a pretty immature way of handling the situation,' she said finally, but she didn't apologise.

She kept me waiting a long while before she spoke again, and when she did I thought maybe she'd jumped topic, wasn't going to answer the question. 'Do you remember that girl we picked up near Indian Rock?' she asked. 'Really dark eyes and all that crazy black eye makeup. Short, dark hair. Kind of wild-looking?'

I looked over. There wasn't enough light to make out the expression on her face but I could feel a shift of mood, something in the pauses maybe, a sort of nakedness; it seemed evident that she was telling me something she hadn't planned to share.

Back when Arlette and I ran around together, I was driving a tan sedan and yeah – couple of times at least – it happened like she said. We'd be out and we might see a girl looking lonesome and Arlette would roll down the window and offer her a smoke. If they took a drag most usually they'd come back with us to party. It worked pretty well.

'So you remember her?' she asked again.

'Maybe,' I said, 'I think yeah.' I gave a slow nod, but really I just wanted to see where this was going.

'Remember her name?'

Nope.

'Susanne,' she said. 'Least that's what she told us when she got in the car. She wasn't a good liar. Is this coming back to you at all?'

'Yeah, I guess. Or maybe not. I mean, it was just one of our things, right.'

Arlette took in a long breath, then released it again very slowly.

She started to talk. About that night, and how the girl – Susanne – climbed in the back seat. How she smelt of unwashed hair and patchouli, sort of feral; I could imagine the smell of her there in the car with us. We drove back to my place and Arlette read Susanne's cards, and we had a couple of joints, Arlette was good at rolling by then, couple of drinks, no doubt talked the usual stoned bullshit we used to talk back then, and Susanne started coming on to her. Really coming on. 'Just me though,' Arlette made clear. 'It was me she was into and she didn't hide it. You might as well not have been there.'

The thought of it was intriguing. 'Go on.'

So the two of them started messing around on the bed. Clothes came off. Susanne kept whispering to Arlette that she was beautiful, telling her real nice stuff. No one had ever talked that way to her, she said.

And me? I'd taken a seat in the armchair, she told me, in the corner where I could keep out of their way and watch the two of them.

Funny, I could recall that armchair all right, a hulking green-upholstered thing someone had left on the sidewalk. Likewise the apartment I was living in back then. A studio on Arlington. I used to keep the bed under the window, no curtains. I had an embroidered Indian quilt I'd picked up in a yard sale, a crimson lava lamp. I wanted to remember this Susanne girl too, but I couldn't.

Even so, it was easy enough to picture the scene she was describing – two girls fooling around on the mattress in the red light, one long-haired, the other smoky-eyed, all of it loose and spontaneous, destined to be forgotten by the morning. I must have lived through a string of similar nights back then. The girls themselves were interchangeable. It didn't need to be Arlette, could just as easily have been some other girl I'd dated, in bed with some other woman.

'She took a scarf,' Arlette continued, 'and then she tied my wrists. You know, to the bed frame. Went down on me.'

'Uh huh?' I said. Her story was definitely getting me a little aroused again. 'You liked it?'

'Yeah,' she said. 'Sure. At first anyhow.'

'And then?'

'And then, just as I was about to come, Susanne broke off and stopped.'

'Stopped?'

'Yeah, she gave me this really weird look, straddled my chest. Pinned me there to the mattress. And it all changed.'

'What do you mean "changed"?'

'I mean suddenly it wasn't about me any more,' Arlette said. 'It was like— Kind of like a telephone line just dropped, you know? The connection broken. And then it was all about you, Ray.' She gave a small bitter laugh. 'Maybe it was about the two of you all along.'

'I don't know,' I said, giving an uneasy shrug, and then frowned.

'So, this girl just left you hanging, didn't get you off – and that was it?'

'No, that wasn't it,' she replied. 'No.'

Arlette had her arms crossed and was rubbing her shoulders gently with her hands, like she was cold or something.

'Well, what?'

'She grabbed my blouse and she held it over my face, really tight over my nose and mouth. She kept looking back over her shoulder, checking that you were watching, making sure. I thought she was playing around at first, you know. But I couldn't breathe, Ray. And she wouldn't let go.'

Arlette's voice was a little thin, spinning off someplace else. Something clicked then in my memory. Holy shit, I did remember it. Like seeing a picture on a TV screen. This girl straddling Arlette, looking back at me over her shoulder, her knuckles white where they held the flowered blouse tight. And Arlette's eyes, wide and frantic as she tried to signal that she was in trouble, her lower half writhing in the red glow of the lamp, naked legs thrashing against the mattress. God, seeing her kick like that.

'It was turning you on,' Arlette said plainly. 'Wasn't it?'

A lot of my memories from that time are hazy; things shift, try to trip you up, it's hard to pin down the details. I didn't let on to Arlette that pieces of that night were coming back, because it's not like what I could recall was all that clear.

'I remember you just watching,' she continued. 'Sitting there, watching. I remember trying to get free, fighting for air. And then everything went black. When I woke up again you were in the bed with me and Susanne was gone.'

She stopped talking then and the room was quiet. The cassette next door had played out.

I thought about the scene a while, tried to rearrange it, to put it together – what I could remember, what she could, the stuff that maybe happened with me and the other girl while she was out of it, and even what if it did, I mean, we were high, a little drunk, and it's not like anybody got hurt. Arlette was just too young, a kid out of her depth.

She shifted away from me on the bed. 'You don't get it, do you?' she said. 'I thought I was going to die. That's why I left.'

I didn't know what she wanted me to say. 'Look, I'm sorry,' I offered at last.

'Forget it,' she said. 'It's no big deal. Why apologise for something you can't even remember?'

'I liked you a lot, you know,' I told her. 'I really did.'

'You know, Ray,' she said after some seconds, 'I think I'd like you to go now,' and she pulled the quilt up to cover herself.

I was tired when I got back, a little hungover from the wine I'd drunk that afternoon. There was a message from Judith on the answering machine, she was pissed I hadn't called her back, and I turned it off halfway through. I opened the fridge but felt uninspired.

In the bathroom mirror I caught my reflection as I took a piss and it made me pause. 'You're looking old,' Arlette had said.

I felt weird all night. Things hadn't exactly panned out how I thought they would and I couldn't let it go. Part of me now wished I'd let Arlette walk away earlier.

I fell asleep on the couch, *Saturday Night Live* on the TV.

Just before I zoned out though, a strange, random image came into my mind, of one of those red fortune-telling cellophane fish. You know, the ones you hold in your hand? At first they lie flat and then the humidity of your palm makes the red slip of plastic writhe up and curl, slap back sometimes, flip, like a landed trout on a dry dock. It's supposed to tell you what you are.

A week or so after the party, I was driving down Solano and I saw the dance studio where Arlette had said she taught. There was a bunch of little girls in leotards coming out the door, evidently just finished a class. I don't know why but I made a U-turn at the next junction and drove back the way I'd come, parking across the street from the studio. The little girls' leotards were the colour of candy. They wore ribbons in their hair and skipped about on the sidewalk. The moms were chatting together on their way out. After some time, the women and girls all dispersed.

I was just about to turn the ignition again when the door opened and out came Arlette. She was wearing a leotard too, with a pair of sweatpants. She unloosed her ponytail as she stepped outside and shook her hair out over her shoulders, then turned to lock up the studio.

Next door was a frozen yogurt shop and she stepped in, the guy behind the counter smiling as though she were a regular there. He fixed her a paper tub of yogurt and she took it over to a high stool in the window. Setting the tub on the desk, she pulled a paperback from her shoulder bag.

'Have you ever been in love, Ray?' she'd asked, as I was putting on my clothes the other night to leave.

I didn't hear the question at first and she had to repeat it.

'Course I have,' I told her, 'what do you think?'

I think she knew it was a lie but she let it drop.

'You told me not to fall in love with you,' she said. 'You remember that? It was one of the very first things you told me.'

'Maybe I did,' I said.

The truth is it's what I tell them all. Let's have a good time, I tell them. Let's have some fun. Let's not get complicated.

She'd turned on the bedside light so I could find my clothes and she watched me as I pulled on my pants then sat on the edge of the bed to pull on my socks. Naked beneath the quilt, her makeup smudged and her hair messed up, she looked young again, more like when I'd first known her.

I found my shirt, picked up my car keys and wallet from the dresser.

'It was good running into you,' I told her.

I was late for work, but I didn't drive on, just sat a while more watching Arlette alone in the shop window, turning the pages of her paperback as she spooned up her frozen yogurt. She glanced out a couple of times, but didn't notice me.

When she was done, she walked away down the block, the sunlight bright on her bare shoulders and curling hair, and from my car across the street I watched until I couldn't see her any more, my hand on the ignition key, wondering how much I was to blame and for what.

TORONTO AND THE STATE OF GRACE

Kevin Barry

The winter bleeds us out here. These December mornings, it is often just myself and the dead jellyfish who are left to the beach. These are the lion's mane corpses that get washed in on the equinoctial gales and they come in terrible numbers some years, as if there's been a genocide out there. They look like pink foetal messes flung about the sand and rocks – kids call the place the abortion beach – and the corpses are so preserved in the winter air they're a long time rotting down. How one's soul lifts on the morning stroll. And then there's the endless afternoon to contend with – mostly, I have the bar to just myself and the radio, and we sit there and drone at each other. Maybe there's a lone customer, a depressed old farmer down from the hills, or maybe, the odd day, there's two. I am at this stage largely beyond caring.

But it was on just such a lifeless and dreary winter day, almost precisely as our ten streetlamps came on to glow against the dusk, that the rental car pulled up outside. I could hear two voices raised in an odd, quivery singing inside the car but they ceased as the engine cut. A slight man in late middle age stepped out and braced himself against the evening's chill. He looked at the sign above my door – it reads *Sullivan*, still, though it's years since there's been a Sullivan here. He came around the car and opened the passenger door and a frail bird-faced old dear in furs emerged. He offered an arm but she was proud to manage without. They stepped up together then to stare through my window and their eyes were lit so madly that my breath caught in a kind of fear or forewarning. They pushed through the doors. They came into my sad pub like a squall of hectic weather.

*

There was a strange manner of cheerful eeriness about them I'd rather not get into. They took grinning to the bar stools. He swivelled a half turn and squinted hard as he read the spirit labels –

'It's a very attractive selection, Mother,' he said.

'Let's not be rash, Tony,' she said.

But she swivelled the half turn, too, and hers drew a slow creak to the room that sounded in a crescent-moon shape, ominously.

'We're going to work our way across the toppermost states,' he said.

'Oh, Tony,' she said. 'Riding the Empire Builder? Again?'

He half rose from his stool.

'Take me back to the Blaaack Hills,' he crooned. 'The black hills of Dakota . . .'

'The beautiful Indian country,' she sighed.

He was fey and thin and in the last gasp of middle age; she had the remnants of a sharp-boned beauty yet.

'He's a dreadful child but kind,' she confided, and she laid her touch to the back of my hand where it gripped with white knuckles the bar top. Hers was paper-brown and cut deep with wrinkles.

'A Laphroaig to set us off from the station,' he said, sitting again. 'Let's strap ourselves in, dear.'

'Laphroaig, Tony? Is that the peaty number?'

'Like drinking the bloody fireplace,' he said.

'Two?'

'Water to the side,' he said.

I set them and they sipped, and they considered each other with the same liquid eyes, and relaxed. She looked at me kindly.

'Our background is theatrical,' she said.

'In all senses of the word,' he said.

'Have you travelled far today?'

'Oh Christ,' he said. 'Was it Kenmare, Mother? Was the last place?'

'Horrendous,' she said, and placed thin fingers to her throat in long suffering.

'Full of horrible skinny Italians on bicycles,' he said. 'Calves on like knitting needles and their rude bits in Lycra. I mean it's bloody December!'

'In fact,' she said, 'we were rather run out of town.'

'There was an incident,' he confirmed, 'over supper.'

'Last night?' she said. 'We're barely in the door and there's talk of the guards.'

'Five-star melodrama,' he said. 'As per. Matinee and evening performances.'

'We had . . . stopped off,' she said. 'En route.'

'We were a little . . . tired,' he said.

'We thought we'd take things a little more gently today,' she said.

'Nonsense,' he said. 'We're riding the Empire Builder. We're taking the high ground. Is that a Cork gin I see?'

It was second along the line of optics from the Laphroaig – I thought, surely they can't be in earnest? There was a line of nine spirits turned and hung there.

'Mine's with just the tiniest drizzle of soda water,' she said.

'Mine's a slice of lime, if you have it,' he said.

'Actually . . .'

'Surprise me,' he said. 'Straight up is fine. Though I may become poisonous and embittered.'

'Given you've a head start,' she said.

'Do you see now?' he said. 'Do you see what I'm dealing with?'

I tried for what I imagined was a half smile and set their gins.

'One yourself?' he said.

'I don't, actually.'

Sobriety was the mean violet of dusk through the bar's window; the mean view down the falling fields to the never-ending sea; the violet of another mean winter for me.

'Toronto!' she cried.

'Oh Mother,' he said. 'It's barely gone five.'

'Anthony was conceived in Toronto,' she said. 'I was Ophelia to Daddy's Prince. We're talking 1953, barman.'

He didn't look sixty. He had the faded yellowish skin tone of a preserved lemon. Pickled, I suppose is what I'm trying to say, but it seems unkind.

*

Their moods came and went with each sip as it was taken. He took a sullen turn on the Cork gin –

'Kenmare was the fucking horrors,' he said. 'I had one of my spells.'

'He hasn't had a spell since September,' she said. 'Though I'm not saying October was a picnic.'

'Five this morning?' he said. 'I'm lying in the bed, my heart is going like gangbusters and there are bloody crows on the roof – crows! And they're at their screeching and their bloody cawing and the worst of it is I can make out the words.'

I couldn't but ask –

'What were they saying?'

'You don't want to know,' he said. 'Suffice to say I've always suspected the worst of crows.'

'A crow is a crow,' she flapped a wrist. 'It's the rooks you want to watch out for.'

'Oh, a rook knows,' he said.

'Knows?' I couldn't but ask.

'The day and the hour,' he said.

'Of course sleep is a thing of the past for me,' she said. 'You'll find this as you get older, boys.'

The bar was empty but for them. I just wanted to lock up for the day and not open for the night. I wanted to drink mint tea upstairs and watch television and go on the internet. But they were making light work of the Cork gin.

'It was a dry town,' she said, narrowing her eyes, 'was Toronto.'

'Hideous Protestant bastards,' he said. 'What's this is next along?'

I turned, coldly; I tried to look stern.

'I'm afraid that's a very cheap and nasty Spanish brandy.'

'How did you know I was coming?' he said.

* *

The moving sea gleamed; it moved its lights in a black glister; it moved rustily on its cables.

'Of course Daddy was several years the senior to me,' she said. 'I was a young Ophelia. He was an old Prince. But impressive. He had range had Daddy.'

'Do you realise,' he said, 'that my father was born in 1889?'

'My goodness.'

'Picture it,' he said, swirling the last of his gin and signalling for two brandies; she'd already finished hers and had her palms placed expectantly on the bar top.

'1889,' he said. 'This was in County Mayo. In a cabin, no less, and in low circumstances. A whore mother bleeding down the thighs and seventeen screaming bastards swinging from the rafters . . .'

'Anthony,' she said. 'Really.'

'To even emerge from such a milieu,' he said, 'walking upright and not on all fours speaks of something heroic in the old lech.'

'He carried himself well,' she said. 'Daddy had class always.'

'Meaning?' he said.

'Apples and trees, dear,' she said. 'You've got some, too.'

'Some?' he said.

Together they tested their brandies with tentative lips.

'Coca-Cola,' she said, and I set a small bottle for a mixer.

'I shouldn't,' he said. 'The caffeine doesn't agree with me.'

He took a hard nip from his Spanish – suspiciously – but smiled then and looked up with new glee and blew the room a kiss. Then he was halfways stood on the stool again.

'When they begiiiin,' he sang, 'the beguine . . .'

He slithered from the bar stool and landed on lizardy toes. He waltzed a slow-shoed shuffle as though with his own ghost.

'*Quiero sentir las cosas de siempre*,' he sang, loudening, and he turned cock-hipped on a heel.

'Julio Iglesias,' she said.

At which point the door opened and one of my poor farmers poked a glance in –

'When they begin,' he came to quick refrain, 'the beguine,' and he waltzed towards the door, and my farmer turned on his own heel and moved off down the village, and quick.

Tony grabbed the door and shouted to the night after him –

'Come back at half past eight, dear! I'll be doing me Burl Ives!'

The chill of the evening faded again as he let the door swing closed and he took happily to his bar stool.

'Toronto?' she said. 'The house was half empty most nights but the company was lively.'

'Evidently,' he said.

'I think it happened the very first time,' she said. 'He'd got his hands on a bathtub gin, had Daddy.'

'The telling detail,' he said.

'Tasted like turps,' she said, 'but it did make one pleasantly lightheaded.'

He squinted again at the line of optics and shook his head.

'Now my wife?' he said.

'Don't, Tony,' she said.

'Oh and by the way,' he said. 'What did you say your name was?'

'I didn't. I'm Alan.'

'Well, Al,' he said, 'it turns out that my darling wife has only taken off with the pilates instructor. A she. And twice the man I'll ever be.'

'You should never have married an actress, darling.'

'So you've been saying this last fourteen years, Mother.'

'Marry the shop girl,' she said. 'Marry the factory line. Marry the barmaid. MARRY THE WHORE! But you never, never marry the actress, Tony.'

'Well it's a little late for it, Mother,' he said. 'Given I can never set foot in Tenerife again. The shame!'

'Nor Manchester,' she said.

'The horror!' he cried.

'Of course in Toronto,' she said, 'there wasn't a great deal to do in the evenings. And the show'd finish for seven!'

'He gave her one down the fish dock.'

'Oh Tony,' she said.

'By the mighty Ontario,' he said.

'Folks,' I said, 'listen, I mean really . . .'

'County Mayo-style,' he said. 'You know what I mean, soldier?'

'Tony,' she said, disappointedly.

'And as for my betrothed? I said, well! I said, this pilates has given you a whole new lease of life, Martina. You've come in glowing and you're up to four sessions a week.'

'What's this is next along the line, Andy?'

'Alan,' I said, and submitted to my fate. The way they moved was sure as a tide.

'It's an Absolut vodka,' I said.

'Marvellous,' he said. 'One minute we're rock-chewing Spanish peasants humping the donkey in a humid night wind, the next we're on the porch of the dacha, it's a summer's evening, placid . . .'

'A light breeze licking the trees,' she said.

'Pine-scented secrets,' he said. 'Cruel handsome souls with cheekbones like knives. Burly intrigue . . .'

'Burl Ives,' she said.

'. . . and some rather fetching Cassock-type headgear. A tubercular old sort about to hack his last . . .'

I poured and set the vodkas over ice – they slammed them back neat.

'Of course Martina's not been right since the change,' he said.

'Her manners are learned,' said the mother. 'There was always something forced about her manners. As if she'd learned them by heart. From a library book.'

'Pilates!' he cried. 'If it wasn't for the kiddies, it'd be a clean break.'

'The kiddies were a disaster,' she said. 'At your age? I don't know what you were thinking, Anthony.'

'Prolonging the noble line,' he said. '1889? Oh . . . Is that a Drambuie, Adam?'

*

The alcohol appeared really to have no great effect – it just kept them at a spinning clip.

'He never talked about Mayo much, Daddy,' she said.

'You could hardly blame the man,' he said.

'Though he told a horrid tale. About the day his father decided the wife was a whore. He stood at the bottom of the stairs and screamed the foullest abuse up at her. She flung a loaf of bread down and hit him on the head. Your daddy, as a kiddie, is watching the whole thing from under a table. The poor infant! And next *his* daddy flings the bread back up again and roars . . .'

She half stood on the bar stool and reddened as she called the line.

'"Feed your fucking bastards with it!"'

'Is it any wonder I turned out the way I did?' said Tony.

'Folks,' I said. 'In truth, I'm not feeling the best this evening, I think it's a virusy thing and I may lock up a little earlier . . .'

'Mine's a Drambuie, Al,' she said.

'Times two,' he said.

I set the glasses and poured.

'He talked about that loaf of bread for sixty years,' she said.

'Martina and I? That first weekend? We never left the bed. Of course this was the eighties and we were extremely tanned and fit. Tenerife, matinees and evenings? That'll keep you in your skinny jeans.'

'Always it would come up,' she said. 'The morning it all went bananas. Back in Mayo. Back in the . . . Was it a cottage, Tony?'

'It was a cabin.'

'From what I could gather that was the last he ever saw of his father. The morning of the loaf of bread flung.'

*

It was by now fully night outside; the road was deserted.

'Daddy did a turn,' she said. 'In his day. As a lady?'

'Oh?'

'Coeur d'Alene,' she said. 'We were hired for the Empire Build-er. Lounge-car floorshow. That was us. And Daddy? In 1957? Oh he was at his peak, my lovers! This was before the tragedy, of course. He went as Dame Delilah. He was got up buxom. He was got up blonde. Tony was still on the bottle. Tony was still in the cot but it seeps in, does talent.'

'I was four,' he said, and a tiny tear came. 'Riding the High Line!'

'I'll admit Daddy's nerves were not right,' she said. 'What he'd been through, the trauma? He had . . . He had what I used to call his *things*. Which were something like Anthony's spells, actually. Come to think of. But Daddy? Well! For example, he couldn't see a shoe on a bed. If he saw a shoe on a bed, he wouldn't be right for weeks.'

'A shoe on a bed? This is new to me,' he said.

'You were four,' she said.

'Now I'm going to have a thing,' he said, 'about shoes on beds.'

She smiled, and she rose up suddenly, at the shoulders, and her eyes brightened ever more madly, and she gasped her last. Then she keeled over dead onto my bar counter. There was no question about it. The way her head snapped onto the counter top. She just went. There was no question of a passing out; there was no question of the one too many. This was death on the premises. A single hard snap of bone on wood. He looked at her. He looked at me. He looked at her again, so coldly –

'Oh you haven't,' he said.

*

The one road along the peninsula is a bad one, and we are at least a half hour from Castletown of a winter's night. Which is an ignoble length of time for a woman dead on a bar stool. Together we carried her to the lounge seating and laid her down crookedly there. Her knees wouldn't straighten. I went upstairs to get a sheet. I didn't know what I was thinking or doing. I was panicked. I fetched a brown paper bag to breathe in. I took the sheet off the bed; it was like wrestling an octopus. But it covered her, at least, and I spoke stupidly then, intemperately –

'I suppose the shock would tend to sober you.'

'Oh no,' Tony said. 'I'm still hilariously drunk.'

He looked up at the optics.

'Where were we, Al?'

Next along the line was a Bailey's, and I poured a pair of them over ice, and I sat with him on the lounge chairs as we sipped.

'They must have been happy in Toronto,' he said. 'Or at least had some sort of fuck glow.'

From the gap in the mountain the ambulance was seen at last to spin its lights and call and as quickly again its men were in the door and about us. Tony went in the back of the ambulance with his mother. The last that I saw, his head was bobbing in the moving light as he yapped and cried and gesticulated.

I went upstairs with the rest of the bottle of Bailey's poured into a pint glass filled with ice. I Googled toxicology reports and I Googled liability. I Googled the Empire Builder and I could hear it as it moved across the mountains and the plains –

Winona.

Wolf Point.

Coeur d'Alene.

I had to get out for a bit. I walked down the cold road to the beach and it was just me and the dead jellyfish and my eyes stung with cold and all the silvers of the sea came and entered me there on the white sand like the surface of the moon pocked and cratered and the jellyfish lay dead and translucent all around me and I just lay where I had fallen into this night of void and stars and I thought oh Jesus, oh God, it's so fucking cold now.

METAPHYSICAL

Ali Smith

It's a cup and saucer, nothing but a cup on a saucer. But it's a very nice cup and saucer, proper porcelain, pure and white, *Royal Limoges France* on the base, good quality, the cup more like a little bowl, it feels good in the hand, the saucer quite deep. The light catches the rims of both saucer and cup, it catches the handle on the cup, a lit capital D, and there's light inside the cup in lightbulb circles, lines of light which move with him when he moves his head.

He's a man who, in the middle of the night in his hospital bed, pulls off the oxygen mask and lets it drop, pulls the tube that's attached to whatever's hanging off the side of the bed out of his midriff, swings his legs out the other side from the tube and the hanging things and stands up. He tests his legs to see if they'll hold him. They will.

He feels his way by holding on to the ends of the other beds till he's at the door of the ward, which is behind him now, dark and full of the distress and noise of the other sleeping people. It's quiet in the corridor, darkened too. There's nobody. Night shift. He knows not to go to the lift that the visitors and other outsiders use. He goes to the goods lift instead. The down button lights when he presses it. The lift door opens a box of light off the dimness of the corridor.

It's a pretty big lift, nothing in it but him. The doors close. He presses Basement. The lift hums. He takes a deep breath in. He breathes it out again.

In the basement he goes through a set of doors heavy to open. He crosses tarmac up a ramp, like a ramp for cars. It takes him

out into the night air, he feels it on his face and feet, his feet are
bare. He puts his hands in his pyjama pockets to keep them up
round his stomach. There might be women. He doesn't want to be
impolite or careless.

But there's no one on the street.

There's a white van, like a work van, with one back door half
open.

He climbs inside and sits down on the bit of metal curved over
the wheel.

A man comes to the back of the van. You right, then? the man
says.

The man knows him. But he doesn't know the man, does he?
The man slams the doors shut and it all goes dark in the back. A
stranger knows him. He fills with pride. Well, it'll be work, probably. Probably a lot of people know him. They'll know each other
from work somewhere.

He sways about in the back. He hopes the man won't need him
to do any work. When the van stops and the man opens the back,
he tells him.

I've no slippers. I've only my feet.

But the van man's dragging a ladder out of the back, off to
do something, someone needing someone to do something, there
always is.

There's a house there. You can't just go into someone's home
uninvited. There's a side path to its back garden. There's grass
under his feet. There's one of those new outhouses at the back of
the house, a hut down the garden.

Well, try the door.

It opens.

He goes in. It's warmer in it. It's new, the hut, the air smells
of newness in it, new wood, clean in the cut. He feels for a light
switch by the door in the place he'd have put the light switch if it
were him doing the work. There it is.

It's a clean white room he's in. Lovely, and a chair, a comfortable-looking one, and on the side up there a kettle, above it a cupboard. He opens its door. Clean wood. There's a jar of coffee, there's tea, sugar, tea things, the kinds of things they keep in a hut to make themselves at home, but it's right nice, they must be decent people. Is there water in the kettle? There's a sink. All you need, and look there, someone's made a table out of a plank and breeze-blocks. That's a good idea. You don't need much.

He settles down in the chair.

When he opens his eyes the light's up outside, it's near morning. He goes out and along the side of the house, leaning as he goes with one hand on the pebbledash. The van's gone. There's an ambulance waiting. Is it waiting for him?

It's a different man. He doesn't know the man but the man knows him. The man helps him up the steps though he doesn't need any help. The man asks him did he have a good night.

I did, he says.

He sits down in the ambulance. The man gives him a wave and shuts the doors. There's no one else in the back. They've sent it out specially for him. He didn't need that.

I don't need this, he says out loud to the metal doors, the stretcher, the machine for hearts, the boxes and packets of medical stuff and the like.

In the bed on the ward with the mask back on he tells whichever of them's visiting him, one after the other.

I took the goods lift up again, he says. I wasn't missed. All night. They didn't miss me. I don't believe they even knew me gone. I made myself a cup of tea.

None of them believes him. They humour him but they don't believe him.

I put the kettle on, he says again. I didn't think they'd mind. I made it in the cup with a teabag, there were teabags on the side, though there wasn't any milk. You can't have everything.

I washed up after myself. I put the things away. They had right nice things. I left it as good as I found it.

*

The smallest of our cats brought in the carcass of a bird that had been dead for quite some time and threw it round the kitchen, the bathroom and the hall. The carcass was full of maggots. I chased the cat out. I put my hand inside a plastic bag and picked up off the top of the broadband box, which is where it finally landed, what was left of the bird.

I took it out to the bins then came back to the house and hoovered up all the maggots I could see. The smell was pretty foul.

I was undressing later in the bathroom for a bath and I was thinking about the plant in the Botanical Gardens which flowers only once every hundred years or so and whose flower is meant to smell of death. Last year or the year before they announced in the media that this plant had flowered; every day on the local TV news they reported the massive queue of people waiting at the gates of the gardens to smell it. There were still two or three maggots, I saw now, there on the bathroom floor. I went for them with a piece of toilet paper; I managed to pick up one. The others disappeared; they must have seen me coming and known to squeeze themselves into the dark of the place where the side of the bath meets the floor.

I looked at the one on the paper in my hand. It was whiter than the bleach in the paper, it was quite small. Did that mean it was young? I knew nothing about maggots. It was ridged, completely white except for the black in it at one of its ends.

Maybe you could charge people to come to smell *us*, the maggot said.

No it didn't, maggots can't—

Yeah, because maggots haven't got a voice, have they? it said with its black mouth or its anus, whatever the black bit is. Maggots can't talk. Maggots don't have language, do they? Even after all that time of us cleaning things up. All the years of us helping with infected wounds etc. All the centuries of us eating dead things away to clean bare bones, all the millennia we've cleared up the rot you leave behind. We're not unhygienic. It's you hoovering up life, leaving each other for dead for all the centuries and centuries in the ditches and the battlefields, in the seas and the graveyards, in the town squares, hung off the trees and lampposts bombed and shot and cut to pieces. It's not us who smell, and that's obvious enough to a maggot brain, but you're not even bright enough to—

I screwed up the paper in my hand. I threw it into the toilet bowl. I pressed the bigger of the flush buttons, the one that gives the longer flush.

I got down on my knees and had a look at the crack between the laminated side of the bath and the tiles on the floor. The tiles were rough marble and quite uneven, which is presumably how those other few had escaped behind the laminate.

I went through to the front room to get something to poke with. I went on tiptoe because I was naked – as if going on tiptoe would protect me from something like the postman, anyone, coming to the front door (which is glass) and seeing me there with no clothes on.

As I did it, I felt stupid. I felt surveilled and self-conscious.

How had a maggot I had just drowned made me feel these things?

I began to feel cruel too. What right had I to decide about life and death of any sort, even a maggot's?

I came back through to the bathroom with a sharpened pencil and got down on my knees again. I put my head sideways on the floor but I couldn't see if anything in there, in the gaps between the floor and the edge of the side of the bath, was moving.

I poked the pencil point in anyway, wherever there was room to.

I got into the bath. That was better.

I ducked my head into the water. I surfaced, shook the water off me and the water still in my ear sang in a high-pitched Brechtian singsong:

can't you hear us in the hoover
making short work of the dirt
hear us in the human skin cells
that you like to call the dust
hear us in our maggot chorus
in a pure white noise of maggots
we don't stay like this forever
nothing stays like this forever.

I told my imagination to fuck off.

I stuck my finger in my ear to get the water out. I got out of the bath and dried myself. Before I left the bathroom I checked all round, all the corners. There weren't any more there alive or dead, not that I could see.

I got dressed, went into the kitchen and opened the hoover. I took out the hoover bag and took it outside to the bins.

I put a new hoover bag into the machine and clicked the plastic clasp shut.

Two weeks later, midnight, I was cleaning my teeth to go to bed and there was a bluebottle on the mirror ledge.

I killed it.

The next day, round about lunchtime, there was another bluebottle, metalled and shining, a little winter-dozy, on the rim of the pot we keep the toothbrushes in.

I killed it.

The night after that I put the reading light on in the bedroom to read a bit before going to sleep. A large bluebottle sang past my head. I got out of bed and hit at it with the book.

I killed it.

The next day there were two bluebottles in the kitchen at different ends of the light fitting.

I killed them by spraying them with disinfectant cleaning spray.

The next night I was in the bath. A bluebottle hummed by my ear and landed on the bristles of one of the toothbrushes.

The next night and the next night and the next day and the next.

AUTHOR BIOGRAPHIES

Kevin Barry is the author of the novels *Beatlebone* and *City of Bohane* and the story collections, *Dark Lies the Island* and *There Are Little Kingdoms*. He has won the IMPAC Prize, the Goldsmiths Prize, the *Sunday Times* EFG Short Story Prize, the Author's Club First Novel Prize, the Edge Hill Short Story Prize, the European Union Prize for Literature and the Rooney Prize for Irish Literature. He also writes plays and films. He lives in County Sligo, Ireland.

Lynn Coady is a Canadian novelist, journalist and TV writer. Her short story collection *Hellgoing* won the 2013 Scotiabank Giller Prize, for which her novel *The Antagonist* was also nominated in 2011. She has published six books of fiction and her work has appeared in the US, UK, Germany, Holland and France.

Ceridwen Dovey's debut novel, *Blood Kin*, was published in fifteen countries and shortlisted for the Dylan Thomas Prize. *Only the Animals*, her first story collection, won the 2014 Readings New Australian Writing Award. She studied social anthropology at Harvard and New York University, and now lives with her husband and two sons in Sydney.

Robert Drewe was born in Melbourne but grew up on the West Australian coast. His novels, short stories and non-fiction, including *The Drowner*, *Our Sunshine* and *The Shark Net*, have been widely translated, won national and international prizes and been adapted for film, television, radio and the theatre.

Damon Galgut was born in Pretoria in 1963. He wrote his first novel, *A Sinless Season*, when he was seventeen. His other books include *Small Circle of Beings*, *The Beautiful Screaming of Pigs*, *The Quarry*, *The Good Doctor*, *The Impostor* and *In a Strange Room*. *The Good Doctor* was shortlisted for the Man Booker Prize, the Commonwealth Writers' Prize and the Dublin/IMPAC Award, *The Impostor* was also shortlisted for the Commonwealth Writers' Prize and *In a Strange Room* was shortlisted for the Man Booker Prize. His latest novel, *Arctic Summer*, was published in 2014. He lives in Cape Town.

Petina Gappah is a Zimbabwean writer with law degrees from Cambridge, Graz University and the University of Zimbabwe. Her debut collection, *An Elegy for Easterly*, won the *Guardian* First Book Prize in 2009. Her debut novel, *The Book of Memory*, was published in 2015.

Sarah Hall was born in Cumbria in 1974. She is the prize-winning author of five novels – *Haweswater*, *The Electric Michelangelo*, *The Carhullan Army*, *How to Paint a Dead Man* and *The Wolf Border* – as well as *The Beautiful Indifference*, a collection of short stories. The first story in the collection, 'Butcher's Perfume', was shortlisted for the BBC National Short Story Award, a prize she won in 2013 with 'Mrs Fox'.

Peter Hobbs grew up in Cornwall and Yorkshire and now lives in London. He is the award-winning author of two novels, *The Short Day Dying* and *In the Orchard, the Swallows*, as well as a collection of short stories, *I Could Ride All Day in My Cool Blue Train*. He is a Fellow of the Royal Society of Literature, and a writer-in-residence for the schools literacy charity, First Story.

Yiyun Li is the recipient of numerous awards, including the PEN/Hemingway Award, the Frank O'Connor International Short Story Award and the *Guardian* First Book Award. Her most recent novel, *Kinder Than Solitude*, was published to critical acclaim. She was selected by Granta as one of the 21 Best Young American Novelists under 35, and was named by the *New Yorker* as one of the top 20 writers under 40. She lives in Oakland, California with her husband and their two sons, and teaches at the University of California, Davis.

Alexander MacLeod's debut collection *Light Lifting* was a finalist for the Scotiabank Giller Prize and the Frank O'Connor International Short Story Award. *Light Lifting* won an Atlantic Book Award and was named a 'Book of the Year' by the American Library Association, *The Globe and Mail*, and Amazon.ca. Alexander lives in Dartmouth, Nova Scotia and teaches at Saint Mary's University.

Ben Marcus is the author of *The Age of Wire and String*, *Notable American Women*, *The Father Costume*, *The Flame Alphabet* and *Leaving the Sea*. His work has appeared in the *New Yorker*, the *Paris Review*, the *New York Times* and *McSweeney's*. He is the editor of *New American Stories*, and a professor at Columbia University in New York.

Jon McGregor is the author of the critically acclaimed *If Nobody Speaks of Remarkable Things*, *So Many Ways to Begin*, *Even the Dogs* and *This Isn't the Sort of Thing That Happens to Someone Like You*. He is the winner of the International IMPAC Dublin Literary Award, the Betty Trask Prize and the Somerset Maugham Award, and has been twice longlisted for the Man Booker Prize. He was runner-up for the BBC National Short Story Award in both 2010 and 2011, with 'If It Keeps on Raining' and 'Wires' respectively. He was born in Bermuda in 1976, grew up in Norfolk and now lives in Nottingham. He is Professor of Creative Writing at the University of Nottingham, where he edits 'The Letters Page', a literary journal in letters.

Guadalupe Nettel's acclaimed English-language debut, *Natural Histories*, was described by the *New York Times* as 'five flawless stories'. Nettel has received numerous prestigious awards, including the Anna Seghers Prize, the Ribera del Duero Short Fiction Award and the Herralde Novel Prize. *The Body Where I Was Born*, her first novel to appear in English, was published in 2015. She lives and works in Mexico City.

Courttia Newland is the author of seven works of fiction including his debut, *The Scholar*. His latest novel, *The Gospel According to Cane*, was published in 2013 and has been optioned by Cowboy Films. He was nominated for the IMPAC Dublin Literary Award and the Frank O'Connor award, as well as numerous others. His short stories have appeared in many anthologies and broadcast on Radio 4. He is currently a PhD candidate in creative writing.

Taiye Selasi was born in London and raised in Boston. She holds a BA in American Studies from Yale and an MPhil in International Relations from Oxford. 'The Sex Lives of African Girls' (Granta, 2011), Selasi's fiction debut, appeared in *Best American Short Stories 2012*. In 2013 Granta named her in its once-every-decade list of Best of Young British Novelists. Selasi's debut novel *Ghana Must Go* (Penguin, 2013), a *New York Times* bestseller, was selected as one of the 10 Best Books of 2013 by the *Wall Street Journal* and *The Economist*.

Ali Smith was born in Inverness in 1962 and lives in Cambridge. Her most recent novel is *How to Be Both* (Hamish Hamilton, 2014), and her most recent collection of stories is *Public Library and Other Stories* (Hamish Hamilton, 2015).

Wells Tower is the author of *Everything Ravaged, Everything Burned*, a book of short stories. He lives in North Carolina.

Alan Warner is the author of eight novels: *Morvern Callar, These Demented Lands, The Sopranos, The Man Who Walks, The Worms Can Carry Me to Heaven, The Stars in the Bright Sky*, which was longlisted for the 2010 Man Booker Prize, *The Deadman's Pedal*, which won the 2013 James Tait Black Prize, and *Their Lips Talk of Mischief*.

Claire Vaye Watkins was raised in the Mojave Desert, in California and Nevada. Her writing has appeared in *Granta*, the *Paris Review* and the *New York Times*. Her short story collection, *Battleborn*, won five awards, including the Dylan Thomas Award. *Gold Fame Citrus*, her first novel, was named Book of the Year by numerous publications.

Clare Wigfall was born in Greenwich during the summer of 1976. She grew up in Berkeley, California, and London. Her highly acclaimed debut short story collection, *The Loudest Sound and Nothing*, was published in 2007. The following year she won the BBC National Short Story Award for 'The Numbers' and was longlisted for the Frank O'Connor International Short Story Award. She has also received the K. Blundell Trust Award for a young writer whose work enhances social consciousness, has been longlisted for the *Sunday Times* EFG Bank Short Story Award, and was nominated by William Trevor for an E. M. Forster Award. Most recently she was awarded a residential fellowship at Schloss

Solitude, which she plans to undertake in 2017. Having spent her twenties in Prague and another year in Edinburgh, she currently lives in Berlin with her husband and two daughters.

ACKNOWLEDGEMENTS

Our huge thanks to everyone who has contributed to this anthology, particularly:

All our authors and their agents.

Clare Conville, Deborah Rogers and Zoe Waldie.

At Faber: Lee Brackstone, Alex Russell, Silvia Crompton, Mary Morris, Hannah Griffiths, Luke Bird, Kate Ward, Camilla Smallwood, Lisa Baker, Lizzie Bishop and Kate McQuaid.

At HarperCollins US: Cal Morgan and Katherine Nintzel.

At House of Anansi: Sarah MacLachlan, Kelly Joseph and Janie Yoon.

Rosalind Harvey and Eleanor Rees.

The Royal Literary Fund.

Luke Brown, Jennifer Custer, James Garvey, Jarred McGinnis, Jon McGregor and Anne Meadows.